fiction

P9-BYG-364

TROPICAL ANIMAL

by the same author

Dirty Havana Trilogy

TROPICAL ANIMAL

Pedro Juan Gutiérrez

Translated from the Spanish
by Peter Lownds

CARROLL & GRAF PUBLISHERS
NEW YORK

TROPICAL ANIMAL

Carroll & Graf Publishers
An Imprint of Avalon Publishing Group Inc.
245 West 17th Street, 11th Floor
New York, NY 10011

AVALON
publishing group incorporated

Library of Congress Cataloging-in-Publication Data is available.

ISBN: 0-7867-1499-9

Printed in the United States of America
Distributed by Publishers Group West

I

The Fiery Serpent

1

A Swedish university had invited me to some literature seminars which take place every spring. Seminars don't interest me, literary studies even less so, but I thought I could use the occasion to get to know the country, all expenses paid. For some reason that I have no wish to try to recall – I think Sweden's social democracy didn't much please those who had to authorize my voyage – I couldn't make my little Scandinavian tour. So I began to exchange phone calls and correspondence with Agneta, the course coordinator. Each conversation was warmer. We were a year at this little game. I sent her some of my poems. Later, she mail-ordered *Dirty Havana Trilogy*, which they sent to her from Barcelona. When she began to read those stories she called me every day, upset. She stuttered into the telephone, and soon everything began to have a much more intimate tone.

By sheer coincidence, I spent Christmas of 1998 in the Alps. I was with a woman friend, a photographer, in a wooden cabin in the middle of the mountains, which might seem like something out of a romantic novel. But no, that's exactly how it was. One gray, cloudy, wind-swept afternoon, I was drinking whiskies while my friend took photos of me. As the alcohol went to my head, I began to take off my clothes. When women look at me naked, my dick gets hard, especially if a camera is involved. That's just the way I am. The photos turned out very well: me, in the snow, totally naked, with my prick stiff. My friend printed them in sepia and I seemed so young, with such an erect and attractive ego, that I couldn't resist and I sent Agneta one of those photos as a Christmas gift.

I am a seducer. I know. Just as there are inveterate alcoholics, people addicted to gambling, caffeine, nicotine, marijuana, kleptomaniacs, etcetera, I am addicted to seduction. Sometimes the little angel inside me tries to take control, and says: 'Don't be such a son of a bitch, Pedrito. Don't you see that you make these women suffer?' But then up jumps the little devil, and contradicts him: 'Go ahead. They're happy like that, even if it's only for a while. And you're happy too. Don't feel guilty.'

It's a vice. I know that seduction is a vice equal to any other. But Seducers Anonymous doesn't exist. If it did, it might be able to do something for me. Although I'm not so sure. I'd probably make excuses not to go near their sessions, not to have to stand up shamefaced in front of everyone, put my hand on the Bible and serenely say: 'My name is Pedro Juan. I'm a seducer. And today makes twenty-seven days that I haven't seduced anyone.'

By March, I was back in Havana. Life was very peaceful. I was painting, experimenting with some recycled materials; by which I mean with garbage I'd collected on street corners. I had a lot of material available to me. In the afternoons, I was drinking rum, smoking my cigars, seducing black women or mulattas. I adore them. You won't catch me writing here that blacks are superior – that would be inverse racism – but I am convinced that we have to mix more; that we have to provoke miscegenation, manufacture more mulattas and mulattos. Miscegenation saves. That's why I like black women. Well, that's not exactly it. When you fuck, you don't give a shit about anyone's salvation. But I do have a couple of enchanting mulatta daughters who corroborate that idea.

Soon Agneta organized another trip to Sweden for me from Stockholm. Though she seemed her usual hyper-efficient self, I also sensed that she had changed. What with the poems, the stories from the *Trilogy*, and my naked photo in the alpine snow, her neuronal rhythms were in an uproar. She called me almost daily and said things like: 'Last night I couldn't sleep. You've got me into a state. Is everything you write true?'

And I answered her: 'Yes. I have little imagination.'

And she: 'Ohhh, will you come in the spring, Pedro Juan? Everything is set up already. Will you come?'

2

She always called me at eight in the morning, Havana time. Two in the afternoon in Stockholm. On the dot. One morning in March, the telephone rang. I had been awake for an hour but I was still lying down; my head propped on three pillows, I was reading Kundera's *Immortality*. Agneta interrupted me on page 69, just as I was reading a fragment about the repression, the brutality and the grandiosity which power engenders: 'Goethe! Napoleon smacked his forehead. The author of *The Sufferings of Young Werther*! While on the Egyptian campaign, he had discovered that his officers were reading this book. And as soon as he discovered it, he became very angry. He reprimanded the officers for reading such sentimental foolishness, and he forbade them once and for all to read novels. Novels of any kind! Let them read history books, they're much more useful!'

Unlike Agneta, I was reading a slow, philosophical novel. I read in the few moments of peace and relief I can find in the midst of this vertiginous, chaotic city.

To Agneta's questions I could only respond with the obvious: 'If you live in a place like this, you can't write slowly. Here everything comes apart in your hands. Nothing lasts. And so you have to go out to search for more. It's like this every day.' She remains silent. Two people only allow themselves to shut up for a while and enjoy the silence between them when they're together, each beside the other. But an international call costs money. Nobody spends money to remain silent. We do. Agneta calls from her office in the university, so we play our sensual game for free. United by silence, we don't speak. Finally, she interrupts the emptiness and asks again, as she always does: 'Will you come in the spring?'

3

We speak little, maybe five or six minutes. When I return to the book, my thoughts go back to the question of *tempo*. You write as you live; it's inevitable. A slow, restful *tempo* is ideal for the way a European writer interprets his material. He lives inside a sedimented, exhausted culture; at the end of something, a period, a historical phase. His is the perception of someone who has come to the end of a road and stops to look back over his long and hazardous journey.

I, in contrast, belong to a convulsive, effervescent society, one with an absolutely uncertain and unpredictable future. In a place where only five hundred years ago men lived in caves, naked, hunting and fishing, knowing only fire. What's more, I live in a neighborhood of blacks; blacks who a hundred years ago were still slaves, and have achieved very little since. Too little in a hundred years unchained.

The result is that my life is a perpetual oscillation between nothing and nothing. Sometimes the experiment becomes dizzying and brutal. I can't artificially separate what I do and what I think from what I write. If I lived in Stockholm, maybe my life would be slow, monotonous, gray. Surroundings are decisive. The only thing I can always do – in Stockholm, Havana or wherever – is carve out my own space. I can never wait for someone to give me leave. You have to build freedom by yourself. How? Everyone has to discover this on their own. I build my freedom by writing, painting, sustaining my simple vision of the world, lurking in the jungle like an animal, preventing others from meddling in my private affairs. The essential, for man, is freedom – within ourselves and in our lives. The freedom to dare to be yourself at any moment, in any place. Freedom is like happiness: it never quite arrives. It can never be fully yours. Only the journey matters, in the pursuit of freedom and happiness. That's how we live. It's all we can aspire to. A few years ago, and for a long time, my life was tied to systems, concepts, prejudices, preconceived ideas, the decisions of others. It was authoritarian, dependent. I was living in a cage, everything crumbling in front of me. I was on the verge of suicide. Or madness. Something inside me needed to change, or I'd have ended up crazy or dead. Yet I so wanted to live. Simply to live. Without oppression. Maybe even with a few happy days thrown in. And to reduce anxieties. This is indispensable: to reduce anxieties. Maybe it's just a matter of changing your point of view. You must be fully present wherever you find yourself, and not always try to escape.

I put *Immortality* aside. I walked downstairs, and I sat for a while facing the sea, on the Malecón. It was Saturday, maybe eight-thirty in the morning. Everything was tranquil and silent. The only thing audible was the radio of a nearby policeman: 'Twenty-four zero twenty-four. Twenty-four zero twenty-four. Twenty-four zero twenty-four. Praaaaacccc. Praaaacccccc. Yesssss . . . come in, zero twenty-four. Praaaccccc . . .'

I headed back towards home. I wanted a coffee. It'd do me more good than to continue to sit on the Malecón watching the sea. I walked a few yards; the two mental defectives were saying goodbye in the door of the building. They're a married couple. Both are retards, borderline, half-crazy; no one quite knows what's wrong with them. Each one has screws loose in the brain, and they enjoy shitting on the stairs and tormenting everyone with their stupid screaming. I enter the hall of my old building. It was built in 1927, with white marble staircases, ample, comfortable apartments, a lift of polished bronze, a facade like those in Boston, and mahogany doors and windows. In sum, impeccable, luxurious and expensive. Now the place is in ruins. The lift and the stairwell stink of urine and shit. On the sidewalk, in front of the door, there's a hole which permanently expels excrement into the street. People smoke marijuana and have long sex sessions in the darkness of the stairwell. The apartments have been divided again and again, and now ten or fifteen people live where before there were three. The cistern is always dry. No one knows why the water doesn't come, and we all haul pails up the stairs. Nothing exceptional; it's the same all over the neighborhood. Filth, stink, disregard, neglect, everywhere you look.

I do what I can to escape from this apocalypse. At least mentally and spiritually. My material, though, remains anchored amid the wreckage.

The retard woman entered the lift with me. I pushed the button for seven and stared at her. It was very dark. The lift is always dark. Like a mineshaft. The light bulbs are gone, stolen. Still, we're lucky it's been running several days without a hitch. Anyhow, light or no light, the retard and I were watching each other. Very disagreeably, a bit in jest, it occurred to me to say to her: 'Elenita, you seem happy.'

Immediately she drew near. She grabbed my arm and pressed against me with her big, solid tits. She was uttering strange little noises. Something like 'Oghn, oghn.' Wow, she had hard tits, abundant, with splendid erect nipples. I grabbed them with my right hand and massaged them. My left hand reached down for her pussy. She had no underclothes – only a thin, frayed wrap. Oh, so good. Elenita must be about twenty-five. She's a strange cocktail of mulatto, white, Chinese, black, with a trace of Jamaican or Haitian. In short, an impenetrable combination. The final product could have turned out very well, were it not for that cerebral defect which brought her close to mongolism. Something failed in the mix. She says very little, but she groans well. Maybe she has sexual obsessions. I don't know. When my hand reached her pussy, it made a marvelous discovery: lots of hair. An abundant pubic furze. It was a big pussy, hairy, wet, and odorous. That's how I'd describe it. I inserted a finger, worked it around a bit, she wet my hand and I squeezed her clit. She sighed. I sniffed my finger. Very nice smell. Smooth and fragrant. Not at all dirty. Crying out for some tongue. I lowered my hand again, reinserted my finger. She sighed more. She was already squeezing my cock from outside my pants, with lots of emotion, and me with a tremendous erection. She squeezed me, massaged me, and kept on making

8

those little noises, like a pig: 'Oghn, oghn.' But there wasn't time for more. The lift had ascended joltingly, suddenly it shook, stopped and, with a great clanging, opened its grate. I got out on the seventh floor. I didn't say goodbye. She went down again. She lives on the third floor. I went up another flight of stairs to my room on the roof. It crossed my mind that the fool might have syphilis or AIDS or tuberculosis. Oh, mother of mine! Why am I like this? I wanted to wash my hands, but there was no water and I didn't want to go down to the street and walk to the corner in search of a pail. At least I didn't kiss her.

I thought about making coffee, but no, I was too exhausted. I lay down on the bed and slept. I dreamt I came to some enormous dark ships, where there were people soldering steel plates, sparks showering in the unreal brightness of the arc lamps. Maybe they were shipyard workers. That was one of my first jobs, when I was seventeen years old: assistant solderer in some shipyards where boats were repaired. I had a steady shift from midnight till eight in the morning. The job lasted less than a year, but it drained me like twenty. I don't want to remember it because I felt like a fucking slave. The bloody shipwrights and the enormous ships and the soldering always come back to me in anxiety dreams. In one corner there was a pregnant monkey, with many little monkeys nursing on her breasts. The male monkey approached her, but she rejected him and kept focused, making milk for her brood. I petted the male monkey, and he drew nearer. I caressed him some more and touched him. He had an erection. I masturbated it a bit. The monkey became calm, clinging to me, enjoying being jerked off. And he came. He shot his wad of semen and soaked my hand. A lot of semen. And we remained a while together. Feeling each other. That's it. I don't remember what happened next. I suppose I slept a bit more and woke up.

4

Three days later, Agneta called again. She had already sent the letters of invitation. To travel, I need an institution to invite me all expenses paid, authorization from emigration, visas, medical insurance, people who will accept legal responsibility for me and make sure that, as an emigrant, I'm not going to loot and pillage. Everything in order, everything under control, that's how it has to be.

Agneta displays her innate efficiency. First she informs me of the arrangements, then she relaxes. On the weekend she and a girlfriend rode horses. I tell her she needs to have more fun. She spends all her time working. Yesterday an envelope was delivered which she sent weeks ago. It contained a graph from the newspaper of January 28. '*Sverige har blivit kallt.*' In Karesuando it was −19°C. In Stockholm −14°C. The snow fluctuated between 51 and 94 centimeters high. Luckily I am not there. We speak of the weather here. It's very sunny, the sea calm and blue, 24 degrees. I avoid the disagreeable. It's better to talk about horses, bicycle riding, my English lessons, paintings. We don't speak much. She falls silent. Maybe she has little to say.

'Did you finish the book?'

'Oh, no. I can only read on the weekends.'

'Why?'

'I can't sleep when I read it. I have a lot of questions to ask you, Pedro Juan. A lot. If I read from Monday to Friday I couldn't work. Your book makes me so uneasy.'

'Ahhh.'

Afterwards I paint a little. There's calm and silence these days and I use it to focus. Solitude. Maybe we write and paint not just to create a space around us, but also to feel communion. Not exactly to break the solitude. It's not about that. Solitude is always there. I feel it, I touch it, I talk to it. It forms part of my life. Solitude is inevitable. And it helps. I concentrate more. I couldn't live without solitude.

These days I'm painting with grays, blacks, ochers, sepias. I want nothing whatsoever to do with red; even less with blue, with green, with yellow. I paint angrily. That always happens. Painting brings out my fury. And I mix the fury into the painting.

By mid-morning a strong wind begins to blow. Then clouds appear. The sea ripples. In less than half an hour everything changes. Thunderous waves break over the Malecón seawall, sending salt spray over the city. I close the windows. Here on the roof it blows hard. I have to lash the windows from inside, bolt them down well. The rain and the wind increase. Water begins to come through the windows and runs over the floor to the corner where I paint. I quickly collect all my painting utensils, put them on the bed. I let the water keep running. I'll dry it when it stops raining. The north wind grows more violent. My door faces east. I stick my head out, and there's the storm over the sea and the city. You can barely see the Morro lighthouse through the waterspout. Everything has turned gray and the temperature is dropping. I feel cold. A red boat leaves the port loaded with containers. It isn't a big ship; it only carries sixteen containers. It makes a slow, dramatic exit, battered about by the wind and the waves. Its machinery is about to explode, but it keeps fighting against the fury of the Caribbean. The captain wants to be brilliant in the eyes of his crew, wants to demonstrate that his little boat is small but courageous and strong. He could postpone his exit until the storm passes, but that's not worthy of a mariner. So there goes the little red boat amid the gusts of gray, cold rain; riding the waves which explode on the deck, crash against the containers. It's a beautiful sight. The little guy, in red, full of pluck, straining with all its might to leave the port in style in the middle of the gray storm; the raging storm trying to knock its opponent upside down. But the little guy won't be defeated, and advances, fighting every inch of the way.

From the opening of the interior patio of the building I hear Gloria's bracelets. She's sweeping and shouting. Her cries blend with the music of a singer in full flow. Roberto Carlos, José José.

I don't know. A singer. There's always a singer bawling away in her house. Love problems and disillusionment. Surely the rain came in the windows and inundated her house too. Those bracelets sound like bells. Maybe they're made of Mexican silver. I like to hear them. They resound when she scrubs the dishes, or sweeps, or cleans. They always ring. I live on the roof, along with neighbors I shun. I don't interest them and they don't interest me. The roof is actually the eighth floor. Gloria lives below, on the seventh, with her mother and her son, and a radio and a tape recorder which never rest, and thousands of relatives who come and go. They are cousins, nephews, godchildren, uncles and aunts, brothers- and sisters-in-law, brothers and sisters, sons-in-law, neighbors of the uncles and aunts, stepchildren of the brothers and sisters, fiancées of the nephews, sons of the cousins with their wives and children. The whole caboodle. They come from all over Cuba. They come to see a doctor, to do business, to scam, to turn tricks, to earn some dollars, to spend them, they sleep over for some days and disappear and others appear. It's the house of chaos. Music. A lot of music. Bolero, salsa, rancheros. I loved you and you abandoned me. I ran after you and you gave me the cold shoulder. Why do you make me suffer, my daaar-ling? Why, why, why, my baaa-by? The music is always there. Feliciano, Gloria Estefan, Luis Miguel, Mark Anthony, Ricky Martin, Ana Gabriel, La India, Rocío Dúrcal, Juan Luis Guerra. And bottles of rum. And no sign of money. The money appears and disappears. It appears again and is gone in a second. And cigarettes. Tobacco, boleros, rum. And people. They come in, go out, eat, shit, block up the toilet, use up in half an hour the small amount of water which comes in the mornings. The rest of the day we do without it. Family, a lot of family, whites, mulattos, blacks, mottled ones, Orientals, Indians.

It looks like the rain isn't going to stop. It keeps coming through the windows. I like to see this heavy water falling like lead pellets on the sea and the city. Gloria keeps sweeping frantically, her bracelets still ringing. Without thinking, I stick my head over the wall and shout: 'Gloria! Gloria!' She doesn't hear me. I keep shouting. The rain is cold. In a few seconds I'm soaked, dripping from head to foot. Finally Gloria hears me. She sticks her head out the window and looks up. Just seeing each other we know. She grins at me and shakes her head affirmatively. Still dripping water, I go to the door of the stairway. The roof terrace of the building has its independence. Gloria's already coming upstairs. She's twenty-nine years old. I'm fifty. She's a very thin mulatta, rather dark, a little shorter than me. With black hair as hard as wire. A perfect body, with small tits, without an inch of fat. She's like a nerve fiber, sweet, smiling, cunning, with her super-white teeth and a deliberate, provocative way of walking, her little ass held high. She's a sly streetwalker from Central Havana. Gloria could have lived here two hundred years ago and she'd have been no different. Perhaps she'd have been called Cecilia Valdés, but she'd still have been the same hustler, with her own custom-made morals and ethics. I like her a lot. What attracts me most is the impression she gives of being free. If all the inventions and conventions of society get in the way of her living, she simply ignores them. As calm as you please. She takes the whole heap of obstacles, moves them aside, and just keeps on walking. That girl does her own thing.

We started playing around three years ago. By now we're out of our minds. It's crazy. It's not just sex. Each day we love each other more, know each other more. I want to write a novel with her as the protagonist. Maybe I'll call it *A Lot of Heart*. Luckily she tells me everything. With me she's uninhibited.

'Pedro Juan, you're crazy.'

'Me? Look who's talking.'

'My house is flooded, *papito*. It's raining harder inside than out.'

'And your mother? Is she crippled or what?'

'Ahhh . . .'

'No, ahh, no. Fuck it. Let her grab a broom and sweep the water out.'

'All right, okay, *papito*, let it go.'

Two minutes later, we're on the bed, naked. We do sixty-nine to get hot. Her pussy always has an odor. It's a strong smell, nothing subtle about it. Mulatta she may be, but she smells black. It's so rich, I can't tear myself away. We give each other tongue like two devils. She's pure fiber, tense. She did gymnastics, and danced in the Palermo for many years, like a madwoman. When I put it in her, she goes nuts. She says whatever comes into her head, and I never know whether it's truth or bullshit. She knows I like stories, her porno stories. She sticks her feet way up. She takes them in her hands and says to me: 'Put it in all the way, fucker, oh shit, knock me up, that's it, that's it, hurt me! Why does it get so big? Ahh, I can feel it in my navel! Oh, this is torture! Hurt me, baby, yes, like that. You're my macho, *papi*, you make me crazy. Your dick keeps getting bigger and fatter, that's it, jam it all the way in, faggot, fucker, son of a whore. Hurt me, goddamn it, hurt me!' I push hard and bump against the depth of her. I love it. I hit it once again. We fuck like two savages. Like a colt and a mare. I spit on her. I drool on her mouth and she goes crazy: 'Yes, shit, spit on me, slap me, you fucker, I want to be your slave, faggot, enter me with your sword drawn, I want to be your slave, you crazy shit. You're a madman, I'm crazy about you, knock me up, knock me up. Stuff it all in, *papi*. Jam it all the way in and knock me up, go on, knock me up.'

I don't want to come yet. I pull it out a little. In control. I relax. I start to give it to her again. She has another orgasm. How many has she had? She doesn't even know. One after the other. When she loses her head she doesn't know what she is saying or doing. I control myself, putting it in and pulling it out so I don't come so quickly. How much time has passed? An hour? An hour and a half? When I can't take it any more, I ask her: 'You want my milk, baby? I can't keep it any longer . . . take it, goddamn it, take it!' She stretches her legs even higher and takes both feet with her hands: 'Yes, give it to me, let it go deep inside me, fill me up, shoot it all the way back, all the way down in there.' And there I go. I let loose one stream and another and another. Ahhhh, I've got nothing left. I pull out of her and fall back, face up, on the bed. As always, she puts it in her mouth and sucks up the last little drops of semen. Glutton. She's depraved. The best in the world. The biggest pervert. She's incredible. She blasts me into space, I bounce against the clouds, and come shooting back below. I fall into bed, spend my come and feel groggy. Knockout. I don't even hear the mandatory nine count.

Nothing. Knockout. I need more time to return to myself. Afterwards, I feel like the most macho animal in the world. Like a bull after mounting a cow. Sometimes, the thought used to bother me: why do we behave like wild animals when we fuck? As if we weren't civilized. I mentioned it to a good friend of mine, a cultured guy, and he gave me this answer: 'Obviously we have to feel like animals. Impossible to feel like an apple tree or a stone. We *are* animals. It just so happens it's not really in good taste to remember that that's what we are, simple animals. Mammals, to be precise.'

If we have rum at hand we drink a shot and I leave the knockout behind in a matter of minutes. But usually we don't have rum or anything else. Just she and I. Two nuts in love. It all began three years ago. With sex. That's all we wanted. We liked each other. But, little by little, things between us began to heat up. Now some nights she comes up, gets into my bed, and we sleep together till morning. It feels good to sleep with someone, to share your nightmares or your dreams. To wake up with someone by your side, both of you naked, and to feel the warmth of that other body, to caress each other. Sometimes I'm an hour or more with a tremendous erection, but I don't put it in her. All I do is caress her. When the gypsy woman possesses her, she throws the shells for me and tells me something of the future. She usually gets it right. Or she brings me up a plate of food. She cooks badly, with little flavor. Incredible but true: fucking she's a ten, but she's the worst cook that human eyes have seen, as Columbus would say.

What I want to say is that we've grown closer, without noticing it. Solitude is terrible. If one can feel affection for a dog or a cat, which are stupid animals, how am I not going to feel affection for this hot and depraved woman? What's best of all is her depravity, her total lack of decency, of standards. If one day I write her biography, I don't know how I'm going to do it because everyone will think it's hardcore porn. No one will believe that it's a real tale of a sweet woman, who curls around my neck and seduces me. And catches me and hypnotizes me until finally the cherubim and the flaming sword appear above our heads and expel us from paradise.

5

When we recover, I stick my head out the door. Now it's drizzling. The wind blows in gusts. The little red boat is nowhere in sight. It won a clean fight, and headed out to sea. The sky is still cloudy, almost black. That's fine. I enjoy a respite from so much sun. Below, on the street, there's an uproar of sirens, firemen, police. They've stopped the traffic with barricades.

'Gloria, something serious is going on down there.'

'Why?'

'They've closed the street and there are firemen.'

'I heard an explosion.'

'What explosion?'

'I don't know. An explosion.'

'An explosion?'

'Yes.'

'I didn't hear anything.'

'Of course not, you were busy shooting your milk.'

'What kind of explosion was it?'

'I dunno. I dunno. I *dunnoooo*. An explosion.'

'Oh.'

I put on my pants and slippers, and start to go downstairs, shirt-less. I like to show off my tattoo. It's not every day that such a tasty fifty-year-old stud appears in the neighborhood. Just then, Gloria starts in with her same old song. Lately she's taken to asking me repeatedly to knock her up:

'*Papi*, my tits are swollen, they itch . . . Come on, try to make it a girl. I don't want another boy.'

'Damn it, girl. Cut it out.'

'No, I won't. If I get pregnant, it's yours. You'll see, you'll see!'

'Shit. I've told you a thousand times that you're a slut; if you get knocked up you won't know who the father is.'

'Sure I won't. Look, I'm no fool and I wasn't born yesterday. It's yours, *papi*. Who else's is it gonna be if I'm so shut up in the house all day that I never even set foot on the street?'

'You're shameless, girl! What about that butcher?'

'What butcher?'

'The little fat one who gave you the eighty pesos.'

'That was months ago.'

'The first time was months ago. And after?'

'Cut it out. Cut it out.'

'Everyone in the neighborhood knows that you fuck like a bunny, so don't play the pretty one with me. We'll see who the hell the father is.'

'Oh, baby . . .'

'Oh baby nothing. I'll tell you once more: you can have all the cocks you want, but with rubbers. The only one who can insert his clean bare dick is me. Is that clear?'

'Yes, sweetie, anything you say. I always keep rubbers in my handbag.'

'Okay, I'm off now.'

'You're very clever. You diverted the conversation.'

'Are you going keep on with the same old shit?'

'No, no, what I'm going to tell you is not to worry. If I'm knocked up I'll know whose it is. If it's not yours, I'll know it right away and I'm not going to accuse you, I don't have to deceive anyone. But if it's yours, it's yours. And be ready to assume your responsibility, *papito*, because I'm not going to raise it by myself, just so you know!'

'Gloria, by your mother. I have recognized three children with my last name and another in Guantánamo that they say is mine. This is getting tired. Don't make things more difficult, girl. Now get going. What's more, it isn't mine, just so *you* know.'

'Oh, lost your appetite, now you ate the coconut candy?'

'And I'd still be eating it, but . . . ahhh, all right, all right, all right. This conversation is pointless.'

'For you, perhaps; but not for me. Far from it. You're already trembling, just thinking about having a little baby girl.'

'Ahhh . . .'

'What's more, I dreamt it. Not just once. I've had the same dream three times. And with me dreams always come true.'

'What did you dream?'

'Get this: I was coming up to your place and there was this trail of debris and wood and a lot of dust – as if it were being demolished. Then you said to me: "I'm so tired, I can't do it any more." You took the bicycle and went downstairs, but in the middle of the debris was a baby's bottle full of warm milk. I stuck my head out from the roof and shouted that you had left the bottle behind. But you were already heading off down the street, on foot, I don't know where you left the bike. And do you know what you were carrying?'

'No.'

'A baby. A little girl, wrapped in the prettiest pink swaddling clothes.'

'And you saw that from way up here?'

'Well, it was a dream . . . in dreams . . . you know. But look, I haven't finished: you were going with the baby girl in your arms, smiling, so happy, and I yelled to you: "Pedro Juan, the bottle, Pedro Juan, the bottle." And you didn't even hear me, because you were so happy with your baby girl.'

'Yeah? And twilight in the background and a little violin music. You get a ten. As a soap-opera actress, you get a ten. You're more dramatic than Torín Cellado.'

'That's just the way it was. You were so happy, you looked like a kid.'

'Turn it down, Gloria, turn it down.'

'Nothing doing. Perhaps I'm not pregnant and all we're having is a nice chat; but if I am, I'm not getting rid of it. Just so you're clear. I am *not* getting rid of it.'

'Gloria, you've had five hundred abortions. What does one more matter?'

'Three. I've had three interruptions. And all while I was with my state-registered husband, the father of my son. But if I'm pregnant now, I keep it.'

'Damn, do you get mad at me!'

'So why all the love and romance when you've got it in me? Yes, when we're fucking you're so inspired and it's "I love you, I adore you, you make me crazy" and blah, blah, blah. But when you cool down, you don't even trust your shadow.'

'Don't count on me, I told you.'

'I don't want complaints after.'

'Complaints about what?'

'My kids don't go hungry, I want you to know that. I'll fuck the greengrocer, the butcher, the guy at the dairy, even the fat old man at the bakery. I'll put out for the entire neighborhood.'

'As you have always done. That's nothing new.'

'Maybe; but my kids don't go hungry. I sell my pussy like you say, but I bring home food every day.'

'What do you want, Mother Courage, someone to play the *Marseillaise* for you and wrap you in a red flag?'

'Go on, make fun of me. God will punish you, you'll see; she'll turn out just like you. Identical. Right down to your strong character and personality. So that when you're old . . .'

'Okay, okay. Cut it and get a move on. I'm going down to see what's happening on the street.'

'Busybody! Typical journalist.'

'Writer.'

'Writer! Writers ought to be cultured and educated and speak nicely, I think. You're more like a savage.'

'Okay, Gloria, okay.'

'Besides, where are your books? I haven't seen one yet.'

'They're published in . . .'

'Yeah, they're published in Spain. Always the same story. And here? What bookstore has them here? What you are is a tremendous con man making out he's a writer just to get some *cachet*.'

'Drop the bullshit, okay, butt-peddler; you'd drive anyone nuts.'

'Sure, okay, split. Let's go, I'm headed home. Oh, my sister brought you some cigars, come and get them when you go back up.'

'All right.'

I went downstairs. Dozens of people were hanging out in the street. The building in front was falling to pieces. During the storm big chunks fell onto the street. The police sealed off traffic and evacuated three families: one group of three, another of four, and another of eighteen. These last ones were blacks. In the neighborhood, people called them *Los Muchos*: 'The Many'. An architect was asking them questions and taking notes. The firemen had nothing to do, they were walking about, talking, laughing; one of them took a little mulatta aside, they were speaking very quietly and seemed about to start hugging and kissing in front of everyone. They were getting hotter by the minute. All the neighbors were gossiping: 'Where are they going to put all these people? They say the shelters are full. *Los Muchos* are out of luck because they don't fit in any place.'

Gusts of wind, showers. That building, all three stories of it, stood right on the corner of San Lázaro and Colón. The salt in the air and the sea wind had eroded it bit by bit. Enormous holes gaped in its walls. It had been that way for at least thirty years. It didn't fall all at once, but in little pieces. The police erected barriers around it, into which debris started to fall, pieces of brick. No one knew what would happen. The building could suddenly collapse. The oldest member of *Los Muchos*, a woman of seventy or more, was as drunk or high as ever. She wobbled around laughing to herself, making short, directionless excursions. The architect and the firemen came and went, and nothing happened. Everyone looked at one another. The old woman muttered: 'I'd like to see what they're going to do with us. You'll see that we end up in the street. And now that it's cold. You'll see, this is going to be just like with Machado, when we lived in the arcades in Monte and in Reina. In the arcades. You'll see.'

Gloria came down, stood next to me and whispered in my ear: 'Leave these good-for-nothings – their problems are nothing to do with you. Come up to get the cigars. Minerva's waiting for you and she has to go.'

'Eh, so what? I'll come up when you let go of my fucking balls.'

'Baby, don't answer me like that. I'm gonna get you some rum. Go up and don't stand around here. All these people have lice, and they'll jump on you.'

'On me? Where?'

'Hah hah hah.'

The lift was broken again. I climbed the stairs, all seven floors. I rang the bell to Gloria's apartment. Minerva opened the door, and whispered in her little-girl voice: 'Oh, it's you. Come in. Gloria will be here soon.'

We sit in the living room. Two big armchairs, a sofa, and a black-and-white Russian television. Everything's in ruins, stripped down. The walls are peeling, filthy. A bulb hangs from a cable covered with flies. Way up on the wall is an old shelf – who knows why they put it up so high. It's probably been there for fifty years. As ornamentation, the shelf has two empty cans of German beer, a small print of the Virgin of Mercies, and a wrinkled postcard of an Italian beach on the Adriatic. The décor of the desperate.

Incredibly, the house is empty and silent. Only Minerva. She sits in front of me. She looks like Gloria's twin, yet she's completely different. Gloria said to me one day: 'Minerva? The most submissive girl in the world. At thirteen, she went off with the man who deflowered her. She left school. And dedicated herself to house and husband. She has three children and thinks the sun shines out of her husband's ass.'

Now she is wearing a white dressing gown, almost transparent. She's very thin, with well-tanned, Indian skin, and black hair. No bra. Her breasts are small, the nipples very black. They look delicious. And she displays them with adolescent innocence. A halo of subtle, delicate eroticism surrounds her. Her expression is that of a virgin about to go floating up and disappear among the clouds. But without the trumpets and without the lights. A cloistered virgin, silent and somber.

She has nothing to say to me. Nor I to her. I look her over and lower my gaze. The married woman, silent, submissive. Most men yearn to find a woman like this. They dream about it, but they don't dare to say it out loud because the rest will think they are reactionary and chauvinist. But she's the best: a hot, sensual, complacent, domesticated, masochistic woman. I'd like to put my cock in her and force a reaction: 'Scream, goddamn it, say something, don't act like a hypocrite!'

She interrupted my thoughts: 'I brought some cigars. Want to see them?'

'Yes.'

She got up and went to find them. I followed her with my eyes. Too skinny. Anemic. The husband must make about four pesos, and the five of them have to survive on this. Gloria says that the guy gives her beatings like a big shot. For the past two months, Minerva's been working in a cigar factory. She has to spend a year as an apprentice twisting Havanas before she gets steady work. Every day she steals a few, and sells them to me. For two Cuban pesos, that is, ten cents on the dollar. She comes back with a pack. Thirty beautiful cigars. Lancers. They're exquisite. She hands them to me without a word. She smiles timidly and lowers her eyes. I stare at her again. I take out sixty pesos and give them to her.

'Thanks, Minerva.'

'Don't mention it. At your service.'

'Minervita . . .'

'Tell me.'

'Put on a little music.'

'No, no. That's Gloria's. I don't know how to work the machine.'

I fix her with my gaze: 'If I were your husband, I'd give you a good thrashing every day.'

'Oh, what for?'

'To knock some life into you or else to leave you half dead. I'd whip you.'

'No, no. Oh, no!'

'Oh, no? Oh, yes. A lot of bed and a lot of leather.'

She looks at me with the sweetest, darkest, softest eyes in the world. She's as gentle as a dove. What a fucking sensual woman! She knows that I lie. If she were my woman I could only seduce her, hypnotize her. Her weakness must be flowers. What is she hiding? What lies behind those eyes? Serenity? Resignation?

Wisdom? Stupidity? She never holds my gaze. She lowers her eyes to the floor. She's an enigma. A closed book.

'Put on a cassette, Minerva.'

'I don't know how to work it. If I break it, what will my sister say?'

I get up. I go to the tape recorder. Luis Miguel. Boleros. 'The Half Turn':

> You go because I want you to go,
> Whenever I want I can stop you.
> I'm not willing to let my love show
> Because, like it or not, I'm your master.

I take her by the waist: 'Come, let's dance.'

'No, no.' But already she's yielded. There's little resistance: 'What if my sister comes and sees us? She'll say nothing to you, but to me . . .'

'Ah, girl, don't be . . .'

I was going to say: 'Don't be stupid,' but I contain myself. Instead, I grab hold of her and press her body against mine. And we start to dance, slowly. Her flesh smells warm. Just like Gloria's. It's a light odor, free of perfume or makeup. No doubt her underarms have a slight aroma of perspiration. She presses against me.

> I want you to go out in the world,
> I want you to know many people.
> I want others' lips to kiss you,
> So you can see if I have an equal.
> If you find a love who understands you
> And feel he wants to be more than friends,
> Then I'll take a half turn and
> Go with the sun when afternoon ends.
> Then I'll take a half turn and
> Go with the sun when afternoon ends.

We dance closely, one against the other. Minerva lets me lead, passive. I have my eyes closed, enjoying it. Suddenly, Gloria explodes at my side:

'Hey, what's this!? Since when do I have to stand for this? In my own house and with my sister!'

She had entered silently and surprised us. We separate. Minerva lowers her head and doesn't know what to do.

'Oh, Gloria . . .'

'No, Pedro Juan, no. This is a lack of respect. Let's see . . .'

She grabs my dick through my pants. It's slightly erect. Not hard, hard, hard, but . . .

'That's a hard-on, you son of a bitch! A hard-on and you're hitting on this bitch here. If I came two minutes later, you'd have slipped it to her. As for you, Minerva, you shameless hussy – you want to see what happens when I tell your husband? You want to see me tell him so that he gives you a beating that'll leave you dead?'

'Oh, Gloria, no, no, no, for Mommy's sake, don't do that, he'll kill me. Gloria, he'll beat me to death if he finds out. Pedro Juan made me. I didn't want to dance, but he grabbed me and forced me.'

'And you . . . well, if you wait one more minute to be born you'll be a complete fool. A fool and shameless at that.'

'Listen, Gloria, don't offend your sister further. You know she's a child of God. Stop abusing her.'

'Oh, now you're going to defend her too?'

'I don't have to defend anyone.'

'I must have shit for brains, going to get you rum. As cynical and perverse as you are! I don't know how I could fall for you! Son of the devil! You love no one. You love yourself and nothing more.'

'That's fine, Gloria. Don't talk more shit.'

'The only thing you want is to screw me so you can write that shitty novel. You think I don't know that? You've spent three years fucking around, asking me shit like if I crap twice a day.'

'Hey, quit yelling, goddamn it, the neighbors are listening.'

'Oh, that's a good one. Now he's worried about the neighbors. What an educated boy he is.'

'Gloria, I'm going to give you two cuffs round the head if you don't shut up.'

'I'm never gonna shut up. And I'm not gonna tell you anythin', Pedro Juan. You're gonna be fucked cause you don't know jack shit. A writer has to invent. What's this crap about putting all the truth down there? Are you crazy? What if people find out that that Gloria is me? Where do I hide?'

'Okay, okay, get a glass, and let's drink rum so you can cool down.'

'Invent. Invent or stop writing, because I'm not sayin' anythin' else.'

'Get a glass, baby, quick, bring me a little glass.'

'No. I'll get two. Do I look like I have a square mouth?'

'Bring one for Minerva.'

'No, not for me. I don't drink.'

'No, the little hypocrite doesn't drink, doesn't smoke, doesn't fuck, doesn't speak ill of anyone, doesn't even like pork. They say the Pope's gonna come back to Cuba to get her. Gonna take her there where he lives, whaddayacallit?

'The Vatican.'

'That's the place! To the Vatican. Saint Minerva of Havana! They're gonna put her on a poster, with that dumb face of hers. Slut! If I hadn't come in time you'd have fucked him right here, on two feet, listening to boleros.'

'Gloria, shut up and get the glasses.'

We serve ourselves and go out on the balcony to drink. Rum from the cask. Pure petroleum. For how much longer will I have to drink this shit? I swallow two big mouthfuls. I make a grimace of disgust and say: 'Uggh, what shit! Blessed Santa Bárbara, Changó, help me to write a bestseller so that one day I can drink whisky.'

'To write a what?' Gloria asks.

'Nothing, nothing. Bring me a lighter.'

I fire up a Lancer. In the background the boleros play on. We're on the seventh floor. In front of us Havana, a bit wet, windy and salty. Ruined Havana, falling to pieces. You get to love a city if you've been happy and suffered there. If there you've loved and hated. And have been without a cent in your pocket, struggling through the streets, and afterwards you recover and thank God that everything isn't shit. Without some history on your side, you're like a speck of dust blowing in the wind.

The day is rainy and gray, somewhat melancholy. I hug Gloria tight to me and am filled with a sense of strength. I feel solid, full of energy. I love this damn bitch, but I'm not willing to admit it. Gloria is a trap, and I know it.

6

On Sunday morning, I went out early to get bread. On the corner of Laguna everything is in ruins. There are some trash containers brimming with rotting garbage, a hill of rubble, puddles of fetid water. In the very center of the street two beautiful models, above it all. A girl and a boy. Very white and blond. About eighteen years old. They were modeling clothes. A team of Japanese were taking photos. The makeup artist was spraying something liquid and shiny on their hair. The clothes were white, pink, and pale blue. Simple clothes. Enchantingly simple. Deliciously expensive. I suppose that, amidst so much filth and with the inconstant sunlight, the charm of those two blond models, as white as paper and sweet-faced and innocent as angels, would shine even more. In the background there was always a collapsed building, some mangy old mutts, and little black kids staring, open-mouthed. The public was present. The neighbors, reduced to idiots, kept a respectful silence. No one approached to ask for coins or chewing gum. Two policemen were also watching, stationed discreetly several yards away. The neighbors were captivated. All of them blacks or mulattos, dirty, downtrodden, contaminated. I stopped to check it out. The Japanese were smiling: pleased and content. From time to time the photographer climbed up an aluminum stepladder and asked the models to move closer to the garbage and debris. The youngsters made disgusted faces because the rotten garbage stank, but they quickly recovered and put on very relaxed little smiles. 'Professionalism' is what I think this self-control is called. Then the photographer took pictures from the top of the ladder. A woman beside me said they were foreigners. She's a very nice black lady who wears seven necklaces and sometimes sells me contraband cigars. I told her the photographers were Japanese but the models were Cuban. And she, very convinced,

27

replied: 'Go on! Don't you see how blond and white they are? Look how beautiful they both are – they're foreigners.' I just knew they were Cubans. I don't know why, but I could recognize their Cuban traits a mile away. From what hothouse could the Japanese have plucked them? I continued on my way. I bought bread. When I got back to the building, Gloria was just leaving, shooting off like a rocket. She was accompanied by a young mulatto dressed in black with a very thick gold chain and medallion hanging outside his shirt. He was a cute little thing with the face of a sodomite.

'What's the rush? Where you off to so early?'

'Oh, *papi*, see you later. I'm in a hurry.'

I inhaled deeply: 'Uhmmmm . . . you must have bathed in perfume.'

'Ha ha ha. Ciao. See you later, my love.' She gave me a little kiss, and ran off. I climbed the stairs smiling. Gloria was off to turn a trick – and I hadn't been to the beach in a while. I put on a bathing suit underneath my pants and headed for Guanabo. A ten-peso van ride and one hour later, I was sitting underneath a coconut palm. There was a lot of wind, but the sun was bright and everything was calm and quiet. How many years had it been since I'd been to the beach? I couldn't even remember. Cans, bottles, plastic bags and empty packs of sweets and fried potatoes were strewn around the sand. The modern world invades us. I took off my clothes and shoes and put them in a backpack. I walked down the beach in my bathing suit, the cold water lapping about my ankles. I splashed on as far as the rocks. It looked like the beach was ending, but no. It was there that, thirty years ago, the Russians decided to dump thousands of enormous rocks that they brought from nearby fields in KP3 trucks. The Russians didn't speak. They simply acted. Some said the Russians did it because they didn't like sandy beaches, only ones with rocks and rubble. Others said the rocks were intended to hamper enemy progress, should the Americans ever decide to disembark on this beach and advance on Havana. No one knew the real reason. Result: a nice piece of beach fucked up, covered with enormous rocks. On the other side, the sand continued. Twenty years ago, there was a decrepit old wooden house there and I took some photos in the late afternoon. I framed them with the enormous rocks, the rickety house and the water, with lots of shadows and highlights, and then wrote a very poetic article saying something absurdly romantic about it all. When it was published in a cultural review, an important woman said that it was so refreshing to find such a beautiful and poetic article, and one with such a creative approach, in our press, and that this set an example for other journalists since Cuba is full of beautiful landscapes. Therefore, she said, all journalists should take initiatives like this and not just dedicate themselves to covering meetings, patriotic acts, and reports about the sugar-cane harvest. I felt very flattered to be complimented by such an important woman.

Now, a few yards from the rocks, a series of very ugly little painted houses had been crammed together. Some workers were spending their holidays there with their families. They were eating and drinking, and many children were shouting and playing, and the fat women were heehawing and scolding the children and cuffing their heads and shuffling in their slippers from the kitchen to the door and from the door to the kitchen. In each little house, they were trying to listen to different music. At the same time everyone was playing dominoes, shouting and slapping the plastic pieces down hard against the wood of the tables, yelling ever louder to be heard above the music. They were bellowing with laughter and saying: 'This time I fucked you, cutie, god-damn it, I fucked you good! Just so you know who I am, you gotta respect me . . . Cookie, bring me another beer here!' It was still very early, but they were drinking liters and liters of beer and rum because they were on their annual holiday and had to have a ball and get high. It appeared the winners were those who occupied a little house painted magenta, yellow and green, with lavender doors and windows. They had put two big speakers in the doorway and they were enjoying, and obliging everyone else to enjoy, at top volume, a selection from the hit parade of the moment:

Lick it oh lick it
Strawberry and chocolate
Lick it oh lick it
Strawberry and chocolate
Lick it oh lick it
Strawberry and chocolate
Lick it oh lick it
Strawberry and chocolate
Lick it oh lick it
Strawberry and chocolate
Lick it oh lick it
Strawberry and chocolate
Lick it oh lick it
Strawberry and chocolate
Lick it oh lick it
Strawberry and chocolate
Lick it oh lick it
Strawberry and chocolate
Lick it oh lick it
Strawberry and chocolate
Lick it oh lick it
Strawberry and chocolate
Now now now. C'mon,
Pay attention, raise your hand,
C'mon move your hand higher,
Ahhhhhhhhhhhhhhhhhhhhhhhhhhh
Lick it oh lick it
Strawberry and chocolate
Lick it oh lick it
Strawberry and chocolate
Lick it oh lick it
Strawberry and chocolate
Lick it oh lick it
Strawberry and chocolate

I walked back on the sand to my coconut palm. A two-hundred-yard stretch. Three uninterrupted streams of urine, grease, and shit ran from the cafeteria and nearby houses, adding to the filth of the beach. A nauseating odor. Shit pursues me.

But a bit beyond, near the coconut palm, everything was tranquil. There was no smell of shit, you couldn't hear the music, and the sea remained blue and clean with little frothy waves and good sun. The only things missing were seashells and an eighty-year-old poet to put it all into rhyme, his white hair ruffled by the breeze.

Really, everything was perfect, and I said to myself: 'What are you complaining about, Pedro Juan? Don't be so conflicted, comrade. Stay on this little patch here, because it's regal, as Cuban Sandra would say, and to hell with the rest. Don't try to fix the world.' So be it. I went in the water, and I swam for quite a while.

The cool blue water did its thing. Half an hour later I was invigorated, relaxed; I had forgotten the anxieties and dark side of life. Now I was functioning at full sail. I lay down to catch some sun, and it was then that the thought occurred to me that thirty years ago I was only twenty. Young, uninformed, and happy. I believed in and aspired to something. What exactly that was, I didn't know. But back then I believed, sought and aspired to find something. I closed my eyes, and I left my mind a blank.

7

I awoke half stunned, alligator-like, drowsing under the sun. I entered the water, swam awhile, and refreshed myself. What time was it? Around me the tranquility, the silence continued, almost no one about. I needed an aspirin and a very cold soda. I started walking. Head back to Havana? No, it was still too early. Soon I found an open pharmacy. I asked the salesgirl, who turned her back, angry for some reason, and answered me between her teeth: 'There's no aspirin. Nowhere, don't even look.'

'But from time to time . . .'

'When they come we're out in half an hour. They bring very few. And for the past three months, nothing.'

I drank two orange sodas and climbed up a hill, heading toward the wooded zone where Evelio and Julita live. I hadn't seen them for years. The last time we spoke, they were running around Havana, from office to office. They wanted to travel to Venezuela and, naturally enough, not come back. Julita had a niece in a little village there, and they had pinned all their hopes on the niece and the village. Problem was, only the two of them were permitted to travel – they'd have to leave their children behind. They prayed to eleven thousand virgins, they swore they would come back, that they wouldn't ask for asylum. All to no avail. They were still here, all the family together.

They live in a lovely place, two hundred yards from the beach. Each house has trees and a garden around it. I crossed a baseball field where some boys were playing. I asked one who was playing center field: 'How's the game going?'

'Sixteen to sixteen in the third inning.'

'Damn, kid, you guys are really bad! Doesn't it make you sad?'

'You know, mister, it doesn't bother us at all.'

I kept going. Backwoods ballplayers. I went toward the thicket. I found the house. In a short time Evelio had gone quite gray-haired. He was doing something with some cages of fine roosters. There were about thirty cages, set in the shade, beneath some mango and avocado trees, next to the house. We looked at each other, but he didn't recognize me. I stopped on the sidewalk and shouted to him: 'Hey, mister, are you selling those roosters?'

'Damn it, Pedro Juan, I didn't recognize you, man!'

'We haven't seen each other in years.'

'Come in, come in.'

'Those roosters are beautiful, are they yours?'

'Yes. Got to keep busy with something.'

'Are there cockpits around here?'

'Yeah, uh huh, the woods are full of cockpits. They run them on Sundays, in secret, you know, just like everything else. You like the fights?'

'Uh huh, ever since I was a boy. But I don't have the patience to breed.'

'You just bet.'

'I bet. When I was eleven I started selling ices in the cockpit at Matanzas. And I got hooked, you know how it is. With your pocket full of pesos, who can resist?'

'You must've bet on the sly, because at that age . . .'

'I placed my bets outside. I had a phony work permit, and I won a lot. I have a good eye for the cocks.'

'Because you like them. A man who likes the birds has an instinct. He knows a winner.'

Evelio had two bottles of *aguardiente*. Supposedly to blow on the feathers of the roosters. It seems he used this pretext to spend the day half in the bag. He told me he went on Sundays to a Baptist church where there was an Alcoholics Anonymous meeting. I grabbed a bottle and we sat on the porch. A nutritive breeze was blowing in from the sea. If you took a mouthful, you could taste it.

'So, where do we stand, Evelio: Sundays you go to church or to the fights?'

'Depends on how I feel when I get up. I prefer the roosters, but I have to give up the alcohol. Else I'll be left without a liver.'

'Evelio, do you have an aspirin?'

'For what?'

'For a headache.'

'Ah, that's easy. Olgaaaaa! Olgaaaaa!'

The neighbor came out on her porch when she heard the cries. Evelio asked her for an aspirin.

'No, what I have is paracetamol. From the States. It's even better than aspirin.'

'Fine. Bring one for my associate here.'

I took it with a mouthful of *aguardiente* and many thanks, Olga. We sat in silence. We had nothing to talk about. Until I remembered something: 'Evelio, what did you tell me about the roosters and the santos?'

'That I have these roosters because when I received my santo years ago, he demanded roosters.'

'Yeah? He asked for roosters?'

'Ah, you don't know anything. Sometimes they ask for goats, sheep, black hens, boa constrictors, doves. But they also take things away from you. For instance, I can't ride bicycles or motorcycles or drive cars. The religion is very complicated. I began with two little cocks and a fine little hen, and already I have a flock which is worth whatever I want to ask. These animals are all winners. The moment they hatch, they're ready to fight.'

Again silence. Two or three more mouthfuls of pure fire *aguardiente*, and on an empty stomach too. Evelio said to me: 'Here, look at this. This is something I never showed anyone.'

He showed me the casseroles, the iron pans, the soup tureens of the *santos*. He'd hidden them all in a little cupboard with doors in the living room. We returned to the porch and continued with the *aguardiente*. Then he leant back in the armchair and looked at the ceiling, pensive. He had in his hands the blue-beaded necklace of Yemayá. He was playing with it. He sat for a moment in silence, before saying: 'A little while ago you made a good decision. And it's going to bear fruit. It was hard, you were very indecisive, you were even afraid they were going to put you in jail, but you have a good guide. Don't be afraid now, keep moving forward. It was a decision with papers and things like that, but this has already passed and, as I told you, you drew a good card. Now . . . I'm going to tell you more . . . you have an African and an Indian always at your side. Both are strong and they won't leave you.'

'That's what I'm always told in consultations.'

'That's because it's true: they are there. They never leave your side. Even though you don't take care of them. Well . . . to the Indian, yes, you pay attention and ask him for things and offer flowers, but you don't even look at the African. You've forgotten about him.'

'Yes, it's true.'

'Ah, you see. But you must serve them both. You are intelligent thanks to the Indian and strong and a fighter thanks to the black man. Both are important for you because they complement each other. One supports the other. You understand?'

'Yes, of course.'

'This black man is real hard. Thanks to him, no one can touch you. He's a big strong black man, naked, save for a loincloth. A loincloth made of jute sack, and a red bandanna wrapped around his head. You have to give him a gourd full of coconut milk with rum or *aguardiente* and a cigar. Not always. When you remember it. That's what this black man likes. He likes rum, tobacco, and women. Speak to him. You have to speak to him and ask him. And, once in a while, offer him a red rose, a black prince. Red flowers are his favorites. Anything red. He's not a festive black, he doesn't rumba. He's a black from the woods. A fugitive. He never shows his face, because he hides in the cane-brakes. But he knows a lot. He's strong, astute, and very brave. He's got balls.'

Then Julia arrived. Evelio had the blue-beaded necklace of Yemayá in his hands. He'd been playing with it while he told me all that. He felt caught *in flagrante*, surprised. He quickly tried to hide the beads, but Julia had already seen them: 'Oh, Pedro Juan, what a surprise to see you here. And Evelio here telling you all that shit about his *santos*, and about his little necklace; making like he's a prophet.'

'Julita, please, at least show some respect.'

'I respect nothin', Evelio. He says he has to consult. Lies and stories. All this is shit.'

'Now, Julita, come on . . .'

'Oh, I see. You believe in all this gibberish too, Pedro Juan. This is shit. Stories. I believe in what I can touch with my hands. But unseen things, things in the air . . .'

'Goddamn it, what about those nights when they were pulling on your feet? And you used to wake up weeping and shitting yourself? You sure came running to me then so I could cleanse you and remove the dead.'

'Oh, those were dreams. I got nervous.'

'Dreams? No, you were wide awake, and they kept pulling your paws.'

'My feet.'

'It's the same.'

'Nah, I just got nervous, that's all. It was the same crap every night. Pedro Juan, this man's an engineer. He studied. He was a professor at the university. Tell me honestly, must he believe in this foolishness of backward blacks from Africa? I could understand it if he was like me. I barely managed to finish secondary school. I was stupid, I didn't like books or studying, but this man is a real scholar . . .'

'Julita, I've told you a hundred times that studies have nothing to do with religion. Pedro Juan, pay attention to what I'm about to tell you. I used to be the same as Julia. At the time, I was teaching at the university, and I was involved with the trade union and the mobilization, and all the rest of it. I didn't believe in anything. Nothing at all. My father was the one who had his *santos*, and with him it was a lifelong thing, ever since he was a kid. But he kept quiet about it. Not for his own sake, but so that it wouldn't harm his children and the family. He kept everything in a room, under lock and key, and the only ones who knew about it were his family. He didn't give readings or anything. What's more, for quite a while my old man was a manager and traveled to Bulgaria and to the Soviet Union. Oh, he was a big shot all right. Anyhow, time passes, he retires, he gets older, and there comes a moment when he starts to lose his mind. All of a sudden. Without illness. He was seventy-two years old, but he was healthy. He lost control, he rambled, he talked nonsense, he even forgot when to eat; he wasn't sleeping, his hands shook. If he went through the woods we had to go after him, else he'd get lost and not return. Then *I* started to have problems: at night they tugged on my feet and I'd go unconscious, and, when I came to my senses, I'd be told that I'd been talking for an hour like a Congo black. Sometimes I'd go running off through the woods, on a mad impulse, to a ceiba tree half a dozen miles away from here. Running! And I'd arrive not out of breath, not even panting. There I'd look for herbs and then crouch between the roots of the ceiba to prepare a tincture. I could be there a couple of hours. When I was done, I'd return home.'

'And you couldn't control yourself?'

'I had no self-control. It was as if I were mad. Exactly the same as happened with my father. It was as if the two of us had lost our heads. So I went to see my father's *babalao*, his spiritual godfather. And he told me: "Your father is going to die soon but before he does, he has to pass all his knowledge of the *santos* to you. Until you receive it, he cannot die."'

'I must have heard this tale seven hundred times, Evelio. Every time you have a drink you come out with the same story.'

'But it's true, Julita. I don't tell lies.'

'And how did it all end?'

'As the *babalao* said it would. One Monday my father passed everything on to me. And he died that Wednesday. Peacefully in his bed, at night. And since then, we're beginning to move forward here, there's nothing lacking in this house.'

'The *santos* know their own business, Evelio. Stop talking rubbish. And I know mine. And no *santo* is going to come down off their altar and put fifty bucks in my hand. Let the *santos* stay here and starve; I'm going to go where I can eat ham. The day we get lucky in the raffle and they give all four of us visas . . . ahhhhh, watch out, boy, because I'm going to throw a party so huge it'll shake the whole of Havana. They're gonna hear the music way up there across the water. Not in Key West or Miami, but further up, in Tampa. They're going to hear the music in Boca Ratón!'

We kept silent, until I said to her: 'You're obstinate, Julita. That's bad. You'll drive yourself crazy.'

'Sure I'm obstinate. I'm crazy, completely crazy. The same as everyone else. Aren't you obstinate?'

'That's her thing, Pedro Juan. The screaming, the craziness: yes, she's crazy; yes, she's going to hustle an old Spaniard so he'll run off with her. And if she's crazy here she can be just as crazy there. Listen, man, nobody can live like that. This woman can agitate anyone. She's got a wild hair that all the African commissions combined couldn't pluck.'

I didn't reply. I had an urge to get the fuck out. Why did I come to visit these people? We fell silent, sitting on the porch, in the cool breeze, staring at the sea in the distance, between the trees. On the baseball field the boys continued playing but they couldn't be heard. Only the wind in the trees was audible. Julia couldn't stand the silence: 'Pedro Juan, if I'm not mistaken, you were writing poems.'

'Yes, sometimes.'

'You don't write now?'

'No.'

'Why?'

'I have nothing to say.'

'You're not in love?'

'No.'

'People write poems when they're in love.'

'Hmmm.'

'I'm going to give you a notebook of poems.'

'Yours?'

'No. A hustler's.'

'Ah.'

'A romantic whore. We rented a room to a Mexican and a hustler. When they took off they left a notebook of love poems behind.'

'Let's see.'

'You can have it. We've already read it. If we leave it here, it'll end up in the bathroom because the kids grab whatever's around to wipe their asses.'

'Julita, Julita.'

'It's true, Evelio, don't make like you're refined, because Pedro Juan is family. Keep it, Pedro Juan. They're very pretty poems. I wish I could write like that. They're really precious.'

I took advantage of the pretext. I grabbed the notebook, said goodbye, and set off back down the hill.

8

The telephone rang: Kurt, from Salzburg. A year ago he translated some of my texts into German. He was crippled, in a wheelchair. Once, on a beach in the south of France, he fell backwards onto some rocks and broke his spine. Now thirty, he's been rolling around in that chair for eight years. He intended to make the best of it. At least not embitter other people's lives. Could we get together this afternoon? Yes, sure. At five.

At that hour I stood on the corner of 21st and 2nd streets, in Vedado. Kurt had rented a small apartment a few steps from there. He liked to be self-sufficient, to move around on his own with the minimum of help. I sat down on a very low wall which bordered a garden. I leaned back and prepared to wait. It was a tree-lined place, tranquil and silent. Clean enough. Obese women were passing, looking like executives, wearing jackets, with pale-colored scarves around their necks, and carrying black attaché cases. Neighbors with decrepit cars were entering and exiting their garages. Well-dressed adolescents, looked like little daddy's boys, that is, seemingly well fed, smiling, not preoccupied. Some were jogging, outfitted to sweat and reduce the excess blubber of their bellies. People strolled calmly beneath the trees. Some seemed a bit bored, walking their lively dogs. The little dogs sniffed at the foot of the trees, raised their legs and peed a little. Sometimes they produced a small strained turd.

Down the sidewalk walked a young black girl, very coquettish and sexy. She wore a very short blue tweed skirt which exposed her thighs, and an equally flimsy blouse which allowed her to show off her belly, her navel and her shoulders. All beautifully black, youthful, smooth, and perfect. She was overflowing with energy and life. She stopped on the corner, and looked one way then the other. There was no traffic at all. The streets were totally empty. She saw me smiling and directed herself to me: 'Are you from around here?'

It occurred to me to tell her yes. It appealed to me to speak with her a moment, that tasty morsel. I thought she was going to ask directions, but no: 'Do you know anyone who wants to trade around here?'

'Around here? No.'

'Do you live nearby?'

Since I had already told the first lie, I went further: 'Here, in this building.'

'Oh, and you have no idea if anyone wants . . .'

'No, my love. This is a very good area. Nobody wants to move from here.'

'Yeah. I know. I live nearby.'

'Ahhh, and what have you got?'

'An apartment with two bedrooms, dining room, bath, kitchen, balcony, and a little interior patio. It's in good condition. With a little paint it would be perfect.'

'You want to expand?'

'No. In exchange I need two smaller apartments. One bedroom each.'

'You're getting divorced?'

'I'm not married. I want to be independent of my parents.'

'They control you too much?'

'Yeah. They don't let me live. I'm an adult now and I've had it with so much control.'

'I ask because I have an apartment in Central Havana and . . .'

'In Central Havana?! No, no, no, no! Not even if I were crazy! I won't leave Vedado for anything in the world.'

'Hey, but listen to me first. It has its advantages. It has a telephone, there are no blackouts . . .'

'Yeah, and a million horny black guys, and police, and crazy old ladies and disgusting old men, and cockroaches and rats and the sewers overflowing with shit. No, no, no, no! You'll pardon me, because I'm black. You're not going to believe that I'm racist, but who *caaaaaares*?! For a black girl like me, enough is enough.'

'Well, my love . . .'

She left in a foul mood, without saying goodbye. I continued waiting calmly, observing the peace in that no-fire zone. It seemed my neighborhood was at war. A low-intensity war. Luckily, I felt very good among the filth and with my Afro-Cuban friends.

It was already five-thirty. Kurt still hadn't shown up. I waited ten minutes. Another ten. At ten to six, I left. I bought a little rum and sat placidly on my roof terrace, facing the sea. A cigar, a glass of rum and the sea. Sometimes I try to think. That's what one ought to do, supposedly: think, reflect serenely. About what? About nothing.

So I continued drinking, bored and in silence. By nine at night there was still some rum and I was feeling no pain. It was cold and windy. I put on a woolen shirt and reclined in a window to contemplate a very murky Havana. Havana in darkness. Full moon and cloudy. A cold wind was blowing as if it were threatening to rain. The telephone rang loudly. Kurt. Very nervous. His Spanish, usually fluent, was incomprehensible. He was shivering.

'Perrrrrrro Guan? Perrrrroh Guan?'

'Yes, yes.'

'Kurt, Kurt.'

'Yes, what's happening?'

'Oh, excuse that I call you. Excuse. Perrrrroh Guan . . . I have no one, I have no one, excuse . . . ohhhh . . . I'm freezing.'

'Freezing? Where are you? Impossible that you're freezing.'

'Oh, it pains me to ask for help. Oh, I'm very nervous.'

'Do you want me to come to see you? Where are you?'

'Can you come?'

'Yes, immediately. Give me your address.'

It was very close to 2nd and 21st, that very peaceful place. I arrived in thirty minutes. It was a very small apartment, in the rear of a basement which also served as the garage for a ten-story building. In an area partitioned off from the garage, someone had constructed a small room with a bath. It was tiny, oppressive, windowless; what's more, for me, it was claustrophobic. When I arrived, the door was ajar. I called out. Kurt told me to come in.

Total darkness. I couldn't see anything. By touch I found the switch on the wall, flicked on the light and . . . ahhh: Kurt lay naked on the floor, next to the telephone, trembling. There was the smell of shit. Fresh shit.

'What happened to you?'

'Oh, I'm so ashamed, Perrrrroh Guan, ohhhh, ohhh . . .'

'But what happened?'

'Please, go to the bedroom and bring me something. A shirt. I'm so cold.'

The apartment had only one small room, divided by a folding screen with panes of colored glass. Behind the screen there was a bed and a closet. This is what Kurt was calling 'the bedroom'. In one corner, a small door led to a disproportionately large bathroom, comfortable, even sophisticated. Everything was on the floor. A stream of water led from the bathtub, which was overflowing with water and shit. Floating turds – that's where the stench was coming from. I looked in the closet. There was nothing. Empty hangers. No clothes, no luggage, no shoes, only some underpants, some dirty socks, and a ragged old pair of canvas tennis shoes. Some papers, an address book, a toothbrush. Even the sheets had been taken. Luckily they had left a woolen bedspread. I took it and went back to the other room, near Kurt. He was shivering. I covered him with the bedspread.

'Kurt, there's water all over the place, but all your things have gone. Were you robbed?'

'Ah, yes. Oh, I was in that cold water for hours. I think I have fever.'

'Sure, you have fever.'

Kurt stank of shit. He seemed to have bathed in shit. I wrapped him tighter. He was totally paralyzed from the waist down. His arms, hands and fingers were functioning with great difficulty. I was able to sit him up on the floor.

'Please, bring my chair.'

His wheelchair was in the bathroom. I carried him there and placed him in it, bundled up in the blanket. He asked me to make a coffee. In one corner of the room there was a small fridge, a gas stove, a table, and three chairs. I prepared the coffee and served two cups. Kurt, distressed, stared at the floor.

'Hey, listen, wake up!'

'Oh, please don't shout. I'm very nervous.'

'Drink the coffee and finish telling me what the hell went on here.'

'Ehh, it was a hustler . . . ohh, no, miserable fucks . . . oh, I'm ashamed, Perrrroh Guan, but I'll tell you the truth . . . ahhhh . . .'

'Kurt, please, concentrate. Drink the coffee, calm yourself and tell me the truth. I can help you, but tell me the truth.'

'Yes, thank you, you are kind. Thank you. I brought them here, last night. A woman and a man, hustlers. I liked them a lot. The boy and the girl. He was very black, very sexy, and she was a mulatta, also very sexy. Beautiful both of them. We had sex, three of us, you know. For several hours. It left me exhausted, so afterwards they put me in the bath with hot water and gave me a massage. The boy was very smart, very cunning; he massaged me in the water and gave me more rum. I did not want to drink more. We had drunk much, smoked weed, you know, everything. But he almost forced me to keep drinking, and . . . well, I fell asleep in the water. I don't know what time.'

'They put something in the rum.'

'Yes, now I think it too. When I woke up, the water was very cold and I felt frozen. I called them, but they didn't answer. Oh, Perrroh Guan, what a problem. I had panic. I couldn't get out of the bath on my own, you know. I kept screaming. I screamed and screamed until I lost my voice, but in this basement there are no neighbors. I was terrified thinking I might die in such an absurd way, so unnecessary. I had much fear to die. Much fear.'

'And you took a shit in the bathtub.'

'Yes. Oh, I'm so ashamed with you. But I can't control my sphincter, you know.'

'Cool it, calm yourself. It's over.'

'Ohhh. Well, finally, I don't know how, I succeeded in grasping the sides and threw myself to the floor. Crawling, I came to the telephone and called you. Sorry, but I didn't remember any other number. Only yours. Thank you for coming, thank you for . . .'

'Okay, okay. Forget the thank-yous and the courtesy. The problem now is what do we do? They took everything.'

'My documents too? Credit cards, passport, return ticket? Oh, no. Please. Inspect thoroughly.'

I did: all they left was the wheelchair. There was no money, no clothes, no passport. Nothing.

'Well, Kurt, there's nothing here. What shall I do? Call the police? And, by the way, we have to clean up, because the smell of shit is unbearable. And you have to bathe again.'

'Yes, oh, no. I'm not sure. I'm confused, humiliated. What humiliation.'

'Forget the humiliation, and come back down to earth, Kurt. React. Do I call the police?'

'No, no, not the police. It would complicate everything more. I'll go to the embassy for a new passport and, oh, I've no money.'

'Listen, forgive my asking, but do you have erections or do you take it up the ass?'

'Yes, yes, with a medicine, very potent. It gives me up to three hours of erection, but I don't feel anything. The girls really enjoy it, you know, I enjoy looking, and you know, the fantasy and, ohhh, what must I do now?'

'I don't know, Kurt. I have no idea what you can do.'

9

Agneta called on Tuesday, in very good spirits.

'Last night I read *My Dear Drum's Master*.' She was sending an envelope by messenger with documents for the seminar. The airplane ticket is for May 13. Oh, how great, the height of spring. I must send the medical report right away for the insurance. We speak of trivial things.

'It's very hot here.'

'Here it's still three or four degrees. I'd gladly go to Cuba. For a year.'

'There's no work.'

'Ah, it doesn't matter. I'll sell my car and make do for a while.'

Later, I don't know how, the conversation begins to heat up. I think it began with me, as always. I like her voice, her hesitant speech, her slowness. It got me hard and I began to shake it softly, and told her so. 'Ah, I like that. Really? You're doing it? Oh, I'm at the office. I can't do anything.' I keep at it, slowly. Caressing my prick, putting saliva on it so it moves smoothly. What I haven't said until now is that when Agneta got that photo of me naked in the snow, with a stiff prick, it began to turn her world around. From the Alps I went back to Vienna. I spent a few days living in an attic on Radetzkystrasse. Agneta called me every afternoon. Darkness comes early in Vienna, but in Stockholm nightfall was at four in the afternoon. I don't recall how, but we got used to masturbating on the phone. I suppose she would look at the photo, and she listened to all the barbarities I told her. For me, it was enough to hear her voice and her sighing.

Now Agneta was speaking of other things: of her boss who'd just returned from vacation in Sicily and was telling stories which made everyone laugh.

'Why do they laugh so much? She's a stupid woman.'

'She came back satisfied from the Mediterranean. Probably had sex with some Sicilian.'

'Not with a Sicilian. She had sex with her boyfriend. Oh, the stupid woman.'

'With her boyfriend who is your ex?'

'Yes, my ex. It's a strange situation.'

'In Sweden it is. In Cuba it's very normal. All mixed up, as the poet said.'

'What poet?'

'*A* poet. That's what he said: all mixed up.'

Agneta remains silent. It's very sensual. It turns me on to know she's there in silence, thinking of me. And when she speaks she says it all so softly, and it's glory. Not Gloria. Glory. Then she whispers: 'Are you still . . .?'

'Yes.'

'The same thing?'

'Yes. You going to leave the hair in your armpits?'

'Oh, no. I tried it for a few days and I don't like it.'

'It's okay. When I'm there I'll convince you. No hurry.'

I keep on but holding back. I don't want to shoot my wad in the air. I'll save it for Gloria or someone else.

'I'll be fired for this. This isn't a business call. We've already been talking for . . . uhmmm, twenty-three minutes.'

'Yes, but how great it would be if you were here, Agneta. Do you have a lot of hair on your sex, on your thighs?'

'Yes. I told you. A lot of hair. I'm very dark, and . . .'

'Ah, catch this, bitch, I can't hold back any longer, watch it spurt out, bitch, slut, horny Swede, cunt, I can't stop myself, fuck, I'm coming all over the floor . . .'

'Oh, and I'm so far away. How is it possible?'

'Ahhh, the last drop . . . How is what possible?'

'How is it possible? Me so far. You finished?'

'I don't like it alone, I don't like it alone, oh, fuck. All this whacking off is wasting me. I don't like shooting my come on the floor.'

Finally it was thirty-five minutes of prattle. I ended up exhaust-ed. Jerking off is a killer. In my adolescence I did it up to five or six times a day and the skin of my cock became irritated and some-times I gave myself sores from so much jerking off. I had some photos of Brigitte Bardot. And sometimes I spied on my neighbor, Estela. Beautiful name. I'll never forget her. I wrote her little love poems. I'd love to reread them, but I don't know where they are.

Searching for these poems, I found a notebook with the begin-ning of *The Frugal Life*. It's an interrupted novel. I don't dare go on with it. It's written in the first person. To write in the first person is like taking your clothes off in public. It begins when the guy, I mean the protagonist, catches his wife with another man. The guy suspected it, but had pretended not to notice anything. The novel begins like this:

'Habitually we ourselves construct our infernos and our par-adises. Thus, anyplace can be marvelous. Or terrible. I spent many years building my inferno. Only I didn't notice it. I did it very scrupulously, but at the same time unwittingly. I mean, for many years, I acted like an automaton. Then I had a time bomb on my hands. And it exploded in my face in the summer of 1990. Of course, it left me devastated; not knowing what to do. One September afternoon, I discovered a happy glint in the eyes of my wife. She moved like a cat. It was evident she had another man and that, furtively, she had just been to see him. She was returning home happy and when she saw me, she grew bitter. Now I can write it without pain and without hate, but at that moment it gave me goosebumps.'

It was terrible. That man, I mean the protagonist, lashed out and smashed everything within reach. He burnt his bridges and ended up completely isolated, a wreck on a desert island. Shattered. The tantrum lasted years. He'd have to die like a dog or rise from his own ashes.

For now it doesn't interest me to write a novel which starts this way and which I know from memory: from start to finish. All I have to do is sit down and write it. To write it with guts and entrails. Spilling it all out on paper. Staining the pages with blood and saliva, and with shit and piss and snot and tears. Usually when an editor receives such filthy manuscripts, he can't understand why you're such a careless pig. But the fact is a novel like *The Frugal Life* isn't written with the brain or the hands. You have to be willing to flay yourself. You strip off your skin until you're raw meat, and then you throw yourself headlong into the novel until you hit the bottom of the precipice. Smashing yourself, skinning yourself, and breaking your bones against the rocks. It's the only way. He who doesn't dare to do it this way is better off leaving his paper and pencils on the table and dedicating himself to selling tomatoes or real estate.

Anyway, for the moment, I couldn't write. I didn't want to. No writing, no painting. I read something by a dirty old man: 'Intuitively, the woman knows that sham survives in our society and therefore she prefers it. All that interests her is having children and raising them in safety.' My fifty years of street life assured me this was totally true. I suppose the intolerant ones, male and female, would keep watch over this old man so as to club him back every time he stuck his snout out the door of his house. The majority of human beings cannot think for themselves. People act by imitation. And there comes a moment when just to breathe requires a leader to show them how to do it. And there always is a leader on hand. This was the leitmotif of *The Frugal Life*. The protagonist had fallen in the trap, and, little by little, automatism was taking hold, growing inside him like a cancer.

I was wandering around like that, incoherent. Thinking twenty different things and about nothing. At this moment Gloria reappeared, very calm, with an innocent smile. More than innocent, it was a candid, childlike smile, but naughty too. She brought with her a package containing paper: a thousand-odd sheets of cheap, yellow paper. Newsprint. Which was fine – it's what I use to write on. And I hadn't any. For years now you can only get it out there, on the black market.

'Damn, girl, you finally showed up.'

'But, *papi*, I was here, at home. How come you didn't look for me?'

She gave me the paper.

'Thanks a lot. How much did it cost you?'

'Nothing.'

'What do you mean, nothing? What did you do to get it, slut?'

'Don't ask. I told you I'd arrange it. And there it is.'

'What did you do?'

'Nothing, my love. Just take the paper and forget it.'

'You want coffee?'

'Sure. But I have no cigarettes.'

'And that gringo you hustled? Didn't he pay you?'

'What gringo?'

'Don't give me that shit. You're gone since Sunday. You went off with that street punk to find a gringo.'

'The things you make up; you're very imaginative. Your head's full of fiction and suspicious thoughts.'

'Gloria, why don't you have cigarettes?'

I knew the response by heart: 'I have no money, *papito*. I was shut up at home waiting for you. And you lost out there, strutting the streets.'

I gave her thirty pesos: 'Buy rum and cigarettes, and get me a couple of cigars.'

'It ain't enough. Give me forty.'

'Forty nothing, try to stretch the thirty. And hurry, I'm gonna make coffee.'

In ten minutes she was back with everything. We sit with our espressos. I really wanted to know the story behind the paper. Finally she was relaxed enough: 'Didn't I tell you that mulatto at the printer's was going to give it to me?'

'Yes.'

'I went yesterday, at five o'clock. He told me to wait a while on the corner until the other employees went home.'

'Slut! So he slipped it to you behind the Linotype?'

'No way. That one slip it to me? Do you know how ugly and twisted he is? He's so ugly that if you saw him you'd run away. He looks like the Devil.'

'You say you don't like good-looking men.'

'That's true. But not so completely gross. This mulatto shattered the ugly-meter.'

'You had to do something. You showed him your tits . . .'

'He took me to the back of the shop, gave me the package of paper, and, without my noticing it, already had his cock out and standing like a truncheon. "Let me see your tits, let me see your pussy," he said to me. Doesn't even know how to talk. If he fell down, he'd start eating grass just like a donkey. But what a huge cock he had! And fat. Really fat!'

'So he did have a saving grace: a big dick.'

'Yes. Not all bad. The truth is it was attractive.'

'So you jerked him off?'

'*Meeee?* No, I'm too decent a girl to do that. He took care of it himself. I showed him a little bit up here and a little bit down there. He sucked my tits for a second and came in two minutes flat. I grabbed the pack of paper and was out of there in no time, wiggling my ass and glad to be rid of that mulatto jerk-off.'

'Well, the paper's here now.'

'If you need more, I'll get it for you, *papi*. I left him hungry. Imagine, even after he came, his cock was as hard as a board. Like a table leg. But, man, is he ugly! He looks like a punch-drunk boxer.'

Now it was me who was horny. And I jumped her. She drives me nuts with her stories. Which aren't stories. They're the counter-story of the official story. The antistory. The suprastory. We like each other a lot. I like her hands, her feet, her hair, her color, her laugh. All of her. I like to sniff and lick her ass. I like to be inside her. An hour, an hour and a half. Two hours. And to talk. She always has a slight underarm odor, which drives me wild. I took off my woven leather belt, and began to hit her lightly on the buttocks. I drooled on her mouth and she flipped. She turned over, offering me her ass. Oh, first it hurt, but she asked me for more, she wouldn't let me take it out, and she told me about her adventures on the street. She really likes it up the ass. I can't describe more. Two hours of madness. She's lovely. She has a dark face, so beautiful, with very white teeth.

'Go on, *papi*, let me live with you and make me pregnant. Calm me down. Get me pregnant, and I promise I'll be quiet and never even look at another man. Just you, *papi*, just you. It's because I have fire between my legs. Ever since I was a little girl. I can't control myself.'

'Brainless hussy! You're going to be an old crone of seventy and still looking for young studs on the street, you're shameless.'

'That's it, my love, that's what I like. And to be in Milagro's cathouse.'

'What the hell's Milagro's cathouse?'

'Ahh, I like to go there, wait in a room for whoever enters. And then I undress. And right away ask him for money. I like that. Them pulling out the bills, hooking them to the elastic of my panties.'

'What's this, mulatta? Tell me the story, you've got me going.'

'And you've got me confused. This never happened to me before. I don't even know what I'm saying. Why do I talk so much?'

'Because you're in love.'

'I'm in love, goddamn it. At home everyone knows. You leave me gaga.'

She was kissing my tattoo, sucking and biting it.

'This red serpent has me hypnotized.'

She put the belt up her vagina and offered herself to me, asking for more and more. All the while kissing the red serpent.

'Don't come, goddamn it, don't come! Give me cock, fuck it, give me more cock!'

She was a porno star, a genius. Wild. When I couldn't take it any more I shot my milk, kicking, screaming, snorting like a bull. I gave her a slap and fell quivering and convulsing to the basement of the building, rebounded and came back to bed, spent, as ground up as mince.

A shot of rum and a good cigar to recuperate. I reclined on my window ledge, facing the sea and the city, the sun shining. She glued herself to my back: 'Oh, *papi*, when you come you're not you.'

'And who am I? When you extract the milk from my medulla, from my brain, from my asshole, from the marrow of my bones, you squeeze it out of me . . .'

'You're not yourself. It's the African. The black that is with you. You pant and you rage and shout and lose your mind. You have no idea what you do. It's the African who's getting off, not you.'

'You're going to tell me about the African too?'

'You already know. I don't have to tell you anything. The African uses you as his horse. That's why you screw like a savage. And, what's more, you're the reverse of most men. The older you get, the bigger and fatter and harder it grows and the more milk and more, you know. Whoever goes to bed with you . . . girl! watch out, cause you're a trap. A trap just lying there, ready to spring.'

I felt myself very macho and very strong and very savage after those encounters. Let Lacan come so we can put him in bed and make a Lacanian sandwich and all be happy.

'Look, *papi*, I bought you a little gift.'

She took out of a bag yellow briefs and a sleeveless T-shirt: violet, yellow, and black. I thought: 'Fuck, that's for carnival or going to Jamaica,' but I didn't say anything.

'This shirt so I can see your tattoo.'

I put everything on right away. 'And this gift?'

'The gringo gave me a few dollars.'

'The gringo from Sunday?'

'Yeah. He's like seventy years old. Very difficult.'

'Where's he from?'

'Ah, I don't know. He says he's the mayor of a town and that he has some wine shops.'

'Probably Spanish.'

'He doesn't lisp.'

'How does he talk, then?'

'I don't know. I didn't even ask him. He has a very weird name I don't remember. My thing is first to take his cash and then make him hot. I strip in front of him and put consolers up his ass. He has a collection of around ten consolers.'

'Consolers?'

'Dildos, all sizes and colors. He has a little satchel full of vibrators and creams. The old guy is nuts. A couple of logs light of a load. I don't know how he can be a mayor or have businesses . . . well, every madman has his thing. Point is, I made a few bucks, and later he tipped me fifty more. I settled things in my house. Now there's enough grub for a week at least so I bought you a little gift too because I always think of you.'

'What you are is a tremendous hustler.'

'I may be a hustler but I love you. You've stolen my heart, and you're my man. So what if I'm a hustler? I told you if you marry me that's over, I'll live for you and only you. For you and the children we'll have together. That's what I want.'

'What you want? You want to be a housewife *and* a streetwalker. The two things at the same time.'

'No, *papi*, no. Just a wife, that's all. At home, happy with the kids. Anyhow, I've never seen a woman spend her whole life as a whore. It's a one-time thing. And those who haven't done it sometimes want to. The trouble is, you're a man and men don't understand how we women are.'

'Ah, drop the theory and don't try to be a sociologist.'

'I'm not. But what I'm telling you is true. Everyone is bad sometimes.'

'You're not bad.'

'But that's how you see me. As if I were a devil.'

'I see nothing.'

'Well, each to his own.'

'Want to go to the beach?'

'Now?'

'Now.'

'I don't even have a peso.'

'And what the old gringo gave you?'

'I already spent it, my love, it was nothing more than a few little pesos.'

'Find some dollars and let's go to the beach.'

'No, no. It's already spent.'

'Find some dollars or I'll smack you.'

I picked up the belt again. I gave her two or three smacks on the back and the buttocks.

'Ah, stop it, don't hit me, you bastard! Abuser!'

'Get the money.'

'How much?'

'Twenty dollars.'

'That's a lot. You want to go to Varadero or Guanabo?'

'To Guanabo.'

'All I've got left is ten bucks.'

I gave her a couple more smacks. I pushed her down on the bed; already I had another erection. We played a little more.

'Oh, baby, how I love you, damn! I want to be your whore, your wife, your bride, your everything. I want to marry you, *papi*, dressed in white and you with a white linen suit. Real elegant. In a yellow Cadillac, with colored balloons, honking up and down the whole Malecón so all Havana knows. So everybody knows and makes a fuss. Give me your saliva, you crazy bastard, give me cock, shove it up to my navel.'

We continued playing like this for quite a while. Enough. We got up. She went to her place, and came back with fifteen dollars which she handed over: 'Take them, *papito*. This is more than enough to go to Guanabo.'

'Or to Santa María.'

'Santa María is full of hustlers and they're going to come on to you, the sluts, and I'm gonna have to pop one.'

'And gringos. Who'll fall for you, the bastards.'

We walk to Corrales. The buses weren't running. We take a little ten-peso van and come to a stop at the same coconut palm as the previous Sunday. Man is a creature of habit. The beach was clean now. Some old women were collecting garbage, throwing it into bags and dragging them across the sand. A guy pulled in on a spectacular motorcycle, all chrome, with, behind him, an even more spectacular mulatta, succulent, assy, tasty, a mass of flesh and muscles. She took off her clothes and ended up with a dental floss buried between her buttocks. Damn, she wound up naked, that body for all to see, and she was laughing! That woman was a ball of lust and perversity. She had ten gold chains around her neck, others on her wrists, on her ankles, and even one from her nose to her right ear. Were these people aliens? They sat in the shade of a coconut palm to drink rum, listen to boleros and *rancheras*, and live out their passion. Not for them the beach, the sea, the sun. Just rum, music, kissing and sucking.

I went to swim for a while. When I returned, feeling invigorated and in shape, I found Gloria playing at wives. She was conversing with a mild-looking lady lying under a coconut palm two yards away from ours: two ladies of leisure who go for a picnic on the beach with their husbands and calmly chat away about everyday subjects: the children's school, how to make paella without shellfish because there aren't any, that kind of thing. The lady was recounting her life in detail to Gloria: she was depressed, a year ago her husband had gone to Miami and behaved very poorly: 'Once he sent me a little note and twenty dollars and that's the last I heard of him.' She kept on badmouthing the guy. He was greedy, tight-fisted, he betrayed her with other women, let her starve. Gloria seemed very interested in the chatter. Meanwhile I was taking slugs from the bottle and looking the other way. Gloria, playing the upright lady, watches me and says, from a distance: 'My love, don't drink any more. It'll do you damage.'

Ah, fuck. Gloria gets so easily corrupted by these imbeciles. I don't like that woman telling her life story, all about her mother's illnesses, the raising of chickens, her depression because men won't go near her: 'I'm only thirty-nine and not that ugly, right? And no strings attached because my daughter is already a young lady and I support her. The problem is men like the young ones.' Then she directs herself to me: 'Your wife tells me you're a writer.'

'My wife? What wife?'

'Yes, she, ehhh . . . and you've published or . . .?'

'Or what?'

'Or haven't published?'

'Yes.'

'Let me explain why I ask. It's a small world, you know. I'm a specialist in Cuban literature, and we're making a dictionary of writers. So, look, what a nice coincidence.'

'Ahhh.'

'We want it to be as complete as possible. Have they made out a form for you yet?'

'For what?'

'So that your name appears in it. We've included everyone. Even those who've won a minor prize for verse in the Flying Ox Municipal House of Culture.'

'Oh, yes? How great. It'll be a big dictionary.'

'Such is our intention, comrade.'

'And those who are abroad?'

'Also. Everyone, everyone. Now it's not going to be like that other time. Uhh . . . And I have to fill out a form for you.'

'No, thanks.'

'But are you a writer or not? Have you won any prizes?'

'I have never won anything. I always lose.'

'Ah, well, if you've never won a contest, some prize, then I don't know what to tell you. Because without a track record, I don't know if the committee will accept you for the dictionary. And the track record matters because inclusion in the dictionary gives you standing, is that clear? What do you write? Poetry?'

'Ahhhh, señora. Would you like a little sip?'

'I'm trying to help you so that your name can appear in the dictionary, because later that'll help you to publish abroad and everything. Is that clear?'

'Do you want a sip of rum? It's good.'

'No, no. I'm taking Trifluoperazina with Amitriptilina. Can't have any alcohol.'

'Gloria, let's get in the water. Señora, can you keep an eye on our clothes?'

'Yes, of course. I'll take care of it. Although now, with so many police around here, there's nothing to worry about. They even have police in the water. But that's fine by me. That way I can feel safe and relaxed. Right? They're there all day long, on top of things, even asking the hummingbirds for their ID. That's what was missing. They ought to have more, many more. Since there's no work, delinquency is on the rise and it's made life impossible for decent people. I believe they should employ more police and exercise more control. See, in my neighborhood . . .'

'Well, señora, with your permission. We're going into the water.'

'Off you go. Water frightens me. I wouldn't go in the sea for anything in the world. I'll watch your clothes.'

I took Gloria by the arm, dragged her away, and we went out to the deep part.

'I'm going to drown you, damn it!'

'No, *papi*, don't get heavy because I can't touch, here!'

'Why the hell did you have to play the wife with that load?'

'Oh, Pedro, she's a decent person, who's studied and all. What am I going to tell her, that you're a struggling artist and I'm a jenny-ass and we're here because I hustled a gringo and screwed him for fifteen dollars? No, sweetie pie, my problems stay at home, that way nobody knows a thing. You're a writer and a journalist and all that and I'm your wife! Everything with lots of *cachet* and elegance. If she tells her life story to the first person she passes on the street, that's her problem. But me? No way. My life is a secret, and it goes with me to the grave.'

'Gloria, when you want to talk shit, there's no stopping you.'

'Why?'

'Because you know your life is no secret and that you're not the Pharaoh's wife or fuck all.'

'What you talkin' about? Speak clear. What's this about the Pharaoh's wife?'

'The Pharaohs took everything with them . . .'

'Oh, *papi*, don't mess up my head with weird stuff.'

'Gloria, damn it, you're an animal!'

'*Papi*, I know I'm kinda thick but you like it like that. Look, I'm gonna tell you something: the best couples are those in which both partners are very different. Where one has nothing in common with the other. You're very intelligent and you play the cultured one who writes and all that, but me . . .'

'Okay, okay. Cut, cut. I feel like giving you some dick right here.'

'I love to screw in the water. It's been a while since I've done it. Yeah, baby, yeah. Lay it on me. Make yourself comfortable. C'mon.'

I got her hot first by rubbing her with my finger. Two fingers, three fingers, four. My thumb I put up her asshole. She got turned on. Me too. Afterwards we coupled, floating, like a pair of lobsters. It's so great in the water. With Gloria straddling my waist, moving ever so slightly, and me nailing her very deep.

10

The trip back to Havana was very entertaining. The little truck was a Ford of more or less 1945 distribution. They had put some wooden benches in, so it held about a dozen people in total. A very young woman climbed up, ready to give birth. Her husband was with her. They sat down facing us. She was almost naked, with an enormous and perfectly round belly and her breasts swollen and voluminous and her thighs and buttocks like jacaranda wood. She was wearing a bikini and on top a very light, almost transparent dressing gown of African batik. She was cupping her stomach with both hands, as if the creature were going to exit at any moment. They were both very young. The guy was a handsome devil with gold eye teeth and necklaces of Changó and Yemayá and prison tattoos. Three numbers on the left arm. He displayed his collection of numbers very proudly. He was just wearing shorts, his torso bare. He was carrying an undershirt in his hand and sweating copiously. A big scar ran diagonally from his left nipple to his navel. Someone had given him a good slashing. It was best not to stare. Anyhow, I was wearing dark sunglasses and could study them at my leisure out of the corner of my eye. The girl was a beauty, a real temptation. I've always liked pregnant women. And this one sitting right in front of me was almost completely naked. The truck didn't go by way of Guanabacoa. It went straight toward the bay tunnel. Then the guy shouted to the driver: 'Hey, man, where you headed?'

'To Havana. Through the tunnel.'

'No, boy, no. I want off at the Guanabacoa light.'

'Ah, I don't go there.'

'Stop, stop. Let me out here.'

They climbed down in the middle of the highway. The girl was having contractions. She was still cupping her belly and walked awkwardly, holding herself so that the fetus wouldn't come out. She was biting her lip and sweating, holding on in silence. The little truck drove off.

An old man said: 'That guy is crazy. The woman's going to give birth on the highway.'

A woman answered: 'He's drunk.'

'You think so?'

'I smelt the alcohol from here. And she must be crazy. If it was me I'd tell him: "You can stay here because I'm going straight to the hospital."'

Another woman butted in: 'It's her own fault. Who'd want to go to the beach when you're about to give birth?'

'It's because some men have no compassion. You could tell this one was an animal.'

'It's youth, it's youth.'

'No, not youth. I have four children; the first one I had when I was sixteen years old. And all alone because, when it happened, my husband was a militiaman and never at home.'

'Young people think that everything is fun. At that age you don't think.'

And on they went about the theme. I switched off. I was returning with my backpack full of mangoes. A family from Cotorro had been selling them. They went to the beach with two bags of mangoes, all the children and old people and bottles of rum. They came in a beat-up little truck, about ten of them, all very thin and tall and black. When the police went away, one of them, the youngest, even though he already had a wife and three children, went around with a bag. He had to ignore the kids who were screaming behind him: 'Papa, take me with you.' His wife rounded up all the children, like a hen with chicks. He hawked his product: 'Look, ripe little mangoes, by weight.' I bought a few. Afterwards he sold me more, at a reduced price. In the end, when the skinny guy had drunk enough rum, he came up to me, very friendly, and offered some rum to me. We drank a couple of shots, he gave me around twenty mangoes which he still had, and asked about my tattoo. He wanted a tattoo of St. Lazarus on his back but, you never know, if the ink's bad after a while it starts to run, and blah, blah, blah. We spoke for quite a while, and he offered me his house. Whenever I wanted it. In a word, a good guy. We speak a while, I end up with a shitload of mangoes and we knock back half a bottle of rum.

I dedicated the next day to eating mangoes. And to divesting my shelves of useless books. They were too much for my little library . . . Lunacharski's opinions about culture, art and literature, *The Fortress of Brest*, *The Way to Forge Steel*, Engels about art, *A Man of Truth* by Boris Polevoy, pamphlets of speeches, harangues in favor of one thing or against another, *Crisis and Change on the Left*, *The Spiral of Treachery of Someone or Other*, *Esthetics and Revolution*, *The Revolution Betrayed* by Trotsky. I was in the midst of this when Kurt called me. He was saying goodbye. Everything resolved. His parents had sent him money. Could we get together in an hour for a drink? He wanted to thank me for all I had done. No, Kurt, thanks a lot. It's really okay, have a good trip.

I had a few calm days. Gloria says that she loves me a lot, but she disappears from the map and not even God the Father can find her. There are always people coming: they telephone, they turn up unexpectedly. The day after Kurt left, Ingrid arrived. They're friends. Kurt asked me to act as her guide in Havana. She visited me one night with her thirteen-year-old son. We have coffee, talk some, have a glass of rum. She asked to use the bathroom. Naturally, I have a strategic peep hole, just in back of the toilet. From there I checked her out. Nice ass. Very nice ass. I offered her more rum, music, and we started to dance. Nothing doing. Ingrid was jumping around frenetically. Armando Manzanero was singing 'With you I learned that the week has more than seven days . . . ', but she kept on laughing and prancing about. She wanted to enjoy herself in Cuba. I gave her more rum, and tried to get her to settle down so I could stick my tail between her thighs. But she was still dancing around wildly and smiling, her face as red as a tomato. I put my hands on her buttocks. Still she didn't get it. I'd had enough – I grabbed her pussy and gave it a squeeze. It was a very big pussy, lots of mass. The attack was too much for her:

'Oh, no, the boy' – she whimpered – 'I'm sorry, I'm sorry, excuse me, *adios*.' And she launched herself down the stairs, forcefully grabbing her little darling by the wrist. I'd tried to be a good host so she could have fun like the Cubans. I did everything I could.

They appear like that. Each one with her story. Some have read the *Dirty Trilogy* and want to tell me something of their lives. Sometimes they leave me letters, cassettes with music, they make themselves pretty and wait for the tiger to pounce and tear them apart. But no, I can't put my tail in all the moist, hairy holes which come my way. Well, I could, but I don't want to take requests like some kind of cabaret singer. Maybe it's because I'm tired of being a buzzard. When I was young, I was a buzzard and I lunched on any carrion. With gusto. I'd snack on any spoils, and to me they tasted like cheese and guava sweets. With age you get more selective and you develop a gourmet palate. For example, Ingrid got me hot because I spied on her through the peephole, but, on calmer consideration, she was too corpulent for my taste, too white, she had too much cellulite. She was an easy-going kind of woman, healthy, slow, good manners. A woman who, when you're nailing her, probably stifles her screams because to scream is not well educated. The educated thing is to hold back. Or, at most, to let out a discreet sigh. You develop a sixth sense for this – that she would not be a good fuck. Others are too masculine or tomboyish and bulky. Not only muscularly but spiritually too. They're not for me. There are many women like this, and some believe it would be useful to have an adventure with a primitive, brutal macho man. They conjure him up in their mind, then off they go to find him. Because, of course, they never have him near. They believe they're cut out for this because when they were young they escaped south with a knapsack and very little money. And they almost became hippies. And they believed it. In the midst of this confusion, some shine with their own inner light. Very few, but you meet them sometimes.

Maura, for example. She's intelligent and masters her surroundings. She's not lost, at least she doesn't seem to be. She's not crazy or anxious or fearful. At least that's not the impression she gives. She's taking a rest after a thirteen-year relationship that has just fallen apart. She's a friend of an old friend who in the most difficult years came to Havana and encouraged me, telling me: 'Go to Malaga with Ana, here you'll go mad.' So then Maura appears with a letter from my friend. Supposedly she was taking a break. The first days she was bored. Afterwards, she told me that a black man with a tricycle mounted her desperately every night. He didn't mount her on the tricycle, but he mounted her. A condom between them. She had already confessed to me that, on leaving Buenos Aires: 'My friends gave me boxes of rubbers so I'd have some stories when I got back.'

'But are you resting or not?'

'Yes, of course. But it's more like spiritual repose. Emotional. The black man insisted so. And he's beautiful. He's very beautiful. What energy, I never would have guessed! All night long! He's worn me out. I can't take any more. What imagination! He's amazing, this black guy, he knows it all!'

When I assumed she'd be happy with her black taxi driver, she appears, mad about a European diplomat. A guy who was the complete opposite: white, cultured, with glasses, a bit fat, suave, delicate, soft, a good boy; he even wore a suit, tie, and black shoes.

She confused me. Supposedly she knew what she wanted. Well, finally, the three of us go out to have coffee. We went to a cafeteria facing the Malecón. We sat. The diplomat went to the bathroom, and I couldn't resist the temptation: 'Maura, which is it to be? The Good Savage or the Cartesian?'

'The Good Savage is fine for a few days . . .'

'For a few nights.'

'That's right. A few nights. But he's too intense. I have a pelvic inflamation, all the muscles of that zone ache. Oh, you can't imagine how intense that negro is. The guy's a genius, powerful, but I can't live impaled twenty-four hours a day.'

'And with this gentleman?'

'Nothing.'

'Nothing?'

'Nothing.'

'A brutal switch.'

'Yes. What's more, he's a bit effeminate . . . ohh . . . I believe it's more than a bit. I believe that he's totally effeminate, but I'm going to Europe with him and that's that.'

'That's fine. You can't have everything at once.'

'That's so, Pedro Juan. You are intelligent. For a man, you have very good intuition.'

'And you can always come to Cuba for a few days when you get very bored.'

'Yes, but I have to find someone who has a smaller one because this negro is disproportionate. It's not human.'

'That's going to be very difficult. Not impossible – but difficult.'

The diplomat returned from the bathroom. He interrupted us. I was about to explain to her what she could do to find someone with a proportion more suitable to her depth. At that moment three guys entered with black uniforms, bulletproof vests, and machine guns. Very serious, very stressed out. Two were on the alert, watching everything, a bit wired. The third headed for a dollar-swallowing machine. One of those in which you put a dollar and it allows you a couple of seconds of action to utilize some robot pincers and try to grab a little furry bear. But you never succeed, the machine chews up the bill, and you never see it again. Okay then, one of the guys opened that apparatus, without letting go of his machine-gun. He removed all the little toy bears, counted them. He noted it on a form. He delved into the intestines of the machine and extracted a number of one-dollar bills. Maybe twenty or thirty. Put them in a canvas bag which he tied and sealed. Closed the machine. Checked that everything was okay. Moved the machine-gun from his left hand to his right. Made a signal to the others, and they withdrew to the truck that was waiting for them: a black delivery van, armor-plated, with a large golden shield and the acronym of their money transport enterprise. The driver was waiting at his post, tense and alert, with the motor running the whole time.

They left. We came back to reality. We relaxed. We smiled again. We ordered some drinks. Maura recounted her Cuban adventures. Not those with the black man. The taxi driver was an

official secret. To reveal it would cost her dear. She related innocent, amusing adventures. For instance, how dozens of hustlers
accosted her to offer matrimony, rum, cigars. 'Every day they
offered to marry me and I told them: "No, take it easy, I'm resting." I don't want to know anything about men after thirteen
years with such a drag. I don't even know how things started
with Luís Mañuel. It's an unexpected infatuation. He has conquered me like a gentleman, but those vulgar hustlers . . . they
don't even know how to speak. I can't even understand what
they say.'

'They're rogues, just like anywhere in the world,' I said, to help
her keep up her performance.

'I don't believe it. There simply aren't rogues everywhere you
go. The Argentinians, yes. We're rogues. We go through life
thinking we're the best in everything, in soccer, in business, in
bed. Really, we're just bores, we annoy half the world and then
people don't want to hear anything more about us.'

'Maura, you're exaggerating.'

'No I'm not, Pedro Juan. We're bores and the same thing is
going to happen to you. Wherever I go, I hear people talking
about the Cubans, saying how they're the best at music, how they
have the most beautiful women, the men the most tralala. Cubans
are everywhere, springing up like mushrooms. And people think
to themselves: "Hey, these Cubans believe the world revolves
around them." I tell you, you'll end up by annoying everyone and
no one will be able to stand you guys any more.'

'Well, perhaps we shouldn't always try to steal the limelight.'

'Maybe the Cubans can manage that, but not the Argentines.
Every day more and more stars.'

'Don't you Argentines get tired? Being a neurotic star is
exhausting.'

'It's a vice, Pedro Juan. Just as others have the vice of power. Or
of money. You convince yourself that you deserve power or that
you deserve all the gold in the world, or that you were sent by
God to save Humanity. And that's it. Done. There's no one to pull
you out of it.'

The diplomat listened to Maura, enraptured. A fat guy came over from another table to greet him and interrupted us. He was a greasy, gelatinous, spongy guy, half queer, covered with chains and rings of gold, with a flowered shirt and a cloying, fawning smile. Despicable. The diplomat greeted him at a distance, but the guy was so conceited he didn't give up. He greeted us all. He presented himself with some name or other and added: 'I'm a purveyor of art and antiquities. Please, accept my card.' He gave his card to Maura. He looked me over closely. He didn't give me his card. Cubans didn't interest him. He turned toward Maura: 'Señora, I kiss your hand.'

The guy had some nerve. Finally he returned to his table, and Maura immediately said: 'That guy is such a drag!'

And the diplomat: 'The Drool Queen.'

'What? You call him the Drool Queen?'

'Yes. Don't you see it? He leaves a string of drool behind him.'

'He says he deals in art.'

'It's something more. Havana functions like a little village. When I first came here they sent me mulattas, many mulattas. Mulattas didn't interest me so they sent me mulattos. Adonises, ephebes, enchanting, sublime. Mulattos didn't interest me. Next, drugs. I don't need them, I'm allergic. Then came the Drool Queen making offers of art: porcelain, bronzes, antique jewels, gold, silverware, furniture, famous paintings. All at bargain prices. The temptation. I almost fell in the trap, but another diplomat warned me: stop, the Drool Queen is poison. And I keep him away from me.'

'And you're so calm?'

'Well, it's not that one is Mata Hari, but you get used to it. If your nerve fails, you have to resign. Diplomats develop tricks to survive. The same as in any other dangerous profession. Paratroopers, astronauts, firemen. Every trade has its tricks.'

'Luckily, I don't care for those more dangerous professions.'

'Yours is terrible, Pedro Juan. The worst of all. The powerful fear ideas and the word. They find them terrifying.'

11

The neighborhood panorama at seven in the morning is very calm. The Chinaman, with his permanently hungover and famished face, beats his hard, encrusted boots to knock off the caked cement. Three or four guys with pieces of wood and nails patch up the building from which they were evicted weeks ago. They say they want to repair it. I doubt it; it seems too ruined. The dealer is on the go early: there's a taxi in front of her pad. She hands a little packet to the driver. Grass or powder. The guy screeches off and vanishes down the Malecón. The two streetcorner hustlers return from the night. One black and one a light-skinned mulatta. Very young, dissipated, chain-smoking, with long glittery, satin dresses and high-heeled gray shoes. They're carrying something in plastic bags: gifts from the gringos. A black man draws water from the hole in the middle of the street. Again the water has vanished from the pipes. It's been six days and not a drop has come to the neighborhood. Cops on the corners. A guy with a tricycle full of flowers; another pedaling slowly by on his bicycle. A ragged street-sweeper, old, filthy, utterly beaten by life, sweeps fetid water from a puddle. The sewers are backed up. It stinks but the sweeper enjoys being in the water and plays at leisure, like a child. That's the impression one gets: he's playing with that shit, standing in the puddle, sweeping slowly, soaking his feet in the fetid, stinking water. The final cold front of the winter hurling wind and a salt-rich spray over the city. The waves breaking against the wall of the Malecón throw up white foam and soak the street and the buildings. Day breaks. The city brightens, little by little. Almost everyone is still sleeping. There is little movement. The neighborhood is almost deserted. Nobody works. Or very few. So there's no hurry. People wake up and slowly start their day. Around ten in the morning there'll be a little more movement. For now everything's quiet.

I walk a number of blocks and, when I get to the house of Rosa, the *santera*, it's ten after seven. There's already a solitary woman waiting on the sidewalk, outside her door. I'm number two. Rosa opens her room shortly after. Greets us. Cleanses with perfume and sweet basil, removing all the evil in the air from the day and the night before. Above all from the night. She freshens up. Takes a mouthful of coffee, lights up a cigar, and comes smiling to the door. She's a thickset, lowslung black woman, dressed in white, ropes of colored beads around her neck and a blue kerchief tied around her head. She might be sixty years old. Maybe older. On the sidewalk there are five of us waiting for her. The cigar stinks. It must be a butt left over from yesterday.

'How many are there? Five? That's it. Not one more. Who's the last one?'

A woman of a certain age raises her hand to indicate it's she.

'Señora, do me a favor, when someone else comes, you tell them to come back tomorrow. I'll finish with you at about two in the afternoon. That's when I have to go all the way to Cojímar to cleanse a house. They're already waiting for me with everything. So not even one more. Who's first? You? Come on.'

The young woman enters. Rosa's room is small. She shuts the door tight. An hour and a half later, the young woman leaves and I go in. I let my eyes adjust from the blinding light of the street to the darkness of the room, which smells of mildew, herbs, and filth. In one corner an enormous altar with all the *santos* and attributes. In the other corner a guy sleeping on a cot, snoring, covered by a ragged, dirty sheet. Rosa is very black. He looks white and a lot younger than her. Before starting with me, she says to him: 'Cheo, when are you getting up? Wake up. You have to buy me the herbs for the Cojímar thing. Let's go, baby, get a move on.'

'Yes, Rosa, yes. Look how you pester me, girl. You don't even let me sleep.'

'Sleep, that's not sleep. You're still drunk from last night! You overdid it.'

'Bring me a little coffee 'cause I'm getting up now. No one can sleep with you talking shit.'

Cheo had a boozy voice. Like sandpaper. Rosa looked at me smiling and triumphant and said: 'Pardon me a moment. He who hopes for a lot, waits for a little, right?'

She got up from her chair. On a table she had a kerosene stove and some pans. There was coffee in a pitcher. She poured some for Cheo and handed it to him. Cheo stretched a bit, sat up on the bed, and drank the coffee. Afterwards, he got up, yawning. He was a few feet away from me, completely naked. Either he didn't notice me, or it didn't matter, or he enjoyed showing off his oversized cock and balls. A bit excessive for that bony, badly treated body. He looked about twenty-eight, maybe younger. He appeared undernourished, with several days' growth of beard and lots of matted black hair. His whole body gave off mixed odors of tobacco, *aguardiente*, filth, semen, shit, sweaty sheets, hunger, fatigue, old drunkenness. Almost groping, he found a grimy pair of pants and put them on. He opened a very narrow door which led to a tiny patio, maybe six foot by six foot. It brightened the room a little. Rosa handed him a jug of water. He washed his face without soap, rinsed his mouth, pissed on the floor. He stretched a bit more, scratched his belly, and, yawning, put on a shirt as dirty and ragged as his pants. He found a pair of worn-out rubber flipflops under the bed and put them on. With his left hand on his forehead he squeezed his temples: 'Ahh, I have a splitting headache . . .'

'There are no aspirins.'

'There ain't shit in this house.'

'Not in this house nor any other. There's no aspirin, Cheo.'

'Fuck, there's not one aspirin in the whole damn country!'

'Shhh, Cheo, don't talk like that. Be aware that there are visitors and that you don't know this gentleman.'

Cheo opened his eyes wider and looked at me.

I said: 'No, there's no problem with me. Besides, he says there're no aspirins – and he's right.'

'Yes, but you never know who you're dealing with. It's best to keep your mouth shut and let the world turn.'

'Rosa, if you're going to keep talking, tell me, and I'll lie down again.'

'No, no. Come on, up, up.'

'Okay, I'll go. Give me the money for the herbs. And stop fucking around.'

Rosa gave him some banknotes and a scrap of brown wrapping paper: 'Look, open your eyes and wake up. Don't tell me later that you lost the money. I've written down everything I need there. Tell Gregorio that everything has to be fresh. Old, wilted herbs won't do and I'll return them. He knows me well but he plays the fool, so tell him very clearly. And open your eyes!'

'Is this enough money?'

'Sure. With two or three pesos left over.'

'No. Two or three pesos, no. Give me five pesos more, so I can get something to eat.'

Rosa searched between her breasts. She was big-breasted. I saw her better in the light which entered through the little door to the patio. To screw that old lady you needed real guts. And she liked boys of twenty. Well, this boy was dog's barf. Life had mistreated Cheo. Rosa continued to search between her flabby tits and finally found a five-peso bill: 'Take it. Hurry because by one we should be leaving for Cojímar.'

'We should? You go. I'm not going.'

'Cheo, let's not argue in front of this gentleman. You have to help me with this. What they've started there is very strong. And what's more, you have to learn. If you don't practice you'll never develop.'

'Ah, girl . . .'

And off he shuffled in his flipflops.

Rosa sat back down: 'He has so much grace! It comes to him through Changó and through Oggún. But he's the medium for the spirit of a dead man who's the best diviner in the world. He whispers everything, everything in his ear. But clearly, so that he hears it all. Me, I'd love it if my dead man would speak to me so clearly. Cheo's gives him the name and age of the people and everything. Well, it's a beautiful thing, it's by the grace of God. And it never fails him. Orula tells him that he has to consult, whether he wants to or not. He has to give consultations. But he . . . you've already seen. He's been with me more than a year, we're together for . . . more than two years carrying on together . . . but he can't get down to it. Trouble with the police, rows, benders. Dealings with bad people. He doesn't have one worthwhile friend. Not even one who is a decent person. They're all lousy delinquents. The police are watching them.'

Rosa was walking about, she straightened up the cot a bit, rearranged some bottles in a corner, opened canisters and looked inside. Finally she came and sat down at the consulting table, but she went on with her monologue: 'I'm teaching him so that he can consult too, but if he gives me any more trouble out he goes and that's the end of it. I'll go on alone like nothing happened. Yes, because bed isn't everything. I've had very few men like that in my life. As far as bed is concerned, you understand me? He's a macho, a bull stud. I'd like to be able to give him a son. To see if he'd settle down. But at my age . . . imagine. But really that's not everything in life. You get disenchanted. Time passes and he does nothing to get ahead and keeps on getting drunk and . . . ahhh . . . well, let's see, you came for a consultation because you have some problem and I'm also in a hurry, so . . .'

Rosa cut her tiresome talk about Cheo and made the sign of the cross looking at the *santos* on her altar. She daubed me with cologne. We bared our heads and arms and she began to invoke: 'Hail Mary Holy Mother of God who art among all women blessed the fruit of thy womb Jesus our Father who art in heaven blessed come here to me Lord and to . . . what do you call yourself?'

'Pedro Juan.'

'Come to me and to Pedro Pablo Lord and illuminate thou who seizest seven rays . . .'

She kept on praying that litany without stopping. Softly rapping the table with her knuckles, blowing cigar smoke at a crucifix placed in a glass of water, and opening the palms of her hands as she continued the invocation.

'I believe in God the all-powerful Father Creator of heaven and earth and of all which lies above and below and . . . hummm.

Humm . . . let's see . . . hummm . . . let's see what I'm gonna say . . . you don't come here for problems of health or money . . . you don't have problems with the law . . . hummm, let's see what I'm gonna say . . . you have a voyage. A long voyage, with water in the middle, and you have many women on this side and on that side of the water . . . hummm . . . Pedro Luis, you don't take care of what's yours, my son. You have to save something for tomorrow. The dead man says that you have Changó and Ochún always in front and you have to pray to them and put flowers on the altar for them and ask their help. You have to speak with them. That's why the women like you so much. And you are potent and powerful. Women offer themselves to you easily and fall in love with you, Pedro José. You don't even have to open your mouth. Only look at them and they come up and offer themselves . . . I'm gonna tell you somethin', Pedro Pablo . . . Did you say Pedro Pablo or Pedro José?'

'Pedro Juan.'

'Pedro Juan, yes. Well, looky here, Pedro Juan . . . hummm . . . the dead man says that you need protection and a cleansing. You ain't got nothin' above to protect you, my son. And to open the paths . . . Okay, yes . . . the dead man says that you have the beads of Obatalá and of Changó, but you don't wear them. Is that so?'

'Yes.'

'Ahh, that's bad. Uhhh. And why don't you use them? Are you a director or somethin'? I mean . . . do you think they can harm you?'

'No, no.'

'You have to use them, my son. But, along with the beads, you need many things for this voyage to happen. And to turn out well. As it's meant to. With money for you and your fine and elegant women and every little thing you want. You want . . . papers. There are many papers, ahhh, I don't get it. Are you a musician?'

'No.'

'And how are you gonna travel if musicians are the only ones here who travel?'

'Ah.'

'No, but yours is different. You have to do with papers, not with music. But you're gonna travel, even though you're not a musician. And a long time. A long voyage. And there's money and success and women and you're gonna eat and drink well and live like a king in fine houses. Everything's good for you. But I see papers and worry. You think a lot, son?'

'I don't know. Normal.'

'No, no. You are preoccupied. Sometimes you think you're gonna go crazy. And you drink a lot of rum. And smoke tobacco. Well, the dead man says that the rum, the cigars and the women come from the African. You have a runaway African, you know, a fugitive, and an Indian by your side. They never leave you and they help you.'

'So they tell me.'

'That's because they're there. At your side. And how they hide, both of them. They're sharp bastards. Don't let themselves be seen easy. You have to know. Hummm . . . let's see . . . The Indian is calmer and he likes silence and flowers, but the African is rebellious and quarrelsome. Are you quarrelsome, my son? Yes. You don't have to answer. We can see you're impudent and quarrelsome. It's because the African was a runaway and died in the bush, naked, wearing nothin' more than a loincloth. He was from the backwoods but lively and rebellious. An impudent, quarrelsome negro. Worthless as a slave. Took off from the farm. Didn't want to work. Rather be dead than lower his head and keep his mouth shut. He was a slave but he broke his shackles and ran to the bush. He'd have died in shackles. He preferred to live like a savage in the bush, even to go hungry. But free. And women were easy for him. Tobacco and *aguardiente*. That was his thing in life. And now he's at your side and doesn't leave you.'

Rosa went on like this some more. I sat silent, without opening my mouth. Until she said something new: 'Look, the dead man says that the women are always gonna keep coming, Pedro Pablo. Some go and others come. You conquer with your glance, your talk, and in bed. You know there are men who don't talk, who

74

play the brute straight away. And women don't like that. A woman wants to be courted. You talk pretty and in bed you're a stud. Besides, you must be a tease, as a son of Changó and Ochún. But to get to the point: the dead man says there's a woman that you don't know. Very fine, tall, white, elegant, very educated. She likes to dress in black and she's fair-skinned, very white. Is that so?'

'I don't know.'

'You don't know, of course. There's water in the middle. She may even be a foreigner. But you're gonna be together and that'll be good for both of you 'cause she's a daughter of Eleguá and Oggún . . . hummm . . . very strong . . . Eleguá and Oggún. But she doesn't know that. You have to tell her and bring her beads that've been blessed for her benefit. Red and black for Eleguá, and black and green for Oggún. You know? Yes, you know this 'cause you're really a believer. Look, Pedro Pablo, go buy the necklaces and bring them to me so I can work on them, prepare them good, and you take them to her and put them on her neck in the name of . . . well, I'll tell you later because you have to say something when you put them on her neck. This woman is waiting for you. And when you two get together, you're gonna open new ways for each other. What a beautiful thing. She's gonna open the way for you and you for her.'

'And what's her name?'

'The name isn't clear . . . Could it be Anita? Kirina? Something like that but he doesn't give her name. She will, though. She's beautiful, tall, dressed in black, walking on a beach or . . . there's a lot of water . . . it's like the sea. And there's a lot of wind and a lot of cold. She's waiting for you. Alone, walking by the seaside . . . hummm . . . There's one other woman and you have to be careful. She's very different. And she's at your side. Is that so?'

'I don't know.'

'You must know, Pedro Pablo! Just tell me yes or no.'

'Yes.'

'Hummm . . . right. The dead man says that this woman is completely the opposite, but she's close to you. And you like her a lot.

75

And she loves you. Don't believe that she doesn't love you. She loves you and you love her but she's crazy. She was born that way. She's short, mulatta, very thin, fun, amusing, always laughing, light on her hooves, a true daughter of Ochún. She loves gold, jewelry, money, music, dancing, men, and religion. 'Cause she has hers in her head. She was born with this grace from the most holy Ochún and her religion is strong. But do not fear. She won't harm you, 'cause she's noble and good. But crazy in the head. She's always gonna have you and another and many more besides. Sometimes she has several at once. You have to choose. If you don't, this woman's gonna drag you down. There's no compromise. Either you split or she brings you to the grave. The dead man says it's difficult but you have to decide.'

The consultation with Rosa lasted almost two hours. I paid her and left with a long list of remedies, treatments, cleansings. I strolled on Blanco until Virtudes and walked down a block. On Águila and Virtudes stands El Mundo. An old and abandoned bar, a bit of a ruin, but I like it. At least they charge in pesos rather than dollars. I ordered a double rum. It reminds me of the bar where I was born and lived my first years, listening to boleros on the record-player. I looked over the list of remedies. Too long. He who follows the path of a *santera* goes crazy. The hell with it. Let that which is coming come on its own. Good and bad, there's strength here to stop a hurricane.

All the *santeras* are the same. Too many herbs, ceremonies, protections, cleansings. After you get the beads, the warriors, the little hand of Orula, your *santo*, your birthdays. And paying well. A month's rent. I get up to a certain point with this. And I go no further. I knocked back the rum and continued on my way to the market at Reina and Águila. Nothing for me. It's already enough effort to attend to my own *santos*. But I bought the beads for Agneta. It was obvious, she's the woman who awaits me. Gloria also appeared clearly and without errors. Rosa stopped just short of telling me that she's a snake who'll wrap around your neck and strangle you. Perhaps the Swede will be fun too and a horny fucker. Ah, what the hell? I'm ready for anything.

I ate a pizza. I checked out the asses of the black girls and the mulattas, squeezed into blue, red, yellow, and black spandex. 'An Antillean watercolor of flesh, color and motion', as a certain ridiculous and venerated orator would say. Beautiful asses. Tempting asses. It's a pickup zone. They look for guys who'll pay, or at least treat them to a beer, something to eat, and buy them a pack of cigarettes. They're whores, and yet they're not.

I went back to my roof terrace. Nothing to do. I connected the television. They were transmitting a meeting of presidents from many countries. I turned it off. I went outside in the fresh air. The sea calms me. The turbulence of the cold front dirtied the blue; and brought masses of seaweed and algae to shore. I'd have liked to be a sailor, to always be leaving. To wave *adios, adios*, until I vanished from sight of land, swallowed up by the sea. *Brammmm!* A sudden, loud noise tears me from my thoughts. A brick-red Oldsmobile from '50 or '51, hand-painted, with a white roof, has stalled in the middle of San Lázaro Street, the end of its left rear axle broken. The wheel went rolling toward the sidewalk, leaving the car like a wounded animal. The end of the fractured axle buried itself in the hot asphalt. Two guys wearing shorts, sleeveless undershirts and rubber flipflops climbed calmly out of the vehicle. They didn't get irritated. It appeared that these disasters were habitual. They raised the car with a hydraulic jack, secured it with stones and rubble, and began to repair it right there, in the middle of the street. Light traffic passed to the left and right of them. In a few minutes the dinosaur bled. A pool of liquid and grease spilt from it. The men reached for some tools from the trunk and got down to work. It was about four in the afternoon. They had sufficient light. If night fell they'd have to grope in the dark.

There I was, completely absorbed by the repair of the dinosaur and, in passing, by an extremely well-endowed young lady who had recently moved to the adjoining building. Her clothes are so tight she must have trouble breathing. She takes off her shoes, puts on music at top volume, and goes out on the roof to fetch pails of water from some tanks. She scrubs, cleans, rinses like a madwoman. Her husband's an engineer. They live in a very small room they improvised out of bricks, pieces of board and fiber cement roof tiles. It's about twelve foot by twelve foot, on the roof terrace of that building. I like to see it in the afternoons, when the sun sinks. The two of them sit outside on the terrace and work for a couple of hours: they make necklaces and bracelets of beads for the *santería*, belt buckles, headbands, ornaments for the hair. They live on this. Their salaries don't even stretch through the start of the month. Sometimes she leaves the guy stringing beads and starts scrubbing the floor. She's obsessed with cleaning. Perhaps she becomes intellectually exhausted stringing beads. Her brain can't stand such intense work and so she abandons it and goes into action, expending her energy scrubbing floors. And she's happy with her ass and tits tightly packed, so that everyone knows she's as sweet as coconut candy.

There's a knock at the door. Trucutú and Pelé. They've come to adjust the antenna. They're young guys, thirty or thereabouts. They were born and grew up here and both know the neighborhood like the back of their hand. Nothing goes down without their knowing about it. For them, to go to Vedado, to Cerro or to Guanabacoa is to take a long trip. Months ago, Pelé put an antenna on my terrace to catch the Miami channels. It's illegal, but he's crazy about Cristina's talk show. All his brothers live in Miami. Trucu has a body shop, and the two are long-time partners. They always hang out together, for better or worse. They work patching tires, washing cars, repairing them, they do anything: mechanics, electricity, plumbing – legal and illegal. Anything to earn their daily pesos. Even so, Trucu goes hungry and is skinny with a hungry face. Pelé is strong and eats a little better. The broken Oldsmobile is right in front of their body shop. From the roof, we observe the two guys at their work. Trucu tells me: 'Since they're good for nothin' tightwads, they'll be at it all night.'

'Why? You know them?'

'No, but I suggested we make the repairs for them and they told me no, they'd take care of it.'

'That's not so complicated. In two or three hours . . .'

'Two or three hours for a broken axle? It's obvious you don' know nothin' about mechanics, Pedro Juan. They'll be there for ten hours at least. Just to save a few pesos.'

'A few pesos, no. You and Pelé would nail them for at least three hundred.'

Pelé interrupted very convincingly:

'That job is worth five hundred, man. I wouldn't do it for less. With a guarantee. We always give a guarantee. That shitty heap could come apart anywhere else but the end of that axle will never break again in this life. For sure!'

'Okay, I believe it. No need for more publicity. When I buy a little car I'll contract you two as permanent mechanics.'

'You gonna buy a little car, man? Why the fuck not? You got some pesos hidden. You're a veteran with personality, Pedro Juan, but don' keep ridin' that bicycle, man. It makes you look like just another bum. Hey man, I'm your friend and I tell you sincerely: what you need is a real pretty little car to give you some prestige, friend. A sweet little car for a white guy with style. You have a high-roller's personality, pops, so we're going to find somethin special for you.'

And Trucutú: 'This is the kind of thing we know about, Pedro Juan, we'll look out for somethin' special. A car that don't give you lots of headaches. What'd be perfect for you is a '56 or '57 Chebrolet painted steel gray, all chrome, imitation tiger-skin seats, a good digital cassette player, extra-wide whitewalls. You'd drive it from here to heaven, my man. It's de luxe. Can you imagine how many chicks are gonna stick to us? And then it's off to the beach to fuck and drink beer.'

'Hey, Trucu, get down off that cloud, my brother. Are you stoned or somethin'?'

'Well, you always gotta dream a little. But it's possible, man. Hey, I close my eyes and I see myself there. The three of us. The three of us! With three stunning twenty-year-old chicks. Eighteen-year-olds. Sixteen-year-olds. Little tender ones. And cans of beer in our hands.'

'Okay, okay. Don't get excited. When I get the rest of the money, I'll make a deal with you.'

'Exactly, my friend, exactly. Take a little trip like the ones you make around Europe and bring home the bread so we can get our hands on a Chebby. And come back, man, come back. Don't go changing your mind when you get your hands on some bucks.'

'You know I always come back.'

'Yeah. The only one.'

'The only one, no. A lot of people leave Cuba and come back.'

'Well, man, don't wait too long 'cause now things are down, but at any moment the prices'll explode again and that Chebby's gonna cost you double.'

They started to clean Pelé's antenna. Salt air oxidizes the aluminum. A box of diodes had become detached. I found some rum and we drank, checking out Superbutt bathing a little dog on her roof. Then Pelé took out some grass, prepared it, and we smoked. The rum was finished. Trucu went downstairs and got another bottle. Pelé went to the kitchen, heated a plate, and prepared some coke. Two lines for each. It had been quite a while since I snorted and it made me euphoric. They had fun with me. I made jokes, I danced, I told stories about my crazy fucks on the beach. Pelé kept drinking rum. He was a glutton. He rolled another joint and smoked it, alone. Trucu and I had had enough.

'Man, today you brought a cartridge belt full of bullets.'

'Tha's all I got now, Pedro Juan. There's nothin' else left for me.'

'What do you mean, nothin' left for you? Find yourself a sweetheart, Pelé. You're young.'

'I'm in love with Patricia. It's three months today she ain't called me. So I'm celebratin'. Look like she found somebody with bread out there and left Pelé to rot in misery.'

He looked sad. His parents died years ago. His four brothers live in Miami. He's been in prison a couple of times. Short stays. A little more than a year on both charges. His wife invented a trip to Venezuela. She did it all on the sly and only told him about it when she was practically halfway to the airport, but not to worry, she said, because she'd send for him and they'd live together, in Venezuela or Miami. It seems she's changed her mind. There's been no word from her. Pelé put on a cassette of Feliciano and sat in the corner listening to it, sadder and more downcast than a black widow.

The Oldsmobile guys were still working down below. By now it was night and nothing could be seen. Or very little. We left Pelé to his drunkenness and depression. Trucu came up to me: 'Let him rest, man. Pelé, sleep it off, bro', sleep it off.' And he told me quietly: 'It's better that he sleeps 'cause otherwise when he's drunk he weeps. Or goes crazy and smashes everything. He destroyed his house. He's got nothin' left. He broke all the furniture, lamps, everythin'. The place is a pigsty. When he busts the television he won't even be able to see Cristina's show, which is the only one he likes.'

'Shit, that woman really did him in.'

'Patricia?'

'Yes.'

'Hey, forget it.'

'Why?'

'She gave him horns and he put up with it, dozens of times. And now he plays the romantic. Man, he knows she was an evil slut who only wanted to take his money.'

'And then what?'

'He's a dreamer. He doesn't like to face reality. He listens to Feliciano's boleros, snorts a little powder and falls in the shit again. Sure, he's my partner, but what can I do? He's livin' in a soap opera, man! Some people are like that, they have to live from drama to drama. If he scores another chick tomorrow, he'll act just as tragic and jealous, doggin' her until she leaves him or starts fuckin' around.'

'You're the strong one, Trucu. You spent a shitload of time out at sea.'

'Seven years. I been six on land now, run aground up to my nuts 'cause a docked ship don't earn freight.'

'They never called you up again?'

'Forget it, friend. Those days are gone.'

'There are boats at anchor in the port.'

'The few small boats which stayed alive. Most of the fleet rotted and disappeared. That's an old story now. Why mention it? Better to forget.'

'You began as a kid.'

'At eighteen, I climbed aboard the *Pearl River*. Seven years on board, always sailin' way up north, towards the ice.'

'That's a tender age to ship out. Did they get your ass?'

'No. No. I'm a man, my friend. There's a lot of respect on board. The whole crew has to be straight. No ship wants any queers. They get rid of 'em.'

'For being queers?'

'No. They invent something so that they can kick 'em out. Queers aren't wanted anywhere, boy. Much less on a ship 'cause they always stir up trouble. The sailors go crazy and fight for their asses. No, no. You gotta be macho.'

'So what did you do? Jerk off?'

'Boy, let me explain somethin' to you. Sailors never talk about this 'cause some things bring bad luck just talkin' about them. But you're my friend and this is gonna stay between us 'cause I know you ain't gonna repeat it. I always had a steady woman. If it wasn't one, it was another, but I always had a woman waitin' on land. Now I'm gonna tell you how a sailor thinks. 'Cause a sailor with a weak brain is a man overboard. Listen to me: I know perfectly well that all women are alike. All of 'em. No exceptions. The thirty to forty-five days that you're on land everything's lovey-dovey and it's "yes, my sugar daddy" and "anything you want, my sweetie" and they spread their legs wide for you every half an hour. So you're contentedly fucking away. You keep shovin' it in her even when you're outta milk 'cause she keeps provokin' you so you won't complain. Well, let's say that you make a thousand or two thousand dollars, that's five to seven thousand Cuban pesos, for six months of work. A sailor makes fifty times, five hundred times more than a doctor, I don't know . . . but, as I was saying, a broad is gonna spend all that in less than a month, man. In less than a month it's all gonna disappear. And all the stuff you brought is gonna disappear too: dresses, shoes, watches, tape recorders, everythin'. Finally, you're askin' for a loan to get through the last week 'cause she's stripped you. The day that you're gonna leave, you already owe money, but the broad doesn't leave you 'cause now she's a mind, a walkin' brain, and she's already plantin' seed for the next harvest, and goes with you very affectionately to the pier with little kisses for her sugar daddy and "you're my baby", and "how I'm gonna miss you and write me every day" and "when I hear that song I'm gonna think about you". All the while crying her little tears. But you're already a savvy beast 'cause this life has taught you quick and you see her stud standin' thirty yards away, with a bicycle, just leanin' up against a post and waitin'. You know him 'cause you've seen him circlin' and you're on the alert. A sailor on land sleeps with one eye open and the other shut. That's how it is. As I turn my back to climb aboard the ship, she's already happy and laughin', the tears disappear, and here comes the other guy, puts her on his bicycle, and drives her away laughin' and sayin': "Damn, at last that dumb shit's gone." And that night the guy wears all your shoes and clothes and your cologne and goes out to drink beer with your dollars which she has hidden by the handful.'

'Ah, Trucu, you're bitter, man. You're exaggerating.'

'Pedro Juan, I'm not exaggeratin'. This I never speak about with anyone. Only with you who I consider my friend and discreet. You're not a gossip. Nobody speaks about this 'cause nobody likes to play the part of the guy with horns. I'm tellin' you what happened to me with five women, one after the other. You say that I'm bitter. What I have is a heart of stone. My heart, my soul, everything is stone. I feel nothin' no more. In seven years at sea the same thing happened to me with five women. So am I the bad guy? Am I the one who's wrong? Am I the son of a bitch and are they the good girls? I even saw their studs, here in the 'hood, wearin' my clothes, my shoes, and my watches, and the broad had the nerve to tell me she'd sold them 'cause she was dyin' of hunger. Lies! They're all whores. There's not one that isn't a whore. All women are the same. They all love to smash the man beside them, use him up. Crush him. Exploit him. Live off him. 'Cause they know everythin'. They like the son of a bitch, the one who beats them till their bones break and doesn't let them talk or look sideways. That's the son of a bitch they like. But if you're a noble guy who caters to their tastes and brings them gifts and gives them money, they destroy you, boy, they destroy you. Me frozen in the North Atlantic. Frozen! Pedro Juan, you don't know what that's like. Frozen! Pullin' up the icy nets. Separatin' fish barehanded and puttin' them in boxes out on deck. Twenty degrees below zero. Thirty degrees below zero. Even your balls freeze. And at night even though your prick's as stiff as a board, you don' dare touch yourself, 'cause if you get used to jerkin' off you die: the work's so hard, the food's bad, and on top of that, slammin' the ham . . . shit, man, you'd kill yourself!'

'So what did you do?'

'Mental control. A lot of mental control. You can't let your brain get the best of you. It's better not to touch yourself. Let the milk flow on its own while you're sleepin'. I woke up stuck to the sheet every day. It comes out like paste. You're always washin' the sheets 'cause sometimes it's a pint a night. Sometimes I felt calmer and it was less. Dreamin' of bein' on land, even for two days, to buy stuff, to sell boxes of cigars, you know how sailors swap things, 'cause if you arrive in Cuba with empty hands, the bandit queen won't even look at you. She makes like a lady but it's bull-shit. She's an actress and a bandit and you have to bring her per-fumes and shoes and all kinds of stuff. If you don't, you don't get to fuck. So, yes, you go crazy. It's an obsession, Pedro Juan.'

'No one can live like that.'

'Yeah. You get used to it. I'm worse off now, knowin' I've already done most of what I wanted to do in this life. Now there's no fleet, no boats, no fish, no work, nothin'. And I got no wife, no children, no money, no nothin'. Not even a place to drop dead 'cause the sluts took it all when I was someone. And the years passin' by.'

'Hey, drop the sob story, buddy. Don't get depressed . . .'

'No, no. I told you I'm talkin' to you honest 'cause you're my friend. And what I tell you is the truth. I'm not inventin' nothin' or makin' drama. You see me workin' at the body shop for a few pesos a day – it isn't enough to eat, Pedro Juan. I know I'm never gonna escape this misery. Sometimes you're thinkin' and you tell yourself: somethin's gonna happen so I can have a mountain of money, an old lady is gonna marry me and she's gonna be loaded and die right away so I can be rich. Nothin'. Stories you invent. Money ain't gonna appear, or a decent woman, or an old lady with cash, ain't no love in this world or nothin'. This is the shit you invent so you don't dive from this roof and get stuck headfirst in the asphalt.'

I grabbed him by the arm: 'Listen, Trucu, what's happenin', man? Get away from there and drop that shit before you start to believe it.'

'Ha ha ha, you actually believed I was gonna jump? I'm just talkin', that's all, my man. You're takin' it way too serious.'

Pelé came staggering out on the terrace and vomited like an animal. He had a lot of garbage in his stomach. He slipped and fell in the vomit. He remained there, sitting on the floor, smeared with it all. We stood and stared at him, completely wasted ourselves. The Oldsmobile guys continued down below. How many hours would the repairs take? I stood looking at the vomit, and then said to Trucu: 'Don't confuse love with property rights.'

'Who told you that, Pedro Juan? Shit, you're a man of the street, a graduate of the university of life like me. You always gotta subdue a woman, Pedro Juan. Always been that way and it's gonna stay like that. She's gotta know you're the man. If your paw's a little weak she's gonna notice it and finish you off. Hey, look at me.'

'The woman makes you believe that. But, actually, she's the one who calls the shots.'

'No, no. You're wrong. Either you call the shots or she does. It's war. This love stuff's a story.'

'Too many years at sea. You may know about cod and hake, but you've learnt nothing about women.'

'How so?'

'They put on a show, they took your money, they played tricks on you like a child. And you still believe that if you show them who's boss, they'll obey you. Women are more intelligent than we are, Trucu, sharper, braver, more decisive, more mentally agile.'

'Where's your evidence for saying that? Haven't you read Vargas Vila? Vargas Vila's books are the Bible.'

'Don't give me that crap, Trucu. Vargas Vila? Don't be so dumb, buddy. They don't call you Trucutú for nothing.'

'But Vargas Vila wrote it very clearly: seduce them, corrupt them, addict them. They're all whores. They have whores' souls.'

'Let's drop the subject since we're both drunk and we'll never get anywhere . . .'

A knock at the door. It was Gloria. When she saw us like this she enjoyed putting on her lady-of-the-house-on-the-way-to-early-morning-Mass act: 'Uggh, what filth! What a drunken pigsty! Pedro Juan, the day you stop drinking I'm gonna light twenty candles to St. Lazarus and remain on my knees before him until the last one burns out. A promise I make is a promise I keep before my Lord on the cross.'

'Ah, don't play the decent one 'cause you . . .'

''Cause I nothin'. I don't get these filthy drunken sprees. Look at Pelé like a dog in his vomit, arghhh . . . and how he smells! Get me a pail of water right now to wash him down and enough of this. Up, Trucutú, get up and help me!'

'Calm down, Gloria. I've got two or three pails of water left in that tank and I'm not going to waste them on Pelé.'

'You're a bigger pig than they are.'

'Leave that for tomorrow. If we're lucky there'll be water in the building.'

'You know there's been no water for a week and that we have to go down and get it. It just so happens that you're a tremendous loafer and a pig.'

'Let me be and don't make like a wife.'

'No. "Let me be" nothing. As long as I'm your woman or as long as I'm with you, things have to be done correctly around here. I'm going to prepare our bath so we can go to bed. Do you want a coffee?'

'A coffee yes, but no bath. I'm going to bed just like this. Trucu, what are you going to do? Nobody's going to be able to move Pelé.'

'I'm gonna stay right here, man. There's still some rum left.'

'You sure?'

'Sure. Don't worry. Go to bed. I'm gonna stay out here and enjoy the breeze.'

Gloria and I went to bed. The room is next to the terrace. I fell into bed like a stone. Gloria opened the venetian blinds, lit the lamp, and began to take off her clothes.

'Hey, slutty whore, Trucu's going to see you.'

'That's why I'm doing it. He's already watching.'

'Ah, shit.'

'And now I'm going to fuck you so he can jack off like a madman. That's the only thing he knows how to do: beat his meat and fuck seventy-year-old ladies.'

'And how do you know that?'

'Oh, don't ask.'

She threw herself on top of me and began to suck me. I couldn't get a hard-on. I felt nothing, I was too drunk. Everything was spinning around me. I fell asleep. A little later I thought I heard whispering next to me. I made an effort and saw Gloria and Trucu on the bed. I'm not sure, but it seemed to me it was the two of them.

When I woke up it was light. Gloria was snoring next to me, naked, satisfied, with her legs apart. I had slept enough. I had a dry throat and a stiff prick. I moved down to Gloria's pussy. Uhmmm, it was moist and had a cheesy odor. It tasted like cheese. I like it better like that. Sometimes it smells like fish. Now it had a good taste. She woke up purring like a cat. And we began. Slowly, in no hurry. I like these morning fucks. I like to get inside of her and hug her hard. She feels like a little bird. She kisses my tattoo. She loves the red serpent. We caress. And talk. She shuts her eyes and releases her brain. She says it to me quietly: she's imagining that I'm her father.

'Oh, yes, he was kissing me and touching my pussy and stroking me. I used to give his cock a good squeeze. My little hand wouldn't fit around it. He had a very thick one . . . oh, no, no, no. Don't believe me, that's a lie. It was Rodolfo who did that to me.'

'It was your daddy, bitch.'

'No, not my father. My father was decent. He was a decent man. Make me pregnant, come on, make me pregnant. I want to marry you and have children.'

'Marry you?'

'You and I. Dressed in white. And if I'm already pregnant, better. In my bridal gown and with a big, six-month belly. Ah, shit, like that, fuck me deep, it's big and thick, you fucker, faggot! I can really feel it! You love whores and sluts. It's huge, *papi*. Knock me up so I can have kids with you and stay home; that's all I want.'

'Like Minerva? That's what you want.'

'Yes, that's what I want. To have a husband and stay at home washing and cooking, *papi*, and to fuck you in every room.'

'And for me to give you four slaps.'

'Ah, that drives me crazy. Hit me, and I'll die for you. But don't tell me about it, you'll make me come.'

'Yeah. Take this, slut.'

I slap her around a bit.

'Go on, hit me with your cruel hand. Make me come like a bitch in heat. Ahh, I'm a mistreated daughter, beat me, I love it . . . take my milk, *papi*, take more.'

She gyrates her hips like a blender. I'm about to let fly. No. I hold back. I turn her over. She lets me do it. I lick her asshole, I kiss it, I get it wet with lots of saliva. And push it in, gently. She has a black anus, very beautiful, with its curly mulatto hairs. And she clenches it and pushes it out. It's a temptation. The girl's insatiable. I nail her smoothly, sweetly, no hurry. I lie on her back and I bite it. And we sweat together. She moves well. Digging it and wanting more and more. Her buttocks are small. Everything about her is small, manageable, perfect, with her tanned flesh. She's a devil, an insatiable witch. She likes it from behind, but not always. You have to seduce her, drive her wild. Really make her hot. Find her weak spot. And strike there. In the weak spot. Then she loses her head and tells me all the filthy things that occur to her. I never know if she's lying or telling the truth. She's the naughtiest, happiest, craziest woman I've ever had. She talks nonstop: 'Take me to the tattoo guy. So that he can put it on one of my buttocks, one of my tits. Wherever you want it, *papi*: "I belong to Pedro Juan." "Pedro Juan is my man." Just like that, to make all my other men envious. So that they'll be jealous. And I'm gonna tell them: "This is my man. He's the number one. The one. My man. I take money from you so that I can take care of him."'

'Really? You want to have a tattoo?'

'Yes, yes. I'm gonna get drunk, smoke a joint, and then they can stick the needle in me. Ahh, how do you get such a tree trunk? It's so fat and big, it hurts, I can feel it in my throat, ahhh, what d'you eat, *papi*? To have such a hard trunk, what d'you eat?'

'Horse meat and hot sauce, sweetie.'

'You're the horse, you animal. Go on, go on. Give it to me.'

All of this drives me mad. I can't take it any more; I let loose my come inside her. *Uffff* . . . I relax. We kiss, we stay a while longer loafing on the bed. Finally I get up and make coffee. On the roof terrace is Pelé's vomit, drying in the sun, the stench growing. Hundreds of flies. I take a little water and wash it down. And here comes Gloria to bawl me out: 'Don't do that. You're not my maid. I don't like men doing women's things.'

'Ah, Gloria, don't fuck with me. I've been living alone for twenty years. Now you're going to teach me?'

'But now you have a woman. Everything about the house is my problem. This looks like a black slave shack, with your drunken benders and your pals. The only things missing are lice and chiggers. Look, go to the market and get rice, pigmeat, something. The icebox's empty. There's not even a bottle of water. I don't know how you can live in this disaster. From drunk to drunk.'

'Gloria, Gloria, stop agitating and let me be!'

She likes to play the housewife: to prepare little meals, clean, wash dishes, care for the kids. In a second she transforms. Changes personality. Superman/Clark Kent. There's nothing left of the big whore with the loose tongue of several minutes ago. But, then again, I don't know if she's telling the truth or a lie. I don't know if she's playing with me or if she really feels it. She confuses me, and I never know where the boundary is between reality and fiction.

She puts on a not-too-clean checked housecoat, ties a kerchief around her head, slips on some old, worn and dirty rubber slippers. And she's the great scrubber. She scolds, commands, orders, sends me to the market to find some food. She takes the lead. And by midday she's satisfied. Everything's in order, the floors polished, the air fragrant. She's even sprinkled seeds in some flowerpots. And, very much at ease, she sits to watch a soap opera. She doesn't even let me joke at a mess of a show with a stupid little blonde who constantly sings to the seagulls. She concentrates, laughs, weeps, bites her nails, immerses herself in the soap opera. I can't bear it. I refuse to cohabit with stupidity. I have to keep myself from throwing her downstairs. But as soon as she concludes her role as missus-mama-housewife, she reverts. She sprouts fangs and becomes the wolf-woman, the great seductress, the devourer of men, the viper. Gloria the Cuban. Gloria the deadly. My madness, my love, the woman I love. The one who makes me feel like a billygoat bellowing with pleasure on the mountaintop.

That's the way life is. Pain and pleasure. I drink a cup of coffee, light a cigar and leave for the market. I leave her with her soap opera. I put on a sleeveless red T-shirt and feel strong as a bull. With my tattoo exposed to the sun. I like to screw hard with Gloria, really hard. A couple of hours sweating, and afterwards go out for a stroll by myself, reeking of sweat, of semen, of Gloria, of bed. Feeling like a strong and healthy animal. A lively, muscular colt striding down Lagunas or Ánimas headed toward Belascoaín. I feel like a bucking bronco, with the spermatozoa sluicing through me, fertile, searching desperately for a way out and into the ovule. I imagine my spermatozoa, merry and playful, my microscopic children, laughing, full of happiness within me, waiting for the gun to fire and the barrier to be raised so they can go swimming off at full speed towards the ovum. They already know. Only one will be able to put his head in, make an effort, struggle and force his way inside.

13

Gloria and I are two souls possessed by the Devil. More and more so each day. The pimp and the whore. The little girl and the father. The vampire and the victim. The light and the shadow. Christ and the cross. The sadist and the masochist. My stiff dick drives her crazy and I just love to impale her, to drink her blood and swallow her saliva. Madwoman and madman. We'll wind up in the madhouse. What will become of us? What are the limits? Who sets the limits? Who invents them? Where are they? How far can I go? When I write the novel, with her as protagonist, what will I be able to say about all of this? What must I leave out, insinuate? Should I tell it all? Do I have the courage to go all the way and get totally naked? Is it necessary? I'm an exhibitionist. Striptease. That's what I do: striptease.

This afternoon I read a fragment of *Don Quixote*, for Spanish Radio Abroad. Today is Cervantes' I-don't-know-what-day. His birthday, I think. I don't like these readings, but one can't always play the spoilsport. There were three of us – writers – and while we were waiting for the moment to arrive, one cited Michel Butor, said something about *The Writing of Disaster*. The other one answered him, tying this book to Lezama Lima. *Ufff*, it's impossible to find a balance point between shit and the clouds. I went out on the little balcony to get some air. At least in Old Havana the landscape is absorbing. When it was my turn I took the telephone, read a piece of the book. At one point they said to me: '*Gracias*, Cuba.' I stopped reading. I waited an instant. The same voice again: 'We're off the air, all well, many thanks.' I went, as if drawn by a magnet, to the bar on Águila and Virtues. I was parched. I drank a few Polar beers. Ice-cold. There were two employees and three or four regulars drinking rum. All speaking very low, almost whispering. A very skinny little policeman, standing on the corner a few yards away from us, was observing us from the corner of his eye. Four little whores, very young, were walking around in circles. They were looking straight into the eyes of those of us who were drinking, elbows on the bar. We were all between fifty and sixty years old. The little whores knew their business. I had an empty stomach. The beers gave me a jolt. I went home and called Gloria. 'She's not here, she went to her cousin's house.' Some minutes later I receive a very nice call. A club of unmarried girls. They got my name and number from the directory, by chance. They're looking for boyfriends over the phone. Overly decent this method. I don't believe it. I ask them: 'Are you señoritas, virgins? From some nuns' boarding school, a convent?'

'No, just single women.'

'Ah, good, okay. Then it's possible.'

'My name is Yamilé.'

And she describes herself: mulatta, thirty-two years old. A sixteen-year-old son, a five-year-old daughter, she works in a cigar factory, rolling cigars. She gave me her number. We spoke some more. She has a lot to talk about. She's nice. Okay, let's get together one of these days.

Gloria appeared at eight-thirty at night, with her short yellow dress, very short, white shoes with heels, and some white panties. Very beautiful, with her skin so tawny and her well-turned legs and thighs. Nothing lacking and nothing left over. She has it all perfect. In exact proportion. Only the hands and the feet a bit uncared for. She's just right. I tell her that from now on she's going to become more complete, more womanly, like a fruit which ripens. Until now she has been just a naughty girl. After thirty, she'll improve. I tell her about Yamilé. To me it's been a joke. But Gloria has told this joke many times: 'A joke nothing. If you call her and you see each other naturally you'll like her and then she's got you by the short and curlies. You see, I've also rung this number.'

'She says it's a club.'

'A club nothing. That's just the rap. I can't leave you alone for even an hour. You're always stirring things up!'

'*Meee?* They come looking for me. I don't do anything.'

She goes to the little book beside the telephone. It's written down: Yamilé, 791952. She tears the page into little pieces.

'Here's for mulattas, black women, white women, for whores and for housewives, for all of them, all of them – I'm here now. Aren't I enough for you?'

'I know the number by heart. You want coffee or rum?'

'Both.'

I went to the kitchen. She came behind me and took the coffee pot from my hand: 'Leave it, *papi*. I'll make it. You have to get used to having a woman in the house, baby.'

It's better to let her make it. After all, I like to see her in the kitchen, her silver bracelets ringing. I'm like Pavlov's dog. My mouth waters and my tail stands up whenever I hear the jingling of her bracelets. Or when I see her walking barefoot around the house. Her feet and her hands turn me on. I'm triggered even when I don't smell or touch her. Just seeing her in a robe, cleaning the house, half naked, in slippers or barefoot, her bracelets ringing and Mark Anthony on the tape recorder at top volume. She works a little and starts to sweat, and her pussy gets raunchy and ripe. I'm a vulgar, unscrupulous type, an alley cat. It must be my vocation. Elegant, aristocratic, perfumed women don't do anything for me.

Well, now that I think about it, I've only ever liked one of those oh-so-special ladies – of the kind you used to see in the red-light districts my rooftop overlooks. It was on a certain autumn night, in the National Auditorium of Madrid, and I was sat in a box, minding my own business. The Berlin Philharmonic Orchestra had a program of Beethoven and Brahms. The concert was to begin with the Fifth, of course. At which point a deliciously slender, lean lady, with black stockings, a short black skirt, and a slight French accent took the seat beside me. She threw her fur coat on the floor, trod on it contemptuously, drove her heels into it, defiling it with dust. I looked at her out of the corner of my eye and enjoyed her sadomasochistic expression. She had the face, the aura, the magnetic field of an old whore. A de luxe whore, an aristocratic whore. We look at each other, we smile, we greet one another: 'Good evening.' We talk about Beethoven, Brahms, the Berlin Philharmonic, that night's conductor: 'And you, what do you do?'

'Me? Many things. Depending on the moment.'

'Ahh. My husband is captain of a ship. A supertanker. Now he's in South America.'

'Very far away.'

'I've grown used to it.'

'It must be difficult to be the wife of a sailor.'

'Of a sailor, perhaps. But I adore being the wife of a captain.'

'It's more lucrative.'

'Ohhh . . .'

The applause, the conductor acknowledging the audience, the final tuning of the strings. And it began. In spite of the music, the exquisite lady arranged to whisper something in my ear every few minutes. She gave me the impression that she was ovulating and had become excessively moist. Later I thought that was impossible. She was more than sixty years old.

'Have you thought what music you'd like for your funeral?'

'Let them burn me. And throw the ashes in the trash.'

'Ohhhh . . . . ehhh . . . I have always asked for the *Eroica*.'

She gave a long account of all the European cities in which she had heard this symphony. She remembered it all in a scrupulous way, like someone who had little or nothing else about which to think: orchestra, concert hall, conductor, time of year, pianist's mistakes, name of the first violin.

While she was talking, I was watching her slender, slightly separated thighs sheathed in black stockings; I imagined myself kneeling before her, putting my head there and spreading those thighs far enough apart for me to arrive with my tongue at point X.

The Fifth continued playing, and she kept murmuring in my ear. I thought we would be able to go to her house. I pictured her bedroom: elegant, perhaps a bit overdecorated in a nineteenth-century style; strawberries and champagne on a little table. And me slowly taking off her clothes bit by bit, in the light of four perfumed candles, and working her only with my tongue and fingers, obliging her to search for a whip. She kept on whispering something or other even as my imagination roamed freely about her bedroom. In the end, I avoided that temptation. I was feeling a bit overwhelmed by some rather aggressive threats, the result of a certain book I'd published that autumn. In sum, the moment was not right. My little guardian angel was watching me from afar, from another box, and when we left the theatre, he reproached me severely for my discourtesy. In fact, I was left with a desire to explore that luxurious lady. But I suppose a second opportunity will present itself. For now, I keep cultivating my usual habits: what attracts me is filth, the smell of sweat, abundant hair in the underarms. Servant girls, little maids, whores, cooks, cleaning ladies, fighters, street sellers, the most common, imperfect, uncultured women, the ones who know about everything and who dress themselves in short blouses, leaving their navels in full view, and who'll entice anyone into letting them give him a ten- or fifteen-peso handjob at midday in the middle of the Malecón. Gloria is all of this. Now she's leaving the hair in her underarms. All that luxuriant armpit growth, like the German girls, and without deodorant, sweaty. Just smelling it I go crazy like an animal and lose control. Her sweaty odor is a stimulating drug.

I draw near her, I caress her, I kiss her, I sniff her, I get her a little hot, and there we go. I turn off the stove. The coffee remains half boiled. I take a mouthful of rum and pass it to her mouth. I take her to the bed, take off her clothes and observe her. I like to look at her from behind. She lies down on her side and lifts her knees to her chin. I start to masturbate slowly. We observe one another. Without touching. Since childhood, she was accustomed to looking at grown men's pricks. Just looking. She has told me about it in detail. Since she was seven years old. She was living in a tenement on Laguna Street. Many people in very few rooms, and only one or two communal bathrooms. Promiscuity was inevitable. Gloria was watching and letting others watch her. In the tenement and its surroundings, the perverted or the perverse abounded. At ten years old, she liked her dance teacher and so she threw herself full force into conquering him. She already had some experience. At least in watching and letting herself be watched. The man resisted her. She insinuated herself on him, intending to excite him, but he knew that it was from five to ten years behind bars for corruption of minors. And at the trial he could never claim that the girl had seduced him because they would accuse him further for attempting to pervert the course of justice and for offending and defaming the innocent.

The poor man dissembled, meaning to go on with his classes. But the innocent creature was diabolically persistent and clever. She was much more than a mere naughty, capricious girl. Gloria was a little monster. One day she entered the teacher's room on some pretext; he lived in the same tenement on Laguna. She came in like a hurricane and, very merrily, went to a water tank which was standing in a corner and poured a jugful over her head.

'Oh, look, Rodolfo, I wet myself! I'm gonna catch cold.'

She took off her clothes and, very quickly, without letting the man react: 'Dry me. Get a towel and dry me.'

Rodolfo stood there astonished. How far would that little girl go? He found a towel. He closed the door tightly. He could only think about jail.

'Girl, by your mother, stay calm, you're gonna get me in trouble.'

'Dry me, Rodolfo, come on.'

When he came near her with the towel, she touched his cock from outside his pants. The girl was not beating about the bush. She got straight to the point: 'Let me see it.'

'Little girl, by your mother, you're gonna mess me up.'

'Come. Look.'

She sat in a chair, lifted her legs, opened them and showed her little sex, with thick black hairs much too abundant for a ten-year-old girl. She offered herself to him.

'Take it out. Let me see it.'

He went to the door. Checked that it was well shut. Came back and took it out. He already had it half hard. She caressed it a bit and then put it in her mouth. She had never done it but, perhaps by intuition, she knew how to act. Rodolfo came in two minutes, and she received a shower of come. Happily. She anointed her body with it as if it were lotion. Rodolfo liked that.

She knew all about jail: 'Don't be afraid. I'm not going to get rid of you. On the contrary, I'm going to care for you.'

'You're going to be my little girlfriend?'

'I'm going to be, no. I already am. Your girlfriend, your little woman, everything you want.'

That relationship between the ten-year-old girl and the forty-two-year-old man lasted many years. But Gloria didn't believe in fidelity. She has always been totally and absolutely unfaithful. And it isn't cruel or intentional. It's something natural, as unquestioning as breathing or drinking a glass of water. Apart from her love with Rodolfo, she turned many tricks in all directions. At fourteen, a boy her age penetrated her. Some days later, she wanted Rodolfo to penetrate her too. He asked what had happened. She told him about it with the greatest naturalness in the world. He took offense. The right of passage belonged to him; that was without question. And not to a snotty fourteen-year-old. The relationship became very tormented. You know: love and possession. The eternal confusion. The origin of the family, private property and the state. Gloria, pragmatic and decisive, ended the affair. She was too young to start to suffer for men. When she related this to me she wound up a little sad: 'I liked him a lot. But nothing lasts for ever.'

'Do you still see him?'

'Yes. He still lives by himself. He's over sixty years old now. He's suspicious of everyone.'

'Far from here?'

'Right there, in the Laguna tenement. I get sad when I see him so poor, so unhappy, so bitter, without children, without anyone to care for him. And what's more, he rejects me. He lives in total squalor. Sometimes I go to see him just to clean his room, to help out, but it's useless. He doesn't let me and he kicks me out.'

'You were in love.'

'Like a crazy woman. In my mind, I pretended that he was my husband and that we had kids and all of that.'

'You were never a girl.'

'Yes, yes. These were a little girl's games. Like playing house.'

'But with a real cock.'

'Ha ha ha. I think everyone in the tenement knew. I was always in his room. I was a little girl of ten and eleven and I washed his clothes, cleaned his room, cooked for him, everything, I did everything for him. But people respected him. He has always been a serious man, very decent. To me, it didn't matter if they knew or not.'

'What if someone had accused him?'

'I'd have denied it and called that person a liar. People are always ready to do damage to others. But there they respect him. He's a serious man.'

'I think you were born a whore.'

'Don't call me a whore.'

'I say it with affection.'

'Once they told me that in a former life I was a woman of cabarets and parties. And in another before that I was a gypsy.'

'And in this life you're perfecting it.'

'That's right, *papi*, I like to have fun with the men. I like to look at pricks. Lots of pricks. Different ones. Is that bad? Look at the dogs, how they do it there, in the middle of the street; it's normal.'

'We're not dogs.'

'It's the same, we're animals.'

Talking like this, softly, I was putting it in her little by little. As we continued caressing each other, I said: 'You're like a little animal. You're warm, hairy.'

'Yes, *papi*, I am a little animal. I like dogs. Ahh, buy me a big black dog, the kind that fight, real ugly and jowly, with a big tongue.'

'For what, crazy little girl? What are you gonna do with the dog?'

'So I can fuck with him in front of you. So I can jerk him off.'

And off went her brain with the black dog. At some moment she turned me around and sucked my butt. She inserted a finger. Two fingers.

'Ahh, crazy daddy, I like it like this, to be your woman and your husband. If I had a banana, a cucumber, a carrot . . . This ass is mine. You're mine, completely. I've never had a man like you, you've got me hooked, you goat.'

I was relaxing myself, giving myself over.

'I'm gonna go back to the cathouse for you, *papi*. For you, yes, I'll do it. Any time you ask me to. I want to keep you. I like pimps, *papi*.'

Gloria is on the far side of glory. We were like this for maybe a couple of hours. We can be like that all the time in the world. She has an incredible imagination. It renews itself constantly. When I can't hold back any more, I gather up my will power. Then I whip out my dick and come in her mouth. She gulps it all down.

'Ahhh, it's acid again. Sometimes yours is sweet, sometimes it's acid. Ahh, it's burning my mouth, like cashew bark; it's so bitter I can hardly talk, ha ha ha.'

I go to the kitchen. I relax, finish making the coffee, and we drink it. We smoke; get started on the rum. Gloria goes to the cassette player and Roberto Carlos enters the scene. When she has a few shots, screws, drinks more rum, and kicks back, she talks a lot. That's when I accumulate material for the novel.

'Tell me something about Milagros' cathouse.'

'You're always asking. Why do you wanna know more?'

'Get dressed. Let's go over there now.'

'It's closed.'

'That's a lie.'

'No, it's true.'

'When did they close it?'

'Months ago. They almost took the house away from Milagros.'

'For what?'

'Ha ha ha. For being a madam. Ha ha ha. Boy, do you live here or in the clouds?'

'Why do you say that?'

'My love, by then the place was famous. People came from all around. Blue bloods in the regime, common field hands, all sorts. All with lots of cash. Peasants with fat wallets, straight from the agromarket! You should have seen how fast we took it! Sometimes I didn't even have to screw them because they drank so much they couldn't get it up. They didn't even notice me taking banknotes out of their pockets. Yes, there the money really flowed!'

'So it was a big place.'

'Seven rooms, and we always had ten or twelve girls. Sometimes more. A lot of coming and going.'

'Was there a bar?'

'They set up a bar in the living room. It was already a madhouse. And when they did away with the law against . . . well, I had no problems because I had already gone.'

'Eh?'

'I wasn't there then.'

'You mean, like a good girl, you went peacefully?'

'Milagros kicked me out.'

'What for?'

'Her husband, he fell in love with me and I had to go off and screw him a couple of times. When she found out, she got rid of me. She did it like a lady, without making a scene, the way decent people do. But I had to go fast.'

'You sure don't make things easy. Who in their right mind would fuck the boss's husband?'

'Me.'

'Yes, only you. Your head is hollow.'

'Me a hollow head? No, *papito*, I don't do anything just for fun. The guy was a butcher and he paid me well. Sometimes he'd give me two hundred pesos for a lousy little five-minute fuck. Am I going to beg his pardon? No way, man, not for nothin' in the world! And I didn't screw him again only 'cause word got round to Milagros and things got fucked up.'

'You were lucky, you avoided messing with the police.'

'Yeah, but the work's still out there. There are little bordellos in the neighborhoods. Lots of them. But because they're small, people with money don't go. Shitty little bordellos, which aren't worth the trouble. I had days in Milagros' house when I pulled down five hundred pesos. That was big time.'

'She'll open it up again. With luck, she'll forgive you.'

'No. I never walk the same path twice. What's more, when I leave something, it collapses. When I was there, the house was always full of men and the money flowed. She got rid of me, and seven days later she had to close; they almost took the house from her and put her in jail. Her, her husband, and the guy who ran the bar. They were even gonna lock up the old lady who cleaned and changed the sheets. They were let go because Milagros greased so many palms he ran out of hands. And all the fuss died down.'

'You're vengeful.'

'It's a gift I have. Whatever I walk away from collapses.'

'Were you going at night?'

'At all hours. I act on inspiration. That's enough now. What do you want to know more for? To make yourself jealous?'

'No, girl, it's for the novel.'

'You and your fucking little novel. You'll probably never even write it.'

'No, I have to begin it some day. I have to decide when.'

'You're not gonna write nothin'.'

'Yes I will, you'll see. The most difficult thing is the title and the first page.'

'You told me it's called *Lots of Heart*. Or have you already changed your mind?'

'Yeah, that title is good, but . . . I don't know what's the matter. I have a lot of material . . . I don't know where to begin. It's like I'm lost.'

'I wouldn't put it past you to include all those cathouse stories and me with my real name.'

'What do you want to be called?'

'In the novel?'

'Yes.'

'Anything but Gloria.'

'Pick one.'

'Katia.'

'I like Gloria better.'

'But people will know it's me. How embarrassing. For God's sake, don't do this to me! At least change my name.'

'Who's going to know it's you?'

'Enough already. You're a tremendous loafer and you ain't gonna write nothin'.'

'Did you like the cathouse?'

'Of course, it's a happy life. No emotional attachments. When did you ever see a whore get emotionally involved?'

'Men enjoy whores.'

'That's a lie. They like whores in the street and in the cathouse, but at home they want a missus: "Private property. Keep off the grass."'

'I like you a lot.'

'Yeah, uhhh . . . to fool around with in bed.'

'No one knows what our destiny is. We may get together . . .'

'Get together nothing. Married. And dressed in white. With . . .'

'Okay, okay. Don't repeat the same foolishness.'

'And have twins, *papi*.'

'Something's not right in your head. I can't stand kids. When did you last see an old man bringing up babies? I already raised three. Not one more, Gloria. Much less twins!'

'Ha ha ha. How funny you get. Like a little boy. You're not old, *papito*. You're a stud.'

'Me?'

'Ha ha ha. What a rogue you are. How you love it when people praise you, ha ha ha.'

'What I love is your laughter.'

'Liar. No man likes it. Men don't let me laugh.'

'Why not?'

'They say it's a whore's laugh.'

'Ah, because you're happy.'

'Yeah, but it makes them angry. They're ashamed.'

'Did you ever get sad in the cathouse?'

'Only one time.'

'With a man?'

'Yes.'

'Why?'

103

'I fell in love. He was a chino. A chino-mulatto. Very beautiful.'

'Was he black?'

'Don't you know what a chino is? Mulatto turning toward chino. Chino-mulatto. He had a really beautiful dragon tattooed on his arm. Our Lady of Charity on his back, and a gold eye tooth. Ahhhh, the craziness, and how he liked to dress in white, always immaculate, like a dandy. And a cock like this . . . like . . . like ten inches. He had cock enough to eat and to take home.'

'And with you being narrow and shallow.'

'Narrow and shallow, me? . . . Don't be a fool, my heaven. I can make it stretch like chewing gum; course I can. He liked to fuck me on the floor. Always on the floor.'

'And why did you fall in love?'

'Ah, I don't know. The way he fucked me was different. He was affectionate, never crude, very sweet. He fucked me like you do, with feeling; he told me pretty things. I don't know. You can't explain it. You're in love and that's it.'

'And he paid you?'

'At first yes, of course. Later no. But he always gave me money. Not as pay, but he was always giving me gifts. He was rolling in money. He was always hanging out on the beaches with the foreigners. He had lots of cash. Later he even came to my house to woo me, telling me he was going to leave his wife and take me out of the cathouse and marry me. It lasted, like . . . a year, just over a year. He took me out for walks, to drink beer, but all of a sudden he disappeared and I heard nothing more of him. I saw him a little while ago. He says he was almost two years locked up. One other time he spent a year in jail.'

'What for?'

'You remember when the dollar was banned?'

'Yes, of course I do.'

'They caught him with two hundred dollars and laid a bunch of years on him, but he served only one.'

'And now?'

'Now he's a gigolo, with foreign women. A second offender. It's that he's so beautiful. I'm glad our affair is over, because I'd have suffered a lot. He's a very showy guy, very macho. When he walks down the beach you see the foreign women looking at him with open mouths. Well . . . he can choose any one he wants. He isn't obliged to screw old ladies or anything. And, just so you know, he doesn't like blondes or white girls.'

'Little dark ones?'

'Ones like me. Brunettes. Any day now, he's gonna strike it rich. He'll marry someone from the States, and they'll take him over there, to live well.'

'You haven't seen him again?'

'Yes, I see him from time to time. But it's all over. Everything passes. He never made decisions, we were always seeing each other in the street, very informal. And finally he lost me. In life, nothing is eternal. Just like us now. I can't spend my life running after you and you playing the pretty stud, 'cause I'm gonna get disenchanted, or someone may come along who I like and who'll decide on me, marry me, and support me and my son and boom. That's where we're at. I don't even want to think about it, but it's the truth.'

'Yes, that's it.'

'It first happened to me with the father of my son. Later with the chino, then it happened with . . . well . . . a few times. And if you go on without making decisions . . .'

'Hey, what's with you? What do you want?'

'What do you think I want? What any woman wants: to get married, to live with you, to have kids, for you to love me and be my husband; to have my house. To have what's mine and organize my life.'

'Next to nothing.'

'You going to keep living alone? You need someone to care for you.'

'To care for me? Do I look like a little boy, a baby, to you?'

'All men are like little boys. They all need a woman to take care of them.'

'Ahhh.'

'I'm patient, *papito*. I'm crazy about you like a bitch in heat, but

105

everything has a limit. Think about it. Start making decisions because everything has a limit.'

'Gloria, things are not so simple. It's only natural that, at twenty-nine, you want to make plans for the future.'

'Ah, don't play the old man.'

'I'm not playing the old man, but we're from different generations.'

'Uhmm.'

'Go do your thing. And don't worry about the rest. But my generation functioned differently.'

'How?'

'They made us concentrate on the others. And forget about ourselves.'

'That's why you're so bitter.'

'And so confused. And so disappointed with everything. At least I haven't killed myself, and that's something. Now cynicism saves me. Every day I'm more cynical and more skeptical. All I want to do is get out of the way. Let them keep throwing rocks at each other. Let them continue with the hate and rancor for the rest of their lives. But let them not fuck with me any more, let them not hit me again in the name of this or that. What I need is four dollars in my pocket and a little love and compassion in my heart.'

'You're melancholy today, *papi*.'

'Melancholy nothing! Why d'you let me talk so much, it only gets me even more bitter. Let's find some rum. Then I'm gonna give you four lashes and take you back to bed.'

'Ah, savage, you always go for the same thing.'

'To dance and groove with the National Philharmonic. Come on, Gloria, come on, it'll soon be too late.'

14

The little matter at the Swedish embassy caused some trouble. I must have gone twelve times. On bicycle by the Malecón. Half a dozen miles there. Half a dozen miles back. Each time I needed new documents, another application form. Agneta had to make some new arrangement or other in Stockholm. At times, I thought they were mocking me. But no, it seems the officials there were simply getting bored behind their bulletproof glass and steel drawers. So protected are they against terrorists, invaders, germs, tropical diseases and other predators that, obviously, they grow weary and have to come up with pranks. At some point the guy, contemptuous, shutting his eyelids, told me: 'I notice Cubans always leave everything until the last minute.' I had a feeling he was provoking me; that he wanted some pretext not to give me the visa. Did I have the face of a delinquent, of Gloria's pimp, of a dope-head? No. I don't think so. Therefore, I ignored his comment. In fact, I could have said to him: 'My dear sir, it's been more than a month that I've been getting fucking nowhere with these papers. Do you think you're granting me entry into paradise? Shove the visa up your ass. I'm not going anywhere. You're the losers. You should want to have a tropical animal like me as a visitor every once in a while.'

But I didn't tell him that, of course. I smiled just like he had, cynically, and asked him, as if it were of no importance to me: 'So, tomorrow?'

'Yes, sir. I promise you that tomorrow I'll have your visa ready.'

When I picked it up the next day, I went to the airline, picked up my ticket, and my mood improved automatically. I sat in a nearby cafeteria, and drank two or three beers to celebrate. I don't know how it occured to me, but right there I wrote a poem to Gloria. It's not exactly a love poem. Maybe it's a bloodthirsty poem. I felt free. My spirit was swelling. At such moments, the little sadistic and cynical Pedros triumph within me.

I am the vampire
who always surprises you
and sucks your blood.
I feed myself on your sweat,
on your tears,
on your semen.
I take your breath away
and penetrate you kissing you
until you don't even know
that I live inside of you.
Like a parasite.
Like a snake.
Like a virus.
I am your heart and your shit.
I am your brain and your hands.
I am your feet and your tongue.
And so I'll keep driving you crazy
like a demon enclosed in your breast.
You'll be mine inevitably.
The woman of the devil.
And while I sleep,
because then I'll stay asleep,
you'll sink your fangs into my throat
and you'll be my vampira
and you'll suck my blood.
And you'll feed on my sweat,
with my tears and my semen.
You'll take my breath away
and you'll penetrate me kissing me
deep as my soul.
And I'll live inside of you.
And you'll live inside of me.

II

The Swedish Lover

1

Now everything is much simpler. I write my notes in a beautiful notebook on soft paper. I read a little book of *Celtic Blessings* which has comforting texts:

> To Christ the seed,
> To Christ the harvest;
> To the barn of Christ
> May we be brought.

> To Christ the sea
> To Christ the fish:
> In the nets of Christ
> May we be caught.

Sometimes I walk up Sveavagen at night. The bar La Habana is just above Radmansgaten. They serve food too, though it's very expensive. A glass of draught beer costs five dollars. But there's always salsa music and black men from Havana dancing with Swedish women. So, for a few minutes, I return to the madness. They tell me how they conquered their Swedish women on the Malecón or in Guanabo, how they seduced them, how they escape now to dance, gamble, and get drunk with other Swedish women. Since they never have a krona in their pockets, they have to invent something every day to survive. Some give dance classes. Others continually ask their women for money. They understand no Swedish. There's one who is white – a depressed anthropologist. He's been in Stockholm four years. He doesn't dance. He hardly speaks. If he keeps on like this, he'll die of grief. 'Why don't you go back to Cuba?' I ask him. 'No, no, no, no!' I think he'll end up crazy or commit suicide. Another guy is just visiting. He lives in Umea. He doesn't work, doesn't understand the language, and he complains for half an hour. He complains about everything. I can't stand them. I quietly return to my little house, by metro and suburban train. I listen to Bruce Springsteen and Lou Reed, eat bread, cheese, and salmon. I drink beer and read an essay by Bertil Malmberg on the history of the Castilian language. Romanic philology. In life, one wastes time on many useless things. I write bad little poems to Gloria. I gather them together in an envelope and send them to her through the mail. Each letter costs more than a dollar. Why is everything so expensive? Or, at least, expensive for me. I suppose it's not so bad for the Swedes. Luckily, the good stuff is free. Agneta for example. She's affectionate, sweet, calm, silent, has nice tits, eats lightly, and takes very good care of herself. She's easily excited. I just have to squeeze her nipples a little, kiss her, and she's already moist and sighing. I suck her, kiss her, play with her pussy. She's finally decided to suck my prick. Not much, but at least she tries it. At first she didn't want to: 'Oh, no. I have never done it. I cannot.'

'Does it give you the willies?'

'The willies? What is that?'

'Does it turn you off?'

'Turn me off?'

'Ah, fuck. Enough of this. Does it seem dirty?'

'No, it is not dirty.'

'So go for it, girl, suck, suckle, absorb, lick, swallow.'

That's how it is. I'm becoming a thesaurus. Even in the middle of a fuck I have to stop to think of all the possible synonyms for the words she doesn't know. Nevertheless, I prefer it. The other option is to speak English. And I can't handle any more English: the television, the books, the people in the street. The more I speak it the less I like it. And in Swedish I can only guess at one word or another. For now, all I say is *tack*: thank you.

We adapt to each other little by little. I arrived in Stockholm very proper. With worn jeans, a thickly woven beige shirt, and a brown sports jacket, like any liberal intellectual. And on my best behavior. Twenty hours by plane from Havana. And shitting myself with fear each time the planes take off and land. It's uncontrollable. I don't literally shit in my pants, but almost. Finally I arrived and, two or three hours later, music, whisky, a sofa; cool and drizzle outside. Little comforts. And to bed with my Swedish lover. I was expecting something worse. But no, there's no need to sacrifice anything. She gets very emotional about it all. She's not as demanding as the Cuban women who want a very stiff, intrusive prick that doesn't droop for at least an hour. If it does, they'll say you don't desire them. 'Already I can tell you don't like me, *papi*. I can see you don't like me enough.' And right there they fuck things up. Many women do it with evil intent: that way they keep the man exhausted so he can't go with other females. Feminine wiles are bewitching. I adore them. And I learn from them.

Agneta is much more agreeable. Some tongue, a little diddling with the fingers, a light brush with the cock, and she gets enthusiastic and comes like a concubine. Abundantly. I didn't expect it. Since it's always said that the Swedes are ingenuous and cold and that they live floating in the air. That's why the saying exists: 'Don't act like a Swede.' Forget it. She's a great fuck. She gives herself over and says to me: 'Oh, what are you doing to me? You make me crazy.'

The only problem is I don't sleep well. Three or four hours only. When I wake up, it's already daylight and I can't sleep. Night falls at eleven. Day breaks before two in the morning. It drives me crazy. In Umea it's worse. I've had to go a couple of times. There it's always light. Later, in the winter, it's always night.

Other than this, nothing happens. The seminar at the university passed without shame or glory. Now I eat salmon, drink coffee and tea, fuck every day. I listen to music, look at the tulips, run half an hour every day to sweat out the toxins from so much salmon and cheese. There's almost always a couple of hours of strong sun at noon. I live in the suburbs. There are woods and soft grass, and little lakes with ducks and gulls which shriek. I come back sweaty, lie down naked in the sun, and smell my pits. It's a strong smell. I close my eyes and there's Gloria, lifting her arms so that I can savor her to my delight.

113

Her memory doesn't let me rest. I'd love to have her here. As consolation I had a little affair in the seminar with a big-assed African woman. Very, very big-assed. Exaggeratedly big-assed and big-breasted. One morning as we were leaving the Parliament after a token official visit, she got her ass caught in the revolving door. This door has four sections. In the section in front of me a Swedish man was exiting, I was behind him, and behind me was the African woman. It seems she didn't have time. Her big ass got jammed, and the door stopped. The Swede didn't see what had happened behind his back, and began pushing to get out. Behind me, the African woman was screaming and swearing, but the door is glass and so you couldn't hear her. The Swede was pushing forward to get out and the African was pushing backward to get out. All of a sudden I forgot all my English. I didn't know what to say and I couldn't act as an intermediary between Europe and Africa. Seconds went by which seemed like minutes. Finally my brain cleared, and I yelled at the Swede: 'Excuse me! Excuse me! Hey, you, come back, come back!' To say this shit you don't have to think. My brain is sluggish. The Swede heard me and stopped pushing. Her ass was freed. All of us acted as if nothing had happened. Elegance is important, especially around the Parliament. At any rate, when we reached the street, the African woman and I exchanged a glance. She was rubbing her buttocks and saying: 'Ohhh.' I couldn't contain myself and let loose a guffaw, and she laughed with me.

A couple of nights later, all of us who had attended the seminar had a small party. All were university professors except me, and they didn't dance. In other words, serious people. They just talked and talked. I had seen the African woman speaking with her husband on the phone. He was apparently a high-ranking military official in her country. She kept telling him: 'Oh, honey, I love you.' Later she showed me a photo of their three sons and the military man with his uniform and herself very pretty in native dress and all that. Anyway, that night she drank too much wine. We had a few glasses, and at some point she came up to me with the sweetest smile in the world and wanted me to dance. But I didn't feel like dancing. She was pressing me close to her and caressing my back and saying in my ear: 'Ohh, very nice, very nice. Ohh, really, very nice.' My back is extremely sensitive. I put my hands on her enormous and very beautiful African ass, and in five minutes we were in my room on the floor above. That was great. I sniffed the dirtiness in her hair. She'd had those little braids for who knows how long. They were very beautiful, with colored beads, but they stank. I concentrated on other regions. It was three degrees outside, but we were sweating. She was inspired, enormously flexible, and she raised her legs nice and high. I had my head down there when she let loose a couple of farts. Loud ones. I was giving her tongue and felt two bursts of pressurized air hit me in the face. I checked. There was no shit. Okay. Onward. She was very eager. She was fondling me with both hands, she wanted some dick. I had a rubber ready. I condomized myself and off I went to the black jungle. Unforgettable. All very folkloric. By the time she left stealthily for her room, it was almost four in the morning. I went down to the ground floor to search for some tea and to smoke a good cigar. There was still someone there. A gay Vietnamese. He was watching the Playboy channel, lying on a sofa. Covered by a quilt. He had his hand under the quilt and was moving it. Vietcong wank in the Swedish dawn. Each of us does what he can. The next day I tried to repeat the dose, but the African was staring at the floor. She wouldn't dare look me in the eye and, in a very low voice, she said: 'Sorry. Too much wine last night. Sorry.'

I tried to play the Latin lover. I told her everything was fine, that she shouldn't feel embarrassed, that it's natural between a man and a woman who like each other. Nonsense like that. But she wouldn't let herself be swayed. She kept away from me for the next few days. So I asked the Vietnamese guy at what times they had the best films on the Playboy channel.

2

Lou Reed said something like this:

> When you pass through the fire
> You pass through humble
> You pass through a maze of self-doubt.
> When you pass through humble
> You can be blinded by the light.
> There are those who never get this.
> You pass through arrogance
> You pass through pain
> You pass through a past which is always present
> And it's better not to hope that luck'll save you
> You have to pass through fire to reach the light.

The sun is very weak behind the clouds. The thermometer goes up to twenty. Maybe today we'll get lucky and it'll hit twenty-two. Agneta drives carefully. Lou Reed is melancholy, singing about magic and loss. She always looks straight ahead. We cross a very long bridge. Several miles. At some point it rises 180 feet high – maybe more – so that large transatlantic ships can pass through in both directions.

'Here many people commit suicide.'

'Many?'

'Fifty or sixty each year.'

'Damn! One a week. Is this bridge in the *Guinness Book of Records*?'

'I don't know.'

'What do they do? Drown?'

'They smash against the water. I don't know. They die.'

For a while, we stay silent. Cars draw alongside, move on ahead. Agneta drives at a steady forty. No more. Two motorcycles overtake us. They bank from one side to another on their big pneumatic tires. They look like rockets, with the guys dressed as astronauts. They disappear a hundred yards ahead in the gray curtain of rain. They must be doing more than 120 miles per hour. Agneta says to me: 'If we have an accident and I die, remember that you have medical insurance.'

'Ah, don't talk shit.'

She smiles timidly, pained to have to speak about this.

'The papers are in the cupboard, next to the television. In the top part. There are other papers, but your documents are in English. In your name. Everything very clear.'

'Thank you very much, honey.'

Now I've caught it. I don't know what to say. I look out the window. Nothing occurs to me. I stretch out my arm. Stop Lou Reed. I look through various cassettes I brought. Pablito F.G., Los Van Van, N.G. I pick one by Omara Portuondo. It warms up the atmosphere. The songs, 'Soy cubana', 'Son de la Loma', 'Siboney', 'Me acostumbré a estar sin ti', bring back so many memories. The cassette ends on a high note, with 'Yo sí como candela':

> Don't play with me, baby
> 'cause I'm a fire-eater.
> I sang in paradise
> and they made an altar to me
> and I would dare to sing'
> to God himself if necessary.
> I write ballads and improvise
> for fools and those in the know.
> I protect myself from any
> and all dangerous situations
> and if you turn into a beast
> I'll lock the door and keep the key.
> 'Cause I'm a fire-eater!

The woods are very dense. Dark green and solemn. Around ten in the morning we come to a deserted beach with coarse sand and stones. The Baltic. Always gray, dirty, cold, with sparse salt and seagulls, and solitary and silent fishermen. Or empty. A solitary sea full of salmon and half-frozen herring, ready to dip in brine.

There are cold gusts from the northeast. It's stopped drizzling but continues to be totally overcast, wet and cold. We walk along listening to the soft sound of the surf and the coarse sand under our feet, and the gulls screeching above. We walk briskly. It's cold. I like to see the flotsam that the sea casts ashore: bits of rope and rusty steel cable, pieces of highly polished wood, plastic bottles. Suddenly I see a brown leather jacket floating. We stop to look. It floats completely open and near to shore, above the pebbles, and is moved rhythmically by the light back-and-forth movement of half a foot of water. It's a bit discolored but it has no tears and nor does it seem worn by use. Perhaps it's been floating for weeks. We don't speak. I believe we're both thinking the same thing: the owner fell into the water and drowned. His cadaver was eaten by fish in the depths of the sea and the jacket, floating smoothly, resurfaced and arrived at this shore. It seems slightly macabre but we think it simultaneously. It isn't necessary to say it to know that we are each thinking the same thing.

We walk a bit further and sit down on some big rocks, facing the sea. At our backs, the wind whistles through the pines. There isn't a single person in sight. I can see for several miles to my left and a similar distance to my right. Nothing. Not even a boat. Absolutely nothing. I have never liked listening to the wind whistle in the pines. I need to break the silence. To speak about anything: 'On the phone, you told me about a friend of yours who committed suicide. Was it on the bridge?'

'He wasn't my friend. My friend is his wife.'

'His *viuda*.'

'*Viuda?*'

'When the husband dies, the wife is called a *viuda*.'

'Oh, yes.'

'Did he jump from the bridge?'

'Pardon?'

Sometimes I forget that I have to pronounce clearly and slowly. When I speak like a Cuban, she can't follow.

'Did he jump from the bridge?'

'Ahh . . . ehhh, no. It was all very strange.'

She got up from the rock.

'I'm cold. Shall we walk a bit more?'

We kept walking on the sand, and she resumed the story: 'Jonas did something very . . . twisted. He went to the woods near his house. He went in his car. He called the police on his mobile phone and told them: "In such and such a place there's a blue car with license-plate number such and such. A hundred yards to the right there's a dead man." That was all. He hung up. When the police arrived, Jonas was hanging from a tree. On his chest was pinned a piece of paper with the word "Anna". And the telephone number of his house. The body was still warm.'

'Who's Anna?'

'My friend. His wife.'

'And that's all?'

'That's all.'

'He left no explanation?'

'No.'

'He didn't think it necessary. The guy was fed up to his balls.'

'From what, Pedro Juan? How do you know?'

'Because I know. He was fed up to his balls.'

'Anna is in pretty bad shape. She has two small children and ahhh . . .'

'That's not a problem. There's good social security here.'

'Don't believe it. That's not everything.'

'And what does she say?'

'I don't know.'

'Don't you call her? She's your friend.'

'I haven't heard from her. I never call her. It's all been so brutal.'

'Everything's brutal, Agneta. Everything. Absolutely everything's brutal. Does death frighten you?'

She doesn't answer me. She just shrugs her shoulders. We walk for another half-hour. My hands and face are freezing. When we return to the house it is fourteen degrees, cold and wet. Agneta made tea. I prepared rum and cola. I can't keep drinking tea all the time or I'll damage my liver. I kid her: 'You should found Teaholics Anonymous and cure yourself. It's terrible this addiction to tea.' She laughed, but put on a disc of Madredeus in Oporto. Portuguese and melancholy. Ah, shit, this woman wants to bring me down any way she can. I wrapped myself up and sat outside, on the little balcony, with my *Cuba Libre* and a cigar to puff. The hooded crows make an ugly screeching. The rest of the birds disappear when it's cold. Only the crows keep flying and screaming as if it were nothing. When I go back inside, my cigar finished, Agneta had caught a cold. She was blowing her nose.

'I guess it was at the beach.'

'Today is not your best day.'

She looked at me in silence. I took her feet and gave her a good massage. All her acupressure points were painful. All of them. She couldn't take even a little bit of pressure. 'Ah, she's really fucked,' I thought.

'Agneta, I'm going to give you a daily massage. To see if I can balance you a bit.'

The long day slowly followed its course. The winter will be the opposite: the long night. But, by then, I won't be here.

Then I remembered the necklaces the *santera* prepared for her. I put them on her and blessed them. She thought they were typical Cuban adornments. I explained what I could. She asked me, smiling in disbelief: 'So then, they are amulets?'

'Well . . . if you want to see them that way. The important thing is that they were sent to protect you.'

'Ha ha ha. They're very typical. The Africans always use them.'

She took them off and placed them delicately on a small white cloth in the bureau in her room. They were there for a few days. Afterwards she kept them in a drawer. She never used them.

3

Snooping about in a closet I find five albums of press clippings. Four have only photos of mangled cars, highway accidents, ambulances, invalids in wheelchairs. In the fifth are articles about horses, tracks, races and, on the last pages, some Snoopy comic strips. On the first page a big photo of John Lennon. I was hoping to find something more enlightening. Porno magazines, for instance. But no. Nothing entertaining. Only death. I'll have to buy two or three porno magazines. Some days ago, I saw one with older women. Very elegant ladies, in their bourgeois rooms, taking off their clothes little by little until they get down to bare flesh. And always smiling at the camera, these complacent little grandmothers. They display their withered tits, their bald sex, the wrinkled skin. I like it. I remember some mischief with women over sixty. Sometimes these dames can teach you a thing or two. When I recounted the story of the National Auditorium in Madrid I wasn't totally sincere. Some adventures you try to forget so as to be able to say calmly: 'No, I've never screwed a senior citizen, I'm a proper fellow.' But the opposite is true: I am improper, and older ladies like young males with stiff pricks and not old men of eighty. Which makes a lot of sense.

One of these women, a ballerina, very slender, well over sixty, seduced me when I was around forty. She did it adroitly. Little by little. Until one day, after a couple of glasses of whiskey, the disgraceful old dame was naked, sitting on a table, her legs spread, and I was standing naked before her, nailing her rhythmically. In and out. The rhythm was so good the lady even forgot her Spanish. She was a New Yorker. She'd been living in Havana for thirty years, but when she felt herself penetrated she began to say things in English, her blue eyes staring at the ceiling. For more than a year we played together frequently, for that lady, so old, so thin, her skin wrinkly despite the tons of creams she utilized daily, had a rosy little pussy, smooth, moist, youthful, and it had a very agreeable little smell, even though it was completely hairless. I'd look at it and say to her: 'Madame, the bald soprano is demanding meat. She needs meat to sing an aria.'

The lady had a lot of fun. She had another lover. An eternal lover, her age. He was a mulatto musician, real laid-back and as perverse as the old New Yorker herself. He liked to masturbate while watching us. I was enjoying myself at that time, a night-prowling street cat, hunting in the darkness of Havana.

I put all the scrapbooks carefully back in the closet. I mean symmetrically. To the millimeter. I left to take a stroll downtown. Combining train and subway, I emerge in Central Station. All the drunks are there. Men and women. Just like everywhere. The eternal drunks. Downtown Stockholm is a fun place, if you have money. If you don't, it's better to go home and look at the trees and the green grass, or hear the hooded crows and listen to *Kings of the Blues*, that kind of thing.

We meet in the afternoons. Agneta always arrives home exhausted. She organizes interpreters, translators, hostesses, and seminar leaders for international meetings and conferences. She contracts them, and is kept busy explaining to them what they must do.

'Ah, I don't know what is happening these last few weeks.'

'Why?'

'Everyone is depressed or has a medical condition. The psychiatrist has asked them not to work for six months. Oh, no. I can't take this. I'm worn out. In the end I accomplish nothing.'

'And your boss? What does he say?'

'He's not concerned. It's my problem. To find people without ailments. Can you say *"gente sana"*?'

'Yes.'

'So. To find healthy people. It is not easy. There are no healthy people available.'

She sighs deeply. I try to cheer her up: 'Look, they sent a journal from a book club.'

'Ah, yes. *Bockernas Klubb*. They always send them.'

'There's a book about shiatsu. It's not expensive. You should order it. That kind of thing is good for you.'

She doesn't answer me. At times it pisses me off that she's so silent. At other times I like it. I take her feet and give her a massage. All her acupressure points are tremendously painful. Afterwards we stay silent. The door to the balcony is open, and a little cold air enters. It's six o'clock. It's already about fifteen degrees or less. I still have her feet in my hands. I send her a little energy. Then I think about Gloria. When we first got together, just over three years ago, a couple of hours of fucking would make her ears ring. She'd get up from the bed and say to me: 'Every time I fuck you my ears get stopped up. They start ringing. That's never happened before.'

'That's because you're overcharged.'

'Overcharged with what?'

'I send you energy.'

'With your cock?'

'With everything. I charge you. You have a lot of energy, but it's chaotic.'

And then and there I'd explain something to her and Gloria would be interested. She was learning. She has a very open mind and nothing surprises her. She inquires about everything. If I tell her 'A UFO just landed on the roof,' she'll calmly go to see if it's true. 'Why not? Anything is possible,' she replies.

Agneta interrupts my thoughts: 'Shiatsu I don't believe. But . . .'

'But what?'

'Ehh . . . I would like to believe in God.'

'What for?'

'Everything would be easier.'

'Certainly.'

'Do you believe?'

'Yes.'

'How can you believe in God?'

'I don't know. It's not something you can explain. I stopped believing at thirteen years old. And then I followed a long, confusing path. I was very confused.'

'You can't explain?'

'There is no explanation. He who tries to explain it is a deceiver.'

'Oh.'

'Besides, I don't like to talk about this.'

'Why?'

'Nobody believes in anything any more. And it shames me to believe.'

'I would like to . . . I need this experience.'

'What you'll find is already there inside you. You need look no further than that.'

4

Writing a letter to Gloria got me overexcited: 'I'm going to kiss your ass, I'm going to suck your blood, you're not going to desire anything more in life. You'll be both slave and queen, you'll love me and you'll hate me and you'll be happy and you'll want to die, and you'll never be able to get away from me. We'll be two lunatics in love. When I close my eyes and think of you, I want to bolt like a wild colt.'

It was all true. I was writing without thinking. Everything flowed from my heart. When I couldn't take it any more, I put the letter in an envelope, went to the box on the corner and deposited it. I came back and stretched out naked on the little balcony. Three in the afternoon. Good sun and about twenty-three degrees. I can't fully stretch out my legs – the balcony is very small – but at least I tan a little. I was still excited. I masturbated. Only a little. Ah, goddamn, fifty years old and still carrying on like an adolescent. I dragged myself to the living room. If a neighbor saw me he might call the police. Though it beats me where people hide themselves here. You never see anyone. They don't even appear at the windows. What do they do? Where are they? My heart is beating fast and I stop in front of a mirror to masturbate a little more, out of my mind with Gloria. I'm nuts. This mulatta makes me crazy. I stop myself in time, and I wait for Agneta to arrive. Why let spill on the floor something which might help someone else get off. The mail arrived. Publicity. It will all go straight in the bin. I read a piece of a novel by a fashionable Italian writer. Excessively slow and tiresome. Each day I find fewer authors I like. It must be my age. One becomes more selective, taste is better defined. Three hours until Agneta comes home and here I am with my prick semi-stiff. What would the Swedes say? Do they have a word to designate this moment of desire in which the muscle fills with blood and thickens and grows without reaching maximum tension? Yes, they must have a word. Music. Eric Clapton. There are some abominable Spanish magazines. The European jet set on their yachts and at their weddings. I'm anxious. I have an urge to drink and smoke, but I resist it. If not, I'd be drunk all day. I grab the Bible. I really like the story of Sarah seducing the Pharaoh in Egypt and passing herself off as Abraham's sister. Finally, the Pharaoh catches on to the trick and returns Abraham to Sarah, expelling him from the territory, but the guy takes all the riches and on top of that provides himself with enormous grazing lands for his cattle and distances himself from his nephew who has also become rich thanks to the trick they played on the Pharaoh. All in all, a very good story. If I write a remake of this subject, people will say: 'Oh, look, what a cynical guy.' But no. There really is nothing new under the sun. Sarah could be a hooker, Abraham a typical Havana hustler, and the Pharaoh a German industrialist with lots of cash. Nothing original. Life is a never-ending remake. Finally, at six, Agneta arrives. We give each other only a little kiss – she always arrives tense. She takes off her shoes and jacket: 'Oh, I can't go on.'

'Eh?'

'The interpreter who was going to come from Gothenburg next week won't come after all. She called me today. She has lumbago. I don't know what to do. Why is everyone getting sick? What is going on?'

There I am thinking about sticking my dick in her, making her come, and she's stressing about this lady's lumbago. It brings me down. She puts on a record. Mozart. Concerti one and two for flute and orchestra. *Allegro maestoso*.

'Do you want a cup of tea?'

'Tea?'

'You prefer coffee?'

'Agneta, a cup of tea at this hour is harmful.'

'I do not understand.'

'It's dangerous. Very dangerous.'

'A cup of tea?'

'Yes, very dangerous. It's no time for a cup of tea! Balls!'

'Oh!'

'It's time for a big glass of rum.'

'Oh!'

And I fix myself a big glass of sake and cola. The price of rum is much too high. Onward with the sake.

'You make it very strong.'

'Don't you believe it. You don't know what a strong drink is. By the way, there's a bottle of vodka in the closet.'

'Ah, yes, for some time . . . ehhh, a friend gave it to me as a present.'

And she begins to blush.

'A friend? A platonic boyfriend.'

'Platonic? Oh, yes, ahhh, I don't know . . .'

Now she turns from pink to red. Her face is on fire.

'Are you embarrassed to have platonic boyfriends?'

'No. He's a friend.'

'All women under the age of eighty have platonic boyfriends. They all like these ethereal flirtations in which there's no touching. Well, sometimes yes, you go so far as to grab a tit, steal a few kisses . . .'

'You know a lot about feminine psychology.'

'I know nothing about psychology. I know about *praxis*. The Devil knows more by being old than by being the Devil.'

'What? I do not understand.'

I had to repeat the refrain several times, in different ways, until she got it.

'Anyway, Agneta, the important thing is he gave you a big bottle of vodka. So to hell with platonism, and if from time to time he wants to nibble a tit, you may permit it as long as he keeps on presenting you with vodka. Or better, next time I hope he gives you whisky.'

'Oh, yes? You prefer whisky?'

'Yes! Scotch. Only Scotch.'

A couple of mouthfuls of sake. I wanted her to try it but I couldn't get her off the tea. Right, that's enough. I throw myself on top of her. A hot time on the sofa. Mozart as witness. More sake.

'Have a touch of the sake, honey.'

'What? I cannot understand. You are drunk.'

'Me drunk? No! I'm happy. Come. Let's go to bed.'

And so we did. It doesn't even come to 20 percent of the great fucks with Gloria, but it's fine. After all, we're only a few kilometers from the Arctic Circle. You can't ask for more, I don't think. I let loose all my milk in her face. Her style is to surrender. She closes her eyes and abandons herself and has lots of orgasms. Silent ones. She just sighs and comes and comes and sighs discreetly and flies like a little bird. With me there on top of her, giving her the rod.

'Agneta, in some former life you weren't a Swede or an Eskimo or a Laplander. I reckon you were a negress from Africa, from Polynesia, from the Caribbean, an Andalusian gypsy.

'Something hotter.'

'Yes?'

'Sure. At forty-four years old, you've had maybe ten or twelve men. It's a good record for here, I think.'

'You think that is a record? No. It is normal.'

'I like that. Here people say little but they're always on the lookout for kicks.'

'I haven't looked. Sometimes I have gone years without a fiancé.'

'I like you very much. You're a voluptuary, you enjoy yourself. I never imagined you'd be so hot.'

'Me neither.'

'Ah, Agneta, no bullshit. You're forty-four years old. You're going to tell me that you've always been a *mosquita muerta*?'

'*Mosquita muerta*? What is that?'

'A dead fly.'

'Oh, no, no. Believe me, I did not know . . . ohh . . . never have I been like this. Never have I felt . . .'

'Never have you felt what? Speak. You always stop in the middle of sentences. Why are you so timid?'

'I am not timid. I have to think. Spanish is very difficult. I never find the word.'

'Okay, all right. Never have you felt what?'

'It is because . . . I always thought that I was, that I am like ice, congealed, frozen. How do you say?'

'Frigid? That you don't feel?'

'Right. Frigid. I never felt so much as now. With you it is different. I do not know what happens and . . . oh . . . I cannot explain. I am confused.'

'You're not at all confused. Drop the neurosis and the drama. Let's fuck and enjoy ourselves because the world is going to end.'

'What are you saying? I do not understand.'

'Enjoy yourself because you already have the menopause hanging over you.'

'Ah, menopause. No. There are still some years before menopause.'

5

Some Latinos who live here insisted time and again, and so finally I had to go out with them. The Peruvian tried to spend the night talking about Latin American politics and *el hombre nuevo*, the divided left, a rebirth of I don't know what. The guy's been in Sweden thirteen years. He goes to his country for fifteen days every six or seven years. The Chilean has similar obsessions. He's been living in Europe almost twenty years. I said to them: 'Oh, yes, yes, good, pardon me.' And then I went to dance with the Peruvian's wife. Later I did the same with the wife of the Chilean. It was a discotheque with few people and salsa music. The two women work in a fish cannery. I dance with the Chilean woman and she begs my pardon because now they're packing herring in mayonnaise and perhaps she smells a bit of fish guts. I sniff her under her hair, on her neck. She gets goosebumps. Actually, I don't sniff, I blow a little and notice that her nipples stand up under her light wool sweater.

We go back to the table. The Chilean and Peruvian guys return to the attack. And I reply: 'Really, I don't enjoy talking about politics.'

'Why not?'

'I don't understand anything about it.'

'That's impossible. Everything is political.'

'That's what the politicians have made you believe. I believe that really politics is nothing. From my point of view, nothing would have to do with politics.'

'Come on, explain yourself, Pedro Juan. That's absurd.'

'I can't explain myself. I already told you I don't like to talk about politics. No one understands anything about it.'

'It's not like that.'

'Yes, it is. The first ones not to know what they're doing or where they're going are political leaders. Generally they can't maintain their direction for more than a year. After that, they're shipwrecked and pulled along by the tide. So then, what is politics? A boat adrift in the middle of a storm. Shall we dance?'

'No, we don't dance; but hold on a minute . . .'

I get up from the table. I leave them with their mouths open, and I go to dance with the Peruvian's wife. She must be the ugliest and strangest Swede in all of Sweden and its surroundings. I can't understand what he did to find such an ugly beast in a country where there are hundreds of thousands of very attractive women – delicious ones, even – waiting for men to love them and make them happy. As if that weren't enough, she alternates her job gutting fish with another as a gravedigger in a little cemetery, next to a Protestant church on the outskirts of the city. She tells me all this enthusiastically, and invites me: 'Come to visit me at the cemetery. You'll like it.'

'The cemetery?'

'Yes. It's ancient. There's a very beautiful oak grove. Come when you're not in a hurry so we can have a chat. I can telephone you so that you coincide with a burial. It's very beautiful.'

'Uhm, nice job.'

'Yes, I really like it. But there are only one or two burials a month, and I don't make enough. I have to continue working in the cannery too.'

That's how it went: chatting about cemeteries and the dead, and the table without a drink. They complain that the prices are very high. The women dance clumsily, that is, they almost don't dance. Meanwhile, the men obsessively recount their adolescent political traumas. I put up with it for an hour. I said I was going to the bathroom for a moment. I took my jacket and left. In an inside pocket I was carrying a flask with a little vodka. I went walking toward the docks. It wasn't far. It was foggy and cold. Seven degrees or less. They were hauling trunks of giant trees on a boat in the misty port, two hundred yards in front of me. I turned up the collar of my coat and took a deep breath. Cold air and fog. It had a good smell. I purified my lungs and stood for some time drinking and observing how they were loading the tree trunks. The fog was dense and static. It always seems romantic and mysterious. There were flashes of yellow light and a disquieting atmosphere was forming between the black of the starless night, the gray of the fog, the dull colors of the boat and the large cargo hoists, which were moving silently like blue pachyderms. Then I noticed that the entire scene, so beautiful, strange and enigmatic, provoked my fear. I was afraid. Of what? Why did it stimulate my adrenaline? Maybe it was the absence of people. Everything was moving in silence, mysteriously. No one was in sight. Nothing was heard. It was fascinating, that light, and at the same time it seemed to me that something terrible might happen. Something unexpected. Everything could disappear. One shot of chaos could do away with everything at once. And then only the immobile fog and the silence and a dim yellow light would remain.

I took off. The flask was empty. I got back to the house half soused at three in the morning. Agneta was deep asleep and didn't wake up. I was out before my head hit the pillow. Pure vodka coursed through my veins.

At two in the afternoon the temperature reaches thirty degrees. Oh, how nice. A record for June. The sun is strong. We sweat. We talk. We laugh. We listen to a long program of opera on the radio. At a given moment, we can't understand why, they cut to a Cuban number by the Buena Vista Social Club. Then it's back to the opera. Very strange, but cool. Agneta reads the horoscope in the Sunday paper: Aquarius, in other words I, will have a new and beautiful love affair and a good offer of work. Sagittarius, she, will have a secret and extraordinary love affair and will work in a team she really likes. Then we drink a white wine from Alsace while we review the real-estate listings in the *Dagens Nyheter*. A beautiful apartment on the outskirts of Stockholm, eighty square meters: two and a half million kronor.

'Oh, I'd love to have that apartment.'

But we know that it's wishful thinking. In the cheapest chain supermarket we buy only what's on sale and potatoes and dirty carrots. We have to count every krona, so it's better to forget the eighty-square-meter apartment in that neighborhood.

I give her a foot massage and, without realizing it, begin to lick her toes and get an erection. I suck them. They enchant me. She thinks it's only hers. No. Feet excite me. Some say that the feet are phallic symbols, or substitutes for the phallus. I don't know. Is that right? Well, it's all the same. I take the time to show off a bit. I love to put on a show. I masturbate. I display my erect prick, slick with suncream and well tanned. I baby it. I put it out in the sun, I play with it, I caress it. To me it's very important. It gives me so much enjoyment that I ought to be thankful. She blushes but she stares at it, enraptured. I get the camera and we take pictures of one another. Naked, sweating, in the sunlight. I'm tanned as an Arab. She's as red as a crab. I leave her with the wine and go jogging in the woods. Half an hour. I come back, take a shower, we eat meatballs, salad and fruit. She goes to vote in the elections for the European Parliament 1999. I nap a bit and read whatever's to hand. I think it's *Hippopotamus* or something like that. I nap a little more. I wake up and smoke a cigar, drink a glass of whisky with ice. At seven it begins to rain and, within minutes, the temperature drops. My hands and feet grow cold. We watch a documentary about Irish fieldhands who weave baskets with willow and hazel branches. At nine we drink beer, we dine on a mushroom omelette, we listen to Lou Reed. And we talk about the enormous rats that live in the old part of Stockholm and on the piers, where she lived in a very old and cold house with her first husband and they had to battle continually against the rats. Then I tell her about shark steaks and frogs' legs, and of how they hunt those little animals in the marshes south of Havana. The temperature keeps dropping. I have to put on my wool socks. She takes a hot bath, saying that she smells of cigar smoke. She drank a glass of warm milk and went to bed at ten-thirty. I went on reading until very late. From time to time I was interrupted by mental flashes: Gloria, consultations with the *santeras* in Havana, and many other memories. People, places, moments. Disorder and confusion, chaos and torment always waiting. They don't sleep. They don't rest. When it happens, you have to control your mind. Madness is always circling. The loss of reason. The best thing is to leave your mind blank and not struggle. Distance from the place of origin sometimes generates disorder. White out the mind. When I finally attain serenity, I lie down. The bed is warm. Agneta sleeps completely naked. She does everything I ask. It's midnight or sometime after. My hands and feet are very cold. I snuggle right up to Agneta to get warm. I touch her little belly. She moves. She coughs a couple of times but she doesn't wake up. And, again, the sensation of madness flutters over me. At times it surprises me and I wonder, 'Will I go mad some day?' It terrifies me to think so. But it's like that. The idea fills me with a terrible anguish and confuses me. Everything inside me becomes unbalanced. It fills me with an unrestrainable desire to go running across the fields, screaming.

This time the feeling was brief and fleeting. I controlled it and went to sleep within minutes.

When I woke up it was six-thirty. As always, I had a perfect erection and, as always, I couldn't resist the temptation to kiss Agneta. And kiss her and kiss her until she awoke. There I was, face up on the bed with my legs spread, slowly masturbating.

'What are you doing?'

'You like it?'

'Yes.'

'Do it to yourself too.'

'Eh?'

'Play with yourself. Let me see your tits. Damn, they're pornographic. Come on, let me see them. Ahhh, just like that, so sweet.'

Agneta likes these private porno shows. After a while, I put it to her and murmur under my breath: 'Come on, Gloria, take my cock. It's all yours, bitch, you make me crazy.' And I give it to her, slowly, so I won't come. Agneta, as always, comes, and comes again, and again and again. Like a young mare. Fucking sweet, the way I like it! When I can take no more it all shoots out of its own accord, one spurt after another. I think of Gloria, my eyes closed, I think of that mulatta and I whisper: 'Take it, sweetie, soak up my milk, bitch. Soak it up 'cause I'm yours.'

Afterwards Agneta and I breakfast on cornflakes, yogurt and a cup of tea. For her it's late. She eats a little cereal, leafs through the paper and says to me: 'In Sweden, only 38 percent voted for the European Parliament. In Europe, only 49 percent.'

'Nobody's interested in politics.'

'I believe it. Even less than in 1995.'

'In 2003 they won't reach 30 percent. You'll soon see.'

'What are people interested in, then?'

'Money, Agneta, money. That's what interests them. For the sake of money, people forget everything and become imbeciles. They're afraid and they think money is the cure. Others have made them afraid in order to control them. The way bad parents do with little kids.'

Agneta keeps coughing. It's been that way since yesterday. She searches for some pills in the bathroom medicine cabinet. She finds them. She reads and wonders whether to put them in her purse or not.

'There are only these. They are very . . .'

'*Fuerte* . . . Strong.'

'Right. *Fuerte*. Even the tongue goes . . .'

'Numb. They're anesthetic.'

'That's right. Yes.'

'Don't take that shit. What you need is another good *pingazo* in the afternoon.'

'Another what?'

'A *pingazo*. From *pinga*, prick. With the prick. Through. By means of. Introducing it. Getting off on it.'

'Oh, slang!'

'Damn right. Yes, my love, Havana slang. A good *pingazo* takes care of many things. At the least, it gets rid of your illnesses, grouchiness, blues, depression, a cough; it makes you forget you have no money.'

'Oh, yes, I believe it, I believe it.'

6

The morning passes slowly, and I listen again and again to a record by Jeff Buckley. It's 25 degrees; I sunbathe on the little balcony, while we roast a chicken in the oven. Behind the building, fifty yards away, there's a small cemetery and a church. Actually, it's a chapel. Sometimes someone visits it, they place flowers on a tomb. Usually, though, it's deserted. Just the enormous ancient trees, the green grass, the discreet and simple tombs, and the silence and the solitude. Very different from those Catholic cemeteries, full of absurd luxury, with marble and sculptures and post-mortem pride, concealing the rot and stench of the cadavers and the worms. I like to observe such a peaceful cemetery and listen to this slow, sad rock.

At twelve, Agneta returns. We dine together, with a very good red wine from Navarre. Round, full, perfect. Agneta wants a glass of milk.

'If you eat that chicken with milk it might be bad for you.'

'Why?'

'Wine aids the digestion.'

'Not at this hour. I have to go back to work.'

That's how she is. At any rate, we enjoy having lunch together. We listen to Jeff Buckley.

'You like it?'

'Yes. You have good music, Agneta.'

'It's been a while since I heard this record. He committed suicide when he was twenty-five.'

'Ohh.'

'I bought it for just one song: "Lilac Wine".'

'And right now you don't want to drink lilac wine.'

'Ha ha ha.'

'Better. There's more for me.'

I stop to think for an instant. Suicide at twenty-five. A tormented guy.

'You have to take care of yourself, Agneta. We take care of ourselves, but the possibility is always there.'

'Of what?'

'Of putting a bullet in your head.'

'Oh.'

'At times it's terrible. The artist's raw material is his own life. It's terrible. A writer, for example, has to stir his own shit. And extract things from there.'

'I can imagine.'

'A normal person lets the shit dry. And forgets it. A normal person forgets about all the shits in his life. About others shitting on him and the shits he took. He allows all this shit to settle and desiccate so that it no longer stinks. But an artist converts his shit into raw material. Construction material. He makes sculptures, paintings, songs, novels, poems, stories. All smelling of fresh shit.'

'Oh, Pedro Juan. Why do you talk like that?'

Agneta pushed her plate away, revolted. I was speaking with my eyes closed and drinking wine by myself. I had eaten enough chicken with garlic. I didn't want more. I opened my eyes. I saw her revulsion. I closed my eyes again. I kept talking: 'It's not a matter of whether or not you shoot yourself in the temple. You put a bullet in your head when you can't take any more, and that's that. But don't do it too young. First you have to fuck around. Let the sons of bitches fuck themselves. They'll have to put up with me. There's nothing they can do but put up with my books and go shit on their mothers. Later I'll decide what I'm going to do. Perhaps I won't even shoot myself. Perhaps I'll sit around on my arse, happily. Until I'm ninety years old. Or until I'm a hundred.'

Agneta came back at six. She made herself a plate of yogurt with cereal and ate healthily, in the sun, on the balcony. I read a bit more, but I can't stand forced inactivity. I succeeded in dragging her, grudgingly, to a nearby canal facing a castle. There they have rowing races between Viking canoes. A little three-day carnival as a harbinger of midsummer. The crews are in costume. The most comic were some parodying Clinton and Lewinsky. They rowed hard and made it to the finals. Other teams dress up as cowboys, vikings, babies, Elvis Presley. Finally, I get thirsty.

'Shall we drink a beer? Come on.'

'Oh, no, no. There's a lot of wind.'

'So what? A little beer . . .'

'No, no. My throat.'

In reality, the problem is not her throat. It's that there are already some rather happy men drinking beer. Drunks terrify her. Alcohol terrifies her. I was just about to say to her: 'So go back to your little house and I'll stay here.' I restrained myself. It's better not to create a crisis. After all, she makes an effort to put up with my savagery. We hurry back. I realized that she was fleeing from the crowd, from the potential drunks. Perhaps she was also wanting to flee from me. I take her arm to slow her down a bit.

'Agneta, what are you running from? Why are you going so fast?'

'I always walk like this.'

She stared at me and it seemed to me that she was a little frightened. I breathed deeply. Patience, Pedro Juan, patience, who knows what her traumas are with drunkenness and crowds?

'We missed *The Simpsons* today.'

'No. I set the timer on the video.'

'Ah, Scandinavian efficiency. How nice.'

Before playing the tape of *The Simpsons*, we watch the news. The dead in Kosovo. In the last few days there are dozens, hundreds of dead. They bury them. Agneta covers her eyes each time the cameras focus on the pale, or a bit blue and purplish, faces of the corpses. Normal people dressed like any one of us who suddenly catch some lead in their livers and die. And they bury them without even knowing their names. In communal graves. They're already half rotten and smell awful. Agneta always looks frightened, or horrified, or disgusted, and turns her face away.

'Does it scare you?'

'Yes.'

138

She clings to me, pressing her head against my shoulder. Death terrifies her. Next, they give the weather report. Cloudy. Twenty-five percent chance of rain for the weekend. Descending temperatures and gusts of wind. A high of 18 degrees.

'Oh, I wanted to go to the forest with you, to take a stroll. A girl-friend of mine has horses . . .'

'It's always the same. On the weekends, the Swedish summer is fucked.'

'I would love to go horseback riding with you. Do you like horses?'

'I like the mares more, ha ha ha.'

'What? Why the mares?'

'Ha ha ha.'

She never gets my jokes. She leans on my shoulder and closes her eyes. I caress her and tell her something sweet. She's a solitary woman. Too much time alone, thinking of death and time passing, eating yogurt and cereal, listening to dramatic operas, saving every krona and thinking that she's a useless person, a shitty office worker, and that she won't have enough money in her old age. She never gives herself even a little treat. Agneta lives cautiously. She's convinced that even the slightest slip might be fatal.

It's impossible to live this way. I like to caress her. When I tell her something tender, her face changes. Or when I put in my prick. If I put it in sweetly. Little by little. Caressing her. Then her face changes. She relaxes. Rejuvenates. My caresses make her feel twenty years younger. It occurs to me to ask her: 'Honey, are you sure you aren't pregnant?'

'Oh, we are thinking the same.'

'Yes? It's about time.'

'For what?'

'For telepathy.'

'You believe in that?'

'Of course. It always happens with the women who live with me.'

'Ohh.'

'Answer me.'

139

'What?'

'Are you pregnant?'

'No, no, no. Please.'

'Do you want to have a child?'

'Oh, no, no.'

'A baby girl? Twins? Triplets? Choose. I'll plant the seed that you wish.'

'Oh, ha ha ha. No, no. I'm worried.'

'The menstruation.'

'Uhmmm.'

'Hasn't come?'

'No.'

'How many days?'

'Three or four.'

'Must be the pills.'

'I hope so. The pills alter me.'

'And if you're pregnant?'

'Oh, no, no, Pedro Juan. Don't say that, please.'

'My children grow up intelligent and beautiful, tall, all three are very . . . elegant.'

'Yes, I already know. No, not me, no, no.'

'Ah, Agneta, it's no big thing. Drop the drama.'

'No, no. I'd kill myself.'

I look her straight in the eyes: 'What are you saying?'

'I'd kill myself. I don't want children.'

7

At ten o'clock on Sunday night I was watching Sean Penn's *The Crossing Guard* with Jack Nicholson, Agneta half-asleep beside me on the sofa. I went to the kitchen. I made myself a large vodka and cola. I went back to the living room: 'Want one?'

'No.'

'Today you slept until eleven in the morning. You can't be sleepy.'

'I am. I've hardly slept the whole week. This cough doesn't let me sleep well.'

'Sleep's not mathematical. The past no longer counts.'

'But . . .'

'If I were to make up for all the hours of sleep I've lost, I'd have to stay in bed for at least twenty years.'

'You've lost that much sleep?'

'On drinking sprees, great fucks with two and three women in the bed, parties, orgies, business deals, friends, work, cutting sugarcane like a slave from six in the morning until eight at night, madness, insomnia, anguish, depression, wanting to hang myself from a roof beam, a little of everything.'

'Ahh.'

'You see these bags under my eyes? The wrinkles? The baldness? Scars. While you are perfect. No wrinkles, no gray hair, the perfect body.'

'I like to take care of myself.'

'Water, tea, warm milk, eight hours' sleep, no children, from work to home, from home to work, opera, symphonic music, nutritive creams, walks through the woods . . .'

'Ha ha ha, you say it like a formula.'

'Agneta's formula for eternal youth.'

'Ha ha ha.'

'You've never smoked marijuana?'

'I've never smoked anything. Not even tobacco. Nothing.'

'Cocaine, peyote?'

'No.'

'Amphetamines?'

'Noooooo.'

'Not even to fuck all night?'

'No.'

'Did you ever put crème de menthe on your husband?'

'What?'

'On the head of his cock. You never tried it?'

'Oh, no. Who would think of that?'

'In Cuba it's normal. It makes a stiff prick grow even harder and thicker.'

'Oh, I didn't know.'

'Porno films? Magazines? Lesbian clubs?'

'No, never.'

'I don't believe you. Agneta, the imagination . . .'

'It's not good. Nothing of this that you say is good.'

'Who invents the prohibitions? Someone invents them at his convenience and decides for you: "You can do this, you can't do that. That thing there is harmful. This is moral and that is immoral . . .", ahhh, they've completely fucked up my life with laws and prohibitions and orders. I don't give a shit about all this morality and ethics and what's correct and what's incorrect. In the end you discover that these gentlemen live like gods on Olympus and squander everything in the lap of luxury. But they do it in secret, so that nobody sees them, while in public they keep making promises that the future will be better.'

'We're different. You're . . . worn out.'

'I've had it with what others think and decide for me. Each of us has to defend his own life a bit more. And has to have respect for everyone else.'

'Are you annoyed?'

'Yes, I am. They've made me bitter with all the shit they've dumped on me.'

We remain silent and watch a bit more of the film. But I returned to the attack: 'Tell me, why don't you suck? I like it when they suck mine. I like it very much.'

'I try to. You ask it of me and I try to.'

'Oh, yes . . . you try: you put the tip of my prick between your teeth and you tickle it. Is that sucking? Sucking is putting it in up to your throat. Tasting it. Enjoying it.'

'I never do it. I do not know how. How do you say "I do it" in the past.'

'I never did it. I never sucked.'

'Exactly. Oh, the irregular verbs . . . so: I never did it, never . . . I never . . .?'

'*Mamé*. Sucked. To suck is not an irregular verb. I never sucked: *Nunca mamé*.'

'I never sucked. The first time was with you. It's an ugly word. It sounds bad: *ma-mé*.'

'Does it disgust you?'

'No, no.'

'Yes. It disgusts you. One of these days I'm going to make you drunk and I'm going to have you suck my ass. You'll see that it cures your disgust. Horse cure.'

'Askkk, arghhhh . . . no, please, don't speak that way.'

'It does disgust you. I knew it. You love me?'

'Yes, but . . .'

'But nothing. If you love me, it doesn't disgust you. If it's repugnant it's because you don't love me.'

'Ohh, no, you are brutal, you are . . .'

'Visceral, radical, violent, cutting, savage. You love that, but deep down you don't love me. What have you learnt from so many men?'

'So many, no.'

'You and I made a count. And it added up to ten or twelve. Yes, it's true, that's not many. But enough to learn something. Were they very boring sexually? Let's see, what did they do? Occupations.'

'Ohhh, ha ha ha.'

'Don't laugh. I'm serious. Answer quickly. Have you had a journalist?'

'Yes.'

'University professors? Businessmen?'

'Yes.'

'Writers, artists?'

'Ehh . . . one. Journalist and writer.'

'Any millionaires?'

'No, no.'

'A poor man, very poor?'

'Yes, one.'

'Which?'

'*Uf*, enough, Pedro Juan.'

'We can't stop. This is a sociological survey of your lovers. Answer quickly, and don't think.'

'Ha ha ha.'

'Tell me.'

'What?'

'The poor one.'

'What?'

'What did he do? Occupation.'

'Truck driver.'

'Truck driver? That was the one! He never fucked you in his truck? Made you suck him while he drove down the highway? Took you to a cheap dive of a bar so you could jerk him off under the table?'

'No, no, no, ohhh.'

'So what kind of a truck driver was this guy? It's an insult to his profession.'

'No, ah, it was a short time. Only two weeks.'

'Have you had another worker? From a factory?'

'No.'

'Field hand?'

'No.'

'Docker, sportsman, fireman?'

'No, no, ha ha ha.'

'All intellectuals, except the truck driver?'

'Yes.'

'Ah, you're missing a lot in life.'

'Are you against intellectuals?'

'No.'

'But you don't like them.'

'As lovers they're not very good in the majority of cases. Some yes, but you really have to search for them.'

'You're an intellectual.'

'Me?! I don't think so.'

'You write books, you paint, you're a journalist.'

'I was a journalist. In prehistoric times. Now I write and paint in my spare time. It's a hobby.'

'I don't believe it.'

'Better believe it because that's the way it is.'

'I don't believe you. It's a joke.'

'It's not a joke, Agneta. I doubt very much that I'll write more than one or two more books. If I have nothing more to say, I'll remain silent.'

'Oh.'

'I think about setting up a fruit and vegetable stand in a farmers' market. There with the black men and a tape recorder playing Pablito F.G. and La Charanga Habanera the whole day and me selling tomatoes.'

8

I spent many days without doing anything. I'd take the commuter train, then transfer to the metro and go downtown to the old part of the city. To sightsee, to walk, to see people, check out the Swedish girls. Some are very beautiful and have great big tits. Slender and without asses they may be, but I like them nevertheless. They have style. Perhaps they consider big asses a vulgarity. In the afternoon, I'd go back to my woods.

Today I was lounging around the house a bit. A day of unexpected clouds, rain and cold. I run awhile through the little forest. I come back exhausted. I take a shower. I have meatballs with biscuits for lunch. I search the bookshelves and find various books by Umberto Eco. One is the English version of his investigation into the history of language in Europe and its relationship to the culture. I read a little, slowly. In Italian it would be easy for me.

Agneta returns earlier than usual and works like mad: she gathers the dirty laundry. There's a lot. She puts on some very old, battered clogs and descends time after time to the basement of the building, where the washing machine is. She takes off her shoes and vacuums. She cleans everything. Quickly. She puts on a CD, *Pavarotti and his Friends*. A damp cloth for the furniture, then she enters the bathroom with lemon-scented foams, she scrubs, she scrapes, she rinses, she cleans thoroughly. I begin to watch her. Ah, damn, she's a scullery maid just like Gloria: she cleans everything, running around like a crazy woman, no shoes on and the music playing at top volume. There it's cassettes of Willy Chirino and of La India; here it's Pavarotti. The same thing. Already I'm imagining her sweaty, odorous pussy. I get horny and remember Gloria. Then I try to rein in my thoughts, calm myself down.

Later we speak of Eco's book.

'Does it interest you?'

146

'Yes.'

'You contradict yourself, you're incoherent.'

'Why?'

'A few days ago you told me you weren't an intellectual.'

'Are you trying to catch me? Let me put it this way: I prefer to sell tomatoes and carrots. My true vocation is business, to keep accounts. To make money. It's the first thing I did as a boy, with my father: selling ices, paper bags and used comics. But sometimes I like to read such intelligent, documented, scrupulous things. It's fascinating that someone could make such a perfect book. I'm a bungler. Do you understand? I like shoddy work. I like to leave my books half done, with their guts out in the open, dirty.'

'Philosophy of a tomato-seller.'

'Could be. I like to walk around in the filth of the market, selling lettuces, tomatoes, whatever. I like those people. I feel good among them. There are always big-assed women, vulgar, provocative, who do anything for a few pesos. Streetwalking sluts, whores, hookers, Havana hot-to-trots. I like these working girls. And if they're negresses or mulattas . . .'

'It's true? You prefer them?'

'Yes. Definitively. The hustlers and the swindlers. You have to learn to protect yourself because they're always out to get your money. Any way they can. They have thousands of tricks. They put on a real show.'

'You're going to do it?'

'What?'

'The tomatoes.'

'Sure. I write one more book and it's over. I don't think I have much more to say. And I don't want to annoy people just to make a few bucks, and then hear them say: "That guy is an imbecile and he writes trash." No. I have one more book in my head and then that's it. I'll sell tomatoes until the end. And maybe keep on painting. When I paint I don't think. And that agrees with me: not to think.'

Agneta remains silent. Finally she asks me: 'What's the book?'

'*A Lot of Heart.* It's sort of a biography of a little Cuban woman. A friend of mine.'

'Very well, I'm in agreement. If you accept me, I'll go for a year to Cuba and help you.'

'Ha ha ha.'

'I'm serious. I, too, need to sell tomatoes and leave the office and learn Spanish.'

'In Cuba you'd learn Cuban. It's a dialect.'

'Ha ha ha.'

'I'm going to Cubanize you. I'm going to colonize you. I'll set you loose among the blacks in the Cuatro Caminos market and they'll Cubanize you.'

'Oh, no. Only with you. Don't leave me alone.'

'That's what you say here. There you'll want me to leave you alone. In a week you'll be Cubanized and digging the folklore and the negritude.'

We return to silence.

'I know Eco.' And she points to the book on the table.

'Yes? Damn it, such select friendships you have! Very good.'

'I only met him on one occasion. He came to a congress that I organized at the university, and he's a friend of my friend in Ireland.'

'Of your boyfriend in Ireland.'

'No, ha ha ha, it's only because . . . both do research, and he he he . . .'

'That nervous laugh . . . you have the house full of books on Ireland, Dublin, flutes, souvenirs, postcards, paintings, records. This place looks like the Irish Consulate in Stockholm.'

'Oh, ha ha ha.'

'I thought that it was over. Are you still with him?'

'Oh, he he he . . . ehhh.'

'That's okay. Don't answer.'

'Ehhh . . .'

I prepare a little vodka with ice and cola. I take a cigar and go out on the balcony. It's a beautiful evening. A lovely girl, about ten years old, plays with a black dog. She does it almost every afternoon. She'll be a beautiful and sexy Swedish woman within a few years. She rolls on the lawn, playing with the dog. She has very tight slacks and her breasts are starting to bud and her little ass is growing. Her sensuality is already noticeable. I light my cigar and savor the smoke as I look at her. Ah, damn, late afternoon, vodka and tobacco. Deep down Agneta is the same as Gloria. Only she was born in Sweden. Equally untameable. That's why she fucks so well and is so sensuous. She's still with the Irishman. And I, the imbecile, thinking about exclusivity. The same thing that Gloria does to me: making me believe that I'm the only one, and sneakily pursuing her whore's calling. Both these bitches are the same. Even their pussies smell alike. Agneta's only disadvantage is that she doesn't suck, but she's learning. Slowly, but she's learning. To come so far to discover this.

Agneta comes out on the balcony. She sniffs the cigar smoke a little. She likes it.

'You want vodka? Can I make you one?'

'No. I prefer to eat something.'

'Sit down. Join me for a little while.'

'Well, only for a few minutes. Then we'll dine.'

'Uhm.'

I look at the sky and show her the waxing moon: 'Look at her up there, running rings around us. She doesn't hide. She runs in circles over our heads.'

'Ahh.'

'I get crazy.'

'I believe it. It influences . . .'

'It influences everything. My spermatozoa rise up to my brain with this moon. It always happens to me.'

'I don't understand. What is sperma . . .?'

'Spermatozoa?'

'I know what sperm is.'

'And -atozoa?'

'No.'

'It's a single word. Spermatozoa. The microscopic children who race so rapidly toward the ovum, to see who gets there first. That's the way life is. It's the first thing that you do: run like a madman, compete, to get to a place. To any place, because nobody knows where it is. These little microscopic children run and run, and they don't know where they're going. Nor can they imagine why they're doing it.'

'Uhm.'

'Finally only one is saved. The strongest, the fastest one. The trickiest one, the one who pushed the others and tripped them up. The strongest and most aggressive and astute.'

'Oh, yes, but . . . they can't run. Excuse the correction, but they don't *run*. They *swim*.'

'Ahhh, Swede of my life . . . exactly: they swim. They don't run. They swim, desperately. Their lives depend on it.'

The vodka made me happy. I put on Los Van Van. I danced a bit. Alone. I can't get her to dance to a little salsa, or son or anything, a little casino. I try to teach her but she doesn't accept.

'Don't you like it?'

'Yes, I like it, but I don't know how.'

'You fuck well and you're very sensuous and you move your pelvis very well when you have me inside.'

'Oh, Pedro Juan.'

'It's the same. To fuck and to dance. Or to dance and to fuck.'

Truly the moon is turning me upside down. It's not a joke, as Agneta says. That night we fuck a lot. We play. She lets herself be played with. She likes to be my toy. Maybe an hour and a half. We sleep like stones. We wake up at seven. And there I am again, with a stiff prick. I put the sugar cane in her. Half an hour. She jumps up, running toward our daily tea. She doesn't have time to shower.

'Oh, I'm going to be late. I'm already out of time.'

'Ah, it's all the same. That's the way it's done in Cuba. We all arrive before or after but no one ever arrives on time.'

'We're in Sweden, Pedro Juan, we're in Sweden.'

'Did you bathe?'

'No.'

'That's it. In the middle of the morning, put your finger there and smell it.'

'Ahh, nooo. You're crazy.'

'It's so very rich. Monkeys smell themselves. And they like it.'

'Oh.'

'There you have my milk and yours. Mixed. It smells very good. You're gonna like it.'

'Maybe it's a good idea. I'll do it. Ohh, it's very late.'

When she's upset she can't speak in Spanish. At ten in the morning, I call her at work: 'Did you arrive very late?'

'Fifteen minutes late.'

'Ah, that's nothing.'

'No, it's a lot. Oh, I don't have time, I can't speak now.'

'You have a lot of work?'

'Yes, yes.'

'Well, I'll see you soon.'

'Ahh, Pedro Juan, ehh . . . I'm not pregnant.'

'It came?'

'Yes.'

'Ah, that's better. Peace of mind.'

'I'll let you go. I have a lot of work.'

'Does it last many days?'

'Yes. Maybe five days.'

'And what do we do? Up the ass?'

'No, no, ohhh . . .'

'Then from the front with blood and all. No problem.'

'No. Oh, you're . . . I'll let you go. You're crazy. Hang up, please. I have a lot of work.'

So I hung up.

9

At noon I run through a forest of pines, oaks, and birches. There's a path next to a canal. The earth is black, smooth, and moist. Covered with moss and pine needles. I feel very good doing my jogging and watching the people paddling in canoes and kayaks. Others swim in the icy water of the Baltic. Today I understood why I like it so much: in an identical forest, in Lithuania, near Vilnius, I had a day of love and abandon with a very beautiful Lithuanian woman. It was all very strange. She only spoke Russian and Lithuanian and not a word of English, French, or Spanish. We met the previous night at a dinner. We danced. I was thirty-five years old and a very emotional man. She was a dancer with a folkloric group and was also very romantic, tall, slender and delicious. It was love at first sight for both of us. We danced some more but we were already like two snakes coiling themselves around each other. Then, naturally, we attempted to go up to my room, on the fourth floor of the hotel. Impossible. A brutal guy at the door stopped her. She wasn't a guest. I offered him some roubles. No. The hotel was only for foreigners. She couldn't go to my room. The Soviets were charming like that. I still can't explain how the Lithuanian and I understood each other; but that night we just walked around and got hotter, that's it. The next day we went for a stroll through that forest. We made love like crazy. We drank wine and beer. That afternoon, half drunk, I sang her 'Nosotros'. I have a fixation with that song. It's as if Pedrito Junco composed it especially for me and not to bid farewell to his sweetheart, shortly before he died of tuberculosis:

> We,
> who love each other so much,
> must now separate

don't ask me anything more.
It isn't lack of affection,
I love you with my soul
and in the name of this love
and for your good
I say goodbye.

She wept. I did too. Then she whispered a Lithuanian love song. We wept more. We drank more beer. The following day I was returning to Cuba and she was flying to Germany with her folk dance troupe. I don't know how we both understood these details. I didn't ask her name nor she mine. No addresses, no telephone numbers. Nothing. We walked through the woods a bit, which seemed to me like paradise, and, weeping without remedy, we took our leave. For ever. We would never see each other again.

Now I go jogging in a similar forest and I think back to that fascinating moment, of love and pain, fifteen years ago.

Off a little dock, three boys are swimming. They're completely nude and must be about eighteen years old. They piss on each other. I stop to observe them, camouflaged among the underbrush and the birches. One climbs up on the dock and pisses on the heads of the other two. Those in the water close their eyes, open their mouths, and receive the golden rain on their faces. When one finishes he dives in the water, another climbs up and does the same. Interesting little game. Nudists, sodomites, and urinators one and all.

They didn't spot me. They were too busy concentrating on their urinary sport. I kept running. Sometimes I peered through the underbrush. Looking for a murdered woman. The first time I walked through this forest, Agneta told me that a few days before they had found a woman murdered. The news appeared in the daily paper, without giving the exact location. Agneta simply told me: 'They found her in this forest.' Now I search for a corpse among the birch trees.

I return home. Agneta awaits me. Mail has arrived. A letter from Gloria. I put it aside without opening it and, above all, without seeming to lend it importance.

The telephone rings. It's her niece who is arriving within minutes. She lives downtown and wants to go walking in the woods with us. Is it possible? Yes, sure, come. Agneta has no children, but two nieces. I get dressed. Twenty minutes later there's a knock at the door. The niece is with Erika, her new baby daughter, around four months old. She is a typical Swedish woman of thirty: slender, big tits, totally blonde, smiling, blue eyes, speaks only when absolutely necessary. Within two minutes Erika starts to scream. The niece sinks into an easy chair, takes out her big, firm, beautiful tits and the little girl begins to nurse. I stare at those gorgeous tits and perhaps my desire becomes too apparent. The two women look disgusted and become very serious, the niece quickly tucks her twin temptations away. The three of us remain silent, each one looking at a different wall. Erika doesn't look at anyone. She sleeps with her belly full.

Finally I get up. I go out on the balcony and look out. Nothing. There's nothing to see. Only trees. What I want is to grab those tits and . . . ufff. I put on my shoes, my jacket, my cap: 'I'm going to get some fresh air. I'll wait for you below.'

'Yes.'

They take half an hour. I'm sure the niece was telling her aunt that she was harboring a delinquent in her house and to be careful, etcetera. Finally they came down. We went walking through the woods. Fifteen minutes, without exchanging a word. I can't see what the big deal is. Almost everywhere men try to look at women's tits. As far as I know this is normal and doesn't deserve such a dramatic reaction. Do they want me to feel guilty? Well, I don't feel guilty, nor will I control my lust.

It's cold. In the forest it's even colder. The niece calls on her mobile phone. We exit onto a narrow road. Ten minutes later, her husband arrives in the car. He greets us through the window. Just a movement of the eyes. We answer him from a distance: 'Hi.' They go. My hands, face, feet, and ears are frozen. We sit on a bench facing the canal. Three hundred feet away, moored to a pier, are forty luxury yachts. Almost all sailboats. With German flags: 'Very beautiful yachts! Buy one of those, Agneta, and let's sail away.'

'Uhm. One of those yachts is worth . . . my salary . . . for the next twenty or thirty years.'

'Shit!'

'They're Germans. They have lots of money.'

'In Europe the Germans take all the blame.'

'No, no, it's that . . . well, at least those who come here have money. Very much money.'

'It's the same everywhere. Those who don't have cash stay at home. And speaking of home, let's go because I'm starting to freeze.'

'Oh, you're cold?'

'Honey, by your mother, when we left the house it was twelve degrees, now it's probably around ten.'

At home, Agneta prepares something for dinner. God willing, it won't be salmon. I can no longer stand salmon, bread, and cheese. I search for music on the radio. Something appears in Spanish. Incredible but true. A station which identifies itself as Match 81.9. A long interview, in English and Spanish, with a Cuban who lives in Washington. This is incredible. The guy is a member of the Spanish Language Academy in the USA. He says that Spanish is becoming a dominant world language. I like to hear that. Even if it's not true. Communicating in English traumatizes me. 'When I came to Washington, about forty years ago, if I heard someone speaking Spanish I would immediately greet him and we would begin to be friends. Today it's different. Today it's normal to find people speaking Spanish in the stores, the restaurants, everywhere.'

We dine on salad and roast beef. It appears the salmon took a night off.

'Do you really like salmon so much, Agneta?'

'Yes, it's traditional. I always eat salmon and caviar.'

'Caviar paste. It's not real. It's like toothpaste.'

'Oh, no.'

'Oh, yes.'

After dinner, I indulge my bourgeois habits: coffee, whisky, and a good cigar. On the balcony, of course. This is what I don't like about Europe. Eleven degrees, but I have to smoke outside even if I freeze my balls.

'Agneta, sit with me?'

'Sure.'

Sometimes it's good to smoke in company, although I prefer to do it alone. To smoke a good cigar is an act of reflection, of meditation. It's like fishing: sitting there, alone, with only the fishing line. You think, you speak, you project yourself within. Cigarettes are complusive. Cigars are philosophical.

In the corner of the building, on the lawn, there are some sandboxes, with hammocks, swings, little wooden houses. City Hall spends a pretty penny for the kids every summer. Now there are two girls and a boy. The two girls swing madly in the hammocks. They get to the top and scream, then come down hard. The hammock has chains of steel and is very safe, like everything here. The girls swing 180 degrees, to the top. They enjoy themselves, they scream, they laugh, they're afraid, they control it. They keep pushing the limit. They're scared, but on they go. To the maximum. The boy is more cautious. He's cowardly. He doesn't dare. He barely rocks himself. The girls, though, are enjoying it and screaming with fear and maybe even peeing in their panties, but they keep swinging to the top. We watch.

'When I was a boy I did that.'

'Yes?'

'To the top. I dove into the hammock and swung as high as I could. I was almost shitting with fear but I was enjoying it. I clenched my asshole and overcame my fear. I like that: to get to the top and remain in command, to have my hand on the controls.'

'I believe it.'

'I've been that way since I was a boy.'

'You do everything the same way. To the top.'

10

Nothing happened over the weekend. I'm bored with this married life: going to the supermarket to buy beer, milk, cheese, bread, eggs, coffee. On Saturday a package arrived: cable television. I install it. Finally we'll be able to watch some porno films. Now we have twelve additional channels, including a French one, how nice. She's more interested in the BBC and CNN.

I hid Gloria's letter so well that I forgot about it. One morning I'm alone, staring at the ceiling. What to do? There's an amazing silence. Incredible. How do the Swedes achieve these absolute silences in a neighborhood where there are so many apartment buildings? Prolonged and perfect silence. Damn, Gloria's letter! I search for it, stick it in my pocket, put on my sneakers, go downstairs and out to the little cemetery. Some of the tombs have fresh flowers. It's a beautiful place: green, calm, with these discreet little headstones.

Near the chapel there's a bench, underneath some enormous trees with copious, intense green foliage. I sit and open the letter. There's a sheet of paper covered with red, brown, gold, silver, blue-green kisses. Two dried flowers and a long letter of four pages: '. . . I'm a diehard sentimentalist. You supply me with a kind of intimate warmth. Deep down we're alike, even though you are what you are, a bit difficult, but that gives me strange pleasure. I always ask God that you accept me just as I am. Sometimes I think I'm crazy, but every night I light a candle and sit down and ask myself a question. I illuminate my inner being and then I know that everything's in order and that my conscience is clean and so I sleep happily without worrying about my loneliness. I have gone to the Church of Charity and Order and to the one dedicated to the Mercies and I have gone on my knees before the Father to beseech him for my father and for you and for everyone, and I ask that He takes pity on us . . .'

I read it many times, and then I become very calm and think of nothing. I walk a bit on the trim green grass and look at the dates on the gravestones. There are many old graves, of people who lived in the nineteenth century. That's what we are in the beginning and at the end: dust and silence. But it terrifies us to know this so we make a lot of noise and a lot of trouble in the middle, between the beginning and the end.

I walk slowly back to the apartment and write a letter to Gloria: 'When I come back I'm going to bring a whip for you. Much love. A lot of affection, kisses, cock and a whip. I'm going to tame you and enslave you. You're going to be my little animal. Never in your life have you had a man like me, nor will you ever have one again. You inspire me. It's something spiritual and physical at the same time. You awaken the angel and the demon within me. So let's make use of the present because the future is now. I'd like to live with you in a big house. Just us, with a black dog if you like. And no shaving your underarms or legs. No deodorants or perfumes. Nothing. Just you and I. Natural. Alone and wild in a house on the outskirts of Havana. Far from all the meddling, inquiring people. And I'll make you pregnant. I dream about knocking you up and possessing you. With your big belly, you're beautiful, adorable. I'm going to adore you. You with a baby and your tits, which will get big, dripping milk. I'm going to love you like you have never imagined a man can love you. You drive me mad.'

Ah, how this woman continues to bother me, even in Sweden. I have three options with her. Turn her into an even bigger whore and be her pimp, enslave her and have her bring me money. She's often asked me to do it. Or take her out of the neighborhood. Find a house in a calmer place, maybe near the sea, where nobody would know us. Have two or three kids and lead a quiet life. She's also asked me for that. The last possibility would be to forget her. Leave the neighborhood and go far away. Alone. And never see her again.

I don't know what to do. It bothers me. It drives me crazy. And the fucking Swede is also infecting me with her virus. Little by little. Every day she's more affectionate and more seductive and astute.

Ugh, I'm thinking too much in this absolute silence. I put on Pavarotti and Bucchero, the *Miserere*. I go out on the balcony. I need to breathe fresh air. It's a beautiful, sunny day. Two girls meet at the corner of the building. One is walking a German shepherd. The other a woolly black bitch. The girls greet each other. The dogs sniff each other and become excited. They frolic, and get tangled on their leashes. Everything, it seems, was planned. The girls had made a date to meet there. They led their dogs inside the little soccer field, properly encircled by a fifteen-foot-high fence, before closing the gate and releasing them. The dogs romp, run, bite each other, growl, bark. They raise their ears alertly, they sniff each other. They run a bit more. The male mounts the female. Just once. Rapidly. The girls don't miss a beat. Each one calls her dog. They put on the leashes. They say goodbye and then go off in opposite directions. The dogs, slightly winded, obey their mistresses and also part. They turn their heads and stare, disconsolate and anxious. The male tries to go back. Both remain completely unsatisfied. A tug on the leash makes him stop. He lowers his head and stays beside his mistress. I remain on the balcony a moment longer and the *Miserere* ends. I go up to the CD player and see on the digital counter the playing time of the piece: 4:15. It all happened in less than four minutes. Maybe the young girls are Swedish virgins – or virgin Swedes – and understand nothing. Even they don't know.

When Agneta arrives I tell her and she answers me with implacable logic: 'How old were the girls?'

'About . . . eighteen or nineteen.'

'They were not virgins. They know very well, but it bothered them that the dogs were happy and not them.'

She prepares a cup of tea. Now she doesn't waste time making me tea at six in the afternoon. She sits down to knit a sweater for me. She's been knitting it for months. There's no rush. That's for sure. No rush at all. We're not going anywhere.

We remain silent for quite a while. She drinks tea without sugar, and knits. I'm thinking of making myself a vodka and cola and having a smoke on the balcony; but it's overcast and the temperature is falling quickly.

'Oh, look. Let's see about this. Maybe we are already rich.'

She has a lottery ticket and rips it open with the point of a knitting needle. Nothing. It's always the same. Sometimes she plays the horses. And also loses. Three or four times a week she comes with lottery tickets or horses.

'Rich? What you're going to be is even poorer if you keep buying these things every day.'

'Not every day.'

'Almost.'

'I want to be an old millionairess, like my mother's neighbor.'

'She's a millionaire?'

'Twelve million kronor.

'How do you know?'

'They publish it in the newspapers. Every year. The people who have the most money and pay the most taxes.'

'That's no good. They could get kidnapped or murdered.'

'That's what they say. But there's freedom of the press.'

'Uhm.'

'My mother has quite a bit of money too.'

'Did it appear in the paper?'

'It's not that much.'

'She ought to share a little.'

'I think she has shares. She buys and sells on the stock market.'

'Really?'

'I'm not sure. We never talk about it.'

'Why?'

'We never speak about money. I suppose she has shares, because she's always looking up that information in the newspapers.'

Today's paper dedicates two pages to a rock festival. I ask her to translate the headline for me.

'A girl died at the festival.'

'How?'

'Suffocated. Too many people.'

'What does the headline say?'

'The police arrested a youth every six minutes on average.'

'That's the headline?'

'Yes.'

'Shall we walk a bit?'

'Through the woods?'

'Yes.'

'It's windy.'

'It doesn't matter. Bundle up, Agneta. And let's go.'

We put on jackets and shoes, and set out for the little forest. The path beside the canal.

'Are you bored in the house, Pedro Juan?'

'Yes, sometimes.'

It's cold and windy. I put my hands in the pockets of my jacket. I have a piece of gum. Only one. I take it out and offer it to her: 'Want a piece of gum?'

'Yes.'

She takes it. I'm left with the desire to chew a piece of mint gum. A sporty sailboat passes slowly through the canal, headed for the open sea. You can hear a symphony coming from the yacht's cabin. It's playing very loud, at top volume.

'That music shouldn't be played like that.'

'It's Mahler. The seventh symphony.'

Something happened on the yacht. The bow made a line for the shore and, within seconds, ran aground amid the mud and the grass. Smoothly but definitely. To free it would require pulling from the stern, with a cable and another boat. Now the bow was scarcely a yard away from us. I stopped to see what would happen. Agneta kept walking. A corpulent man, in shorts and a cap, came out on deck. The guy was having difficulty maintaining his balance, completely soused. He leant over the gunwale and almost fell into the water. It had been a while since I'd seen anyone so drunk. When he saw that the bow had run aground on the bank of the canal, he put his hands over his face and moaned. It seemed to me he would weep. He collapsed into a canvas chair and remained there, staring into the void. I continued to observe the situation, wondering what I could do. I thought that maybe the yacht could be pulled by a rope attached to the stern. No. That would bury it even more. It would have to be pulled by another boat from the middle of the canal. That was the only solution. Well, at least one could give him some encouragement. The guy seemed to be alone on the yacht. To be drunk and weeping wouldn't solve anything. I yelled to him: 'Hey, man, it's no problem.'

Agneta had kept her distance. When she heard me yelling she came running back, grabbed my arm and tried to pull me away.

'Hey, let go of me!'

'Don't get involved with problems, Pedro Juan.'

'It's no problem. I'm trying to help.'

'He's drunk.'

'So what? Anyone can overdo it and get rum-dumb.'

'What are you saying? I don't understand.'

'Anybody can get drunk. He's in a jam, but it's easy . . .'

'Let's go, let's get out of here. You must not get yourself involved in other people's problems.'

On board the yacht, the Mahler played on, deafeningly. I looked at the guy. He was weeping, collapsed in the canvas chair. He had covered his face with his hands, and was sobbing like a lost child.

11

After lunch, I go out on the little balcony. I take off my clothes. Coffee and a cigar. Agneta comes out, sits facing me. She brings coffee and little chocolates. She sees my prick and: 'Oh!'

She looks around. Perhaps some neighbor is watching.

'It's no problem. The neighbors can't see me.'

I have calculated it. I'm hidden by the railing. I open my legs and exhibit myself. Agneta looks at me and her eyes shine.

'You've never had a husband as naughty as I.'

'Never.'

I like to display myself. My prick thickens, stretches, begins to rise like the trunk of an elephant. Well, not quite. Like the little trunk of a baby elephant. Agneta sighs: 'Oh, Pedro.'

'Look at this, baby, you're making it stand up without using your hands. By telepathy.'

She continues watching, captivated, as the animal lengthens and fattens: 'Oh, Pedro Juan, you are obscene.'

'Ah, how elegant.'

'What?'

'Obscene. Beautiful word. It sounds very nice in Spanish: *obsceno*. It's such a beautiful word for describing supposedly dirty things. And I like how you say it: "Oh, Pedro Juan, you are obscene. Slightly obscene."'

'Not slightly. Totally obscene. Very obscene.'

'Crudely, profoundly obscene. I finally understand. It has never occurred to me to think in those terms. I believe I'm a very normal guy.'

'But . . .'

'But what?'

'I like it a lot.'

'Because it's obscene?'

'I think so.'

'Of course. You've always had educated and discreet husbands. And you're still missing something.'

'Missing what?'

'Sodomy. When I sodomize you, you'll belong to the select Club of the Obscene.'

'Oh, ha ha ha.'

'Go on, laugh. Soon you'll be weeping. With pain and pleasure.'

'No, no, it's a joke.'

'Don't worry. I'll slip it in you with Vaseline.'

'What is Vaseline?'

'Grease. And that's it for today. Look at the woods, and let the animal relax a little. Want to go to the little country house?'

'Yes, let's go.'

I dress on the balcony. I stand up. Agneta gets agitated: 'Pedro Juan, the neighbors . . .'

'Don't worry. They're all hiding behind their curtains, masturbating.'

'This is serious. Here they can call the police.'

'The show is free. Would you like to bet something that they're hiding, watching and masturbating?'

'You're mad.'

'Ha ha ha. Let's go.'

The country house is half an hour away by car. Luckily, neither her sister nor her nieces are planning to visit it today. Just us. It's completely isolated, next to a large farm with pastures and sheep. The nearest house is at least a hundred yards away. In between there are stone fences and bushes. We put down some deckchairs in the back garden, strip in the sun, and read a little. Within twenty minutes it gets overcast and a cold wind starts to blow. The little party in the sun is over. We go inside. In an hour it goes from 25 to 15 degrees. Luckily, the living room has two soft sofas, fluffy carpets and the walls are lined with planks of hazel and walnut. The fireplace is ready, although now that would be a bit much. Several large windows afford a view over a beautiful landscape. We are on a hill. In the distance lies the Baltic, gray and foggy. Just over five miles separate us from the sea: an enormous stretch of green pasture, fields of wheat, potatoes, onions; woods, neat red-and-white-painted farms and stables; cows, sheep, and a narrow road where cars and trucks speed by. I put on my jacket. Agneta concentrates on her reading.

'You're going for a walk?'

'Yes.'

'Are you bored?'

'No, Agneta. My eyes are tired. I'm going to stroll a bit.'

I cross the road and walk slowly through a field. Two hundred yards away, beside the road, there are various houses displaying a sign: *Loppis*. Flea market. There is an immense plain and the cold northeast wind blows the grass, the brambles, and the flowers. A little beyond the road, at the end of a short and narrow path, there is a large mound of rubble. It's an accumulation of bricks, clay, dust, pieces of doors and windows, broken glass, pieces of old wood. It contrasts with the delicate and minimalist beauty of this savanna covered with minuscule multicolored flowers, and with green, sepia, white, and yellow brambles. Little trembling plants and lichens and mosses cling to the rocks.

I walk on further and come close to the *Loppis*. There are tables and chairs, three white poles with Swedish flags. On one side, a line of ugly, filthy corrals built with pieces of old wood, planks rescued from a fire, pieces of wire. There are a few hens, roosters, rabbits. No one in sight. All I can hear is the wind and my steps on the gravel. There's a big canvas tent billowing in the wind. It makes a strange sound. In front of the tent, out in the open, are a hundred or so very old and rusty bicycles. None of them is worth two cents. A bunch of junk, but each one has its price taped to the seat. I look at them carefully, comparing the prices. I have no idea why. I enter the tent. There are used clothes, overcoats on a rack, wicker baskets, clocks, lanterns, mirrors, electrical cables, skillets, typewriters, flatirons, lawnmowers, circuit breakers, useless doorbells. Everything is old, broken, covered with dust. In one box there are whips made of braided leather, maybe nine feet long. The ten-odd whips are at the bottom of a big cardboard box on which they've inscribed the price in black crayon: 10 kronor, a little more than a dollar. I pick one up and look it over. Perfect, flexible, almost new. I quickly roll it up and put it in the pocket of my jacket. I'm not going to pay a single krona. I want to steal the whip.

I leave, and I enter another tent. Nobody around. It looks like the place is abandoned. In this one there is nothing but old Swedish books. A few in English. And more useless, dusty junk. Toasters, scales, little baskets, Christmas-tree ornaments, small fixtures and odd bits. The dirt floor is covered with some filthy old carpets. The wind blows hard and shakes the tent. It looks like everything might fly away at any moment. There are things which remind me of very strange moments in my life. There are ancient records in their covers. Old records of mediocre North American singers. I remember that, at the end of the 1950s and the beginning of the '60s, my aristocratic uncles had all these records in Havana. Shelves stocked with hundreds of American records and all they listened to were tiresome operas and symphonic music.

There are also some bad, imitation-leather portfolios, probably from the 1960s and '70s. They're cream-colored and remind me of socialist Bucharest. In the '70s, a lot of men were walking around the streets of that city with these portfolios and ties and cheap polyester suits. Usually the portfolios contained only a small garlic and oil sandwich, a small jar of yogurt and a pack of insipid cigarettes.

The third structure is solid brick and mortar. At the entrance, there's a little counter and some tables and chairs. They sell coffee, chocolates, sweets, soft drinks. Finally there are people. Two of them, sheltered from the bitter wind. At one of the tables sits a corpulent man, very stout, in his shirtsleeves. He looks about sixty. When I enter a bell rings. The man looks me over slowly. There's something aggressive and confused about his gaze. It seems he has a sluggish brain. I say 'Hi' to him. He doesn't move. He doesn't look at me. He doesn't respond to my greeting.

At another table there's a fat and dwarfish woman, with the face of a mongoloid. She looks like the dwarf in Goya's *Las Meninas*.

She mutters something to the man in Swedish and looks at me out of the corner of her eye. She's drinking coffee and eating a roll. She belches loudly when she lifts her head and looks at me. She belches again as she makes a face and inclines her head. There's a lot of dust in the air. You can see it clearly in the light coming through the dirty glass of a large window. In back there are more accumulated objects, amid the dust: plates, caps, hats, ashtrays, useless ballpoint pens, empty bottles, used magazines and comic books. There are several boxes of beautiful magazines from the 1940s. They have articles related to the war. Almost all the destroyed objects on sale are from this period. Some might work as decorations. But it's impossible. Everything is rusted, broken, exhausted. A few candelabra and small bronze pieces were beautiful in their time. There is a cupboard full of stones. Hundreds of small, common, ordinary stones. A yellow sign announces that each one is worth five kronor. Alongside it, another cupboard has thousands of old, dirty, water-stained postcards with ragged edges. I walk out slowly, hands in my pockets. I touch the whip. I look out of the corner of my eye at the old man and the dwarf. They remain silent. In the same positions. I say 'Hi' again. They don't look at me. They maintain disagreeably reproachful expressions. I sense the old man is about to ask me to leave and never darken his door again.

The bell rings again as I open the door and emerge into the fresh air. I return on the gravel path, listening to my steps. Now I have the wind in my face. It feels very cold. With my right hand I caress the whip in my pocket.

I get home and find it very warm and comfortable. I open a can of beer. I look at the thermometer. Fourteen degrees Celsius. I have an urge to shit, and I hurry to the bathroom, but Agneta calls me from the living room. She is holding an album of photos. The country house in the winter. In different years. On the first pages Agneta and her sister are very little girls, playing in the snow. 'That was Christmas, 1955. The snow came up to the window, over six feet high.'

'*Uf*, that little house must be an ice-box in the winter.'
'What?'

I clench my anus so I don't shit in my pants, and answer: 'A freezer.'

'Yes, but, sometimes . . .'

'Agneta, I've got to shit.'

'I like the landscape. Winter is very different.'

'I wouldn't like living here when it's that cold.'

'Sometimes it drops to twenty-five below.'

'I'm about to shit myself!'

'Come. Let's look at the photos.'

She takes me by the arm and directs me to an easy chair.

'I'm about to shit in my pants. Do you understand?'

'I don't. What are you saying?'

'*Cagar*. A first conjugation verb. Like *amar*.'

'I don't know.'

'I'm going to the toilet.'

I run off.

'Oh, yes. Sorry, sorry.'

I enter the bathroom and ah . . . what relief. What pleasure. I feel lighter. It's a very small bathroom. I close my eyes, rest my forehead against the corner of the washbasin, and listen to the wind whistling outside. It makes the wallboards creak. It's a small lament. It whistles continually, interrupted by the bleating of the sheep. In the afternoons the sheep come near the house. They're grazing and remain awhile on the edge of the property, moving about and nibbling on the grass. I listen to the gusts of wind from the Baltic and the bleating of the sheep, and shit a little more. I concentrate until I let loose all the shit, then I listen to the creaking of the wood, and I feel very empty. How nice.

12

I was running through the birch grove without touching the ground. It was a long stretch paved with narrow boards attached to little pilings. A foot below the boards was swamp. Few people passed through there and the marsh grass was tall and tangled. I was running blindly, pushing the grass aside, the boards shaking with each stride. I was breathing hard. Fleeing from something. I don't know what. It wasn't necessary to know. I was running out of air, and I accelerated until I slipped and fell into the swamp. I sank into the mud. I kicked a little, but it was too thick. I sank steadily up to my shoulders. I tried to grab onto the boards but couldn't see anything. Suddenly it was night and I was feeling a terrible anguish in the dark, sinking into that disgusting, frigid swamp. The mud was up to my chin, and I kept on sinking. I couldn't scream. I kept opening my mouth, but I was so scared that I was paralyzed and couldn't make a sound. Somehow I managed to get my arms out of the mud and began to paddle desperately. Then I woke up. Paddling and yelling. Agneta woke up also. I had hit her in the face. She was sitting on the bed to my left, moaning: 'Oh, oh,' while clutching her nose and attempting to stop the blood. It seems I gave her a good cuff: 'Did I hit you? Are you hurt?'

'Oh, yes, many times. Many times.'

I had to laugh. I was still startled by the nightmare, but it made me happy to see her bleeding and beaten. My sonofabitch appears at the most unexpected moments. Agneta takes such good care of herself and leads such an aseptic existence that it can only be good when something happens to her.

She had to get up. Whimpering, she went to get some cotton wool. I went to the kitchen and drank a glass of water. It was already light. Unbearable. Daybreak at three in the morning. And nightfall at eleven p.m. I go to the bathroom, urinate, and return to the bedroom. Agneta is still sitting on the chair with her head hanging, sobbing. If it were Gloria I'd give her another punch and fuck her just like that, bleeding, and I'd lick the blood to have her taste in my mouth, like Dracula. That would turn her on, and she'd get crazy with me and tell me: 'Put it in deeper, goddamn it, all the way in and hit me again, hit me again.' And with every slap she'd have an orgasm while I was sucking her blood. But Gloria is crazy and she makes me even more deranged than I've ever been. I think about all this in a flash while watching Agneta sobbing and staunching her little nosebleed. I squeeze my prick a little. I massage it and it swells. I have the urge to fuck her and to punch her a couple more times, so that she keeps bleeding instead of making such a fuss over such a little thing. But I contain myself. If I allow myself to follow my urge, I'll be back in the Caribbean within twenty-four hours. No, Pedro Juan, cool it, daddy, cool it. It's not her fault that she's so delicate and so fine and so foolish. Cool it, Pedro Juan, get a grip on yourself, baby, come back into focus. Come on, it's over, my boy, it's over. Be cool.

I breathe out, I relax. I go to the kitchen. I drink another glass of water. I look out of the window at the cemetery. I close my eyes and concentrate for a few seconds on the space between my eyebrows. Then I go back into the bedroom with a glass of water in my hand. Very affectionately, I say: 'Okay, Agneta, enough, enough.'

'Oh, oh.'

The cotton was soaked with blood. It seems I gave her quite a sock; I let loose another guffaw. A little too loud for the Swedish dawn.

'Oh, Pedro Juan, why do you laugh? The neighbors can hear. They'll complain. Why do you laugh? It really hurts.'

'Oh, sweetie, pardon me. I gave you a hard one? Forgive me, my angel, it was a nightmare.'

'Yes, yes. Blows. Many times.'

As always in extreme situations, her Spanish goes haywire and she only manages to say disjointed words.

'Many times? Ohh, what a shame.'

'Yes.'

'Ha ha ha ha ha ha ha ha ha ha ha ha ha.'

I can't contain myself. Again noisy guffaws.

'Oh, but, how is it possible? Do not laugh, please. Do not laugh.'

'Ha ha ha ha ha ha.'

I couldn't control myself. She gave a strained smile. When I finally pulled myself together, I felt really good.

'Let's see, sweetie, tilt back your head.'

'What do you say?'

'The head back, Agneta, the head. Back.'

I took another piece of cotton and helped her. I stroked her head. And in two minutes the bleeding stopped. I looked at the clock. Quarter past four. She was tired. I convinced her. We lay down again. I covered my eyes with a black handkerchief. I caressed her a little. Both of us naked. We'd had a good screw at eleven o'clock when we went to bed. And now it was hard again. I can't touch it. I put her hand on it so she'd rub the animal a bit. She likes it. She caresses it with a special sweetness and makes like a cat. She almost purrs. Okay. This will make her forget the blows and the bloody nose.

'Okay, Agneta, okay, I'm tired.'

'Yes, yes. Sleep. *Excusa.*'

'*Excusa?*'

'Sorry.'

'Go to sleep, and don't say you're sorry, or I'll make you suck my dick right now and you'll forget about your manners.'

'Pardon?'

'Nothing, go to sleep.'

The alarm clock rang at seven. I feel her warm by my side. I caress her. I kiss her. She kisses me with her mouth closed, but I give her some tongue. I like her sleepy breath. She's inhibited. She's so aseptic that she knows nothing of odors. I go down on her pussy. It stinks with all the come of the night before. I suppose I'm licking a cemetery of spermatozoa. It smells very good and tastes even better. I give her some head which launches her off the planet. Like Saturn: devouring my children. I make her float in another galaxy. She comes. And she comes. And she comes. And then I go to give her some cock. Holy shit! She's such a voluptuary. She closes her eyes and loses herself. Let's herself go. I fuck her for quite a while until I finish too, panting like a horse.

Ugh, this hermetically sealed apartment. I'm suffocating. Claustrophobia overwhelms me. I jump up, covering myself with the quilted robe. I look at the clock. Seven-forty. I open the door to the balcony. Damn, fresh air! Fresh air or I'm going to suffocate. I can't stand these drawn curtains and the doors and windows always shut. The thermometer reads twenty degrees. The green gardens, the brilliant sun, the quiet, and the calm. The blue sky. The birds singing. No one in sight. Absolutely no one in sight. Where the hell are the Swedes from this neighborhood? Sometimes I think they have secret tunnels and move about underground, like moles.

I go to the kitchen. I prepare my coffee and her tea. Agneta runs around desperately: 'I don't think I have time. Oh, oh.'

'These morning fucks run counter to employment stability.'

'Ohhhh . . . I don't understand, please, later.'

'The tea. It's ready.'

'I have no time.'

She gives me a kiss. Two. Three. She hurries downstairs. The next local train passes at seven fifty-six. She's in time for it but she'll get to work very late. Maybe by eight-thirty. I think I have to be more careful with these morning fucks. If they fire her, I'll never forgive myself. I can be a son of a bitch, but not that much.

I'm alone now and go out to the balcony. Fresh air and coffee. Then something occurs to me and, without giving it another thought, I go to the bedroom and lay down my red handkerchief on the floor in one corner. I put a little glass of vodka, a cigar, and my necklaces of Changó and Obbatalá on top of it. I light a candle and put down the little images of St Barbara, St Lazarus and the Virgin of Copper Charity I brought with me. I pray, offer up blessings, and beseech. Also for the African and the Indian. I get a chill. Someone is asking for water. I bring a glass of water and bless it too, with certain prayers which I know from memory. What a shame I have no conquer root, no chinaberry or sweet basil. I read the prayer to the Just Judge for men three times. A few days before I left Havana, Gloria copied it on a piece of paper and gave it to me: 'I see my enemies coming, but I repeat three times: though they have eyes, they cannot see me. Though they have hands, they cannot touch me. Though they have mouths, they cannot speak of me. Though they have feet, they cannot reach me.'

13

They often show on television the Floyd Patterson–Ingemar Johansson fight, New York, 1959. The Swedes remember that massacre with pleasure. Johansson knocking the black man to the canvas. The guy gets up. More right hooks. He's down again. He gets up. More short hooks. Right in his face. He hits the canvas. Jabs to the guts. He's down again. I don't know how many times. The television repeats these film clips, until the referee declares the American knocked out. Then you see the two of them now, forty years later, old and fat, smiling, remembering that night in Madison Square Garden. They became friends. Patterson came to Sweden many times. He learnt Swedish, married a Swedish blonde. Johansson always winds up saying the same thing: 'A champion is always a champion.' The papers publish photos of those times. In one, Frank Sinatra and Floyd Patterson appear very young and happy, stepping out of a bar into the Stockholm night.

I like looking at those films and photos. Back then, I was eight years old and my parents were having a having a hard time making ends meet. We were living in a minuscule apartment in Matanzas. It had a little balcony and the only good thing was that the sea, the whole bay, was ten yards away. The building had many rooms and small apartments and two common bathrooms. There were Lebanese, Spaniards, Poles, an old policeman, an old sailor, a pair of old, out of service whores. A lot of down and out types in that seaside building. There was also a whore living there who had a lot of clients and the same name as my mother, Zoilita. The men would send her messages written on scraps of paper: 'Zoilita, I'm in Mayito's bar. Hurry. Ernesto.' Things like that. They would send them with some kid. Sometimes these boys would come to the wrong door or ask: 'Where does Zoila live?'

Someone would point them to our door. The first time that happened was at six in the afternoon. My father was at home and I don't want to, nor should I, remember the row. He almost murdered my mother. Luckily my mother has an agile mind and understood what had happened within two minutes. She ran out into the corridor, trying to stop the boy who was going downstairs. The little boy kept running and my mother went and rang Zoilita's bell. She opened the door and my mother very politely handed her the message: 'Is this for you, señora?'

'Ah, yes, pardon me, the boys get . . .'

'We have the same name, but I'm a housewife.'

'It doesn't matter . . .'

'It may not matter to you, but it does to me. Explain to your friends exactly where you live. I don't want any more mistakes.'

At any rate that's what happened, because from then on everyone knew that the *puta* was the other Zoilita, not my mother.

I liked that neighborhood. I had a lot of friends. As a kid, I had the run of the place. Later almost everyone went to Miami. At night they stole the yachts and the waterski launches which were anchored near the docks of the Nautical Club and two days later they would phone from Florida. We stayed put, with our passports and visas stamped. But that's another story. The important thing was that Concha, who lived downstairs, was the unhappiest and most dramatic person I have ever met. If, one day, I would write a novel about her life it would be a total failure, because no one would believe such a long series of disgraces from the cradle to the tomb. A woman as hopeless as a flattened cockroach. She was a rural schoolteacher living in a shitty house in a little backwater town. She was out before daybreak and returned to her room at night. Three or four nights a week she was visited by Cheo, her eternal lover. He was a fat guy, paunchy, crude, about fifty. What is more, he had a red Cushman motor scooter which resembled him. He and the scooter were like twin brothers. Cheo and I shard a mutual antipathy. The only television set in the whole neighborhood – an ugly Hotpoint with a tiny screen – was one Cheo had given to Concha. I'd go downstairs, say hello to

Concha, ignore Cheo, and sit down to watch the fights. This was professional boxing, ten rounds. Tremendous fights. Sometimes they were transmitted from Madison Square Garden. Cheo hated me because I would come in with my fresh face, not look at him, the owner of the television, and impudently watch all the fights, from first to last. Years later it occurred to me that maybe the guy liked to screw Concha while watching the fights, and I was interrupting them. But, as my grandfather used to say, it's God's guess. It was a sacrifice for me to have to put up with the shit and piss smell of Concha's dogs and cats and, on top of that, the ugly puss of that old fart. Those nights were the basis of my pugilistic studies. Later, when I was in the army, I began to box and, although it's immodest to say so, I had a very elegant and precise technique. They called me 'The Dandy', but my punch always lacked power. The manager was always telling me: 'less elegance and more muscle'. Now I watch Patterson and the Swede mix it up and remember those moments. Obviously, I'm getting old. The young have nothing to remember, while I have too much. Sometimes I think my memory is excessive. However, I prefer to see the positive side of this: a great memory is like a great root. It sends sap to the body. And this juice floods through me and sustains me.

Agneta telephones and pulls me away from all this. Anyhow, thinking about this nonsense leads to nothing.

'Can you come with me to the Saint Jacques prison this afternoon?'

'Saint Jacques? Where is it? In France?'

'No, here.'

'And why is it called that?'

'I don't know. Can you come with me?'

'Ohh . . . a prison . . . ugh, that's like a morgue . . . I don't know . . . you have someone locked up? A brother, a nephew?'

'Please, Pedro, please. In my family . . . ehhh . . . you see, I belong to an organization which offers help. I'll explain it later. I must bring magazines and books this afternoon. I need your help. There are three big bags, very heavy.'

'Oh, if that's it . . .'

'I don't like to go alone.'

'They might rape or kill you?'

'I don't think so. There are excellent security measures.'

Ah, shit. She never gets it. She takes everything so seriously.

'Okay, okay. Yes, I can go and help you.'

She gives me high-precision instructions concerning the place and time.

'Please be punctual, Pedro Juan.'

'Of course, am I not always on time?'

'Sometimes no.'

'But sometimes yes. Ha ha ha ha ha.'

'Ha ha ha.'

Finally she smiled a bit. We met at the exact hour in the exact place. We took the exact train. At five forty-five in the afternoon, Agneta pushed the button on the main door of Saint Jacques. They asked questions over the intercom. She responded. We waited two minutes. To make their job easier, we stared into the television camera above us. They opened the door with a buzzer. It's a small, clean prison. A single-solid four-story edifice, painted light beige and white. Surrounded by a large wall with rolls of barbed wire on top, and all the windows adorned with white bars. It also has a well-tended lawn and gardens, trees and flowers and two small playing fields. Everything clean and beautiful. We were greeted by a delicious and very manly young woman named Pernilla, according to a name tag she wore on her chest. My view was from head to ass. Hard and compact. She certainly doesn't like to do it from the front.

Naturally, they check us at the entrance with metal detectors, look over our documents, stick tags on us and let us pass forward with our bags of magazines and books. Corridors and more corridors. A staircase. Everything absolutely spotless. The barred gates open before us, with the help of the electronic card Pernilla carries. And close behind us. It's very disquieting. I have some experience. We had to go through five barred gates. Medium-security jail. I know that we are in a labyrinth that, gate by gate, is turning into a claustrophobic nightmare. Why the hell did I get involved in this? It's triggering powerful, very unpleasant memories. I am able to control myself by repeatedly placing in my mind a simple thought: I am only here for a few minutes to deliver these books and then I'll be back in the fresh air. Easy, Pedro Juan, nothing's going to happen.

We finally arrive at the game room which, from all appearances, sometimes serves as a Lutheran chapel. We have to wait for someone who will sign the receipts, once again check the bags and receive the contents. Pernilla goes to get the guy. I don't know why, but I think it will be a very serious if likeable chaplain, dressed in black.

In the room there was just one man, with a cheap, faded gray suit. He had the face of a recluse, and was shooting pool by himself. The guy didn't look at us when we entered. Agneta sat in a corner, next to a window. I stood next to a bookcase. There were various table games, all very worn and dirty. Two decks of cards and some ragged periodicals. The only new things were ten Bibles and ten books of psalms. I thought the chaplain must have a hard time doing his job. I looked at the guy and caught his eye. He made an almost imperceptible gesture with his head and eyes, inviting me to play with him. I smiled to help him relax: 'Oh, yes, sure!'

'Do you speak English?'

'Yes.'

'Good. Welcome.'

Balls were missing, the green felt was torn in three places, and there was only one cue. We tossed for the break and began. With my first shot, I pocketed a ball. It had been years since I'd played, but I love it. More than anything I like to set up the shots. It's a game of great precision. You have to practice a lot. I'm concentrating on what I'm doing, and the guy asks me: 'Are you new here? You're not Swedish.'

'I'm Cuban.'

'Uhh.'

'I'm visiting. I brought magazines and books.'

'Do you speak Swedish?'

'No. I came with her. She's my girlfriend.'

'Uhmm.'

We play a little more. In silence. Agneta is on the alert, but doesn't move an eyebrow. Now I ask him: 'How long have you been here?'

'Six and a half years.'

'And how much time did they give you?'

'Thirty.'

'That's a lot. Murder?'

'Yes.'

There were four balls left on the baize. Two and two. It was my turn. While I lined up the shot, I asked him: 'So how was it?'

'What?'

'How did you do it?'

'Drunk. A very strong blow. To the head.'

I look at his eyes as he makes an abrupt gesture, smacking his right fist on the palm of his left hand. His face is tired and full of hate.

'What did he do to you?'

'He liked my woman.'

'And she?'

'I don't know. I don't want to know.'

'Thirty years for one minute of fury.'

'Bad business. If I had to, I'd do it again.'

'You would?'

'For sure.'

'You have friends?'

'I have no one. My woman disappeared. I have no visitors.'

'Never? In six and a half years?'

'Never. No one. Nothing.'

I tried to concentrate on the ball again. I wanted to finish the game. Pernilla returned just then, accompanied by a fat cop, big-bellied, heavy, and with a nasty face as if he had just got up. The elegant, serene chaplain, dressed in black, existed only in my imagination. Agneta called me. I don't know why. I asked the guy to excuse me. The fat cop said nothing. He took everything out of the bags. Inspected it closely. Filled out a receipt. Signed it. Handed it to Agneta. He turned and walked away without a word. In all that time he never opened his mouth. Pernilla, Agneta and I put the magazines, periodicals, and books on the shelves. The first book I took out of the bag, in English, had a pretty disturbing title to be sent as a gift to Saint Jacques: *Free Live Free*. As we were leaving the room, I went quickly up to the guy, gave him a handshake and a smile: 'Good luck, man.'

'Thank you, man.'

Pernilla said something to Agneta. She seemed very authoritarian. Of course, I didn't understand. I sensed she was bitter. We retraced the whole of our path in silence. Finally we got to the door. Pernilla disappeared without a farewell. Agneta and I crossed the garden. At last we came to the main gate and went out into the street. Then Agneta asked me, in a very bad mood: 'What did you say to that man?'

'Nothing. Nonsense.'

'In English? You can speak nonsense in English?'

'It's the *only* thing I can speak in English.'

'It's prohibited to speak with the inmates. They told me that in the future you will have to wait by the door. You cannot enter again.'

'Who told you? Pernilla?'

'Who is Pernilla?'

'The chick who accompanied us.'

'How do you know her name?'

'She had it on her name tag. Didn't you see it?'

'I saw nothing.'

'Agneta, you never see anything . . . eh . . . well, it's not worth the trouble. Okay. The deal is that they won't let me go in again and no one can talk with the inmates.'

'That's it.'

'Why?'

'They are dangerous. Almost all the inmates are murderers.'

'Like that guy.'

'Yes?'

'Aha. He killed a man.'

'Ohh! And so he is very dangerous. And you playing pool . . .'

'I could have done the same thing that he did.'

'You?'

'Sure. So now I could be locked up in Saint Jacques, with a thirty-year sentence.'

14

For breakfast I only drink a cup of black coffee. Agneta has cereal with yogurt, tea, and a slice of bread with cheese while she reads the paper. It's the same every morning. I believe we've been doing the same thing for years. And it's extremely boring. In fact, we've been together for less than two months.

We finish. She kisses me and runs out the door. I turn on the radio. Brush my teeth. Shave. Take off my robe and look at myself in the mirror. I'm getting thinner. I weigh myself. Seventy-five kilos. It's good for me to lay off the rice and beans for a while and eat something more nutritious here. Too many carbohydrates are a disaster. I look at myself again in the mirror and rub my prick a bit. It gets fat and sassy. If I weren't so old, I could earn money doing porno shoots. Anyhow, I still have a pretty cock. They called me 'Golden Cock' in Havana not too long ago. Well, finally, I get dressed. On the radio they're playing a song in Spanish:

> There's no going back,
> So forget, forget.
> There's no going back
> Nothing remains behind,
> So forget, forget . . .

It's got to be some Puerto Rican salsa singer from the Bronx. A bit neurotic. I turn off the radio and read something I have to hand: 'love is born from loving gestures'. I believe it's a French proverb. That's what happened with Gloria. It all began with an erotic longing. Just a little lust. At first I managed it carefully so as to avoid love's entrance. But those small gestures began: some flowers, some books for the boy, a meal together, some sticks of incense for the *santos*, a conversation about religion. And, above all, freedom. That's the most important thing. I let her be free and she let me be free. Letting the loved one be free is a sign of spiritual grandeur. So everything kept changing, little by little. Now I have solitude, distance, silence, and a lot of time to reflect. There are no problems in the vicinity. What will happen when I return? Deep down I want Gloria just for me. I don't want to share her. I think she feels the same. I suppose. I don't know.

Will the same thing happen with Agneta? We share so many of these gestures of love, one after the other, but I don't think it goes beyond that. The heart can't be divided into pieces. The only sure thing in my life is confusion. It's been constant my whole life long: confusion, chaos, complications. I always thought that one day I would come to be an adult and that all this would end and I would be able to lead a calmer life. Now I read something that Colette said in Paris to Truman Capote: 'that is the only thing that none of us will ever be able to be, adults . . . Voltaire, even Voltaire, carried a child around inside him his whole life, an envious and evil-minded child, an obscene little boy who was always sniffing his fingers; and Voltaire carried this child to his grave, as all of us will carry ours.'

The ringing of the telephone interrupts me. It's a Brazilian journalist. He's calling me from *Bravo* magazine in São Paulo. One of my books will be released there in the fall. He interviews me over the phone. For more than half an hour I answer questions. At one point he asks me: 'I see your novel as an honest book but one without any friendliness or political concessions. How was it received?'

And my reply: 'I have no reason to be friendly or to make concessions. A writer is basically a bitter, confused guy with no answers to anything; a guy who doesn't care whether or not he's understood, sympathetic or antipathetic, has money or is dying of hunger. If you're a writer you have to know that these are the rules of the game. Otherwise you're a clown. And you're always going to have someone around you who'll try to turn you into a clown.'

The day continues to be cloudy. Not even a little sun. And today is June 1. Full summer but not in full sunlight. The day passes slowly; pleasant, boring, without alarm. Perfect for someone who wants to be a corpse. It's terrible. It makes me anxious. Agneta comes home at half past five. We go out to walk through the woods next to the canal for half an hour.

We return home. My face and hands are frozen. I read the thermometer fifty times a day. Now it's 15 degrees. So much for summer! I turn on the television and once more try to find some porno on the cable channels. Half an hour surfing from channel to channel. I go back to check the brochure they sent with the equipment.

'Nothing pornographic.'

'But Pedro Juan, do you really enjoy it?'

'Yes, of course.'

'We can watch CNN.'

I'm disillusioned. I thought I would see a porno film every day. Well, that's life . . . illusions and disillusions, just like the romantic ballads. Suddenly I have an idea: 'Agneta, my love, today is Friday. Shall we go out?'

'If you wish.'

'Let's go dancing.'

'I don't know how to dance.'

'You have to dance.'

'I know a Cuban music place, La Habana.'

'No, it's very expensive.'

'You know it?'

'Of course. It's full of black men from Havana. My associates.'

'Ohhh.'

'Uhhh . . . let's go to La Salamandra Loca. It's cheaper.'

'I don't know where it is.'

'I do.'

We went to La Salamandra Loca.

15

That night we didn't go back home. We met a very odd couple at La Salamandra Loca: Elena, a young woman from Seville, happy, confident, great dancer, a colleague of Agneta's at the office. And her husband, a bald Swede, thirty years her senior, unable to dance. He wore a white shirt, a gray tie, and a black suit. He told me his name was Svensson and that he was the business director of some big stores. I danced salsa with Elena in the middle of the dancefloor and we had a great time. When Agneta got too jealous, I danced a little with her. Svensson didn't even try.

At three in the morning Elena insisted that we go to her house: 'It's very near. You can sleep there and we'll all have breakfast together.' We agreed and set out on foot. Daybreak in Stockholm and nothing happens. Some classic cars from the '50s drove by – Chevys, Cadillacs, Fords – full of noisy drunks. A guy was putting up posters for a heavy metal concert. At Svensson and Elena's place, we drank a little more. Agneta preferred a cup of warm milk. And so to bed. They put us in a little room. It was already day time. Four in the morning with the sun shining and a clear blue sky. Agneta went straight to sleep. I wasn't even drowsy. Half drunk, I sat by the window. There was a kino club across the street. Some men came out, very discreetly. If I had a key to the house, I'd go to drink a final glass or two with the Thai ladies. All these kino clubs are the same: a little porno shop and, in back, a staircase, guarded by a Joe Palooka bouncer bulging with muscles. Ten steps down is the club, the most expensive drinks in the world, music, a little bit of light, and whores of all kinds with fixed rates. They're also the most expensive whores in the world. Even the condoms are the most expensive in the world. Suddenly a beautiful black car pulls up in front of the club with two very slender Thai women, professional, elegant, about fifty years old but very well preserved. They jump out and enter the club in a hurry. Two minutes later they exit, accompanied by two employees carrying bundles wrapped in large plastic bags. Dirty sheets and towels. They put them in the trunk of the car. The older of the two women directs the operation. She's energetic, the kind of woman who can run a bordello or just as successfully head the opposition party in Parliament. Her elegance is dissolving because she's so angry. She screams at the two employees, pushes them, threatens to hit them. The men, submissive, allow her to do it. After venting her anger, she climbs into the car and takes off like a rocket. It's obvious that something wasn't right. That lady needs a better breed of worker in her kino club. I lie down, shut my eyes and fall asleep in a second.

I wake up with a pain in my neck, exhausted and hung over. I go to the bathroom and run into Elena. She's already up and ready to rumba, even though it's nine-thirty in the morning. She doesn't get tired. Even when she's sleepy she talks incessantly and laughs at everything. Amazing. If I had a husband like Svensson, I'd never stop crying.

During breakfast, I look over at a small table on which sits the wooden skeleton of a dinosaur – just to have somewhere to look. My hangover won't let up. Svensson asks me: 'Are you looking at the dinosaur?'

'Eh?'

'The dinosaur.'

'Ah, yes.'

'It contains a whole philosophy. I have another on my desk, at the office.'

'And?'

'They disappeared millions of years ago. But they're not necessary. Everything is fine, maybe even better, without them. At least for us it's better without such gigantic animals. Well now, we can disappear too. And everything will be the same. Or better. Therefore, dear friend, anything can happen. Anything. So we ought not to take ourselves so seriously.'

'Very well, Mr. Svensson. Thank you for sharing your ideas with us.'

He was so pleased with his explanation, so absolutely satisfied with the brilliance and originality of his ideas, that he contradicted his advice. Yes, he was taking himself very seriously. If Elena were to leave him suddenly, the guy would go to pieces and shoot himself. The fact that his hands trembled predicted it. He seemed to read my thoughts: 'Flowers every Friday. That's the secret.'

'How so?'

'Every Friday for the past seven years, I have given flowers to my wife.'

Elena nodded, smiling, very complacent.

'When Elena meets my friends' wives, she asks them if their husbands give them flowers. They say no. Then Elena tells them: "Ah, well, my husband does. Without fail, whatever happens, I get flowers every Friday."'

I kept quiet. Observing him. Then the guy delivered his triumphant conclusions: 'So it's an excellent investment. We must not cut corners in this, dear friend. I invest one day per week and take profits on the other six. This is the secret of our happiness.'

We all remained silent. Elena and Svensson satisfied, amorous, smiling, spread butter on their toast and gazed at each other sweetly. I would have liked to be inside that woman's brain. How could she stand such a guy and, on top of that, seem happy and spiritually serene? A husband like this could drive a woman to madness, depression, or suicide. Or maybe not. Perhaps the guy had given her the perfect brainwash and completely subsumed her in his mediocre pragmatism.

The silence was prolonged. I fought the urge to excuse myself and head straight for the subway. But I decided to annoy him: 'I see you have a kino club across the street.'

'Uhm.'

'But it's very quiet. Almost all the women are Thai.'

Svensson ignores the subject. He busies himself with the marmelade. Elena enters the conversation: 'The girls in the kino club? No, they're from all over. There are Swedish girls too.'

Agneta, half asleep, is also not interested in the kino club. Elena asks me: 'Are you interested in prostitution?'

'Me? Well, if you put it that way . . .'

'No, no. Let me explain. Everyone talks about prostitutes, except the women themselves. It's a sociological fact which must be studied.'

'Oh, I don't know.'

'I do. I know something.'

'Ah.'

'I'll tell you. Two years ago a social studies institute in Stockholm held a seminar about prostitution. I was there the whole time. Psychologists, sociologists, judges, all giving their opinions. They agreed that poverty obliged women to walk the streets and so forth. And that there aren't enough rehabilitation programs. Then a very beautiful woman stands up, dressed a bit extravagantly, and says: "Well, you know what? I'm a prostitute and have been one since I was very young. It's been a lot more than twenty years, maybe thirty. And I adore my profession. I love my work. It agrees with me. This stuff about unemployment, lack of work is not right. None of it. I'm a prostitute because I love my profession. I'm Brazilian and I do very well in Sweden. I wouldn't want to do anything else."'

We finish our breakfast. We go out into the little back garden. We talk about the flowers and how beautiful everything is in summer with the tulips and the sunflowers and finally say goodbye. On the way home in the train I began to feel a little better. The view of the countryside covered with grass and flowers and the brilliant sun refreshed me. My mood improved. Agneta told me something about her work and the boss, who grows more unbearable by the day.

'The old bag needs a good bang.'

'I don't understand. You know my boss. Do you remember that . . .?'

'Yes, I remember it. That afternoon I went to your office and spilt sugar on the carpet. She became hysterical.'

'Uhmm.'

'She needs a meat injection.'

188

'A what?'

'A poke. It's the lack of a husband. And she's still nice-looking, elegant.'

'Ahhh, Pedro.'

'If I gave her a shot, you'd see . . .'

'You better forget it because I'll kill you both.'

I was joking, having fun, playing around. But it seemed to me she was speaking seriously.

'I'll kill you and I'll throw you off this bridge into the water. At night. And while I'm at it, I'll kill the American too and throw him off up ahead.'

The American is a Californian who works in the same office. He was Agneta's boyfriend. He jilted her for the boss. It appears that Agneta has not forgiven him. She has turned acid in five seconds.

'Ha ha ha, and you'll go to jail.'

'I don't care. I'll go to jail.'

'Damn, you woke up violent today!'

'Yes. What's more, I won't tell anyone that your final wish is to be cremated. So you'll be buried. It will be one more punishment. The final punishment. You'll rot in the earth. And in Sweden. Maybe I'll arrange for them to bury you in Lapland. Icy ground. So far from the tropics and your supermacho friends and your black women.'

'Wow, the last punishment of the Latin lover!'

'Exactly.'

'Too many crimes combined. You don't seem Swedish.'

'Yes, very Swedish. Very, very Swedish.'

She's very serious. I don't think she's pretending. I look out of the window for a while. The train is moving very fast. Part of me wants to wander through these woods and get lost and not care where I'm going. I close my eyes, breathe deeply, let all of the air out, and say to her: 'That's the way it is, Agneta. Life goes on, and we damage ourselves and everything builds up inside. That pain can do away with us.'

We sit silently, looking at the woods through the window. I sense her anger but I am serene. Four minutes later, we arrive at our station, get off and walk home without haste, exhausted.

16

Agneta took fifteen days of vacation and now we are together all the time. We have little to do and not much to speak about. We listen to Radio Match. The disk jockeys speak English and Swedish simultaneously and play lots of rock and country. We fuck two, three, four times a day. Naturally I'm out of milk, but it doesn't matter. I know a lot of little Chinese games and we entertain ourselves. At times I get morbid and ask about her former love life. Nothing. She doesn't want to talk. I've been thinking that I could write a two-novel series: *A Lot of Heart*, with Gloria in Havana. And *The Swedish Lover*, with Agneta in Stockholm. Perhaps both books would turn out to be interesting. Gloria talks about everything in abundance and makes things easy, while Agneta is a tomb, the slut. She won't speak about her lovers for anything in the world. A writer can always speculate, but reality is more convincing. If I invent everything, you won't like it. Well, maybe I'll never write *The Swedish Lover*, but at least I'll have fun. I insist that she learn how to suck. Not to *amar*, but to *mamar*. Little by little it's happening, but as for the asshole – nothing doing. She freaks out each time I get close with my finger. Even with a finger.

'It's the first time I do it with the mouth. Believe me.'

'I don't believe you.'

'Why don't you believe me?'

I do believe her but I like to be contrary so I can knock her off her pace. In the afternoon of the first day of her vacation, I mix vodka with tomato juice, tabasco, lemon, and salt.

'Ah, a Bloody Mary.'

'That's what it's called?'

'Yes. It's the first time I've drunk one.'

'I've been drinking them since I was a newborn baby. They gave them to me in my bottle. But I never knew its name.'

'I don't believe you.'

'I'm serious. I was born in a bar. My father had a bar-restaurant and we lived in back, on the other side of the kitchen.'

'Ohh.'

'I was raised among the drunks and the whores. They bought me an ice or a Coke so that I would dance cha-cha-cha and mambo. I got used to being an exhibitionist from a very young age.'

'A dancer is an artist.'

'And what is an artist? An exhibitionist. A good artist always gets naked in front of everyone. And enjoys it.'

She tries the cocktail: 'Uhm, how nice. It's delicious.'

'In Cuba we make it with rum. You never tried it? Then how do you know its name?'

'In theory. I know lots of things in theory.'

Sometimes we stay silent for hours. I read. I discovered books in Spanish in a nearby library. They have I don't know how many hundred books in every language. Even in Chinese, Korean, Japanese. It's really perfect. There are about three hundred books in Spanish. The classics. It's incredible how these Swedes find out about everything. If people read these three hundred books, they'd have the classics of the language in their brains.

Agneta invents things to do: she washes, cleans, cooks special little dishes, knits my sweater. She bought a bag of compost, we went up to the attic, found some flowerpots and potted all the plants. She organized a salsa party in the home of a supersexy friend, who currently has lovers in Paris, Stockholm, Gothenburg, and St Petersburg. I had to dance nonstop, with three women who alternated, from six in the afternoon until three in the morning. I spent several days nursing muscle pains in my legs. Best of all was that the supersexy Birgitta was off and flying with a few shots of whisky – and I think she sniffed something else in the kitchen – and called me 'Oh, macho, macho' and rubbed me with her tits (big, beautiful, natural tits, made in Sweden, of course). And squeezed me like I was bread and she was a baker. Tremendous slut, Birgitta. Agneta laughed out loud and said to me in Spanish: 'You told her it was a macho dance and she took it seriously.'

Birgitta didn't let me rest the whole night. She attached herself to my neck and almost bit me. She put her tits on top of my arm and squeezed me against her. She whispered in my ear: 'Oh, Peter, no problem, Agneta is my friend.' At the end of the party, Birgitta wanted to organize an excursion to La Habana nightclub: 'Let's go everyone, I like it there. It's a macho dance. Let's go to La Habana and dance with the men.'

But, usually, Agneta and I are alone and silent. Or with a little operatic music. I've told her twenty thousand times that I can't stand opera, that I'd rather listen to symphonic music. But no. She insists. Sometimes, to break the silence, I recount some shifts of fortune which I've survived here and there. If it's not convenient to say that they happened to me, I tell her: 'This happened to a friend.' There's no reason to always tell the truth. I've had a really intense life but a large part of it is unpublishable. Top secret. Many stories I strip of their sexual parts before I tell them. In this way I avoid her little attacks of jealousy. Despite the makeup I apply, she guesses that I'm hiding pieces of the story, and says to me: 'Sometimes you lie quickly.'

'Meeee?! Nooooo!'

'Yes, you. Don't pretend to be surprised. You are able to tell lies easily.'

'Ehhh . . . yes. We can all tell lies. We all lie.'

'No.'

'Ah, no? You never tell lies? The perfect Swedish woman.'

'I am not perfect. It's because I don't like them. I can, but it's difficult for me to tell lies.'

'I only tell little, minimal, compassionate lies.'

'That's not so. You lie quickly and very well. It seems like the truth.'

'So, I'm dangerous?'

'You frighten me, Pedro Juan.'

'Don't be afraid, my love. I don't tell lies to people I care about.'

'That in itself is a lie about lying.'

'You're very sharp today.'

'I don't know what to think. It bothers and scares me that you're like this.'

'I'll give you the key: watch my eyes. When you think I'm telling you a lie, look into my eyes.'

'Yes, yes.'

I suppose she wants to say: 'No, no.' She knows perfectly well that no one gratuitously gives away the key to their safety deposit.

17

A small museum is showing a retrospective of a very well-known painter. The guy is a born transgressor of the kind who disturbs for disturbance's sake. The pleasure of fucking around. The most scandalous piece in the show is a large oil painting: the mother of the Swedish king with her skirt raised and her black hairy pussy in full view. In front of her a guy in a suit and tie, with his fly open and his big, thick, hard, and healthy cock. In the background another couple screwing, she with her tits exposed. Everyone elegantly dressed, in a very chic drawing room. I like that. There aren't many people in the museum. We go downstairs to the bottom of the building. I'm already a bit aroused, and the solitude arouses me even more. I kiss Agneta, lick her neck, grab her tits. She seems surprised: 'Ohh, here? Nooo.'

'Yes, right here. If you were Cuban, you'd get down on your knees right here and suckle like a calf.'

She gets mad every time I say 'If you were Cuban you'd do something or other.' That's why I say it.

'Oh, if you were Cuban, if you were Cuban. Fool.'

'And if you were Cuban you'd wear a skirt so I could put my finger in your pussy. These jeans traumatize me.'

My prick is already as hard as a nail. I take it out.

'Look, sweetie, give it a lick.'

'No, no, no.'

'Grab it, cunt, squeeze it, it's all yours.'

'No, no.'

'I'm going to fuck you in the supermarket, slut. I'm going to slip it to you in the fitting rooms.'

'Oh, but . . .'

'You want it now? Let's go to the bathroom.'

'Pedro, they might have cameras. Maybe they are watching us. Oh, please.'

I put it back in my pants. I kiss her. We play. I play to relax her. She was really startled. We continue downstairs. We look at the books in the museum store for a little while.

'Agneta, I invite you for a little espresso out there, in the sun.'

'No, thank you.'

'Girl, don't be *pesá*.'

'What is *pesá*?

'Nothing. Accept my invitation and relax.'

'Good. I accept. What is *pesá*?'

'Heavy.'

'Oh, I'm not . . .'

'You don't want to fuck or suck in the stairwell, you don't want a coffee, you make a sour face. You're heavy, sweetie. Relax, please.'

A few minutes later we have coffee and chocolates under a tree and talk about the paintings we just saw.

'He has always been a kind of rebel, with a lot of energy. He's over sixty now. Sixty-seven, I think. And he married a woman of forty-four.'

'Like you. That's good.'

'Uhm.'

'He's an interesting guy, an artist. Wouldn't you marry a man like that? You at forty-four. A man of sixty-eight, let's say.'

'Ehmm . . .'

'You'd have a bit less sex than with me. Or none. Or just games. I don't know how it is at sixty-eight. I have no idea. Maybe tongue and fingers.'

'Ehm . . .'

'Would you marry? No sex, but a guy who's different and original.'

'Eh . . . No, I think not. Not now. Definitely.'

'Not now?'

'A few months ago I would have married him. But not now. Now sex really interests me.'

'A lot?'

'A lot.'

'And before?'

'Before no. I never thought about sex.'

We return to the house loaded with food, beer, juices, proteins, everything. Here it's not a crime to have proteins in the refrigerator. No black market like in Havana. Here the refrigerator is full. I mean legally full.

At seven in the evening, we sit down to watch *The Simpsons*. We make like it's a game, but both of us know perfectly well that every day it's more like a marriage. What is a marriage if not a system of complicity? Essentially that's all it is. All the rest may or may not exist: love, children, great or lousy sex, routines, daily habits, mutual trust or distrust, jealousy, memories, confessions about the former life of each partner, secrets which are never revealed, preparing food together, a beer, a glass of wine, watching the golden light of late afternoon. Perhaps these are little, unimportant details. But, bit by bit, a system of complicity is constructed between two people. And everything, even watching the fading day together, is an element in this system. And before you know it, with or without legal papers, you're a cog in the machinery of marriage. I know what I'm saying. It's happened to me quite a few times.

How many days have I been here? Since May 14. In four days it will be two months of togetherness. And, in another three weeks, I will leave. Nevertheless, it seems to us that we've spent a lot of time together and that there's lots more to follow. It's an illusion. We make plans. 'Maybe you can get a job in the embassy in Havana,' I tell her. 'Yes, it's possible, I know a little Spanish and I have experience in working abroad, I speak English, French, and Russian,' she tells me. I tell her about my house, of what we could do on the weekends. We get enthusiastic. Deep down, we both know that there's more illusion and dream than reality in this. It's not exactly impossible. Just improbable. Like winning at roulette.

I go to the balcony with a beer and a cigar. On television they are showing the news. Pictures of a submarine. I think it's English. It crosses the equator and they put poles up the asses of the new crew members. They replay the image various times; it's been taken by an aficionado, certainly a fellow sailor. There are three sailors, naked and face down on the deck of the submarine. Some guys dressed in white sheets and wearing crowns of Neptune insert the poles. Maybe they're rubber cylinders. Anyhow, they're long and solid. They brutally hammer them so that they penetrate the recruits' assholes. Belly down, the recipients wiggle their butts. We can't tell if it's from pleasure or pain. Then the newscaster comes on the screen, very serious and removed in his blue suit and tie, and launches into another theme.

I sit serenely on the balcony with my beer and my cigar. Dusk is always a good time for drinking, smoking, and not thinking.

I stop thinking and arrive in paradise. I hear Agneta bustling about in the kitchen, making supper. That's what I like. She makes money. She pays. She drives the car. She takes care of me. And I drink beer and smoke. She's right. I'm a bit of a chauvinist and a bit of a pimp. I feel great.

18

We had to take the roundabout route to get to Sodertalje on a less traveled highway. The more direct route from Stockholm was jammed with traffic on a beautiful and sunny Saturday in early July. It's a nice place. There's a deep canal next to the town which enormous transatlantic liners cross on their way to the port of Stockholm. Sometimes I come to fish. I'm sitting on the shore, casting my line with the rod in my hand, when one of those gigantic ships slowly passes barely thirty feet away. The sailors are on deck looking at the people, and we acknowledge each other with a slight nod, as if we'd known each other for ever.

Agneta drives carefully. On the little pier where I fish there are a few ragged drunks slugging wine. We pass through the town. An old friend of Agneta's has invited us to dine at her country house, near the mouth of the channel. When we arrive, it seems they have been waiting for us with some impatience. We apologize for being late. The meal is served right away. Only six of us at the table. While we eat, we talk about the house which is peaceful and impressive. It's more than two hundred years old. It's a splendid place. A few yards away are some artificial pools where a neighbor raises crayfish and salmon to sell. Agneta's friend tells me about the ghost in the attic. It seems he's something of a prankster and makes all kinds of noises at night. At times he allows himself to be seen as a luminous white mass going up and down the stairs. At other times, he makes noises with the pots and pans in the kitchen. When someone goes to check, nothing has happened. Everything is in order. It's a classic haunting. He's a typical practical joker who repeats the same tricks over and over. Nothing original. I tell them that it would be simple to get rid of him: a glass of water, flowers, a candle, perfume, a prayer for this tormented soul, dedicate a Mass to him at church. Actually, there are many ways to help this spirit gather light and find some rest. It often happens that dark spirits have an excessive attachment to their house and family. 'No, no,' the mistress of the house says to me, 'he's a good spirit who takes care of the house. There's no reason to throw him out of the attic.' 'If you say so, that's the way it is,' I answer her with a smile. And keep quiet. I think all dark spirits are the same, in Havana or in Sodertalje, but this lady believes she knows better. No explanation needed. I change the subject, we talk about fishing in the canal and I tell her I always catch something. Which is not true. They never bite. She asks me: 'Do you like to fish? Do you have a sea in Cuba?' I stand there not knowing what to say. Agneta intervenes: 'Cuba is an island, in the Caribbean.' 'Ahh, I didn't know. Well, I suggest that we have coffee and cake on the canal. We have a small yacht.'

We go to the canal. The small yacht is almost forty feet long, has two diesel engines and luxurious cabins, with all the frills. It could make a little trip around the planet, no problem. We climb on board, walk about, drink coffee, liqueurs, eat pastries, talk nonsense such as 'Oh, the Swedish summer is beautiful but every season has its charm.' We take photos, drink more coffee, more cherry liqueur. A little wind begins to blow, and we return to the dock. One of those transparent days in which nothing happens. The majority of days are like that. They have no importance. Important days are rare. And it's just as well. If everything were transcendent, convulsive, terrifying, we would all go mad. The weight of the intensity would crush us.

We return to the country house and all sit on the porch to drink some more. Agneta and I flee to the orchard and the greenhouses, behind the stable. We explore the old stable and the small abandoned house. Everything covered with dust and cobwebs, perhaps for the last hundred years or more. Rustic tables and chairs, simple unpolished kitchen utensils, a very antique pedal organ. We enter the greenhouse. Suffocating heat and humidity. There is a gorgeous tropical plant with dozens of flowers. Astoundingly beautiful. So incredible it doesn't seem real. 'Is it from the Amazon?' I ask. 'I don't think so, they travel a lot in Asia and

Africa,' Agneta tells me. I get close to the plant. Is it carnivorous? It was absolutely beautiful, phosphorescent, magical, with unimaginable colors. It seemed a trap for the heedless. It looked like it could change into a gigantic mouth at any moment and swallow me in a second. But I wanted to touch it in any case. I prodded a few stalks. And suddenly, from under that immense bunch of stalks, leaves and flowers, snakes began to crawl. They were calmly and unhurriedly slithering in all directions. Not as big as boas but not so little either. Damn! I got out of there in a hurry. Agneta followed close behind me, laughing. She shut the door of the greenhouse and brought me back to watch them through the window.

'They are not dangerous. Come here.'

'Holy shit! I didn't know there were snakes in Sweden.'

'They are not poisonous.'

'What do you know about snakes, Agneta?'

'I know something.'

'In theory.'

'Ah, yes . . . Look, there are more.'

I looked through the glass. More were emerging. There was a very big nest underneath the tropical plant. I counted them. Fourteen snakes. Each one three feet long. Some even larger. They moved slowly, sleepily. They hid themselves in other corners.

'They're drowsy from the heat.'

'Are there snakes in Cuba?'

'Of course. *Jubos* and *majás*. Most of all *majás*.

'Poisonous?'

'No, the *majá* gets very fat and makes good eating.'

'Argh.'

'Ha ha ha. I prepared them. In the cane-brakes, when we were cutting sugar cane.'

'Oh, but is it a tradition or . . .?'

'Tradition nothing. Hunger. Cutting cane twelve hours a day, sometimes more. And all we had for food was a little cornmeal and two tablespoons of beans. To catch a *majá* meant a party. I was always the one who prepared them.'

'Uhm, who taught you?'

'Hunger. That's the best teacher. If in one month you lose ten or fifteen kilos of weight . . . Once a *majá* appeared. They caught it in the cane-brake and no one knew how to prepare it. Then I thought: "Damn, it's just meat!" So I said: "I know. My father taught me." In reality, those snakes terrified my father, but I convinced them. From then on I was the chef of the *majás*. And we used to catch one every four or five days.'

'You are always telling lies. How did it occur to you in a situation like that to speak of your father?'

'I'm not lying. I said that then on the spur of the moment, out of a sense of survival. I never learnt how to prepare a cat, even though I ate them. Cat with fried potatoes and a little *salsa*. But other people cooked them.'

'Uggh . . . I cannot believe it.'

'It's because we were very hungry, Agneta. In the '60s everyone was hungry. Boys from sixteen to twenty years old cutting sugar cane like animals and eating a few grams of cornmeal and beans.'

'You could not protest?'

'In the army there is no discussion.'

'Didn't you get sick eating that garbage?'

'No. Quite the opposite. I was stronger than now. We worked like mules all day and at night we went out to fuck calves and mares. And on Sunday afternoons we boxed for hours without stopping. Once I knocked out two in a row.'

Agneta's face showed astonishment or revulsion. She interrupted me: 'I do not believe that you . . . calves and mares?'

'Ha ha ha. At that age, you fuck whatever you find or spend the whole day jacking off. It's normal.'

'No. It is abnormal.'

'In one of the harvests, in Morón, to the north of Camagüey, there was a black calf close to the camp. She was so cute, I'll never forget her. She had a little pink cunt. But there were a lot of us. When my turn came, the line had grown from five to twenty and her thing was so full of come it went "cloch, cloch, cloch" when I put it in her. Ha ha ha. And there were others after me. I guess thirty or forty a night. Maybe more.'

'Oh, please, do not continue. You have no scruples.'

'At that age, no one has scruples. Scruples are acquired.'

'Ah, don't justify . . .'

'Besides, the calf was enjoying it. She got very quiet. She didn't move. It was as if she were concentrating so as not to miss anything that was happening. With the mares it was different because . . .'

'No, no, please. That's enough.'

'Fine, okay. Don't make a drama. I was very young. I hardly remember.'

I think I talked too much. Her face changed. She became melancholy. What is normal for me, is abnormal to her. I'm sure Swedish adolescent country boys also jump mares, pigs, and calves. If there are only harvesting machines and tractors, they'll have to beat their meat like everyone else. That's the way it is. It's not necessary to complicate things needlessly. Luckily, I didn't tell her about the bitches I screwed when I was thirteen or fourteen.

We stayed silent. One minute of silence, two, three. I say to her: 'Well, let's go.'

'Yes.'

We say goodbye. We jump in the car and retrace the long route to detour around the highway. It's a narrow road, with very little traffic. We cross an impressive landscape of enormous, dense, green forests. We're tense, the radio broken. Total silence, and those forests so interminable and oppressive. Finally I ask: 'Are you angry at me?'

'No, but I need . . .'

'What?'

'I don't know how to say. I need . . .'

'Assimilation time. A mandatory eight-count, like the boxers.'

'Exactly. I cannot seem to be relaxed because I'm not.'

'I promise you I won't speak about my past any longer. You don't do it. It's best not to.'

'That's not it. Yes, I speak.'

'But not about important things.'

'I like to know about you. About your past, everything, but . . . sometimes it's very difficult.'

'You're very intelligent. You want to know everything about me while I know next to nothing of you. Speak, little Cuban, speak! The big Swedish woman has picked me! Ha ha ha.'

We laugh. I'm half asleep. I lie back and ask her: 'Are you sleepy?'

'No. I never sleep when I drive.'

'Sure? If you're tired I . . .'

'No, no. Sleep. Rest a while.'

I lie back and close my eyes. So I think I'm lucky I didn't tell her about the dog. I jumped that bitch in my grandmother's house, in the country. Whenever she saw me she would begin to groan. Those summers in the country were very good. Once Granny caught me masturbating on the porch. 'Ah, that's why you were so quiet! Do me a favor, save it. You're going to go crazy. Come here. Help me carry the slop for the pigs.'

Many years later my son would also masturbate, in front of the television. Any time he wanted. Even looking at the news. He thought that no one was watching. His mother caught him one day and began worrying herself sick: 'Oh, he's crazy. We must do something. We'll have to take him to the psychologist.'

'We don't have to do anything. It's normal.'

'Everything is normal to you.'

'Well, yes. A little wank now and then is normal. At that age, it's normal.'

And now that I think of it, at my age too. Sometimes there's no other solution.

19

I was working in the fields and the mud was sticking to the soles of my boots. I had to work hunched over. I was digging in the mud and pulling out potatoes. The day was gray. It was drizzling, and I was very cold. The hooded crows were shrieking. Their cries seemed very close. Picking those potatoes was a punishment. My arm was up to the elbow in the cold black mud. Then I saw that some big leeches, as black as the ground, were secreting their viscous liquid and very slowly crawling up my arms, my neck, my face. I felt them climbing up my back. Some were sticking to my skin and absorbing. I felt the leeches sucking my blood, but I couldn't get rid of them. I couldn't stop working. I had my right arm buried in the mud, picking potatoes. The left one was totally covered with disgusting black leeches. You couldn't see the skin. I felt as if I were transforming, little by little, into a leech. I woke up yelling and thrashing about and began to get rid of the leeches, but they were no longer there. I got up. Agneta muttered something, turned her back to me and continued sleeping. I went to the kitchen to drink water. I urinated. Two in the morning. I looked out of the window. There was a little wind and the cypresses, birches, and oaks in the cemetery were moving. Clouds were hiding the moon, but it was a luminous night and you could see the tombs very clearly. I counted them. Twenty-seven. Others remained hidden by the trees and the little Lutheran church.

I drank some more water, closed my eyes and thought: 'I'm sleeping badly. Let's see, it's only been two and a half hours since eleven-thirty.' I went back to the bedroom and lay down quietly. I ought to sleep a bit more. Then I remembered that the dream of the leeches had been in color, with odor, touch, sound, temperature. But I was walking through a dirty back street with a friend, I don't know exactly who he is, but he's a friend. A young whore urinates against the wall. Strange for a woman but not impossible. She was sending a steady stream against the wall. She finished and then went inside the building. They were all displaying themselves in the window. It was a bordello. All naked, on their beds, writhing lasciviously, opening their legs and showing us. Just then the girl who had pissed in the street came in. It was Gloria. She didn't see me. She had a diabolical face. A perverse expression. She stripped and lay down, opened her legs and displayed her sex through the window. With her eyes half closed, she had no idea who was watching her. She just wanted money. And I ached, it pained me so much to see Gloria doing that, with an expression of fake lust and satisfaction masking real hate and vengeance. I felt destroyed inside and began to weep. Tears, sobs, and snot were flowing out of me. I couldn't contain myself. I knew that Gloria was no longer mine and that I could never touch her. I was losing Gloria at that moment and she kept writhing lasciviously on top of that bed. I looked around and found some brickbats. There were stones and rubble all over the street, as well as a lot of dogshit and all kinds of filth and vomit. I began to throw the shards of brick and stones at the whorehouse window but it didn't break. I threw them furiously, weeping and raging with pain, but no one was aware of my pain or my rage. It was horrible. I woke up crying like a child, sobbing, inconsolable. Gasping for air, I sat up in bed. Finally I managed to control the weeping and convince myself it had only been a nightmare. 'It was only a nightmare,' I repeated over and over. It was thundering. I went to the living room and sat on the sofa. It was two-thirty. The thunder sounded dry and hard. Without echo or resonance. It sounded like an avalanche of big rocks hurtling down a hill. A crackling of light. For a second, the dark clouds were visible through the big living-room window. And then came the dull, dry noise of the thunder. A few seconds of silence and darkness and again the whiplash of light and the rumbling thunder. It began to rain.

For three days I haven't shaved or bathed. I sniff myself, but I remain the same. I need to smell my odors but here it's difficult. The air is so dry I hardly sweat. Impossible to have strong odors.

When I smell my sweat, strong and bitter, is when I get savage. I'm becoming soft here. The way I'm headed, I'm going to keep weakening. And that's fucked up. I want to be the oak trunk, the whip, the Devil's sword, balls and cock! I walk a bit through the woods while I think about all this. How can people live such dull lives? I try to calm myself. I go back. Agneta is working like crazy: she's vacuuming, washing clothes, running down to the basement every fifteen minutes. Carrying clothes up and down. She takes two rugs out in front of the building and beats them. All at the same time. At noon I make lunch: Mexican salad, salmon, cheese, bread, and beer. The sun comes out, the sky clears, the temperature increases. Now there's heat and a bit of humidity. We go to a little nearby beach. That's one way of saying it. Really, it's a big stretch of lawn with a few dozen people basking in the sun. There's a large forest, the lawn, and a wooden pier which juts out a few feet into the Baltic. Some adventurous types dive off and swim for a few minutes.

We pick a clear space to spread out a red sheet and some towels. The sun is strong. We cover ourselves with oil. The nearest person is a woman of about sixty, maybe sixty-five, several yards away. She has a bicycle and a large knapsack beside her. She has taken off the top of her bikini and has dark, wrinkled skin with thousands of freckles and blotches. Her nipples are very long, dark, and erect. Once she had large, full breasts. Now they are flabby bags which hang abundantly to either side. She has her arms raised, a few long white and blond hairs in her armpits. She lies there with her mouth open, her teeth yellow and stained. So abandoned, so distant, with such wrinkled skin, so immobile, so naked. She looks like a corpse. I fix my gaze on her and yes: she's breathing. It's like the cadaver of an ugly old woman. The cadaver of a body used and wasted. A continuous light breeze comes from the sea, smelling of sulfur. There's a lot of silence. Only the murmur of someone speaking near us and the very light noise of the waves breaking against the stones of the shore. There are no gulls or birds. The breeze doesn't even move the trees. No children either. Oh yes there are some, but they don't play, they're very docile. The only noise felt is the throb of a tanker which passes quickly through the sea before us leaving a wake of white spume. I feel alone. Completely and absolutely alone in the world. It's discouraging to have this feeling of total solitude. I read a bit, drink coffee, toast myself. Agneta tells me that she can't be in the sun for very long.

'It has been two years that I do not take sun.'

'So long?'

'Or more. Maybe three years. I do not remember.'

'Well, don't worry. In a little while we can sit in the shade of the trees.'

'No, no.'

'Ah, your allergy.'

'Yes, a lot of pollen. I don't want to get near those weeds.'

'Uhm, I'm going to swim a little.'

'It's icy, maybe you won't like it.'

I return in fifteen minutes. Now there's more wind and the smell of sulfur is stronger. The cadaver-lady has remained in the same position. Has she died? It's impressive to see that body, so destroyed and naked, abandoned on the grass. She's hardly breathing, absolutely immobile.

'Agneta, take off your bra.'

'What?'

'The brassiere, the top part of your bikini.'

'Ah . . . no, no.'

'Why?'

'No.'

'So that you tan evenly. Your tits are white.'

'No.'

'Are you ashamed?'

'Yes.'

'You're so Swedish about other things. You act like a country girl.'

'I am a country girl.'

On the other side of the channel, some trucks are dumping dirt on the rocks near the shore. There are three gigantic trucks and they make an infernal noise. They dump the dirt, raising dust, and leave. There's a factory there. Everything falls silent once again.

An hour later we go back home. Agneta prepares dinner and I mix a screwdriver. I take my glass and go to the living room. I turn on the television. It's too early for *The Simpsons*. There's a police show on. An African stole a little toy car in a store. The manager called the police and now he wants them to take him away. The black man takes out a banknote. He wants to pay for the little car. The manager doesn't want him to pay. He wants to screw him so the police will arrest him. I don't understand. They're speaking Swedish. The African defends himself and speaks, gesturing that the guy wants to take him by the throat and strangle him. He just wants to pay for the toy and have done with it. The two calm policemen speak too. The camera angle changes and we see that it's Christmas. Next, the African appears outside, talking to the policemen near the patrol car. They're standing in the snow surrounded by Christmas trees. Agneta calls me. Dinner is ready. I turn off the television and finish the screwdriver.

20

Imperceptibly, things are changing. Now Agneta likes to go to the supermarket and have something more than bread and salmon in the refrigerator. Sometimes she even buys food from the delicatessen like feta cheese and enormous, seasoned Andalusian olives. She enjoys going bra-less with her nipples pressing against her blouse. No longer does she freeze and save everything she cooks. Her niece with the lovely tits came around and seemed surprised: 'Oh, Auntie, you've never had such a well-stocked refrigerator. How nice.'

And she jokes with me about her millionairess neighbor: 'Each year she appears in the paper with more and more millions. Last year she had twenty-two million, but now she has a husband. Sorry, I can't do anything for you, ha ha ha.' I ask her: 'What if she is widowed suddenly and becomes lonely and sad and needs company?' 'We will go immediately to live in Karesuando or Lapland, ha ha ha.'

Her humor has improved. She reads the horoscopes every day. Sagittarius and Aquarius. She and I. And draws conclusions. Or we go to the track and enjoy betting on the races. She plans to work in Havana for a while. Yesterday we ate on the balcony. There are pots of flowers on various balconies in the building, and she says to me: 'The neighbors have lots of flowers.'

'All except the neighbor with the dogs and you.'

'Uhmm . . . I can have flowers too. I'll buy some soon.'

We remain silent for an instant. I say to her: 'It seems to me that when I came here you were either bored or sad. I don't know which.'

'Yes, a little.'

'You didn't care what happened.'

'Uhm.'

'Now I notice you seem more alive.'

Her eyes redden and she looks like she's about to cry. She goes to the bathroom. I wait patiently. Finally she comes out. I tell her something comforting: 'Don't worry, baby. We all go through periods of sadness and desolation.'

She comes close to me, hugs me and kisses me. For the first time I see a sweet expression on her face. I caress her too: 'Ahh, *qué rico*.'

'I love you a lot, Pedro.'

We silently caress each other. My cock hardens and touches her thigh, but I don't want to screw. It's like a heatwave between the two of us. Love, silence, and peace.

Later that afternoon she bought bags full of flowerpots and a big bottle of fertilizer. We worked for quite a while and revived her wilted plants. Afterwards we sat and I spoke to her about a nude beach which is quite near: 'Don't ask me again. I don't want to go.'

'Are you embarrassed?'

'Yes, of course.'

'Ah, girl, humor me. We only have a few days left together. We separate within a week. And who knows? Maybe I'll never come back to Sweden.'

She gets tearful. Sometimes Pedrito the manipulator lets fly and breaks the bastardometer. I caress her a bit here and there. A few little kisses, and she says to me: 'I don't know where it is.'

'Call your lesbian friend and ask her.'

'Lesbian? How do you know?'

'You can see it a mile away.'

'Oh, appearances . . .'

'Are sometimes deceiving. And sometimes not. I like lesbians. I feel at home with them. When I was very young I had two or three romances with lesbians . . . Oh, they were superlesbians, just like little hoodlums.'

'Oh, please, enough. Don't tell me more. How can you like a woman who looks like a man, who acts like a man?'

'They looked like little hoodlums but they weren't. They always asked me to sodomize them. They adored sodomy. I still like these very masculine lesbians. And transvestites also. I have fun with . . .'

'Oh, enough, please. I do not want to know more. You are a . . . a . . . I don't know how to say it.'

'A sexual pervert.'

'Yes, that is it.'

'But my sexual perversions charm you. And you only know the opening pages of the catalogue.'

'There is even more?'

'Of course. This tale has a second and third part, ha ha ha. "Hot Shit from Havana."'

She called. She found a map, pinpointed the place and analyzed the roads. She consulted the weather forecast and prepared what we would take. The only thing missing was a satellite navigation system. The next morning we were in motion. She was a bit irritated, going against her will.

Absolutely nothing happened at the beach. I felt cheated. There was not one handsome person. Only old men and women with bellies so big they could hardly walk. We took a little stroll observing this rather disheartening panorama, and Agneta said pathetically: 'I don't understand. Do people get excited by this?'

'Do these naked old folks make you sick?'

'Yes.'

'Because you're getting morbid. Ignore them. They're over there and I'm here.'

'I know, I know.'

'The beach is very nice. There's a tropical sun, there's silence, the nearest neighbors are fifty yards away, so what are you complaining about? Take off your clothes, and make yourself comfortable.'

'Everything?'

'Everything. So that you can be all one color. You have white buttocks and white tits.'

'Ha ha ha.'

The beach covers several miles. The greater part for people with clothes: one on top of the other, like little sardines, the children yelling and pestering. Then there are some enormous rocks on the shore and a tiny wooden sign which says: 'For nudists only.' On both sides of this sign there is limbo, in other words a big piece of deserted beach. Then the territory of sin begins. That's where we are.

In a while her mood improves, we swim, drink something refreshing, I squeeze her tits a little, kiss her, caress her, run my finger over her pussy which is already wet, look out of the corner of my eye and yes: a couple of old folks are staring at us. We all enjoy playing the voyeur. Evidently the old folks were having fun.

On our way back that afternoon she invited me to dine in an enormous resort hotel, which announced with much fanfare its huge marina with capacity for five hundred yachts and its twenty-seven-hole golf course and restaurants specializing in Chinese, Japanese, and Mexican food. In sum, everything perfect. I'm charmed by women who know how to spend their money. We ate on the terrace, facing the sea. An enormous Caesar salad with shrimp, a bit of veal, red wine. The wine and the resort atmo-sphere relaxed her sufficiently for her to come out with certain confessions that she had hidden until then. I suggested that we live in stages. Nothing lasts for ever. If one is conscious of this, each moment becomes more enjoyable.

'That's right. I had never thought of it. I have had big houses with three stories and nine bedrooms, racehorses and trainers, dogs, yachts, gardens, jewelry, we entertained on Friday after-noons at five during the summer, we appeared in the newspaper . . . ah, those were beautiful years.'

'Your husband was an actor or . . .?'

'No. A businessman. Shipyards for yachts, a hotel and I don't know what else. I live at another stage now. That's all.'

'Now you're at the frugal stage. Your old jeans, the broken shoes . . . now I understand why you don't speak about your past. I have all the luck: stoic in Cuba, and frugal in Sweden. Both ways I'm fucked.'

'Ohhh . . .'

'You should tell me everything and I'll write a novel. How the Swedish lover evolved from the most revolting consumerism and existential emptiness to the frugality of whole-grain bread, raw carrots, sugarless tea, and a tropical paramour.'

They brought us coffee and the bill. She paid in cash.

'Let's go, Agneta, it's whisky for me. Let's buy a bottle and get drunk.'

'Oh, no. I'm driving. But you can drink.'

'No, on the contrary. I want you to drink and get inebriated. Then you'll tell me everything and I can write *The Swedish Lover*.'

'There's nothing to tell. My life is very boring.'

'Gloria says the same. That's how it always is with the great sinners.'

'It's true. It was always very boring. That novel would be so stupid no one would be able to read it.'

Without willing it, my thoughts go to Cuba and Gloria. If I proposed to her that we should buy rum and get drunk, we'd do it in a second, go to the seashore and while she knocked back a shot or two, she'd get started on her adventure stories. One after another. She's impetuous. Agneta and I walk through the town on the other side of the marina. Excessively touristic. I forget the whisky and remember my youth: 'This town reminds me of Varadero.'

'Varadero Beach?'

'You know it?'

'It's very well known. Many Swedes go to that beach.'

'I lived there until I was thirty. Between Matanzas and Varadero. My lesbian romances were on that beach, in the '70s. The Gray Decade. For me it was the Decade of Spoils. The Perpetual Orgy.'

We passed in front of a jewelry store. They were displaying a beautiful collection of gold chains. I said to her: 'Let's look at those chains.'

'You like them?'

'I've always wanted one, but they're too expensive.'

We go in. They attend to us with panache. I like the thick ones, of hammered gold. The prices are too much for me. We keep walking.

'Too expensive. In Cuba maybe I can buy it for half as much.'

'So cheaply? Impossible.'

'Yes, but not in the stores. On the street, from someone in the neighborhood'

'Oh, but . . . they could be stolen.'

'They are stolen. What's more, from tourists.'

'Oh, that is not right. You must not buy it like that.'

'Why not? They're the cheapest.'

'I have a colleague at work who was robbed of a gold chain in Havana. Three hours after she arrived, walking down the street. They pulled it from her neck. She had it insured and bought a better one but . . . it is not right.'

'Why?'

'You are an accomplice to the robbery. You should not do that.'

'There are many things in this world which shouldn't be done. But they are. And we're all accomplices. When you were rich, did you know where your husband got his money?'

'From his businesses. It was honorable money.'

'Do you know how many miserable salaries it paid and how many people he was obliging to work like mules? He was stealing in every way possible.'

'I do not believe it. He was honorable. A very good person. And he is dead. He was a very decent man.'

'No businessman is decent. No politician is decent. No one is decent. What is decency? Don't fuck with me, Agneta! I'm going to buy the chain from the one who sells it cheapest! It doesn't matter to me that it was stolen from a tourist who displayed her gold in a country where people are starving. Hunger and anemia! That's what's indecent!'

'Then what you are going to do is indecent: to wear a gold chain in front of your hungry neighbors.'

'At least I recognize I'm an indecent and self-serving individualist. And I admit it. I don't start moralizing. Fuck it. I accept the world as it is.'

We stayed angry and silent. We kept walking.

'You want a coffee? I'm buying.'

'No, thank you. Save your money for the chain.'

'Ah, you're going to start again?'

'No, please, we can have coffee at home.'

21

We arrived, annoyed and in silence. Mutually offended. I sat on the balcony but anxiety ate away at my guts. I went to the kitchen, mixed a gin and tonic. I lit up a cigar and sat down again. Agneta was watching the news on television. I thought seriously about going to the travel agency the next day and changing my date of return.

Then her mother arrived. We had seen each other only three or four times, but we got along well. She's a likeable lady of seventy-six. She always waits for me to give her a kiss or tell her a joke. Today she comes in with huge dark sunglasses, very well groomed, a pearl necklace, at once elegant and discreet. I greet her with a big smile: 'Oh, Liz Taylor in my house! How are you?'

We all laugh. I give her a little kiss, as always, something totally unusual. The Swedes don't kiss. On television, they are saying something about the stock market. It's her favorite subject. We talk about shares, and I tell her: 'Scania is climbing quickly.'

'Don't fall for it. Volvo is going to buy Scania.'

'So then you should buy shares in both.'

'Wrong. Only in Volvo. It's very solid.'

'You have a lot of experience. It's better to do what you say.'

'And you are always up to date, Pedro Juan. If you knew Swedish, it would be magnificent.'

'If I knew Swedish and had a million kronor, you and I would make a championship team.'

'Oh, yes. Would you like that?'

'I work no more. I dedicate myself to cooling my balls and play-ing the market.' (I said this last part in Spanish.)

'What? In English, please.'

'That I bring luck. I bring lots of luck to everyone else.'

'This has nothing to do with luck. You have to analyze.'

'Fifty–fifty. Analysis and good luck.'

'You think?'

'Sure. We'd make a good team.'

Agneta serves coffee and pastries.

'Mama, we'd have to leave Agneta off the team. She doesn't know much about the practical life.'

'No. She's never known anything about money.'

'She likes money, but she doesn't know how to make it.'

'No, son, she doesn't like money. She has never liked money or the good life, or anything. I don't know what she likes.'

'As for me, I like to live well. But I don't want to work any more.'

'You are intelligent.'

'Mama, I've spent my whole life working, since I was a child. And what do I have? A rusty old bicycle, corroded by the salty wind.'

'Oh, you don't have a car?'

'I had one for many years. Now it's a super luxury. So it's just my old bike.'

'Ohh, impossible.'

'Now I only write and paint. It's very easy. The good life.'

'You have to write a bestseller, Pedro Juan.'

'Good idea.'

'And with the money in hand, I can give you some investment suggestions. There are some very secure companies.'

'Many thanks, Mama. I'll talk to my publisher. Maybe I can cook up a bestseller. Anything's possible. Ha ha ha.'

I skip the coffee. After the gin and tonic, I continue with vodka and cola. Mama comments that the day before she had been with one of her granddaughters to visit a very luxurious cruise ship which was in port.

'My granddaughter has a job on this boat. She begins tomorrow.'

'What will she do?'

'She's a twenty-two-year-old girl. Tall, pretty. Bet you can't guess what she will do.'

'I can't imagine.'

'Dealer.'

'Ohh, how nice. In the ship's casino?'

'Ha ha ha. That's right. She speaks very good English and German. She's prepared. They picked her from more than two hundred hopefuls. She's deft with the cards and a good judge of character. You have to have a sixth sense.'

'Very nice. An interesting job and travel.'

'And with people who have lots of money. Germans and North Americans, millionaires. Let's hope she finds a millionaire husband.'

I look at her and she smiles. The same old story: pragmatic grandmother looks for a rich husband for her most beautiful granddaughter. It's the same everywhere: in Haiti, they say that we Cubans live well. For the Cubans Miami is where you can be fat and happy. In Miami, they say you have to go to Chicago or to New York. In New York, they tell you that it's the Germans, and in Germany that it's the Japanese, and in Japan they say that it's Switzerland. And that's how it goes. It's a chain. People always think that their neighbor lives better. What's fucked is that it's often true.

Mama leaves. Agneta and I remain seated on the sofa. I was slightly drunk after various vodkas and cola. She caressed me. I kissed her. Her mouth tasted like coffee. I had vodka and tobacco on my breath. It occurred to her to go to the kitchen and return to the living room with a bowl of warm milk and oatmeal. She sat next to me eating that shit. I had to prevent myself from slapping her face and hurling that bowl of disgusting pap to the floor.

It's impossible to understand this woman. I'm half soused. She caresses me, gets me hot, my prick starts to get hard, we're putting the argument behind us. I suppose she's also hot and wants a good fuck to reconcile us. But while I figured she'd return in a romantic mood, wearing a transparent black negligee and carrying a snifter of brandy, she suddenly appears with a plate full of oats. Ah, fuck, I give up, I can't make it with her. It's impossible! She doesn't have the slightest idea of what to do to be in the moment. This woman was born out of somebody's asshole!

'Agneta, for Christ's sake! Are you really . . .? Cunt, prick, what an imbecile you are!'

218

'What? I don't understand.'

'Do me a favor, take that oatmeal out of my sight. Get rid of it! And put on a porn flick, suck my cock, do something . . .'

'Porn? We have none. You know we don't . . .'

'I'm going to give you four lashes on the butt with my whip and you'll see, you'll go running off on all four paws to buy fifty porn flicks.'

'Oh, no. You're drunk! What are you saying?'

'Drink. Have some vodka.'

'No, no, ohh.'

And she begins to weep. Lately she weeps about every little thing. At the thought of a possible whipping, my cock comes to life and I start to remove her clothes. I put her on top of me but she knows so little. She remains motionless, rigid, as if she had no joints. If she could see the rumba that Gloria dances on top of me, impaled like a suckling pig at Christmas!

'Let's go to bed, Agneta. You're the one who's going to fuck me.'

I lie face down. I put her on top of me.

'Do it. Fuck me. Make a tortilla on my ass, stick me with your pepita.'

(In the midst of my little high I remember she doesn't understand slang.)

'Rub your clitoris here on this little bone. Make a tortilla, goddamn it, or I'll kick your ass!'

'No, no!'

She seemed terrified. I didn't care. How hard I've worked teaching this bitch to screw! But I'm too impatient to be a teacher.

'I'm gonna teach you, bitch. I'm gonna take you to Havana so you can fuck all the black men you want. Twenty, thirty, fifty. You'll learn how to get off if it kills you.'

'Oh, but what's come over you? What are you saying?'

'That I'm going to find you two or three black men and they're going to make your head spin. We'll hang out at the Palermo one night and, you'll see, you'll wind up warbling boleros.'

I achieved nothing. I had to turn around and give it to her in the classic style. The same as always. Ah, Gloria, love of my life, you're such an artist, how I'd like a piece of you now, you little slut! I fell into a drunken slumber at some point. I can't remember when. I slept like a rock. Vodka always anesthetizes me. It never fails. I woke up late, exhausted and with a headache. Beside me, Agneta was watching with a sweet and puzzled expression. She didn't know what was going to happen next. She was as confused as I. I kissed her a bit to calm her down and asked her for water, coffee, and aspirin.

Everything has been rushed and transitory. There seems to be time, silence, and solitude. But the truth is it's happening to me the same as always: life, people, circumstances rush by and over-whelm me. I'm actually as confused and lost now as I was at the moment I landed in Stockholm three months ago. Everything I do to try to clear my mind is thwarted. At moments like this, hung-over, chaotic, and confused, I understand that I can't offer any resistance. My life is chaotic. I have to accept it as my due.

Agneta brought me aspirins, a glass of water, and coffee in bed. She kissed me lovingly, and asked me very sweetly: 'Why do you get so wild?'

'It's the alcohol.'

'Partly. But there is something else.'

'Mixed cultures.'

'No. It is something more personal. It is you. You wanted to beat me with a whip.'

'I did? I don't remember.'

'Yes. With the whip.'

'Oh, no. I've never hit anyone.'

'You were a boxer.'

'It's been years since I've boxed.'

'Precisely. You have a lot of desires, accumulated over the years.'

'Oh, please.'

'You must remember. You wanted to beat me last night.'

'Okay, yes. I'm a sadist. So what? I'd like to give you four lashes, and you'd love it too. And after that I'd piss in your face. And you'd like that even more. You'd be crawling after me, begging for more. Shit!'

She wept like Mary Magdalene. Was she really suffering or was it theater? Crocodile tears? Women weep easily and ultimately you never know. I let her cry for a while: 'That's it, cry, cry a lot. I'm going to give you twenty lashes so you can cry some more and get it over with.'

I go to the bag which I have in the closet. I grab the whip and threaten her.

'Oh, no, no.'

I give her a couple of soft ones on the back. And she likes it, the big hussy. She grows restless and sighs like a bitch (I don't think bitches sigh, but just the same that's what Agneta does: sighs like a bitch and purrs like a cat). She lets herself fall, face down, on the bed: 'Oh, you're crazy. You make me crazy, ahhh . . . you're a sexual pervert.'

'No. I'm sexually tormented. Stormy. A sexual hurricane, ha ha ha.'

I give her a few more soft ones, and she continues to sigh. She seems to have an orgasm. Just with the lashes. Deep down, she's as big a slut as Gloria. I mount her from behind and yes, when I stick it in, her pussy goes 'chucuchucuchucu'. It's like molasses, very rich.

We finish. We stay like that a while, feeling each other. I think I dozed off and heard her ask me: 'Do you want vegetable soup for lunch or cream of mushroom?'

'Either.'

We sleep a little, coiled like snakes, then take a shower. Agneta made lunch in twenty minutes. I exit the bathroom wrapped in my plush beige robe. An Albinoni concerto is playing and the table is perfect: cream of mushroom, roast beef, salad, toast, red wine, fruit. The silence of the neighborhood and the light and the summer sun. Before I sit down at the table, I pour myself a glass of wine, listen to the music, and look out of the window. I always return to the cemetery. It's the peace. From here I can see all of it, and I tell her: 'That cemetery is very beautiful.'

'You like it? I thought you detested death.'

'It attracts me and I fear it. Peace and quiet. Serenity and emptiness. The void. At first you're afraid when you face the void.'

'I like having it here, so close to the house. In the winter it's so beautiful, covered with snow. Everything in white and gray. Snow and gravestones.'

'I believe it's perfect. Stones, earth, grass, trees, and wind. The eternal equilibrium: earth, air, fire, and water. You understand, Agneta, how much pain is blotted out by death and reborn again? Pain forms part of our spirit. It generates the equilibrium.'

I kiss her on the head. I caress her sweetly: 'You know what's happening, Agneta?'

'No.'

'It's the law of the survivor. The equilibrium of this cemetery amazes me. I like to know that it exists and that it's there. But we don't live in cemeteries or in eternity. This fragment of time, or eternity, which is called life, is brutal, savage, and painful. And you have to survive. Whichever way you can. With tooth and nail. You have to defend yourself and struggle.'

'You're a bit aggressive.'

'As I need to be.'

'Sometimes the place where you live . . .'

'Always. It's decisive. You can't imagine what it's like living another way. In a very poor country. With no work and very little money, there's no food, there's no solution, every day you have to get some dollars however you can. Poverty is a vicious circle. A trap. Morality and ethics are a heavy burden, that's why you put them aside to leave your hands free, to struggle with tooth and nail.'

'I would do the same.'

'Naturally. Anyone would. Unless you had water in your veins.'

'Well, let's have lunch. The soup is getting cold.'

She served me. I tasted it: 'Uhmm, it's very nice. When you want to be, you're a good cook.'

'Thank you. When you want to be, you're a gentleman.'

22

A gallery in Gothenburg was going to inaugurate a group exhibition of four painters. They would include ten of my canvases. I rev up my batteries to be there personally, arrange the show and sell all ten of them. I can't go back to Cuba with empty pockets. The trip would be quick and easy in the non-stop train from Stockholm to Gothenburg. But there was something I hadn't counted on: my beloved little woman wasn't about to part with her prey.

'Ah, Pedro Juan, we can go in the car. I'll drive.'

'It's too far. You're going to be exhausted. And in the summer, with so much traffic, so many accidents. No, no!'

'It's not far, and I won't be tired. Fine . . . if you want to go alone. It's up to you.'

She makes a face halfway between rage and grief and falls silent. Ah, shit, this woman sticks to me like an Amazonian leech. I give her a little kiss and caress her: 'Sure, honey, sure. Don't get upset. We'll both go. Okay.'

And right away she reveals her plan. She had it all prepared! She has a brain, this bitch: 'Well, if you want, we can leave early tomorrow and stop on the way for a night at my girlfriend's farm. They live in a very beautiful forest area. You'll love it.'

She calls her friend to tell her we'll spend the night. She packs a bag for the trip. She takes care of everything with maximum efficiency. I don't have to think. Well, after all, why should I complain?

The next day we leave the house by mid-morning. That afternoon, after getting lost on little roads and trails through huge groves of trees, we finally arrive at the farm: it's beautiful. Agneta had given me a briefing on the situation: 'Margaretha was a press photographer for years, married to a fat guy, crude and covered with tattoos. They say he spent many years in prison. They had two children but no one understood that marriage. Finally they divorced and she began a new life. She left journalism, bought this farm, came here with her kids, began to work as a freelance photographer and started to have lesbian relationships.'

'And you also started to . . .?

'To what?'

'You began too?'

'I don't understand.'

'You had an affair with her?'

'Me? Oh, ha ha ha. No. We haven't seen each other for many years. Just talked on the phone.'

I began to think of things. I imagined that the farm was a little brothel and that I'd be able to do as I pleased. Wrong. Margaretha is a gentleman farmer, strong, serious, masculine. She looks like a man. She's through with photography. She has a partner. They sell milk and make ceramics. They're tiresome nature-lovers. They give the impression they don't even have sex on Friday nights. We had a soirée with herb tea and symphonic music. I very graciously allowed the three women to speak Swedish, saying: 'Ah, it's fine with me,' but with a growing desire to whip out my prick and whack off, fuck Agneta right there, do something to stir things up so they'd live a little. I was in need, at least, of a little vodka and a cigar. I seemed to be listening to Mozart, but I was starting to freak out. That's when Agneta told me: 'Pedro Juan, Margaretha wants to show you a very special collection of photos. She worked six years as a photographer in an institute of forensic medicine and she wants to do a book.'

'Ah, yes, fine.'

'Not here. I don't want to see them. You really want to?'

'What's the mystery?'

'They're corpses.'

'And why don't you want to see them?'

'Oh, no. Oh, no, no.'

Margaretha and I climbed up to her studio. She showed me her files: 'There are about forty thousand photographs here.'

'Six years of your work.'

'Exactly. I have a selection of two hundred photographs in this folder. The book will be entitled *Death*. Only photos, no text at all.'

'I see.'

I took the folder in my hands. I sat in a very comfortable easy chair. Margaretha arranged a lamp so I would have good light and sat far from me. They were horrible photos. All in color. I had never seen anything like it. Putrified cadavers half buried in the woods, old hanged men with their eyes bugging out, children murdered with hatchets and their parents, suicides, beside them; two gays embracing each with a knife in his back; the corpses of drowned people eaten by fish; a policeman who shot his wife and then killed himself by smashing his head against the wall.

Margaretha asked me: 'Are you afraid?'

'Nauseated.'

'That's what I want. If you'd like to stop, it's all right.'

'I want to go to the end.'

'It's hypnotic.'

She was right. I was looking at it completely hypnotized. I came to the end and went back to look at some. A series of four photos of a mass murder especially bewitched me. It was an orgy. Eight cadavers. There were whips, leather gear, dildoes, vibrators, an enormous bed, everything all over the place. A guy had been videotaping it and had suddenly pulled out a pistol and murdered everyone. Then he killed himself. The horror and fear in those rotting bodies were terrible, some still on top of others, it was infernal. The police discovered the place a month later. It didn't look real. It was revoltingly fascinating. I would have liked to have those photos myself. It would have turned me on to have been there and taken those pictures myself and to have seen the video again and again.

'Will you publish the book, Margaretha?'

'Three publishers have seen it. They don't want it. But I keep trying, I think it's a good book.'

'I think it's splendid. Too brilliant for such a politically correct age. You won't find a publisher.'

We go downstairs and rejoin the others in the living room. Now I need a whisky and a good Havana cigar. Right now. But all we have is herb tea and silence and this impenetrable darkness surrounding the house.

23

What happened in Gothenburg was predictable enough: I put on my white slacks and a carnivalesque tropical shirt, and walked around smoking an odorous cigar. I had remembered to bring some salsa tapes. They didn't want to put the music on and everything was much too solemn, especially since the other three painters were figurative. Excessively figurative, if you ask me. And what's more they were wearing suits, ties, and black shoes. So I kicked up a fuss worthy of an A-list artist and suddenly there was a nice tape deck. I put on my cassettes. There was nothing but wine. I demanded that they buy a few bottles of rum. The owner of the gallery energetically resisted this second outrage. He refused to spend so much money. Very well. We'll make do with wine. I put on my Caribbean show. I love to be the mambo king. I danced salsa with the most daring ladies and really enjoyed myself. I had a ball in Gothenburg, even though I drank too much. A lady appeared with a lascivious face and pearls and jewels up to her nipples. She was interested in three paintings. We danced, we talked. She had a Warhol and a Rauschenberg in her collection and I don't know what else. Piles of money, probably. And me playing the gigolo to sell her my humble little paintings. She wanted us to dine together. Impossible. Agneta was drinking liters of sparkling water and wouldn't leave my side for a minute. I introduced her as my European agent. I was a bit drunk. She, stone-cold sober, rapidly added: 'We have a beautiful relationship. I am his fiancée as well as his representative.'

Incredibly, she pretended to be drunk and repeated the same sentence first in English, then in French, and, finally, in Swedish! The lascivious lady disappeared in a minute. The end of the story is that I sold only one unimportant painting. Hey, man! I can't go on like this, with this dame running after me all over Sweden.

When I get back to Cuba, everybody's gonna think that I have my pockets full and if I don't throw myself a tremendous welcome-home party, they're gonna say I'm a cheapskate and a tightwad. Ah, cruel world, how unjust you are.

We return to Stockholm, and the next day I take her with me to a tattoo parlor. It's in a basement, close to home. The usual: the walls covered with thousands of drawings. They do piercing, they have a terrarium with a black widow immobile in the dark, lying in wait for a grasshopper. An old slot machine. Heavy metal playing at full volume, trophies the guy has won at European tattoo competitions. Industry magazines. Bronstein, the owner and designer, is a mammoth Viking who has tattoos on his eyelids. We look around, check the prices, and leave. I want to engrave Agneta with a red heart crossed by a banner which says: 'Pedro Juan'. On one breast, two millimeters from her nipple. Wow! It really ought to say: 'Pedro Juan is my man', but for the moment I don't want to frighten my dove. I'll get her another one later which states everything clearly. I'd like a big eagle with its wings spread, or a roaring panther. Black, on my left arm, high up, next to the shoulder. We are discussing this as we leave: 'I like the black eagle for you, but not so big.'

'The smaller one looks better on a woman.'

'That big is very vulgar.'

'And I'm a distinguished gentleman? With the face of a guy who jerks off on the roof.'

'Oh, Pedro Juan, I don't know . . .'

'Would you like it if I belonged to the Rotary or the Lion's Club, like your father?'

'No, no, please, no. But I don't want you to be vulgar either.'

'Each of us is what he is. And don't fuck with me or I'll get pissed, buy the ink, and do your tattoo myself.'

'You? You don't have a machine.'

'Like in jail, with a pin.'

'Oh, how painful. My grandmother had a tattoo like that. She told me that it hurt a lot.'

'What a tremendous old lady!'

'When they did it to her, she wasn't old.'

'Uhmmm.'

'She was five, and her ten-year-old brother grabbed her and tattooed an anchor on her arm.'

'That bastard! He was a son of a bitch from birth.'

'A friend helped him. They restrained my grandmother. She wasn't my grandmother yet. They grabbed the girl, tied her up with a rope and . . . with a pin.'

'The guy was sadistic. Is he still alive?'

'We don't know. When he was fourteen years old, he disappeared. He said he was sailing to America, as a cabin boy, to make his fortune. These were poor country people. No one believed he would do it. But, a few days later, he disappeared and that was the last they ever heard of him. Maybe I have relatives in America.'

'When was this?'

'About 1900 or a bit later. There was a lot of poverty here. People were emigrating to America.'

'Be careful. I'm a sadist, just like your great-uncle.'

'Oh, no, please. Don't get like that. Once is enough.'

'You'll like it. You'll discover your masochistic side.'

'Pedro Juan, sometimes you are a wild gorilla.'

'All of us gorillas are wild. Some of us seem to be domesticated, but it's only a trick to be able to live in the city.'

'Ha ha ha, crazy man!'

'I like you a lot, Agneta.'

'You don't love me?'

'It's very difficult to love. I believe the word has no nuances in English. All you can say is "I love you". But in Spanish we have them.'

'Which ones?'

'"*Te quiero*" and "*me gustas*" are less serious than "*te amo*" or "*te adoro*".'

'All of those are on a scale?'

'At least in *my* Spanish it's like that.'

'Then you explain this to me to tell me you don't love me?'

'The semantics of love. I want you and I like you. That's it. Don't rush me because I'm slow.'

'As for me, I love you. Totally. I love you.'

'Better. You start suffering now. I'll catch up to you later.'

We went often to the nude beach. With my very dark sunglasses, I can act like radar. Finally Agneta takes off all her clothes. I ask her: 'Does it excite you now or are you still repelled?'

'Ha ha ha.'

She's Machiavellian. When she falls silent it's because she's thinking about things she doesn't care to reveal.

'I like to see you naked in front of everyone. We're fine. We're a fuckable couple.'

'Oh, Pedro Juan, don't speak like that.'

'Why do you think we fuck two or three times a day? Because you excite me, I like you, every day you're more affectionate. Put them all together. And the tits. What I like most about you are the tits and the silence.'

'The silence?'

'Yes. A silent woman is the ardent desire of every man. Silent, with nice tits. A luxury!'

'In the *Dirty Trilogy* there's a woman with big tits and afterwards you don't like her.'

'Explosive affairs. It was a true story.'

'Completely true?'

'Completely. Her saggy tits discouraged me and I couldn't get a hard-on. She got very offended and was angry with me for more than two years. But we had to see each other and speak to each other almost every day at work and so we remained friends.'

'Ah, what a life you've had! My life is very gray.'

I remain silent. I haven't told her the whole truth. It grieves me. What really happened was that, after the affair, I insisted on retaliating. The immaturity of the tropical male. If it were now, I'd forget in two minutes. But I went so far as to insist that we be friends. I mollified her with roses and gladioli. She agreed to go out with me two or three nights. A friend lent me his car, and that's when I put it to her. In the dark of the road I couldn't see her tits. I suppose it was dark, I can't remember. The truth is we had sex frequently. All very normal. Nothing memorable. The short story has a calm and placid ending, but really it was a disaster. It went like this: the crisis and the hunger started at the beginning of the '90s. She lost her job because they closed up the fire-extinguisher plants. She began to sell on the black market. Sometimes I bought beef or horsemeat from her. But she cheated me on the weight. It was always half a kilo light. I pretended not to notice and let it go. If we were having sex together, I wasn't going to appear ridiculous by complaining about a piece of meat. But one day she shorted me four kilos. It was too much. I lost my patience and we had a big fight. We offended one another. It was definitive. We're no longer even friends. We began bad and ended worse.

That's how it goes. Life is much more complex than literature. But also less intense. Literature has to go full speed ahead to keep up the tension. Otherwise it would be a tiring, boring trip. You select fragments, write, and try not to be boring. Ultimately, intuition is the only guide I have. A bit of intuition. And that's not much to go on.

24

I spent the whole morning reading. Agneta went to look at an apartment for rent nearby. Similar to this one but less expensive. By eleven, I was tight and needed to move my muscles. I ran through the woods awhile. When I returned, there she was making lunch. I showered, opened a can of beer, put on Pergolesi's *Stabat Mater*, and went to the kitchen to help. There was nothing left to do. Lunch was salad, cheese, bread, and smoked salmon.

'You haven't mentioned the apartment. Did you see it?'

'Uhmm . . .'

'Very bad? Dirty?'

'No, it would be perfect. Cheaper than this one, bigger, but . . . it's impossible.'

'Why?'

'The woman who lived there committed suicide three days ago. Her sister showed me the apartment as if nothing had happened.'

'Naturally. If you startle a possible tenant . . .'

'That's not it. Everything was exactly as she left it: clean plates and glasses in the draining rack. Invoices and bills stapled and put in order on the table. The bed made. The soaps and toothpaste half used in the bathroom. Everything in its place, as if the woman were going to return at any moment. Today is Friday. Tuesday morning she got up, had breakfast, put everything in meticulous order, went walking along the railroad tracks and flung herself from the precipice of the second bridge.'

'That bridge always impresses me. It's so high.'

'She seems to have done it all with a level head. Calculating every step, as if she were going to buy a refrigerator. Her sister was very calm. They buried her on Wednesday and, an hour later, hung the sign on the balcony "Apartment for rent".'

'Very rational. That's good. And if you want, I can go with you and help you decide.'

'Not for anything in the world. Even if they gave it to me as a gift, I wouldn't live there.'

'Neither would anyone in Cuba. But we are emotional and superstitious people. You would think the Swedes . . .'

'Ah, don't simplify things, Pedro Juan.'

'I think it's the same everywhere. People who die violently keep wandering. They're dark spirits. They need light to detach.'

'The spirit keeps wandering?'

'That's what the mediums say.'

'That's how it felt to me.'

'Really?'

'When I entered the apartment, I felt something strange, disagreeable. I felt bad. Slightly depressed, melancholy, I really don't know how to describe it. We began to look at the rooms, and this woman is telling me about last Tuesday's suicide, very matter of fact, as if she were speaking about someone she didn't know. Then I noticed that the feeling of heaviness was growing stronger.'

'And you left in a hurry.'

'When I got out on the street, I began to breathe easier and everything was all right.'

The music in the background was still the *Stabat Mater*. The final moments were playing: *Quando Corpus Morietur*. I immediately replaced it with a record of Pablito F.G. singing erotic salsa.

We continued eating. She was drinking tonic water. We spoke about quinine, stimulants, ginger.

'They say it's an aphrodisiac. In Havana, there's a down and out bar in Cuatro Caminos which sells ginger tea with quail eggs.'

'I don't believe in aphrodisiacs.'

'I do.'

'It seems absurd to me.'

'Everything may seem absurd. Or not. There are borders which you can only cross by yourself. When you want to share them with someone else, they vanish.'

'I don't understand.'

233

'What you have just finished telling me about this errant and depressive spirit.'

'Oh, but it's totally true. You know that I don't tell lies and I'm not crazy.'

'And if I tell you that the first time I was in Mexico I knew nothing of chilies. And I was eating chili pepper sauce and had an almost permanent erection. I was astonished. I thought I was going to go mad. I couldn't imagine what had happened. It was like a hypersexual energy. Finally, on the fourth or fifth day, a Mexican told me that, in some people, chilies act like aphrodisiacs, and so I immediately stopped eating them.'

'And?'

'The erections diminished. I couldn't take it any more. I'd wake up in the middle of the night with my prick like a roofbeam. I was jerking off three or four times a day. I thought I was going to die.'

'Oh, I believe you.'

'Of course. You have to believe me. I also believe your story about the spirit. I've had many experiences like that. And worse. But I don't like to speak of the dead. In this bar in Cuatro Caminos there are always old guys drinking ginger with quail eggs.'

'But these old men should not be interested in sex.'

'These guys are. They're old hustlers. Street people. And they like to stay in shape. Many of them die fucking a little slut. They say that's the perfect death: cardiac arrest with a hard cock while fucking a little slut for a few pesos.'

'Oh, how horrible!'

'Nothing horrible about it. The ideal death. Whether you're ninety or a hundred, you're an emotional animal. It's the last vagina of your life. But you don't know it'll be the last. Your prick is stiff. And suddenly your pump fucks up on you. You grimace and you die. In these cases, the whores, who always charge in advance before removing a single article of clothing, make three hundred signs of the cross with their right hand, reciting the Lord's Prayer and Hail Mary Full of Grace and, with their left, they pull out the cock and flee, leaving the dead man lying there for others to find. I'd like to die like that.'

234

'So they can burn you later.'

'Exactly. No rotting under the earth. Purifying fire.'

'I have never understood that about men. They can separate sex from everything else. I cannot have sex with someone I do not love.'

'It's not a matter of men and women. It's a question of point of view. I have always enjoyed sex. Love is another matter. It has happened with women who really turned me on sexually. But it was only that moment. It would be a useless complication if love, tenderness, and good feelings were added to sex. Don't you agree?'

'No. For me, it's the opposite.'

'How so?'

'I would have preferred it with some men if they had been less cultivated and had more . . .'

'Sex?'

'Uhm.'

'Sex?'

'Uhm.'

'Yes or no?'

'Yes.'

'And it scares you to say so? That's normal.'

'Ohh.'

'Speak, use the language. Sure those men were very refined, but they didn't know to thrill you so you never had an orgasm. What's worse, they were unaware of that and always very pleased with themselves.'

'Yes, but, ohh . . .'

She blushes.

'And with me it's the opposite. Nice cock, but half savage.'

'You're not half savage.'

'You say I resemble a gorilla.'

'Sometimes.'

With this conversation and the erotic salsa playing, I became aroused. I lifted up her blouse and she wasn't wearing a bra. She doesn't need one. Her tits are beautiful, large and firm. But I don't want to repeat myself. Someone might think that I'm obsessed with sex. The only problem is, I have to control myself. I get upset when I see she doesn't want to give me head or let me sodomize her. One of these days I'm going to lose control and slap her around until she lets me. And that's not right. I need to control myself. All women aren't the same. Gloria has her wildest orgasms when I give her a few backhands, spit on her, throw her to the floor, stomp on her, piss in her face. Or give her a few resounding smacks on the ass. She digs them and comes like a bitch in heat, telling me: 'That's it, *papi*, beat me some more, come on, I'm a battered daughter, beat me some more.' But that's a crazy, passionate mulatta. If I did the same to this Swede . . . Well, who knows? Maybe she'd surprise me and do the same as Gloria: come like a bitch in heat and even begin to ovulate. Who knows? At least now she likes the whip.

25

We wind up wasted and fall asleep, for half an hour at the most. Then it's back to business. This is what turns me off. She's so passive that I'm always the aggressor. Not that I mind that much. We sweat like a couple of beasts and, finally, it all happens. To tell the truth, I made a firm deal with myself not to write about these intimacies. I have to make an effort because I'd like to describe everything in great detail. But I won't. I suppose Swedish vibrations are moving me in the direction of moderation and silence.

Later we take a hot shower and adjourn to the balcony, with coffee and ice cream. She insists that we go for a walk. I don't want to. I pick up a book and try to read. Really, I feel tired. I no longer have the prowess for two consecutive fucks, but I don't want to admit it.

'I want to see some paintings in a gallery. It's near here.'

'No, Agneta, no. Go by yourself.'

'No, not alone.'

'Are you anxious?'

'A bit.'

'Go take a walk. I'm relaxing.'

'I'm going to the supermarket to buy milk. You want something?'

'No. I'm fine.'

She leaves. I'm anxious too. A little restless. But I don't want her to know. It's getting close to the end. There are only a few days left for me here, and I'm weary. Too much sex. We're exhausted. Sometimes I think of moderation and discretion and am on the verge of creating a program to control my eating, drinking, tobacco, sex, and physical exercise. But I continually violate it, and give in to my excesses. Perhaps that's at the root of my restlessness.

I lie down. I can't take a siesta, I'm too wound up. Mr. Nice Guy is missing. I put on Radio Match. The announcer offers up a vertiginous promotion of supermarket summer sales followed by 'a new CD by Orlando Contreras, famous Cuban bolero singer'. This borders on the absurd. A bolero by a Cuban from Miami broadcast by a small station on the outskirts of Stockholm. I jump up to tape it:

> Wherever I happen to be
> I always yearn to return.
> Some day I'll go back
> to the place where I was born,
> from which they made me leave.
> And I'll go back
> to the place of my loves
> where I left the flowers
> faded without my heat.
> Oh, holy God,
> why make me suffer?
> Look, I want to go back.
> I don't want to die here.

Next they play 'So long, Marianne'. Today somebody very nostalgic is programming Radio Match. I tape the bolero and listen to it a couple of times. Often we try to change life. To have more control, to anticipate things. To foresee the consequences of each decision. But no. We're like those crazy ants which run over each other in the garden and lose their way again and again. That night we went to a place in the countryside to dance salsa. It's something like a clearing in the woods, with an old wooden floor on which to dance. They were selling food and drink and the Stockholm Soneros were in charge of the music. They're Swedish, the singer is Uruguayan, and they play Cuban music. They're not bad at all. We danced a little, said hello to some people we knew, bought a couple of beers. The late afternoon was very slow and beautiful. It began to cool down, and we returned to the car to get our jackets. There was a melancholy vibe between us. It was inevitable. We tried to avoid it by dancing, laughing, talking with our friends, but the angel of sadness was flying silently overhead. We put on our jackets, locked the car, and walked back on a path through the woods. It was very still and peaceful. All at once Agneta took my hand and squeezed it hard to stop me. She looked into my eyes and said: 'Don't leave.'

'What are you saying?'

'Don't go back.'

'Ah, Agneta, you don't know what you're saying.'

'We can get married tomorrow.'

'No, no, no. Don't even think about it.'

'Ehhh . . . if we did you would be legal. They would give you citizenship.'

'I told you no.'

'Why not?'

'It's not in my plans.'

'You have no plans. You don't like to plan or to wait for anything.'

'Don't complicate things. I don't want to live here.'

'Because of the language?'

'Because of everything.'

'Because of me too?'

And the tears began to flow.

'Hey, wait a minute. No weeping or drama. Things are clear between us, so no last-minute desires.'

'Speak more slowly, please. I don't understand.'

'No weeping. No more tears.'

'You are an animal and a . . .!'

'A what?'

'A stupid man. You are a stupid man!'

We were raising our voices. She dropped my hand and headed back toward the dance floor. I followed her, slowly. And with my mind a blank. I had been very clear about it from the beginning. Stay in Sweden? No fucking way! Then a little light bulb went on in my head. I caught up to her: 'Let's go to Cuba.'

239

'I've already thought about it. It's impossible.'

'Why impossible?'

'I wouldn't be able to work. Here it would be good for both of us.'

'If I have to stay here, I'll die like a little bird in a cage.'

We stood there together for a while in silence. The orchestra was playing a rumba.

'Let's not speak any more about this subject, Agneta. It's not worth the pain.'

'Fine.'

We returned home early and spent some time on the balcony looking at the stars. We each took a turn in the bathroom, and then went to bed. I was tired but I was traveling in crammed buses and carrying very heavy bags and knapsacks. People were pressing against me and I had to take care of all that baggage. I was standing in the aisle and couldn't see through the windows. I was surrounded by many people. It was claustrophobic. I was feeling short of breath, so I got off, dragging my bundles as best I could, and found myself in a strange city. Around me people were speaking, but not in any language I recognized. I understood nothing and didn't know where I was. I climbed on another bus as crowded as the last one, dragging those bags and knapsacks full of stuff. I hadn't come from anywhere nor did I have a destination. I was going nowhere but I couldn't stop moving. I had to keep on like this forever, hauling those bundles, without being able to rest and without understanding anything. It was agony. It was a sentence. I was condemned to travel for ever on those airless buses packed with people, never knowing why. I stepped off some and I climbed on others. I had to keep going and going even though there wasn't enough air and I couldn't breathe. I woke up frightened. What had happened? I fought a desperate impulse to get out of bed and go to the balcony to get some fresh air. There was a little light in the room. I lay staring at the ceiling, trying to calm my breathing, Agneta warm by my side. I sensed her big tits and remembered a photo of Dracula, with his black cape and his fangs and his diabolical eyes. He was carrying a very beautiful woman in his arms, getting ready to sink his teeth into her neck. Gloria has this image, hidden under a piece of black cloth, on her altar, next to other images of saints and a crucifix. On one occasion, I found myself alone in her room and I decided to check it out. She had mixed her Catholic saints with her African deities. I lifted up the black cloth and there was Dracula. I put everything back in place and told her nothing. A few weeks later, Gloria and I were talking about a gold chain I wanted to buy: 'I've wanted one for years, but I never have enough money.'

'Buy a cheap one.'

'I don't wear junk, Gloria. It has to be thick and good gold. A masculine chain. And with a gold crucifix.'

'No, sweetie, no crucifix.'

'Why?'

'Don't wear crucifixes because you'll look too noble. Kind of a fool.'

'I will?'

'Of course. You have to keep the Devil inside. If you're too noble, they'll crush you.'

Staring at the ceiling, I remembered that: 'If you're too noble, they'll crush you.' That's it. I have to pull myself back together and continue to be as diabolical as ever. 'The son of a bitch I carry around inside of me has been sleeping in this country,' I thought. 'I have to get out of here fast or I'll turn into an imbecile.'

I drew Agneta to me, and we snuggled up even closer. She was completely naked and warm. I had a lovely feeling of well-being. I closed my eyes to go back to sleep and again began to think about Gloria's Dracula. I mustn't ever forget him. I can't let the son of a bitch sleep.

Sometimes I'd like to retire to a monastery and withdraw from everything, but I know I couldn't take too much solitude either. The past, the present, and the future overwhelm me. I try to take control but it's useless. I never control anything. I cut off the Hydra's heads and more and more heads replace them. It appears there's no solution. In the end, just like everyone, I have a long list of all kinds of conflicts, problems, hates, fears, and fuckups. I'd like to forget about them and live in purity but I can't. Deep within, I don't want to. To live happily is naïvety. Sometimes I understand that I'm going to drag all this around for ever. They're like tattoos that are etched so deep inside that you can never remove them. They're there for ever. I continued my deep breathing and I believe I finally went back to sleep.

The following day we went fishing in the canal. When we got there and threw out our lines, there wasn't a single bite and a cold breeze began blowing, so we took off. On the way home, we had time to kill. We made a detour down a very narrow road and visited the remains of a farm from the Iron Age. It's a protected archeological site which dates from about 700 BC, maybe even a bit earlier. All that's standing are the ramparts of four buildings built with enormous stones. They think that a fire razed the farm. The archeologists have constructed a model. There were four big naves, about one hundred and fifty feet long by twenty or so feet wide. Some very simple low walls: just stones piled on top of each other and, above them, a roof of wood and straw. Everyone lived together: men, women, children, cows, sheep, swine. They forged some objects from iron, brewed wheat beer, made soup from herbs and onions. Three or four men and one or two women lived in some of those houses. They'd all make love together, I suppose, and have children between them without ever knowing who was whose father. And they would be infinitely grateful for a simple glass of beer or a little warmth or that the snow melted with the coming of spring or to be able to satisfy their sexual desires. They would die young. A cold or an infected molar might consign them to the brief memory of oblivion. They knew they were no more transcendent than one of those pigs with whom they shared a roof, warmth, and food.

The farm is in the midst of a beautiful, dense forest. I walked through there in silence and understood their way of life like a flash of light inside me. Two thousand seven hundred years have passed. It's nothing. A breath of wind in the galaxy. The thousandth of a second in the universe. That instant had been enough to fill us with aspirations and desires. Enough for us to consider ourselves very important, decisive, transcendent, infinite. I enjoyed that Iron Age farm.

III

Fury and Bolero

1

When I returned to Havana, I needed a number of weeks to readjust. I prefer to forget those final days in Sweden, Agneta's continual weeping, my uneasiness. Sometimes it was contagious and I started to cry myself. Crocodile tears but nevertheless. Afterwards, I traipsed around Germany with my fucking paintings but nothing came of it. I didn't sell anything. Finally, after almost six months in Europe, I landed with two hundred shitty dollars in my pocket. After being closed up the entire time accumulating humidity, the reception in my little house in Central Havana was authentically tropical. The plaster walls were falling to pieces and the bathroom pipes were blocked. When it was used, the dirty water leaked through the ceiling of the apartment below and through the outside wall which was covered in mildew and seemed about to collapse. To avoid using it, I had to go back to the primitive custom of shitting in a paper bag and throwing it on the neighbor's roof.

I called Gloria three days in a row. Her mother kept my hopes alive by telling me: 'She went on an errand. She'll be back soon.' I knew that she was out there somewhere with a man. On the fourth day she appeared, looking scared. She flung herself around my neck, kissing me, but I felt her trembling: 'Oh, *papi*, you're back at last!'

'*Papi* my dick! I came back four days ago and you've been gone. Where were you?'

'Oh, sweetie, we haven't seen each other for six months and that's the way you say hello? Don't be rude.'

I grabbed her, kissed her and, as the smell of her armpits reached me, my rage was forgotten. We climbed into bed and it was the sweetest, most beautiful fuck in the world. I'm nailing her deep inside, when she says to me: 'You're going to pop my ovaries, you fucker, give me more, give it to me. Ah, it's so hard! That's what

I call a prick. That's it. Make me come, fucker. You're going to be my man for the rest of my life.'

You have to be both a bull and an artist to make her come. She knows all the whores' tricks to get her client excited and see to it that the guy pays first, has a quick orgasm and leaves the runway free for the next landing. And she's as fresh as a lettuce. But, after three years, I know her ways. I know how to do it. Finally we finish two hours later. I open a bottle of aged rum. Two glasses. On the rocks. I love seeing her like this: a cinnamon-colored mulatta, naked, thin as spaghetti, drinking rum, smoking. Her hands and feet are unkempt and a bit ruined from walking the streets so much and from scrubbing and cleaning. She's a vulgar, lowlife slut and I adore her. I think about all of this while I'm taking sips of rum and smoking a good cigar. She puts on a cassette of boleros. We sit silently, worn out, resting. Someone sings:

> I know you lie when we kiss,
> That you lie when you say: 'I love you.'
> Lie to me eternally because
> Your wickedness makes me happy.
> Does it really even matter
> Since life itself is a lie?
> Lie to me some more because
> Your wickedness makes me happy.

'I've always loved that.'

'To tell lies and deceive all the women?'

'No. To sing boleros.'

'And I to dance. Now my cousin wants me to start dancing again. In the Palermo. Will you let me, *papi*?'

'You like to play the wife: "Will you let me, *papi*?" And in the end you do whatever the fuck you please.'

'Oh, no, baby, don't say that. Don't be crude.'

'Listen to this bolero. That's what you do to me. "I know that you lie when we kiss, that you lie when you say: 'I love you.'"'

'What a beautiful voice! Continue, continue. That male voice knocks me for a loop.'

'Hey, I came back four days ago. Where the hell were you?'

'Oh, baby, you want to know everything. That cannot be.'

'Yes it can be because I'm your husband, you little slut, and I have to know everything.'

'You my husband? Not by a long shot.'

'Where did you go?'

'Why didn't you let me know you were coming? You should have told me to wait for you at home.'

'I couldn't.'

'You don't trust me. You wanted to surprise me.'

'Of course I mistrust you, you're a streetwalker. I caught you off base.'

'Don't treat me like this, my darling.'

'Where were you hiding?'

'And back he comes to the same thing.'

'Speak.'

'Ahh.'

'Ahh nothing. Speak.'

The whip came into play. I had it in the bottom of my bag.

'What is that?!'

'This is for you.'

'You told me in a letter that . . . ah, shit, don't hit me hard!'

'Turn over on your front.'

'Ah, no, no. Don't hit me hard.'

She turned over on her front. I gave it to her softly on the buttocks. She went crazy.

'Oh, it's so good, you're my superman, billygoat, whore's son, fucker, you're the man, give me some cock, shove it up my ass or wherever you want.'

I started licking her ass, sucking her pussy, and whipping her softly.

'Ah, give it to me, I want cock, you madman! Whip me more. It feels good!'

'Speak first, and then I'll give you more cock. Speak.'

'What do I say, what do you want, *papi*, what do you want?'

She turns face up, opens her legs, and puts me inside her: 'I was with a Mexican, *papi,* in Guanabo. Stingy and miserable like his mother's cunt.'

'How much did he give you?'

'Only a hundred dollars. And I spent four days with him.'

'I'm surprised a spider like you could fall off the wall.'

'That's it, that's it, hammer it in deep. I took a bunch of stuff out of his suitcase. I got him drunk, he snorted a lot of coke and sank like a stone. I took everything: clothes, towels, perfumes, the son of a bitch tried to have his way with me and I fleeced him, ha ha ha. I left him in his underwear.'

We keep at it a little longer. We take a break.

'Baby, I got you some red Mexican jeans. And a very good watch.'

'And they'll fit me?'

'Of course. He thought he could fuck with me, the good-for-nothing son of a bitch. He wanted to screw for free.'

She went down to her place on the seventh floor and brought them back up. A gold, automatic wristwatch and fiery red jeans. I put them on without underpants. Another bolero was playing:

> When you really love someone
> Like I love you
> It's impossible, my angel,
> to live so far apart.

I start to dance very slowly and let down the pants little by little. Through the fly of the red jeans my pubes appear bit by bit and then the thick, dark, excited beast. Very slowly, it inches out, until everything is completely exposed and the jeans fall to the floor.

'These are the Cuban Boys! Just for you. Secretly, exclusively, from the tropics. The Cuban Boys, ladies and ladies, only for you. From Havana, Cuba!'

'Ha ha ha. Where did you learn to do that, you fucker?'

'In D.F.'

'Where's that?'

'In Mexico.'

'Really?'

'A cabaret just for señoritas and señoras. Señoras with lots of money. There were four of us.'

'You never told me that.'

'You take what you can get, Gloria. We did three shows at a hundred dollars a show. For Mexico, that's good. With my three hundred bucks, I went to Tijuana. But that's another story. I was forty years old then.'

'You were harder than now.'

'More muscular. But the star was a skinny little black guy with an enormous prick. The Mexican women would get carried away and scream and come all by themselves. All they did was look, but you could smell their juices in the room.'

'How you have done things, baby. You're a little box of surprises.'

'Just to get those pesos. The same as you, shitty hustler.'

'Me a hustler?'

'No?'

'No. This Mexican crossed my path and I screwed him, but I'm not dedicated to that, *papi*. You're the hustler.'

'Me?'

'You hustled the Swede.'

'Don't talk like that.'

'It's true. An old hustler. How often do you see that? And there's you pretending to be decent and serious. Anyone who sees you on the street would think you're a gentleman.'

'Gloria, what is this crap you're talking?'

'That Swedish broad paid for everything, you lived off her like the tremendous hustler you are.'

'But she was happy with my golden dick.'

'And the men who pay me are happy with my pussy and my art.'

'Hmm.'

'Does it hurt you to hear the truth?'

'Hmm . . . I'm not a hustler, life . . .'

'Life obliges us? Then I'm not a whore. So drop the drama and come back to reality. What do you want me to do, die of hunger?'

'I adore you, baby, it's all the same to me if you roll a gringo or whatever else.'

'I adore you too, baby, keep hustling the Swede. But don't stay over there.'

'I'd die if I stayed there.'

'Really? It must be nice.'

'It depends what you mean by nice. I missed you so much.'

'Me too. Every day I thought of you, at least twenty times.'

'You may be a whore, but I love you.'

'An artist, an artist. What is a whore? An artist, an actress. It was perfect in Milagros' cathouse. They didn't know that theater was my thing. I staged a different play for each client. And they hung around. I took care of three or four a day. They hung around and paid more, ha ha ha.'

'We're from the same trade union.'

'We're two artists, baby. When I was dancing, it was the same. Me and my erotic dances. I was the star of the Palermo. Nobody knew if it was the truth or a lie. Not even I knew if what I was dancing was fake or really erotic.'

'Just like me with my novels. Not even I know what's real and what's a lie.'

'In the end everything is true.'

'Hmm.'

'You're a whore, Pedro. You're as much of a whore as me. You sell a lie and pretend that it's true. Ha ha ha.'

'A whore with balls. In other words, a pimp.'

'The Swedish broad isn't a whore, you hustled her.'

'Forget about the Swede. I'm your pimp.'

'The Swede's gigolo and my pimp. You're a star, made to order for me, my sweet hunk of man. Give me more rum.'

We drink a little more. She was right. The Swede furtively handed me her wallet under the table and I paid with her money. I liked that, and it excited me. It seemed to me it got her wet too. She never allowed me to spend a single dollar. In my bag, I find some robots that I brought as a gift for Gloria's son.

'Oh, baby, how beautiful. Wait until he sees them. That's what he likes: action figures and little trucks.'

'Like all little boys.'

'I like dolls too.'

'You're a streetwalking slut.'

'I'm your little girl. You want to be my *papi*? Take care of me, baby, buy me a little doll.'

'I brought you some shoes and a Chinese robe.'

I show them to her. It's a red silk dressing gown with an enormous flower embroidered on the back, and some high-heeled shoes. She puts on nothing but the robe and the shoes. *Belle de jour*. The ideal whore. She takes the whip and curls it around her neck, with her hard African hair sticking out after our love-making. This mulatta is irresistible. She has talent and I adore her, fuck it, I adore her!

'I'm going to make a book of photos with you.'

'Naked?'

'Just you. Naked and clothed. I'm going to take the photos over time. *The Woman I Love*, that's the title.'

'Oh, *papi*, everyone's going to see me. Naked, ohh.'

'They've already seen you. You, doing everything, with a very poetic, very brief text. You're my muse.'

'What's that?'

' . . . I don't know . . . my inspiration.'

'Ah, I'm an artist, *papi*.'

'An artist in bed.'

'Don't be vulgar, honey. A ballerina. But my father took me out of that. He said I was going to become a dyke.'

'At any rate, a whore.'

'Well, I don't know. Those were his ideas. My thing is to dance. And yours is to sing boleros?'

'I sing off key.'

'I hope I can keep dancing. Are you really going to do that book of photos?'

'Of course. Now I have a camera and I have you.'

'My cousin wants me to dance at the Palermo with her little group. Are you going to let me?'

'I'll see. I just arrived. Don't nag me.'

2

One night, around eight, Carmita calls me. She lives in Lawton. She's feeling lonely. Her last husband left after eight months. She can't take it any more. Years ago we had a brief relationship. She baptized me 'Golden Cock'. The first night she came to my penthouse, she drank a bit of rum, we kissed, I touched her, she stimulated me, lowered her hands and, when she felt that it was hard, knelt down, unzipped my fly and took it out for some air: 'Oh, how pretty. That's a Golden Cock!'

She told her whole family in Lawton: 'I'm seeing a guy from Central Havana who has such a beautiful cock, it's a Golden Cock.' I don't like to go to Lawton. Her family numbers more than three hundred people, among them whites, mulattos, mottled ones, blacks, Indians. Every time we meet, they greet me slyly. Anyway, we didn't last long because Carmen insisted on using the roof terrace to raise chickens and pigs. She immediately checked out the price of fodder on the black market, found metallic wire for the cages, and bought twenty chicks. I had a hard time getting her out of the house and ridding myself of the pigs and the chickens shitting on my roof.

We continued as friends. Every time she breaks off with a husband, she gets lonely and calls me. Now she's whistling the same old tune: 'Oh, Pedro Juan, everything was going so well but he began to get impertinent and to make unreasonable demands.'

'What demands?'

'That I stay inside the house. He wanted to know where I was going and tried to control me, jealous as a dog. No, no, I'm old enough that I don't want anyone making such demands.'

'You have no patience with men.'

'Nor do you with women. Look what you did to me.'

'We're talking about you, Carmita.'

'It's always the same. They start with lots of love and we fuck four times a day. And it's "how I love you, Carmita", and "this is the way it's going to be for ever". Afterwards, little by little, they get soft and fall into a routine . . .'

'And you can't stand the routine and the boredom.'

'No. I want emotion. I need to fuck a lot, romance, drunkenness, music playing, boleros, a life of adventure. Ah, Pedro Juan, I'm no good at being an old woman!'

'You're going to be a disgraceful old lady. Like so many others. There are many in this world.'

'You think so? It seems to me I'll never be able to settle my head.'

'Well, try to act with more intelligence and less emotion. Because you're going to end up alone and old and . . .'

'Hey, don't frighten me!'

I hear her sobbing on the telephone. I stay silent for a while. I let her vent. She goes on and on. Finally, I interrupt her: 'Carmen, why are you weeping?'

She sniffles and answers me: 'I feel bad, Pedro. I feel very old and alone. I'm getting wrinkles. At least my tits are small so they won't sag.'

'What you are is immature. Do you think you can go on being an eternal adolescent? You have to get used to all this. It comes with age.'

She begins to sob again, harder. Sniffling, she tells me: 'I call you for help and you crush me. I don't know what kind of friend . . .'

'Yes, I'm your friend and I love you, but you're full of drama. You're neither old nor alone. What about your kids?'

'Keep my kids out of this. I'm starting the menopause. It's been three months since I had my period.'

And she sobs and weeps and sniffles.

'Carmita, stop crying. Maybe you're pregnant.'

'No, honey, no. I've already been to the doctor. It's the menopause. I get hot flushes and perspire a lot and I'm nervous, at night I can't even sleep.'

'Shit, you've grabbed all the symptoms for yourself! You're a medical encyclopedia.'

'Ha ha ha.'

'Don't be a drama queen.'

'Oh, don't say these things to me.'

And she keeps weeping into the phone. She's uncontrollable.

'Damn, you're so sensitive I can't even talk to you.'

'Treat me more delicately. Don't be so coarse.'

'Fine, what I want to say is, when another man appears, don't fall in love as if you were an adolescent. Be more intelligent. Do you remember that sailor?'

'Luis. Where are you going with this?'

'The one with the imitation porcelain elephants.'

'Yes. Luisito. Who knows where he is now? I've never had any word from him.'

'If you had acted with more patience he would still be your husband. Sexually, he drove you wild, and he was a nice guy.'

'They're all nice guys and they all drive me wild sexually.'

'You're a crazy dame.'

'Life has granted me that grace.'

'I wrote a story about you and that sailor.'

'I don't believe it! Son of a bitch, what will people say? You used our names?'

'Sure. Carmita and Luis.'

'And you published it?'

'It's called "The Return of the Sailor".'

'I can't believe that you'd be such a son of a bitch. You're a hyena. You're a cannibal. You use your friends, you fuck! Dracula!'

'Ha ha ha.'

'And you have the nerve to laugh . . . let me read it, at least. Where's the book? Did they publish it here?'

'No, over there, in other countries.'

'Lend me one.'

'I have none left. The publisher only gave me ten free copies.'

'What a miser. So I'll go to your house someday soon and read it. And what did you write in this story?'

'The truth. Come whenever you want and read it. And, at the same time, tell me your latest adventures.'

'So you can keep writing my story?'

'If you're lucky, you'll become immortal, like Dulcinea del Toboso.'

'Who's she?'

'Quixote's woman.'

'Ah, are you dumb or what? I don't give a shit about immortality or Dulcinea. A husband with money who'll take care of me and give me some good cock – that's what I need now. So I can get some happiness back in my life.'

'And your oldest boy? Is he still working in the cigar factory?'

'Yes, he helps me a lot. But he has to support his wife, his son, and his mother-in-law on a single salary. Plus little Adrian and me.'

'How old is little Adrian?'

'Fifteen.'

'Already. Any minute now they'll take him away and put him in the army and he'll be off your back, ha ha ha.'

'Boy, how can you be so cynical and so . . .?

'Well, listen, I've got to go. Come by whenever you want.'

'I will, Pedro, take care of yourself.'

I spent the rest of the night without incident. I went to bed early and dreamt a lot. At one point I was fishing in the canal at Sodertalje and got tangled up in the nylon line. That's how it went all night long. Sometimes I dream that I'm falling downstairs or that I'm playing with a tiny little dog who starts to grow, turns into a tiger, knocks me on my back and, now an enormous and exaggeratedly powerful beast, eats me ravenously, tearing me to bits. Luckily, it's been a while since I've dreamt of the stairs or the tiger.

The next morning I arose with an aching body. Perhaps I had fought with the tiger and fallen downstairs but, if so, I couldn't remember it. All my muscles were painful. I made coffee and went out on the roof with a cup. The day was dawning, and Gloria's bracelets were jangling in her seventh-floor kitchen. It was seven o'clock, but she was already playing a cassette of Marco Antonio Solís at top volume:

> There's nothing more difficult than living without you
> living in the hope of seeing you arrive
> My chilly body yearns for you
> but I don't even know where you are.

Gloria had started a tremendous row and was yelling louder than Marco Antonio. Only pieces of what she was saying reached me: 'How stupid can you be . . . I'm going to the police . . . you're so feeble . . . a bandit and a thief.'

I went to the other end of the roof terrace: the lighthouse and the infinite blue sea. It's better to awaken in silence and tranquility. If Gloria and I were to live together it would be difficult. She's too noisy.

In a little while she leaves. I hear the door slam. She takes the boy to school two blocks away. She comes back right away and starts cleaning and washing. I'm quietly painting. Through the opening of the patio I listen to her rubber sandals flopping against the floor. I like this flopping and the sound of her bracelets. Sometimes just hearing those sounds gives me an erection. It's incredible how much I like this mulatta. Around nine, she comes upstairs. She brings a piece of bread and a big jar of tomato sauce. The storm seems to have passed. That's how fickle and volatile she is. Now she's laughing happily.

'What was all the shouting about this morning?'

'What shouting?'

'You were having a row with someone, in the kitchen.'

'You heard me?'

'The whole building heard you. You and Marco Antonio Solís, singing a duet.'

'Nothing, my mother's a pain.'

'Why?'

'Last night a guy I once threw out of the house came back and took an antique bronze lamp. And she let him have it. Stupid idiot!'

258

'There was an antique bronze lamp in your house?'

'Yes, in the middle of the mess. It was in the dining room.'

'I never saw it.'

'Because it didn't work. I had it hidden in a closet. I knew it was worth a shitload of money and that son of a bitch lifted it.'

'I don't understand anything.'

'I was already in bed, sleeping. It was twelve at night. Gilberto arrives and tells my mother that they're going to give him a hundred dollars for the lamp. She believes his story and gives it to him.'

'And now?'

'Now nothing. We lost the lamp. She knows this guy is a bandit and a thief and a swindler and a son of a bitch. I know him well and had to kick him out of my house because of this.'

'It's your fault for taking up with delinquent husbands.'

'I met him in prison, baby, and afterwards he stuck to me and it was a lot of work to peel him off.'

'When were you in prison?'

'I wasn't in prison.'

'And how did you get to know him?'

'Why are you asking so many questions?'

'I'm not asking. You started to tell me the story and now you want to drop it right in the middle.'

'*Papi*, this is the past. It was before I knew you.'

'Cut the theatrics because I'm not jealous. Any husband of yours who's jealous is going to die of heart failure.'

'Why?'

'Because every day there's something new.'

'Don't live in the past. Live in the present, like I do. With your feet on the ground.'

'When you're my age, you're going to say what my friend Yolanda says.'

'What does she say?'

'She's fifty-five years old, and she says that she's fucked one half of Havana and fantasized about the other half.'

'Ha ha ha.'

259

'You're going to be the same.'

'Me? Nothing doing. I'm going to say that I had two husbands, nothing more: my son's father, who is a very decent man and drives the number 195 bus to Guanabacoa, and you, who is going to be the father of all the others.'

'And the rest of your husbands?'

'They'll be forgotten in the night.'

'An extra-long night.'

'Fine, they'll be forgotten in the nights. Maybe there'll be ten thousand nights. But the only ones who'll remain alive are you two, my children's fathers, who are really decent people.'

'And the guy who was in prison?'

'Hey, you don't forget anything! You're a real pain in the butt!'

'Speak.'

'Damn, boy, it's been a while, this was before . . .'

'Yeah, yeah, "before I met you, sweetie".'

'Hey, don't get heavy. A friend told me there was a black guy who'd give twenty dollars and a bag full of clothes and shoes and ladies' stuff to any woman who'd pay him a conjugal visit.'

'And you snapped up the bait.'

'Yes.'

'Did you need papers?'

'No. The guy was in prison for being a con man. He's a brain and had everything rigged. I met a guard at the gate who took me straight to his cell.'

'Were you there a long time?'

'I went in at nine in the morning and got out at five or six in the afternoon. But it was non-stop. Black men are very greedy.'

'You had to fuck a lot for twenty dollars.'

'Too much. He said he wanted me to ask Changó to spring him from jail. All those fucking guys are the same. They think they're sons of Changó and the majority, actually, are sons of Ochún and Yemayá. Which means they swing both ways, with women and men. Fucking a woman or taking it up the ass – makes no difference to them; even though they're always pretending to be so macho.'

'And what was in the bag?'

'The bag was worth more. There were jeans, blouses, perfumes, tennis shoes. Sometimes it was thirty or forty dollars more.'

'Ah, good.'

'The guy was a big shot in the prison. He dressed like a prince, wearing Adidas sneakers, and he had gold caps on both his eye teeth.'

'All of this inside the joint?'

'Yeah, and more. A lot more. You can't even imagine. The guy was managing all kinds of outside business from inside.'

'What kind of business?'

'Wait, wait. You want to know everything.'

'Speak and stop playing the good girl.'

'A little bordello, *papi*, but it slipped through his fingers. I can't remember how long I was with him . . . less than seven months, I think it was. Then he escaped or they released him, I don't know which. After that, he installed himself in my house, broke, without a cent.'

'That complicated things.'

'Finally, I was able to get away from him. I left the house for a few days and called him on the phone, threatened him with the police if he didn't get lost. He had to go.'

'And now he reappears looking for a fight by stealing your lamp.'

'I'd already forgotten all about him. And he's such a fuck that he comes just to steal.'

'You going to go to the police?'

'No! They'll ask me how I know him, check my background and, before I know it, I'll be tangled up in it too. Give me some coffee, baby. It's going to get cold.'

'With a lot of sugar?'

'Mine yes. Stop playing the gringo.'

We drink a couple of cups. She lights up a Popular.

'Gloria, it's too early. That black tobacco is . . .'

'Ah, well, you have to die of something.'

We fall silent for an instant. I know she can't stand silence or calm. She thrives on constant noise and movement. I've clocked it: thirty seconds is the maximum amount of silence she can stand.

'Oh, I haven't told you. I have a job.'

'Dancing or at the hairdresser's?'

'I wish.'

'Selling fresh ham sandwiches?'

'Not even. You won't be able to guess.'

'What is it?'

'In the morgue at the emergency hospital.'

'God forbid!'

'It has nothing to do with the dead. I have to keep a record book.'

'That's all?'

'That's it.'

'You don't have to puncture corpses?'

'No.'

'What kind of records?'

'Oh, shit, I can't remember the word. Analysis of some kind. They told me to come by and take a test this morning.'

'But it's almost ten o'clock already. Why didn't you go earlier?'

'Easy, Pedro, easy. Don't pick a fight. If it's for me, the santos will give it to me. And if not, they'll take it away.'

'Fine, whatever you say.'

She left. I went back to painting and to silence.

I was fine the rest of the morning. Two black men arrived at noon, one young and the other older. They said that they were plumbers. A lady on the third floor sent them to me with her recommendation. I took them to the bathroom.

'The toilet bowl is blocked?'

'Yes.'

'We have to take it apart.'

'Is there no other way?'

'No, we have to do it.'

I wasted the afternoon watching them work. They cut through the floor, found the discharge pipe, and cut that open too. It wasn't blocked. The bathroom and a corner of the bedroom filled up with rubble and shit, and they still didn't know what to do. Then it occurred to me: 'Maybe it's the bowl.'

'No,' said the younger one.

'Why not?'

'The blockages are always in the pipes.'

The older guy gave it some thought: 'Let's check the bowl.'

They check it. Of course, the toilet bowl is blocked. I can't contain myself: 'Come here, boy! So you guys broke all of this up for the hell of it?'

'No, we're going to straighten it all up.'

'No, get out of here. It's already night.'

'Listen, mister, we're not going. You have to pay us.'

I take out fifty pesos and hand it to them: 'Take this and get going.'

'Are you crazy? This job is three hundred pesos.'

'And three hundred more that I'm not going to give you makes six hundred.'

'Listen to me, we're speaking seriously.'

'I'm also speaking seriously. You worked for the hell of it. You took it all apart and, when everything was finally disconnected and in pieces, you didn't know where you were.'

The young one grabbed a sledgehammer and became aggressive:

'Hey, little white man, what's going on? You can't screw me like that.'

'I'm not screwing you, damn it. It's you who are screwing me. What the hell are you charging me three hundred pesos for?'

The older guy got between the two of us: 'Hey, hey, cool it, cool it, nothing's gonna get settled that way. Look, mister . . .'

'Mister nothing. I'm no "mister". They call me "comrade", comrade. I'm a police official, and you better call me "comrade" too. I think I'm going to call the unit now, and we'll take care of this another way.'

The younger one dropped the sledgehammer and shut up. The older guy was speaking: 'No, no. Wait a minute . . . there's been some mistake here . . . Aren't you the journalist from the penthouse? Because Marisol told us . . .'

'No, that's my neighbor. He's still in Sweden. That house is closed. I'm a policeman. But forget about that . . .'

'It's all right, mister, it's okay, I mean "comrade", comrade, it's all right, comrade. Give me the fifty pesos, and we'll come back tomorrow.'

'Take them. And don't come tomorrow.'

I was barely able to contain my laughter until they left. I laughed for half an hour. It was already nine o'clock at night. There was a tremendous stink of shit. Everything was in pieces, and if they find out the truth, they'll be back again to discuss it. So I split. I went down all the dark little side streets, with garbage containers overflowing with putrefaction on every corner. In the bar El Mundo on the corner of Águila and Virtudes, I had a couple of shots of rum. This bar has a very philosophical name. I like it. I like it so much that, even when I'm strolling around with no plan, I always seem to stop there. It's a magnet. I continued on to San Miguel and Amistad and the Palermo. On the billboard there were two big photos of the dance troupe and the orchestra. Some very lovely mulattas. The show began at ten. Okay. I got there on time. I pay the sixty peso cover charge and go in.

3

I sat at the bar for two or three hours, playing it cool, drinking bad rum. And looking at the dancers who were looking at the few gringos sitting at the tables who didn't get it at all. In other words, there was nothing for me. When I'd had enough, I went out on the street to breathe some fresh air. On San Miguel, near Prado, is the old Rex inn. The only thing left is the name painted on the wall. It makes me remember Mignón and the great fucks we had there in the '70s. I had just finished four and a half years in the army and I was nuts. Mignón and those twenty-four-hour orgies were like an electric shock treatment. Now the inn no longer exists and Mignón is dead, maybe, or a dirty, ragged old woman. She'd be fifty, like me, but I'm sure, if she's still alive, she looks seventy. Some day I'll have to gather my courage and go to her house. A little further on is the Okinawa bar. The street is in ruins and covered by an enormous pool of slimy green water that smells like shit. The bar proudly exhibits an enormous placard in front: '3rd Category'. I like it a lot during the day. Now it's closed and dark. There are three black guys and a black chick, all very young, sitting on a couple of large boxes on the sidewalk. This stretch of San Miguel, in back of the Hotel Telegraph, is too dark for my health. They seem to notice that I'm slightly drunk. One of them yells to me: 'Come here, my friend.'

'You come.'

'Come here, buddy. This little girl isn't going to eat anybody. Come close so you can see her.'

The girl opens her legs with a lot of assurance and bursts into peals of laughter. I stand there. The guy draws near. I'm on the sidewalk facing him. He has to go around the huge pool of rancid water and shit. I touch the Swiss Army knife I'm carrying in the pocket of my pants. He wants to come closer to me so he can whisper. I move one step back: 'Keep your distance and speak!'

'Don't be scared, white boy, we're in business. We got whatever you want here.'

'Like what?'

'Rum and reefer on hand. If you want a little powder I can get it fast. And with this little lady you can do anything you like.'

I stay silent, watching him.

'Don't worry, it won't cost you much.'

I remain quiet. The guy thinks that I'm indecisive and says to me: 'If you want to eat rooster meat, speak up. You can pick any one of us here, and he'll get you hot.'

'Hey, I don't give a shit about "rooster meat"? That must be your trip.'

'Ha ha ha, no, it's just that you looked like you couldn't decide what you want.'

'Don't worry, I know. Let's see the grass.'

'All right, come over here.'

'No, bring it here.'

There's no one else in sight. While the guy is crossing in front of me, I have time to turn toward the wall. I pull the biggest blade out of the knife and put it back in my pants' pocket. Now two of them approach. I keep them at a distance. They show me the grass. I smell it.

'That's fine. Give me two.'

'Two bucks.'

'Do I look like a gringo or what? A buck for the two of them.'

'Shit, white boy, you're a sly one tonight. Let me make a living, my friend, don't squash me.'

'A buck for two bags.'

'Okay, hand it over.'

I give him the dollar.

They insist: 'Come, so you can see the girl. She's a little chocolate bonbon, fifteen years old. And we have another one, even more of a baby. Twelve years old, a real cream puff.'

'No, I'm going.'

'They'll do whatever you like. Both of them.'

They try to come closer, smiling, making like friends. They advance a step. I take out the knife and wave it in the air menacingly.

'I'm leaving!'

'Hey, look at white boy, he's hip! He's flashin' a blade at us!'

'Move it, let's go, I don't want to complicate things tonight.'

The other one rises to his feet and shouts to them from the door of the bar: 'What's with white boy? Is he starting to act tragic?'

'No, no. He's cool. Just a little nervous.'

'Nervous my dick. Get out of my way.'

They retreat. They walk around the stagnant pool and stand in the middle of the street. They're furious. One says to me threateningly: 'Listen, white boy, don't ever come this way again 'cause I'm gonna mess with you. I like blades too. I'm crazy about stilettos, just so you know.'

'I'll keep coming here whenever the fuck I want to. This is my neighborhood too.'

'Move. Get going. I'm gonna mess with you and put a hole in your hide. I'm gonna be on the lookout, riding high in the saddle with a stiletto in my hand.'

'You boast too much.'

'You can't get away with threatening me like that! I'm Little Roland from Havana. The tough guy. Today you caught me acting like a good boy 'cause I'm unarmed. Pullin' a blade on Little Roland? You fucked up bad, white boy!'

I walk down San Miguel to Prado. They don't follow me. On Prado and Neptuno there are three little chicks. Jail bait. They look at me and I look at them. Super cuties. I'd love to get all three of them naked in my room. I stand close to them. The skinny little white one says to me: 'Go with me, *papi*, I'll do whatever you want.'

'How much for the three of you?'

The blackest one of the three says: 'A dyke scene? Not me, baby! I don't do tortillas.'

I look her over and start to leave, not caring. I'm smashed. The other two come running up in a hurry: 'Listen, you want a scene with the two of us?'

'You're both under age.'

'So what's the big deal? You ain't got no money!'

'Right. I got nothing.'

'I'll beat your meat for two bucks.'

'Do I have the face of a jerk-off?'

'You don't need a face for that.'

'What I like to do is fuck.'

'Fine, let's fuck, but make up your mind. You can fuck me all you want for five bucks.'

'Get away from me, little girl. You're a minor. Look at the cop over there.'

'He's a friend of ours. Okay, three bucks. Let's go, we could be at it by now. That's a special discount for you.'

'Yeah, sure.'

I keep walking. When I put some distance between us, the other one says loudly: 'Let him go, China, he's gay.'

I turn and tell her: 'Gay like your father, your grandfather, and all of your brothers. What's wrong with you?'

'Deadbeat, tightwad, cheapskate, dirty old man! Go shove your dick up your ass! How dare you walk on the street without money? Pederast!'

It's obvious they don't like to waste their time. I keep walking slowly. Observing the menagerie of sluts, drunks, transvestites, police, old panhandlers, and thinking about *A Lot of Heart*. For the last few days, I've been thinking about the novel a lot. I sit on a bench. I know very well that just thinking isn't going to resolve anything. I have to sit down, organize the thousands of notes I've taken and make a start. Then I remember that I have two bags of weed in my pocket. And there are cops all around me. I walk to San Lázaro. There's a lot of confusion in the neighborhood. I'd better head home.

I climb the stairs one by one. I'm dead drunk. Ah, shit, now I remember, I haven't eaten anything! On the seventh floor, I knock on Gloria's door. I knock several times. Finally, I hear someone coming. 'Who is it?' a voice asks. 'Pedro Juan.' The door opens. It's Gloria's mother. I ask: 'And Gloria?'

The old lady blocks the door and says to me, hesitantly, a little nervous: 'She didn't know you were stopping by today. It's three o'clock in the morning.'

'And so?'

'Well, it's because . . .'

'Let me in.'

'No, it's because . . .'

'Let me in. She has someone in her room.'

'Speak softly, or you're gonna wake her. And you know how Gloria gets.'

'To hell with speaking softly! Let me in.'

'Pedro Juan, it's three in the morning. Let me explain something . . .'

'I don't want to push you. Get out of the way and let me pass.'

In the midst of the shoving match, Gloria comes out of her room, half asleep: 'What the fuck's going on?'

'Fucking nothing. Your mother won't let me in.'

A man in his underpants comes out of the room behind Gloria. When I see him my blood turns to ice. He's white, short, and as hairy as a bear. He must be about my age, maybe a little older. I stand there, not knowing what to say. Paralyzed. It's like the whole building is collapsing on my head. I make a half-turn and continue upstairs to the roof. The door closes behind me. I feel humiliated. I open the door, my eyes welling up. Who the hell would think of falling for a whore? A man of my age should act more judiciously. Think a bit more. When the hell am I going to learn not to be so romantic? I throw myself down on the bed without taking off my shoes, repeating: 'You have to keep your distance, Pedro Juan, you have to keep your distance, you have to keep your distance, you have to keep your distance.'

Later I sat in a lovely saloon bar from the '50s. Very similar to Sloppy Joe's, but quiet and elegant. Gloria was the waitress but she didn't know me. This Gloria is different; a bit older, more elegant and silent. A guy who looked a lot like Humphrey Bogart was sitting in another booth drinking whisky on the rocks. He was lost in a reverie and paying no attention. Maybe it really was Bogart. It seemed like a movie. The light accentuated the warm colors and the shadows. Gloria was slightly taller and thinner, discreet and even more desirable. She served me a hot sandwich, a ham and cheese melt on toast with pickles. I was terribly hungry and devoured it. I was drinking beer straight from the bottle and feeling very good, in that movie that wasn't exactly a movie. Just Gloria, Humphrey Bogart, and me. Then I heard music. Debussy's *Prelude to the Afternoon of a Faun*. I don't know what happened after that. I can't remember.

4

It's eleven o'clock in the morning when I wake up. The sun is beating hard on the fiber cement of the roof. The room is an oven. I get up and open doors and windows. It's already February but it's hot enough to be August. The sea is as flat as a plate and not a breath of air is stirring. Dead calm. If the Swede had been rich, I'd be sailing a beautiful yacht around the Caribbean now, instead of battling the blacks at the Okinawa bar. Ah, shit, well, at least I brought two hundred aspirin from Germany. I take two with a glass of water. Something is better than nothing: I don't have a Swedish yacht but I'm the owner of two hundred German aspirin. Of a hundred and ninety eight, to be exact. I have a violent hangover. That rum is pure acid. It corrodes my guts. When the hell will they make a decent *aguardiente* for the poor of the earth, those with whom I choose to cast my lot? I have a headache, I'm thirsty and hungry. I make coffee, and go out on the roof. I like the sea when it's dead calm. The time I dedicated to kayaking and sailing in Matanzas was one of the most beautiful periods of my life. I was an ignorant and asinine sportsman. That's a guarantee for spiritual tranquility. I'm on the roof drinking my coffee and watching the dead-calm sea when, suddenly, butterflies begin to appear by the thousand. They're flying in over the sea from the northeast. Maybe there are hundreds of thousands. Have they crossed the ninety miles from Florida? It seems so. They fly rapidly over the building and head south. They're looking for the fields to the south of the city. Their colors sparkle in the sunlight. I never thought such a thing could exist. How great! The bitter coffee brings me back to life. Then I hear Gloria's bracelets. They jingle like sleigh bells. I lean over the patio opening and see her through the windows. But down below, on the sixth floor, a dog sees me and begins to bark, looking straight up. On the fifth floor, there's a new tenant hanging clothes. She's a twenty-year-old mulatta and her husband is a sixty-five-year-old Italian. They make a fine couple. The guy has remodeled the entire apartment for her and she lives like a queen. The damn dog continues to bark as if they were killing it. Gloria calmly cleans the floor. She's acting all innocent. A few days ago, a boy said to her on the street: 'Girl, you have pornography written all over your face. You can't hide it.' The first thing she did when she got home was to repeat his pickup line to me and ask: 'Why would he say that to me, *papi*?', pretending to have no idea. Now I call out to her: 'Gloria!' She looks up, smiles, and blows me a kiss. She has this perverse ability to destroy with one hand and heal with the other. I motion to her that she should come up. In two minutes she's beside me. She's more cynical than I am. She arrives with a smile and a cigarette, and asks for coffee.

'No goddamn coffee for you, Gloria. I'm fresh out.'

'Oh, please don't play the angry guy who doesn't give a shit about me.'

'No? Then whom should I give a shit about? Who the fuck was that guy? Not was, *is*. Why is he still alive?'

'Are you going to kill him?'

'If he keeps getting in the way I may have to slice him up. Where did you find him?'

'Are you serious?'

'I'd like to slit his throat. So he bleeds to death in a minute. I don't waste time.'

'Oh, don't say that! Jesus, Mary, and Joseph.'

She kisses her knuckles and knocks on wood.

'Gloria, I've been locked up twice for stupidities. It doesn't matter to me what I do.'

'You can't be serious. I don't believe you . . .'

'Ha ha ha. I'm fucking around. But if I catch him with his dick hard I'll cut off his air by slashing his throat, so there are no finger-prints. That way he won't even have time to say: "Pedro Juan did it." Ha ha ha. But never in cold blood. You think I'm a murderer? A madman?'

'You're gonna wind up crazy writing those little novels of

yours. But not with me, sweetie. With me, you have the soul of a pimp.'

'No, no.'

'Yes, yes! Who found me all of those gringos? The two Italians, the German, the Mexican, the two Spaniards, that Austrian imbecile . . .'

'All right already.'

'Now you want to forget, and you don't want anyone to know it, but you brought them to me, *papi*, and you told me: "Hang on to this guy until you can grab his bucks." True or false?'

'That was to help you. It's been a while since I've brought you anyone.'

'I know it was to help me, but I had to put out for all of 'em. Down there, in my little single mother's bed. And crank up the drama, and put on condoms and take off condoms and put on condoms and take off condoms, ha ha ha.'

'Yes, the ones I brought you plus the ones you were hustling on the side. And the ones your cousin from the Palermo brought you.'

'That's my problem. And leave my cousin out of this. I'm talking about the ones you pushed on me. To prove to you that you're a pimp and I don't really interest you. It's all the same to you if I go to bed with you or two hundred others.'

'Have I ever taken money from you?'

'No.'

'Have I asked you for anything?'

'No.'

'Then I wasn't your pimp.'

'Because you didn't need me.'

'Ah, cut the crap. If you see that I'm flat broke, you head straight for the Malecón every night. I lived off Luisita for quite a while. So you can't claim victory yet.'

'Aha, you see, you're my little pimp. So don't pretend to be decent and chaste.'

'Will you do it or not?'

'Just for you, baby. For you, I'll do anything. Anything you ask. With men, that's the way it has to be.'

'Not with men, Gloria. With me.'

'You're all the same. You know what my boy said to me yesterday?'

'No.'

'I told him I'm going to start dancing again in some bar around here. And he asked me: "Do you get naked in front of men?" And I tell him: "Naked, no. I wear a bikini." And he makes a sour face and says to me: "Better not 'cause I'm gonna go there and grab you by the hair and take you home. And never speak to you again."'

'Now that's a he-man!'

'Too much of a he-man! He's only seven years old and he talks to me like that. I don't know what's going to become of my life. My father took me out of dance class. You won't leave me alone and now even my son threatens me.'

'Read Simone de Beauvoir and start a revolution.'

'What's that?'

'Nothing, nothing.'

We are silent for an instant.

'You told me you were going to work in the hospital.'

'Ah, don't mention that! It's nauseating, revolting, and sick!'

'Why?'

'I swear by your mother, there are pieces of dead people preserved in jars. Yuck!'

'In the hospital morgue?'

'It's like a vault of horror, like a Frankenstein movie. Oh, my God! Jars with eyes, with tongues, pieces of heart, entire hands, brains, bones, ears. They bring this all by on a cart. And I have to sort them out, enter them all in a registry book, and arrange them on shelves. It's been a while since they've had any employees there, because they pay two hundred shitty pesos a month. Who the hell is gonna work there like Dracula for ten measly bucks?'

'It's because you're so sensitive . . .'

'No, no, if it was you, you wouldn't even enter. If it was you, you'd stay by the door and leave right away. There were five hundred putrid jars. So I had to remove all the little rotten pieces of people, burn them, wash the jars and sterilize them so they could be used again. No, no, no!'

'It's because they pay so little.'

'I wouldn't do it for a thousand pesos a month. I was there two hours and I left. I caught a fright that's gonna take me nine days to shake!'

'It's not your thing.'

'Dead people walking around there. Coming and going. Always the same four.'

'What are you saying, Gloria?'

'Oh, *papi*, I've told you about this several times. I see the dead sometimes. I don't like it, but that's how it is. Dark spirits that can't find peace. In the two hours I was there, there were four spirits walking around and around. Wandering as if they were lost.'

'It's all in your mind. You have too much imagination.'

'It's the same to me whether you believe me or not, but I have to talk about it. At least I know you won't make fun of me.'

I give her coffee. She drinks it and lights a cigarette. She sits staring at the floor, thinking, and says to me: 'Let me dance at the Palermo.'

'No.'

'Fine. I have to make a living because with you it's a lot of love, a lot of tenderness, and the juiciest prick in the world, but my son and I . . .'

'Yeah, I know. Money.'

'And Hairy Tony is disgusting. He makes me so sick I can't stand it. Every time I see him on top of me, shoving his tail into me like a savage, I get the urge to kick him off. And he's always asking me: "Why is your pussy so dry?" But I have to hang on to him because he's a decent person and told me he'd be able to give me eighty or a hundred pesos a week. He's a straight shooter.'

'Listen, that's enough! Don't mention that idiot again!'

'Oh, don't play the tough guy now when just last night you were weeping.'

'Me weeping? Me?'

'Yes, you, you! Bawling like a little girl. You think I didn't notice. You made a half-turn and left so I wouldn't see you.'

'You like it. You love it when men cry over you.'

'Don't speak to me that way, baby.'

'And how do you want me to speak to you?'

'Decently.'

'When you deserve it. Meanwhile, you're a slut and a street-walker.'

The telephone rings. It's Agneta. She calls me once or twice a week. She wants me to come back to Stockholm in the summer. Or she'll come to Cuba. I'm not much interested either way. Now, very happy, she says: 'I have a surprise for you.'

'What is it?'

'I made a plane reservation, to go to Cuba within twenty days.'

'Don't be cruel, *mamita*!'

'What are you saying? Slowly, please.'

'That I'm very happy.'

'Just for fifteen days. It's not much but . . .'

'It's enough, it's okay.'

'It's still not certain. I haven't paid.'

'Why not?'

'I'm afraid.'

'Of what?'

'Of going to Cuba and being with you. I will not know what to do.'

We speak a little more, then we say goodbye.

'How sugary sweet you are with the Swedish broad. And, according to you, you're just hustling her. If it was love, you'd be jerking off on the phone together.'

'Cut the nonsense, Gloria.'

'So what does the decent, educated Swedish girl have to say?'

'Ah, balls . . .!'

'What's the matter? You gonna kill yourself for love?'

'Worse.'

'What?'

'She says she's probably going to come here in the next twenty days.'

'Oh, really? Don't tell me the romance will continue?'

'Don't play the jealous wife when you take Hairy Tony to bed. And your mother, the old goat, covering up for you and playing the fool.'

'Leave my mother out of this. She's a child of God.'

'Yeah, your mother and your sister are both semi-dimwits. So the family's only black sheep is what's left for me?'

'If I wasn't what I am, we'd all be in the middle of the street, begging for alms. You have no idea what a family of fools I was born into.'

'So you move all the men into your house so you can really show off.'

'I'm not a woman of the street. I may take all my men home, but you're my husband. Tony is about money. And he knows it. He pays and I let him stick his tail in now and then. It's never free of charge or when he wants it; I ration it out and present him with the bill.'

'Oh, don't pretend to be nice.'

'And don't you play the fool. Every woman does the same thing.'

'Not all.'

'Yes, all of them. Some are lucky enough to find love and money with the same husband. But most of them have two: a husband they love and another who pays cash.'

'Damn, but you're intelligent today. Since when have you been like this?'

'My whole life. No one lives by love alone. You know the saying, "love, health, and money"?'

'Gloria, Gloria, when you try to be intelligent it's a disaster!'

'Shit, a cultured guy like you doesn't know that one? It's in the Bible.'

'What's in the Bible?'

'That thing about love, health, and money.'

'Don't bullshit me, Gloria. In what part of the Bible?'

'I don't remember now. Look it up. But you're changing the subject. I don't want the Swede to come here.'

'You jealous of her?'

'Yes, of course I am. You're my husband! You're my man! Let that Swedish broad come here, and I'll put four black guys with big dicks on her tail and drive her crazy. They'll take everything, down to her shoes and her last dollar, and she'll go back naked and shivering with cold, ha ha ha. Let her come. Haven't you told her that you have a wife and that you're gonna have a family with me?'

'Gloria, for your mother's sake, take it easy.'

'I already know the black men I'm gonna set on her. She's never gonna want to come to Cuba again.'

'Gloria, Gloria, Gloria! I have a blinding hangover. I have a headache, I'm hungry, and I'm thirsty.'

'You thirsty, *papi*? Come on, I saved two beers from last night.'

'From last night?'

'From the ones Hairy Tony brought.'

'Oh yeah?'

'Of course, baby, he works at a market. What do you think, he's dying of hunger? Not at all! He's got a lot of pesos and lives like a magnate. Along with cash, he always brings shampoo, beer, sodas, and cookies for the kid . . .'

'Everything he can steal.'

'Yes indeed. I wish I had a job like that. You wouldn't need anything. I'd bring the whole market home to you!'

'Enough, Gloria, you're squawking like a magpie.'

'Oh, honey, don't treat me like that. Come on, let's go to my house. You drink those cold beers, they'll fix you right up.'

'No. I'm ashamed to see your mother.'

'Why?'

'She'll say I'm a cuckold.'

'Oh, baby, come to my room and you'll see. The cuckold is Tony. And he knows it. You're-my-superman-my-husband-my-sugar-daddy-my-little-boy. Ha ha ha. I'm gonna show you something you're really gonna like.'

We go downstairs. Her house is peaceful. A cousin is breeding carrier pigeons on the balcony. We greet each other and chat a bit.

Everyone in the neighborhood breeds pigeons and the birds get trapped and stolen. Many people get by like this. They steal pigeons from other breeders and sell them, generally to people who worship the *santos*. There are dovecotes on most of the roofs. I take the time to play every number from last night's dream. The cousin is a numbers runner. I put two pesos on 44, beer. And five pesos on 65, food. Gloria tells me: 'Play five pesos on 49.'

'What's 49?'

'Drunk.'

'Who was the drunk?'

'Humphrey Bogart. They gave you the three numbers, *papi*, you wait and see, they're gonna pay off tonight.'

The bed is large. They came straight here from the little twelve-by-twelve-foot room they had in the tenement. For years, Gloria's mother took care of a little old lady who lived alone in this apartment. One night, during an electrical blackout which lasted many hours, the old lady (she was eighty-two at the time) got very frightened of the dark and of her husband, who had died twenty-two years before. She said that the dead man would come for her several times a day and that he would knock on the door and call her by name. She died of a cerebral aneurysm, trembling with fear. She left the apartment to Gloria's mother in a legal testament that appeared, unexpectedly, three days after her death. Now Gloria has a room just for herself and her son. It even has balconies and large windows with views of the Malecón.

The building dates from 1927. It's been forty years or more since they've repaired it, or even painted it. It's a complete shambles. There are sheets of cardboard and planks where there used to be window glass. The walls and the ceiling are covered with soot and cobwebs, the furniture, from the 1930s, destroyed. There are bundles of worn-out clothes everywhere, the wires in the mattresses stick you in the back. The dog sleeps on some old rags in the depths of the closet. In a corner of the room, Gloria has her *orishas*. Reigning from above, in pictures glued to the walls, are the Virgin of Charity, St Lazarus, and St Barbara. In a little wooden chest, Elegguá, Ochún, Changó, the warriors, offerings for Orula. She keeps the gypsy somewhere else, in a privileged place facing the door, protecting the entrance to the house.

I went out on the balcony to see the pigeons and talk to her cousin. For some time, I too managed to live by selling pigeons and snails to the sons and daughters of the *santos*. Gloria brought me a cold beer and ushered me into her room: 'Look, *papi*, so you can see that you're my only man, my superman.'

The *orishas'* and the *santos'* nook is in a corner of the room. Among their images are various colored photos of me clipped from newspapers and magazines. She had asked me for those interviews. I figured she was saving them as a way of remembering. But no, she cut out the photos and pasted them on cardboard. It's very strange. I wouldn't have imagined it. Me among the pictures of Jesus Christ, St Barbara, St Lazarus, St Judas Thaddeus.

'What is this, Gloria? Are you out of your mind?'

'No. Why?'

'What am I doing among these saints?'

'Sweet baby, you're a saint and a demon at the same time. I put the Virgin of Charity over you so she would always protect you and never abandon you.'

'So I see . . .'

When you don't know what to say, it's better to shut up. We shut the door. We get naked and play a little on top of the bed. We savor each other, and she lets herself go. The little boy interrupts us three or four times. He knocks on the door for any reason: demanding his towel, his shorts. Finally, he speaks through the closed door to Gloria: 'Mommy, did you already tell him?'

'No, Armandito. Stop pestering me and leave us alone, damn it!'

The little boy seems to go away.

I ask Gloria: 'Doesn't Armandito go to school?'

'Today is Saturday.'

'What does he want?'

'A little brother.'

'Oh, yeah? And you?'

'I want three or four.'

'Don't joke around, Gloria.'

'I've always told you. I want your son.'

'Maybe one, but not three or four.'

'Let's have one first, and then we'll see.'

At this point Armandito returns. He's made meringues. He brings us a plate of the toasted sweets. Gloria first offers two to the *orishas* with special dedications. Then we eat the others. I watch her licking bits of meringue off her fingers. I like her hands, rough and ruined by detergents.

'I like your hands.'

'They're so ugly.'

'I don't care for anything that's beautiful, perfect, or clean. You know that.'

'You always tell me that, but I don't get it.'

'Your hands have more life.'

'I've worked a lot.'

'At what, besides whoring?'

'Oh, Pedro, don't be a fool. Real work. In cafeterias and the houses of people with money. In the Vedado neighborhood and near Miramar beach. Scrubbing, washing, cleaning.'

'Yeah, everything but cooking.'

'And how do you know that?'

'Because you're a terrible cook.'

'Nobody taught me.'

'You haven't been able to learn how to cook. You were twenty years old when the crisis began, so all you've ever known is rice and beans.'

'Hey, I'm living well when there's rice and beans.'

'That's no way to learn.'

'You cook really well.'

'I'm older. I've had more time. When people are able to eat again in this country, you'll learn. The important thing is to have food to hand.'

'Are you gonna teach me?'

'Of course. Get a job in a cafeteria. So you can send Hairy Tony back where he came from.'

'Ah, it's always the same.'

'What's always the same?'

'Pedro, I've worked in at least . . . ten or twelve cafeterias. All the administrators are the same. The only thing they want is to dip their wick. They give you the job so they can fuck you every day. Until they get bored. Then they invent any pretext to fire you and leave the position open for someone they fancy so they can start in on them. And it's the same thing if you want to dance in a club or in a cabaret, and the same if you work for the folks with money in Nuevo Vedado and in Miramar. All they want is to slip you some cock.'

'Not everyone is like that. I imagine that . . .'

'Have you worked in cafeterias? Have you been a servant to the rich bitches in Miramar? Have you been a dancer?'

'No.'

'Then don't talk about what you don't know.'

'Uhhh.'

'Men are assholes and opportunists. That's why I like to service them and take their money.'

'Me too?'

'No, not you. I love you, but I don't know what to think.'

'You still don't know?'

'I don't know. Sometimes I believe you and sometimes I don't.'

'I love you a lot.'

'Me too, but I don't know what to think.'

'Well . . .'

'I'm suspicious, Pedro Juan. They promise and promise when what they really want is to stick it in, get off, and keep walking. And if you get pregnant, they say that it's not theirs. You know how many abortions I've had?'

'No.'

'Two before the boy was born, and three after. Because you all like to let your milk loose without thinking so we're the ones who . . . Ah, what's the use talking about this?'

'You have a heart of stone.'

'Maybe.'

'They've crushed you and you've crushed them.'

282

'You're very loving, *papi*, but you have the soul of a pimp and a son of a bitch. You like sluts and serving girls. You get me confused.'

'I'm confused too.'

'You really don't know what you want, Pedro Juan.'

'No one knows what they want in this world. We live in chaos and confusion.'

'That's true. At times I feel so lost. I don't know what I'm doing or why I'm doing it.'

'You've never had a man like me: murderer, butcher of women, sadist, pervert. That's why I write novels. I write about what I really want to do: serve Gloria for lunch.'

'My God, what a horror! I have to leave you, you louse, but every day I want you more.'

5

I won eighty pesos on number forty-nine. Humphrey Bogart brought me luck. The other numbers didn't pay out. I had to go to the bookie's house to collect, on a narrow street behind the university. He made we wait quite a while, standing in the doorway. There were two huge publicity billboards on the corner. One said, in gigantic letters: 'We must build a party of steel'. The other had a picture of some mulattas dancing, and announced: 'Havana Night. World Tour 1999–2000'. And, in red letters, on top of the mulattas, 'Made in Cuba–Made in Cuba–Made in Cuba–Made in'. When I finally collected the eighty pesos, I went back home. As usual, I had nothing to do. Night was falling, and the corner of San Lázaro and Perseverancia was dark and peaceful. It was about eight o'clock. Police on every corner. Peace and quiet.

Suddenly a black woman appeared, causing a commotion. She was accompanied by a skinny, undernourished mulatto, drunk as a skunk. Crossing his arms and without saying a word, the guy leans against the wall to keep from falling. And the woman continues to berate him: 'Come on, gotta go, gotta go, you ain't gonna stay here! Come on, come on, keep movin', keep movin'!'

The guy was looking at her, but he was seeing four black women in front of him for sure. He had drunk so much alcohol that he understood nothing. Three policemen were observing the situation from a distance. The black woman saw them out of the corner of her eye and kept screaming as if they were skinning her alive: 'Come on, walk, walk, get a move on, don' stop!'

She was slapping his face and pushing him. The mulatto dropped his arms and said to her in a faint voice: 'Scram. Leave me alone.'

It was like an explosion. The black woman started to push him and to yell even more, like a madwoman. Completely hysterical, she threatened to knock him to the ground. A policeman approached: 'What's going on here, citizen?'

The guy sees the policeman and opens his eyes very wide, astounded. He makes an effort and manages to articulate another sentence: 'Tell her to leave me alone.'

The woman keeps pushing him and yelling: 'Come on, come on, get a move on, get a move on!'

The policeman insists: 'Citizen, I repeat, what's going on here?'

The guy is anesthetized. He doesn't answer. The woman raises her voice even more: 'You see? He's impossible. He's quarrelsome. I don't know why I took him as a husband. I don't learn! I don't learn!'

The policeman, very serene: 'Citizen, for the third time, what's going on? And give me your identity card.'

The anesthetized man looks at the policeman with his glassy eyes. He searches in his shirt pocket, hands him the card, and crosses his arms again. The policeman takes the card, moves a few steps away, and calls the station house on his radio. The other two policemen observe from four yards away. The woman keeps yelling: 'See him? You see? He's quarrelsome.'

The policeman asks her: 'Is he your husband?'

'He's quarrelsome. You see? It's always the same. He's a trouble-maker.'

The mulatto remains silent, his arms crossed, leaning against the wall. A patrol car approaches, draws to a halt. The policeman helps the man into the car and he is taken away. The black woman walks away calmly, saying to the policeman: 'That's what has to be done. Well done. Let him sleep at the station house. He's a lot of trouble, a lot of trouble!'

The policeman rejoins the other two and they talk quietly among themselves. The four or five of us who stopped to watch the scandal continue on our way. I enter my building and start to climb the stairs. I always think the same thing as I walk up the stairs: 'Let's be positive, Pedro, this is good for the heart. Head for the top like a little goat.' Eight flights. I get to the roof. What to do? I have no rum. I put on Mozart's *Requiem. Introitus: Requiem aeternam.* I listen to a little more. *Kyrie eleison. Dies irae.* God, no! Too strong! It overwhelms me. I remove the disc. I put on Celine Dion. Then I turn off the machine and go out on the roof. The sea is dark; there's a cold wind from the northeast. I'm anxious. I have nothing to do. Nothing to think about. Solitude, anxiety, and uncertainty. Incomprehension. I put on Mozart again. *Rex Tremendae. Confutatis Maledictis.*

Someone knocks on the door. I open it. It's a strange guy, very thin, with a beard and long hair, dressed all in black, wearing little round sunglasses like John Lennon's. He uses a deep, professional voice, and says to me: 'Pedro Juan?'

'Yes.'

'I am Baltasar Fontana, film director.'

'Oh . . . come in.'

He seems to have a Spanish accent. It should be Baltasar Fuentes. Who knows why he has an Italian surname. He wastes no time. He sits down and cuts to the chase: 'I read your book and liked it. It was like watching a film. I think we should work together. I just finished shooting a short here.'

I watch him and listen to him, thinking: 'It's really fucked to live downtown. What the hell does this guy want?'

Baltasar keeps talking, with Mozart in the background: 'I want to do a road movie. A young guy, sixteen years old, buys a car and drives all around Cuba. From Havana to Santiago. He's very much a rebel. He fights with his parents. And returns to Havana a winner. The car has to be a classic: maybe a 1950s Chevrolet. The guy triumphs in the end. It has to be a happy ending.'

'And what else?'

'That's it, that's all. A road movie.'

'No, no. I'm not interested.'

'Think about it. I liked your book.'

'You want a coffee?'

'Eh?'

'You want a coffee?'

'Water, please.'

I serve him a glass of water and remain silent. I have nothing to say. I hope he drinks the water and leaves. But no. The water gives him strength and he gets talkative. He tells me the entire plot of the film he just shot in Cuba. Now it's being edited. It's the story of a very beautiful mulatta who is a worshiper of the *santos* and lives in a lovely house by the sea, on a tropical beach, and has visions of medieval castles and the Crusades in her dreams. Then she is transported to that epoch, and she has a romance with a wandering knight. Finally, she comes back from her dream with the knight transformed into a modern man and it ends with a sunset, the two of them walking on the beach. Baltasar finishes, telling me: 'It's a lovely film. Very beautiful.'

'You could have made it in Hawaii.'

'It's very cheap here. Very cheap.'

'Ah. And do you come up with many scripts like this?'

'It's very difficult. To find good scripts is difficult.'

'Do you want to adapt some of my stories?'

'No, no. Too much sex.'

'People are the same everywhere. Sex is normal.'

'Yes, you're right. I'll confess something to you: I live in Madrid and when I read your book I did an experiment. I put a personal ad in a national paper with large circulation. And I paid them to publish it three days in a row. It said: "Old woman, 62. I could be your grandmother. I'll bring you more pleasure than you can imagine. Ten thousand pesetas for everything. Rosa Maria." Plus the telephone number. I made a recording of "Rosa Maria's" voice on an answering machine. In one week the little grandmother received forty-three requests for service on the answering machine. Another eighteen hung up before the recording was finished and didn't leave a message.'

'You can make a film script out of that. It would be called *The Little Old Erotic Lady*.'

'No. That would be pornography. I am an artist. I want to make a road movie in Cuba. And I want the boy to listen to Lou Reed.'

'No one knows Lou Reed in Cuba. And boys of sixteen can't buy cars. In that film the old lady would never appear and there would be no sex. It would just be you and your inner torment. You conducting your experiment in Madrid. Titles are created to confuse the public.'

The *Agnus Dei* concluded and a vigorous rendition of *Lux aeterna* started up. I kept quiet. I wanted him to notice that it was enough already. And he understood. He left me his telephone and his e-mail. He said goodbye. He shut the door. I ripped up the piece of paper with his particulars and listened to the finale of *Lux aeterna*.

I went down to sit on the wall of the Malecón. The cold northeast wind was still blowing and waves broke over the seawall. There was a guy facing the sea, playing a saxophone, practicing scales. He began to play a little jazz, very slow and melancholy. He was improvising. In the midst of the pink light of the Malecón, in the silence and solitude of the night and with a cold wind blowing. There was something unreal about that guy blowing his slow jazz and the music getting lost in the blackness of the sea and the night. That's what's good about reality: it permits luxuries forbidden to writers. Reality doesn't have to be convincing. I repress the desire to take note of the scene and of the atmosphere for *A Lot of Heart*. Too difficult to remove it from the reality and make it credible on paper. I must not overcomplicate my life with this bitch of a novel. I repress the desire to go to El Mundo and drink cheap rum distilled from gasoline. I cannot get sickeningly drunk every night. I repress the desire to look for Gloria. At this hour she must be out there hustling her ass.

I went to bed early, a repressed mess. I woke up at five-thirty in the morning with my prick as stiff as a board. I felt wide awake. I played with myself a bit but cut it short of spilling my seed. A man of fifty gets thriftier and more cautious every day. I controlled myself and got up. I wanted to organize the notes for *A Lot of Heart*. I know how to begin but I have no idea of the end. I can't write like that. I have to know where Gloria is going to stop. I put away all of the notes and start to paint. At seven, I hear her bracelets. She's running around in the kitchen. I stick my head out.

Through the broken glass of a window I see only her hands. I like her hands very much. It's exciting watching her work, making coffee. I call her, and she answers me: 'I'm going to take the boy to school. I'll come up after.'

She finally comes up at nine o'clock. She arrives with a booklet: *Horoscope for the Year 2000*. She reads my sign: 'Look, *papi*, what it says about Aquarius. "The pernicious side will manifest itself in either an incorrigible dreamer or a dangerous, perverted being with neither conscience nor feelings but, rather, a frigid wickedness."'

'Damn, Gloria, don't fuck around! I'm not like that!'

'What do you mean? You're worse!'

'Let's go to Mantilla's. I want you to get the tattoo.'

'No, no. What if I get AIDS?'

'If you haven't contracted AIDS up to now with all your vaginal, oral, and manual services . . .'

'Hey, guy, don't get heavy.'

'You're immune. Let's go to Mantilla's. At least the man knows what he's doing and uses good materials. They send him everything from the States: needles, ink, all of it.'

'Will it hurt?'

'No.'

'Well, we have to take rum and grass. Get drunk first.'

'Let's go, quit fucking around.'

Two architects specializing in restoration knock at the door. We have to wait. They take photographs, measure, and praise the building as a classic of its kind. One, the guy, is Italian. The other one is a little Cuban girl. I notice immediately that she's hustling the Italian. Maybe she'll get a scholarship to Rome out of it. The intellectual hustle. It's obvious that she's seducing and snaring the Italian. The guy is at a disadvantage. He's from the north, from Milan. If he were from Naples, he'd be the one hustling the little Cuban girl and coming to live in the tropics. In the last few years, we've had German, Spanish, Italian, and French architects pass through here. They take videos and photographs. I have a feeling that to live on the Havana coastline is fast becoming a luxury. To see the Caribbean easily from my roof terrace is a privilege. When will it end? Finally they're finished and they leave. We go out to Mantilla's. As we're headed downstairs, on a landing between the sixth and the fifth floors there's a big, fresh, smelly pile of shit.

'Damn, the idiot took another shit.'

It's Elenita, the idiot who lives downstairs. She climbs up and shits on the stairs. She's been doing it for years. Gloria gets angry: 'She's not going to do it any more, you'll see. Wait for me here.'

She goes to her house. She gets a piece of cardboard. She returns. She scrapes up the shit with the cardboard. She goes downstairs to the floor where the idiot lives and hurls the pile of shit against the door of her apartment. The shit drips. It smells revolting.

'I'm going to do this every time she shits on the stairwell. It's the only way she's gonna learn respect.'

We walk down Galiano to Fraternity Park. Every day there are more beggars asking for alms. Sometimes they invent something ingenious. Today's gold medal goes to a mongoloid who drools nonstop. His father sits him on the ground, propping him up so his back is against a wall. The boy seems to be about twenty years old. He seems as soft as pudding and soon collapses into a form-less mass. The father, patiently, puts him back in an upright posi-tion. They repeat this several times. He takes off the boy's shoes. The idiot has twisted feet. Then the man lights four candles around his son, placing pictures of saints and virgins under each. He hangs a notice, written in pencil, around the boy's neck: 'I yam incapisitated. Hep me eat. I was borned into the werld is not my fawlt. I son of saint lasaris. Tanks.' The father winds some neck-laces of Obatalá and Elegguá around the boy's right wrist and moves a few steps back. He observes his work. He is pleased. He puts a plate between the boy's legs, drops some coins on it as a reminder and withdraws a couple of yards. People begin to stop and stare at all this and the coins accumulate on the plate. The father stays abreast of the action. Each time a candle goes out, he runs up and lights it again. The idiot boy seems alone and aban-doned. They've managed to create a heart-rending scene.

I fell into a reverie seeing the preparations and observing the first people throw their coins on the plate. Gloria brings me back to reality: 'Are you going to stay here all day?'

'Poor kid.'

'They're a pair of scoundrels.'

'The guy is an idiot. It's not his fault that his father is using him.'

'Ha ha ha. The idiot is you.'

'He's not an idiot?'

'Of course not. That mulatto's a jerk-off. When I was working in the Trocadero pre-school he was always there, with three or four other ham-slammers.'

'What were they jerking off about?'

'Us, *papi*.'

'How come?'

'To entertain us a little. There were five or six hardcore jerk-offs. And that mulatto was one of them. Maybe he became an idiot from so much self-abuse, the imbecile.'

'Gloria, your brain is fried.'

'*Meeee?* They were the perverts. They stood up on some walls and showed us their pricks, and we opened our legs for them. And they started firing away then and there. With their eyes wide open like weirdos. Ha ha ha. The same thing every afternoon. They were addicted, ha ha ha.'

'I don't see what's so funny. You're an addict too.'

'Oh, baby, it was such a boring job. Taking care of children all day.'

'So he's not an idiot?'

'A good-for-nothing jerk-off and a rogue. And the other one's his partner, not his father. Damn!'

At Mantilla's, they put the tattoo on her right shoulder, running down her back. The guy drew a flaming heart on her, all red and yellow. In the center, in blue, he wrote: 'Pedro Juan'. We were there for three hours. Gloria drank half a bottle of rum so it wasn't painful. And we left. When we got to the building, we saw two boys exit running. They were two of the neighborhood pigeon thieves. We knew them. They saw us and ran off, passing by us like meteors. We were half soused. Then we heard the shouting and sobered up in a hurry. Fire on the seventh floor, in Gloria's house! Someone threw a bottle of gasoline with the fuse lit against the door. Gloria's mother and her cousin got buckets of water and put it out in time. The fire had burnt through the door. Gloria's mood changed, and she screamed at her cousin: 'I told you not to steal any more doves from them! Those boys are dangerous!'

'How do you know it was them?'

'Because they were running away. It was the two of them.'

The cousin didn't answer her. He grabbed a steel bar and took off downstairs like a rocket.

'Oh, Pedro Juan, he's gonna kill them. If he catches them, he'll kill them.'

'They won't get caught so easily. Come on, let's go!'

We go running down the stairs. We get down to the street door in a minute: no sign of the arsonists. Gloria's cousin furtively dropped his steel pipe when he saw the police on the corner. He calmed down and came toward us: 'I know who they are. I'll get them. Let them hide for now.'

'Why did they do it?'

'Because of a dove I stole from them. It's been a while. Now they're coming for their revenge.'

Gloria began to fume: 'That's not the end of this! They burnt the door of my house and I saw them. We're gonna go to the station house so I can make a statement.'

6

The row about the fire and the pigeon keepers lasted three or four days. There were a number of arguments in the street between Gloria, the cousin, and other relatives from both sides. Tenement rabble. I distanced myself from the matter, and everything gradually dissolved into nothing, as usual. One afternoon, Gloria came up for coffee. She likes to sit on the floor while I heat up the coffee pot. She's wearing very tight, short shorts and a skimpy blouse. I serve a little rum. I like to see her like this, sitting on the floor, listening to a cassette of José José. She lifts her knees, opens her legs and provokes me with her big, black, curly bush. I get hot. I pass a shot of rum from my mouth to hers. I expose a little bit of my prick. She pulls her shorts to one side and shows me her pussy. I take out my cock and start to stroke it softly.

'Ah, *papi*, that drives me crazy. How I love it.'

'Damn, but you have the most beautiful, hairy pussy! That's what I call a pussy, so snug and so tight! And what a money-maker you've got with that little beauty . . . I bet you average five hundred pesos a month.'

'More, much more. Look how your thing is stretching out, how pretty!'

'Suck it, and it'll stand up higher.'

She licks it a bit.

'More, sweetie, much more than five hundred. It's a money-making pussy, ha ha ha. And there are some I let use it without charge.'

'I'm ready to come. Where do you want me to put it?'

'No, hold it, hold it.'

We keep playing some more. I'm expert in giving it to her slowly. She plays with herself too. Finally: 'I can't hold it any more! Tell me!'

She opens her mouth. I let loose my spurt. She swallows it, gulps it down to the last drop.

'Ahh, it's pure acid . . . ahhh . . . it's like cashew bark. I've never tasted milk like that.'

'It's my runaway slave making mine acid like that. Ha ha ha.'

'Don't play with your dead man or he's gonna punish you . . . fine . . . it's up to you.' The coffee pot almost explodes. The coffee has evaporated. She laughs.

'Give me more rum. Forget about the coffee, ahhh . . . now you've got me going . . .'

'Why?'

'That always arouses me. It's been my lifelong obsession.'

'What?'

'To have them jerk off in front of me while I show them what's between my legs.'

'Because you've grown accustomed.'

'Since I was a little girl. I ripped a hole in my knickers, and my mother didn't know it was me who did it. So that when I opened my legs they could see my little twat.'

'You're beyond repair. You're completely bent.'

'It's not so bad, it's a game like many others. I don't like playing ball or dominoes. My thing is to go to the beach and display a little bit of pussy, a tit, a buttock. Right away, the jerk-offs come out of the bushes and surround me like madmen. And if I'm feeling perverse on a given day, I call them over and say to them: "Cough it up, twenty pesos each. Or the show closes and the cast goes on vacation."'

'And they pay?'

'Damn right, baby. Some of them give me double or triple what I ask and tell me: "I want this to last for a long time. Can you sit there for an hour without moving?"'

'So you're modeling.'

'That is my art, sweetie, to dance, to model, to display myself. It doesn't matter to me if they sketch me or play with themselves. The important thing is that they pay . . . a l'il money, a li'l money. "Help the Cuban artist!" as my father would say when he played guitar in the bars.'

She trembles with a chill: 'Ahhh, yes, speak . . . let's go . . . give me a little rum and find me a cigar.'

She sits on the edge of the bed. She takes her time, with her eyes closed. She drinks a couple of shots of rum, lights up the cigar, smokes peacefully, opens her eyes and tells me: 'There's a woman in your house who's always writing, sitting at your desk. She isn't old. She may be forty or a bit older. She wears good perfume and you can see that she was an elegant woman, but one who led a double life. She had a secret life at night and was very romantic. She smokes cigarettes and enjoys herself. She likes to laugh a lot. She's always in a good mood, fun-loving, optimistic. Sometimes she plays with you and you smell the fragrance of her perfume or her cigarette smoke. This always happens when you are sitting at your desk, writing. Then you are very startled and you go to the altar to pray and ask the dead men to leave you in peace.'

'Damn it, Gloria, how do you know this?'

'I'm seeing it. So shut up, don't interrupt. This woman is sitting at your desk writing. She's very elegant and doesn't want to look at my gypsy. She ignores her.'

'What is her name?'

'I don't know. What she didn't dare write during her lifetime, she's writing now with you . . . She has . . . a long black dress, down to her ankles, with a high collar and long sleeves. Her hair is gathered in a bun. It's possible that she died a hundred years ago, who knows? You can see by her dress that she's been dead for quite some time . . . She says to begin the novel and not to be afraid . . . She says that she writes through you. She asks you for flowers.'

'Sometimes I . . .'

'Shhh, be quiet. You put flowers on the altar but they're not for her. This lady wants white and yellow flowers in a glass of water, and wants you to put it on the table where you work, in front of you . . . and she says you shouldn't be upset by the perfume and the smoke . . . She helps you . . . and . . . Listen to this: do you sometimes feel like there's a force which is pulling you so that you write on and on without being able to stop? And you think about one thing but write another so that what comes out is something different?'

'Yes, many times. It's like a trance and I can't stop myself.'

'Because it's not you. She's the one who's writing. She's says that, in life, she had no time. One last thing: she repeats to me that you should begin the novel because she is always there. Give her white and yellow flowers . . . Oh . . . She's gone.'

Gloria got up, put on one of my shirts, and went out on the roof to get some fresh air. She took some deep breaths and came back much calmer: 'Look what that does to my hands.'

I touch her palms. They're burning. They must be forty degrees or more.

'It's not so bad. When my head gets that hot, I end up with a pain in my temples. And it's a pain that doesn't leave me for the whole day. When she enters through my head, she stays much longer. Sometimes I'm talking for half an hour.'

'The gypsy is strong.'

'She's strong, but I don't serve her like I should. I forget about her.'

I light a cigar, pour more rum, put on a very old record of Ñico Membiela, and we lay on the bed awhile. I sniff her underarms. That smell of wild African female, sweating in the jungle, is a drug that thrills me. If Africa didn't exist, the black women and mulattas, what would humanity be? We would surely be extinguished, dissolving like ghosts in a desert.

I inhale deeply and fill my lungs with her sweaty fragrance: 'Ah, Gloria, I wouldn't even look at you if you were white and blonde.'

'Because you like black women, you dog, but I'm a cinnamon-colored mulatta. Don't confuse me with them!'

'You're more racist than the Nazis.'

'Yes, I'm a racist, so what? I don't like black people. In my entire life, I've only had one and he lasted four days. And that was only because it was carnival in Santiago and I was drunk the whole time. A week of drinking and carnival and fucking.'

'And you're a mulatta, if you were black . . .'

'If I was black, I would have had no one.'

'Why?'

'Because they're liars, bums, useless pigs, and their pricks are so long they give you pelvic inflammation. What's more, they haggle about the price and don't want to pay. No, no, big pricks and small profits. Let the black women have them, they're not for me.'

'Gloria, that's the worst kind of racism.'

'But it's true.'

'It's not true. There are whites . . .'

'Ahh, save the theory for your little books. Maybe a black man with money and a university degree, all hoity-toity, but it's best not even to look at the blacks in this neighborhood. Impudent, worthless jerk-offs.'

'Damn, you're a Nazi!'

'So now you understand? Ha ha ha. You know what I did to the black guy in Santiago?'

'No.'

'I slapped his face and told him: "Pull it out, pull it out, get off me and go wash your pits, you stink." And, afterwards, he came back like a puppy. He even put on a deodorant. Now I was on top: "Nothing, there's no more pussy for you. Go get some money. Bring me money and rum and cigarettes and grass. Bring it all or I'll punish you. I'll get dressed, I'll leave and you'll never see me again", ha ha ha. Tears were running down his face. That's what I love: to humiliate them. To treat them like slaves.'

'Why are you such a bitch?'

'All of us are bitches and sons of bitches and we all like to have someone below us, to crush beneath our feet. Don't pretend to be innocent. You're worse than me. If you got to be president of the country some day, you'd tie everybody up in chains and gag them so they wouldn't protest.'

'You're a fascist, Gloria. You've got an abnormal little brain. I can't write about this in *A Lot of Heart*.'

'So you're going to write down everything that I tell you in your little novel?'

'Everything.'

'It's gonna be way too heavy. People don't want to know the truth.'

'I know. People prefer baseball.'

'Be intelligent. Don't be sore just because they make your life impossible and you have to leave Cuba. Ha ha ha, a big shot like you!'

'Me, a big shot?'

'Yes, you. You could have stayed in twenty countries and lived like a normal person. Ah, but no, like a cock-eyed animal, you always come back to the filth.'

'I don't want to live anywhere else.'

'Oh, such a sentimental little boy!'

'It's not sentimentality, it's a choice.'

'It's stupidity. You can live better over there than here. How come you didn't stay in Sweden?'

'I live well here.'

'Well? Selling a painting every six months and me hustling the gringos?'

'Even so. I feel good here.'

'Yeah? Well, watch what you do, 'cause when I get pregnant I'm not hustling any more. I'm already sick of gringos. I only want to be with you. With-you-and-no-one-else. Get that into your head.'

'Ah, drop the drama.'

'Drama nothing. It's the truth. You're not gonna be my pimp for the rest of your life and I'm not always gonna be a whore.'

'So now you're going to be a decent woman?'

'I've always been decent. Poor and from the tenements, but honorable. I've always worked for my money, ever since I was a little girl. And don't get me off the subject: you're gonna be my husband and I'm gonna be your wife. So come up with a plan to support the whole family: you, me, and three or four kids.'

'Damn, Gloria!'

'Put your feet on the ground, and stop the paintings and fool-ishness.'

'I'll have to set up a vegetable stand in the marketplace.'

'I'll help you. I have a tremendous gift for selling. Business is my thing.'

'The only things you know how to sell are ham sandwiches.'

'No difference. It's the same if I sell cold water, or a building, or a hand job for twenty pesos. I like doing business. By the way, speaking of business, let me call Margot.'

'Who's Margot?'

'A friend.'

'The one from Guanabo?'

'The same.'

'Tremendous hustler.'

'I'm the tremendous hustler. She's a dumb bitch . . . Hold on . . . Is Margot there, please? . . . Yes, thank you.'

She waits a while. Finally, Margot comes on the line.

'What'd you end up doing last night?'

'. . .'

'And you went with that pig?'

'. . .'

'How much?'

'. . .'

'I'm glad. That's what happens when you try to be nice. I could see by his clothes that he was a phony. Margot, my love, you still have a lot to learn. First, that gringo never takes a bath. Second, his feet, his armpits, and his mouth all really stank. And third, he bought one ice cream for three people, ate half of it himself, and then gave us the rest. Does that tell you anything?'

'. . .'

'That's what he wanted? A free tortilla with the two of us?'

'. . .'

'And what did you tell him?'

'. . .'

'Now you see why you're a complete retard. Tell him to fuck himself and go ask the slaves in Africa, if he can find them. It'd be even better if he found himself in a tribe of cannibals and they ate him alive.'

'. . .'

'Margot, don't tell me that. As a whore you're a failure. Get another job.'

'. . .'

'No. Forget it. On the street is bad and they'll pick you up and send you back to your hometown.'

'. . .'

'Palma Clara, ha ha ha. Where the hell is that, girl?'

'. . .'

'In Baracoa? It doesn't even show up on the map. Take care. I'll see you, 'bye.'

She hangs up. She smiles at me and says: 'She's too noble, still too much of a little country girl. If she doesn't start turning tricks soon, she'll starve to death. She doesn't know that, in Havana, you've got to walk on fire and not get yourself burnt.'

7

I woke up with a wicked hangover. My diplomat friend, Juan del Río, had invited me to an 'aphrodisiac scene' the previous night. I tried to correct him: 'In Cuba we call it carnivalesque.'

'What do you mean?'

'Rabelaisian. Excessively tropical.'

'No. Just the opposite. It will be minimal, but explosive.'

And so it was. He had confessed to me that he and his partner, an eight-foot-tall black man and martial arts graduate from I can't remember what institute, masturbated each other while reading certain passages from the Brazilian edition of the *Dirty Havana Trilogy*.

'Why in Portuguese?'

'It's much more sensual. As Pessoa said, it has no bones.'

I very much doubt that the karate kid would be able to understand anything about languages with bones or without them. But it shows what kind of sybarite this diplomat is. He adored his partner, most of all because the guy penetrated him calmly while watching some television show or another. Juan del Río adored his style: 'Oh, he's a genius. No one has ever humiliated me more! He shoves it in and he can be there half an hour without stopping and without even looking at me. He moves back and forth automatically and only watches the TV screen. He's mesmerized by Bruce Lee movies and *Roadrunner* and *Bugs Bunny* cartoons.

Dinner consisted solely of lightly steamed shellfish with fine herbs. Spicy sauces and wines in abundance. For dessert they served pastries of mandrake root and ginseng, a Mexican cheese stuffed with chilies and peyote, and very strong, genetically treated Dutch marijuana. I smoked one joint of that postmodern pot, sprinkled with cherry brandy, plus the peyote-cheese. I had to restrain myself from doing a striptease. I succeeded in controlling my innate exhibitionist vocation. There were eight or ten of us, including a certain fiftyish, or sixtyish, Spanish writer with her twenty-year-old hustler, as drunk as, or drunker, than me. I spoke. We spoke. And I was losing my memory. At some point, Juan del Río got aggressive with me and grabbed my balls. I removed his hand: 'Careful, you're in enemy territory.'

'Ah, baby, you're a ferocious wolf in your books, but a little lamb in real life.'

'Leave my little lamb alone and don't fuck around. Don't you get off with that big black stud?'

Afterwards I spoke to the writer a little. The last thing I remember was the diplomat asking her: 'What's Pedro Juan saying? Why is he speaking so low?'

And she, tongue tied: 'He's talking in my ear. Private things. He says that he takes care of his penis. That he bathes it in the sun on his roof garden every day.'

And the diplomat, enthusiastically: 'Oh, Pedro Juan, invite us to your roof. It must be spectacular.'

I don't remember anything more. I don't even know who brought me home, how I got up the stairs or opened the door and fell into bed. I suppose that, finally, no one violated me. When I awoke it was two in the afternoon and I felt as if a bomb had gone off in my brain. I made a vow not to smoke any more Dutch marijuana. The only kind I have always been able to handle is the local stuff, from Baracoa. I had a horrible thirst. I was able to get up. I got some aspirin, made coffee, and called Gloria.

She came up right away. She gave me back the whip. She'd had it in her house for weeks: 'Here, *papi*, put it away.'

'Why? What did you do with it?'

'Nothing. I slept with it between my legs.'

She remains silent while I finish the coffee.

'You're enigmatic today.'

'What's that?'

'Ehhh . . . mysterious.'

'Ah, no. I'm not mysterious.'

'Sad.'

'Yes.'

'Why?'

'Sometimes I get this way.'

'For no reason?'

'When I think too much. I don't like to think because I get sad and feel like crying.'

'If you cry it's because someone is hurting you.'

'You and my father.'

'Eh?'

'My father has been in Mexico for four years.'

'You've never spoken to me about this.'

'What for? You never knew him. He's a musician. He was sixty-five years old yesterday. And I know he's not well.'

'Has he written you that he's ill?'

'No, but I know it. The gypsy whispered it in my ear. She's told me two times this week.'

'And you want to go to be with him?'

'He has no money to send me or for anything else. He sends us thirty or forty dollars every month. That's it. I know he's dead broke.'

'Uhmm.'

'That's the problem, sweetie. Him on one side and you on the other. And the boy. No, no, no! I can't think so much because it makes me crazy. Three men in my life! One is seven, the other is fifty, and the other is sixty-five.'

'Have some coffee, and let life run its course.'

'Yes. Thinking solves nothing.'

I have a pot of aloe vera on the roof. I cut a couple of leaves.

'The tattoo is also painful.'

'Still?'

'It's only been four days.'

'No, it's been longer.'

'Yes? Ah, I don't know. I lost count. But it hurts. I had a little antibiotic salve, but it's finished.'

'Come here and I'll cure you.'

I prepare a cream with aloe vera and camomile. I explain to her how to use it. I caress her, kiss her, fondle her a bit. She purrs like a cat: 'You're the first affectionate man of my life.'

'Me, affectionate?'

'No one has ever written me a poem or given me flowers, or . . . nothing, nothing.'

'I don't believe it.'

'Not even my son's father. And we were married and lived together for three years. Nothing. He'd lay me on my front. And put it in my pussy, up my ass. That's what he liked. He'd come in two minutes and then go about his business. Ahhh, they're animals, I tell you.'

'But you were happy.'

'Yes, but he wasn't delicate like you. He didn't fuck me slowly and tenderly, piss in my face, beat me with a whip, and drool in my mouth.'

'You really like the whip?'

'You know how to use it, *papi*. It's so wonderful. You know what you're doing.'

I sit watching her in silence. It pleases me and I love her very much. I remember the beginning of that poem and I whisper it in her ear: 'I am the vampire who sucks your blood.'

'It's so beautiful. Continue.'

'I can't remember.'

'But you wrote it.'

'I forget everything I write.'

'It's a crazy poem. Honey, be careful because if you keep writing like that you're going to become hopelessly mad.'

'I already went nuts once. It wouldn't surprise me if it happened again.'

'Well, in the meantime keep caressing me and giving me flowers, because when you go crazy maybe you'll buy me flowers and eat them instead of giving them to me.'

'Ha ha ha.'

'Yes, yes. I have to live now.'

'It's lack of affection, Gloria. You're living in a very fucked-up, hungry time.'

'I have to get over my disgust with the gringos because . . .'

'Ha ha ha. The leopard never changes her spots. It's because you've had to survive ten violent years.'

'Ten, no. Thirty, the whole of my life! Remember that I was born in the Laguna tenement. Papi with his music and his drinking and his women out there. Mami with her shit. My brothers running the streets . . . Ahhh . . . Why talk about it? I don't like to drag out stories. If you write the whole truth in *A Lot of Heart*, nobody's gonna believe it.'

'And there's more to come because this crisis has no end.'

'Well, on we go. The only thing we can do is fight for our little pesos day after day. It's never gonna end.'

'I don't believe it.'

'Why not?'

'I illuminate those who surround me.'

'Are you a saint?'

'One of the little Pedros inside of me is a saint.'

'And another is a devil. That's the one I ended up with.'

'You ended up with all of them. I've always said that inside me I have a devil, a vampire, a son of a bitch, a black African, an Indian saint, a woman, a wild animal, a madman, a destroyer, a visionary . . .'

'Okay, okay.'

I put my hand on her pussy and massage it a little. We start to get hot. I have the whip nearby and I caress her with its leather: 'Come live with me. I'm going to subjugate you, slut.'

'Do you want me to get my high-heel shoes and black stockings?'

'Yes.'

'Wait for me. I'll be back in two minutes.'

She went down to her house and brought the new gear. She put it on and began her little show.

'All the men like this, *papi*. How they pay when they see me naked with nothing but heels and stockings! I had a Spaniard who brought me black stockings and panties by the dozen. They call panties *braguitas*.'

'Forget the Spaniard and stop talking shit. Come here. Look at what you've done to my pole.'

'Oh, *papi*, what's this? The veins are swollen like . . . ah, like that, shove it all the way back there. It's that African inside you, damn it. There's no one who fucks me like you. You have the black man inside.'

I show her a good time. I spit in her face. I give her a few slaps. I have an olive canvas belt from when I was in the army. That's the one she likes because it stings her more.

'Give it to me with the belt, baby, on my buttocks.'

'You want the whip?'

'It's the same. Whichever one you want, but don't pull out. Fuck me more.'

We play like this a while. I kiss her feet, her asshole, her soul. I adore her: 'No more hustling, Gloria. I want you all for me.'

'I do what you tell me, sweetie.'

'If things get tight for us, then you'll have to fight.'

'I do what you want, my darling. Tie me up! Tie me up!'

I had two pieces of rope in my hand. We had a lot of fun. My hangover totally disappeared. Afterwards, I left her napping and went down to get some rum and a couple of cigars. In the rum dispensary, I ran into an old friend from Guanabacoa. We worked together in Dinorah's sugar-cane juice bar, behind the Quibú River, peeling stalks of cane. Partners from the hard years. Later I was in the same cell as Basilio; he and Basilio used to steal horses together.

'My man Jesús, what brings you here?'

'Damn, Pedro Juan, what's up? Nothin', my friend, just hangin'out. I'm lookin' to trade my place for somethin' near the center of the city. I like this neighborhood.'

'And I want to move out of town.'

'Yeah?!'

'Yeah.'

'How's your place?'

So, finally. Incredible but true. Exchanging houses usually means years of searching, tangles, negotiations. Jesús and I traded ours in four days. He moved very happily to the roof terrace and I went to his farm. It's small but nice. With mangoes, avocados, oranges, and cages of snakes. He had a business raising Cuban boas. He sold them to foreigners and to the *santeros*, for witchcraft. Jesús called them serpents. What's more, he left a gigantic watchdog, a gang of rat-hunting cats, and a cow. In exchange, I gave him a double cassette player and the complete collection of Mark Anthony and Juan Luis Guerra, who are indispensable for the roof.

After a whole life in Central Havana I feel a little strange here with so much silence and the wind which comes from the sea. You can see Bacuranao and Guanabo in the distance, between the hills. It's a healthy and extremely tranquil place. It all went very fast and unforeseeably. I need time to adapt to the calm and serenity. The closest neighbors are a half-deaf old man and woman, two hundred yards away. They grow flowers and corn.

Gloria was unable to help me with the move. A girlfriend called her and she took off like a rocket for the red-light district. The Pacific saloon was full of sailors on a training ship from I don't know where. They wanted rum, whores and brand-name cigars in that order and in industrial quantities. Gloria vanished for three days with that little business. I left the new address with her mother and finally she reappeared, very pleased: 'Hey, sweetie, look, two hundred bucks. Plus everything I left at home.'

'You said you'd be gone a while, but not three days. Didn't you say that the gringos make you sick?'

'Tremendously sick, but the first one offered me a hundred bucks. And it was tempting. I took it, put a condom on him, and closed my eyes. Business, *papi*, business! I was with three guys in all . . . No, with four. But I left with three bills. And everything they gave me. They're splendid. They'll be back within six months.'

'There's no stopping you. You'll be this way for ever.'

'I'm not going to be this way for ever. That was a temptation. And don't you complain. We have enough here for two months. Make me pregnant. I've told you so fifty times. Get me pregnant and rule me with an iron hand. I want a nice tranquil life with you, *papi*.'

'Fine, but I warn you: if you misbehave, I'm going to put you in a cage with the serpents for shackles.'

'No, honey, don't do that to me, I'll be good. Let's start up a business. Buy two more cows and we'll sell the milk.'

'You know how to milk them?'

'No, but I'll learn . . . It's gotta be like jacking off a dwarf.'

'Well, we'll see. Maybe it's better business to raise serpents, like Jesús.'

'Hey, sweetie, speaking of serpents . . . That fuck with the heels and black stockings . . .'

'*Coitus interruptus.*'

'What's that?'

'We cut it short.'

'So come on. Let's continue right now. And out here I can scream and sigh when you fuck me. Are there any neighbors here?'

'Some old folks, half deaf, two hundred yards away.'

'That's great. 'Cause when your dick's inside me all I wanna do is shout!'

And we went about it. I don't know, if I knock her up maybe we'll have two or three children. I don't know if I'll have a telephone. I believe I'm incommunicado because I see no lines or poles in the vicinity. The good thing about this is that it threw the Swede off my trail. Back in the woods, out toward Campo Florido, there are two secret places where they have cockfights and sell cheap rum and cigars for a peso apiece. What more do I need? I don't want computers or e-mail, or Internet, I don't want anyone to fuck with me ever again. I just want to be left alone and in peace. At the moment, I have the lines and hooks ready to go fishing. From here I see some very beautiful reefs and the sea is calm. Better yet, Gloria wants to go with me. That way we can keep on talking about her life. Perhaps, some day, I'll make up my mind to write *A Lot of Heart*. But, for now, I don't dare start since I haven't the slightest idea how it ends.

Havana–Stockholm 1999/2000

Pedro Juan Gutiérrez began his working life at the age of eleven as an ice-cream vendor and newsboy. The author of several published works of poetry, he lives in Havana. He is also the author of *Dirty Havana Trilogy*.